Murmured In Dreams

Stephen Bacon

First published by Luna Press Publishing, Edinburgh, 2019

Cuckoo Spit. *First published in Black Static 27.*
None So Blind. *First published in Shadows & Tall Trees 3, reprinted in Best Horror of the Year 5.*
Apports. *First published in Black Static 36, reprinted in Best Horror of the Year 6.*
Lord of the Sand. *First published in The 11th Black Book of Horror, reprinted in Best Horror of the Year 8.*
Somewhere On Sebastian Street. *First published in Horror for Good.*
Bandersnatch. *First published in Black Static 48.*
Fear of the Music. *First published in Something Remains.*
The Summer of Bradbury. *First published in Terror Tales of Yorkshire.*
The Devil's Only Friend. *First published in Horror Uncut!*
Pennyroyal (original to this collection)
Husks. *First published in Murmurations - An Anthology of Uncanny Stories About Birds.*
The Children of Medea (original to this collection)
What Grief Can Do. *First published in Crimewave.*
The Ivory Teat. *First published in The First Book of Classical Horror Stories.*
Double Helix. *First published in Ill at Ease 2.*
The Cambion. *First published in Cemetery Dance 72.*
Happy Sands. *First published in Postscripts.*
Rapid Eye Movement. *First published in Fear the Reaper.*
It Came From the Ground. *First published in Darkest Minds.*

www.lunapresspublishing.com
ISBN-13: 978-1-911143-73-4

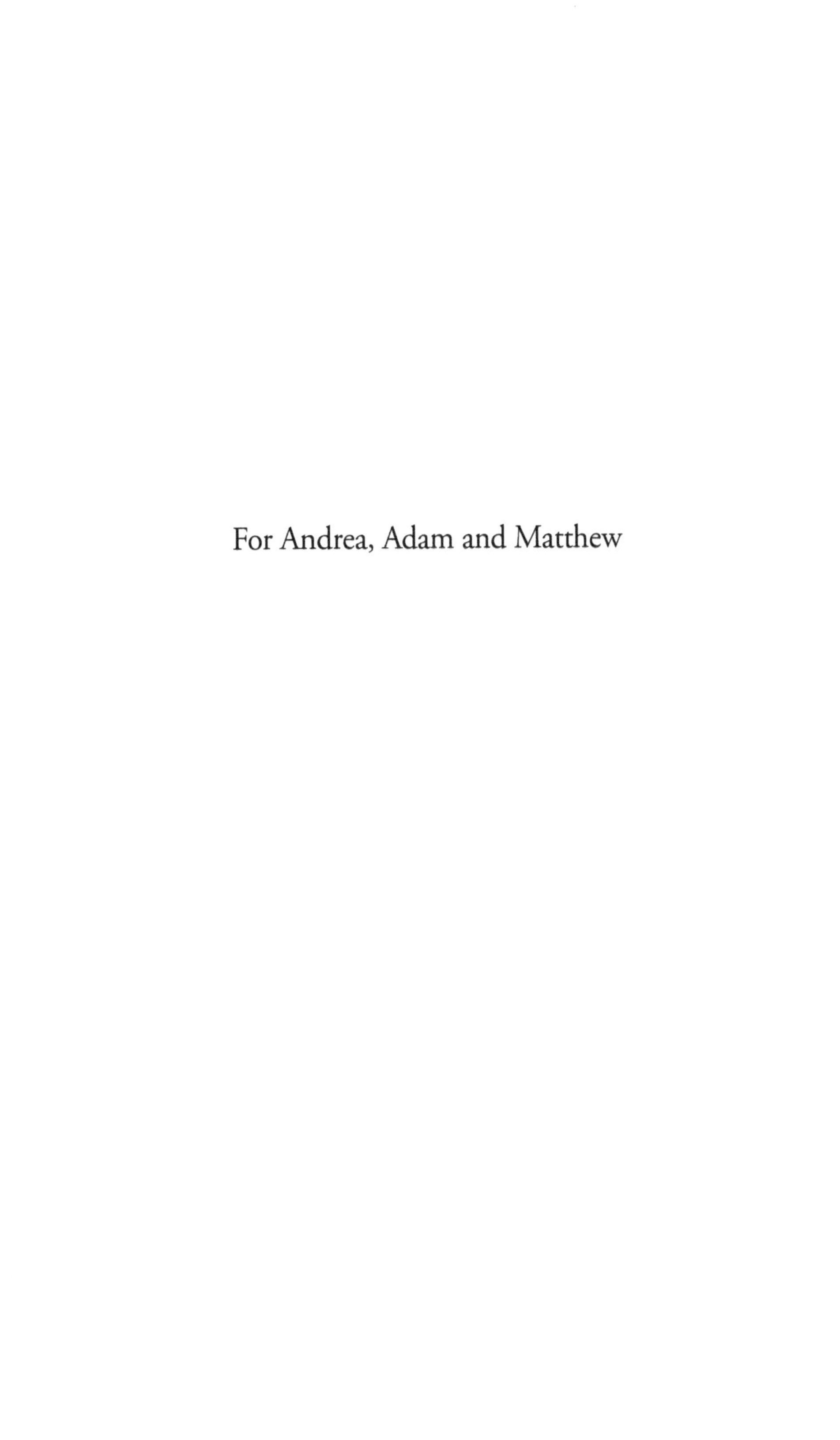

For Andrea, Adam and Matthew

Contents

Introduction

Stephen Bacon is a modest man. If you meet him he won't tell you that his work has appeared in prestigious venues like *Black Static*, *Crimewave*, *Shadows and Tall Trees*, Paul Finch's *Terror Tales* series, *The Black Book of Horror* collection and *Cemetery Dance*. He won't tell you that he's been reprinted in several of Ellen Datlow's *The Best Horror of the Year* anthologies and by JJ Adams in *Nightmare*. He won't tell you that he was nominated in the Best Newcomer category of the British Fantasy Award in 2013 for his first collection "Peel Back the Sky".

What he will talk about is horror. In spades. His passion for darkness is in everything he writes. His love of writers like Stephen King, Ray Bradbury and John Wyndham is on every page.

With "Murmured in Dreams" Stephen Bacon takes us everywhere. Science fiction, the supernatural, the mythic and the horrific collide with both a future Britain and that of the not-so-distant past, with the quiet breezes of a Greek island and with war ravaged Rwanda and Chad.

I read some of the stories in this collection when they were first published, but rereading them has made me realise how beautifully understated and elegant Stephen Bacon's writing is. The ugly is observed in disquieting detail (He could feel the blood rattling in his lungs or A Bull Terrier shivered a pale turd onto the grass). In "Cuckoo Spit" a whole family dynamic is revealed in the simple act of a woman patting the empty spot behind her on the bed. In "The Ivory Teat", Stephen Bacon conveys the things unsaid between a man and a woman, the possibilities of their relationship, with a pair of identical mugs on a table, one of them marked by lipstick. "Bandersnatch" exposes the dark complicity between siblings by them quoting their favourite children's book to each other.

Stephen Bacon doesn't shy away from difficult subject matter—abuse is seen through several prisms, as are incest, infidelity, cruelty and revenge. But there's also hope for redemption, justice, and love at the end of the world. .The thing I find ever present in this collection though is the past. It revisits his characters again and again in the form of previous sins, transgressions, family feuds and promises. The past makes them come out of self-imposed exile, makes them revisit childhood haunts. Even when they run, it pursues them without mercy.

If we are never to be free of the past, if we are always to be haunted by it, then "Murmured in Dreams" is an extended nightmare and we aren't murmuring. We are screaming.

Priya Sharma

Cuckoo Spit

Like a repulsive wart, Jackdaw Cottage crouched on the highest peak of the moor, tainting the natural beauty that surrounded it. As the miles between them closed, Megan felt its grip of malevolence tighten.

Her car topped a rise and she caught her first glimpse of the cottage for nearly 23 years. The house looked just as ugly in real-life as it had in her memories.

It nestled in a hollow, surrounded by a thin copse of skeletal birch trees, rendering the scene russet and melancholy. The intervening years had allowed ivy to smother the exterior of the house, virtually obscuring the brickwork, leaving it almost camouflaged. As if nature was trying to claim it.

Instinctively Megan studied herself in the rearview mirror, her eyes tracing the imperfection of puckered scar that traversed her cheek. It was a challenging look.

The track meandered between heather-flamed hillocks as her Qashqai negotiated the final stage of the journey. Her joints popped as she moved. It had been an arduous trip. Patterdale lay deeper and further into the Cumbrian wilderness than she'd cared to remember. Relief pressed her foot to the accelerator. She drove through an open gate and pulled to a halt in front of the house, next to a mud-spattered 4x4.

She switched off the ignition and yanked on the handbrake. The dashboard clock said it was half past two, yet the November sky seemed to suggest it was dusk. Grey clouds gathered indifferently, stealing the colour from the surrounding moorland. A frantic barking started up from within the house, and she inhaled sharply, gripping the wheel. She appraised the building through the fly-speckled windscreen.

Ivy was encroaching across the window panes. The roof slates looked greasy, fringed by lichen. A coil of smoke rose languidly from the thin chimney. She suddenly had the absurd feeling that dense ivy was concealing the true nature of the cottage; that instead of stone and brick, its walls were constructed of gingerbread, its slates were rolled liquorice. Hysteria bubbled in her chest. *It must be nerves.* A light burned in one of the downstairs rooms.

Megan climbed out and approached the front door. The light was sufficient for her to notice something glistening in the ivy. The foliage appeared to be coated in streams of white froth, which clung and looped from the leaves. She recognised it as cuckoo spit—natural lather created by an insect to protect its young. Probably the foliage was infested. She made a mental note to keep the windows shut.

The door opened and a woman appeared. Her face looked vaguely familiar. "Megan? Come on in, love." The peal of barks started up again.

She hesitated, feeling the frantic pounding of her heart. "I'm sorry—the dog—is there a dog in there?"

The woman chided herself. "Ah, sorry, Megan—I forgot. Yes, there is. Don't worry—I'll lock him in the room." She disappeared for a few minutes before returning. "Come on in, love."

Megan stepped over the threshold tentatively, staring around the kitchen/diner. Little had changed since she'd last been here. Everything seemed timeless, as if she'd been transported back to 1988. It felt like someone's recreation of the original room from memory, almost a pastiche.

"The dog's as daft as a brush; he'll be more likely to lick you to death than bite you, but your mum *did* tell me about your… fear." The woman looked to be in her early sixties. She was dressed in a tie-dyed dress and flat shoes. Her hair was an unruly mop of frizzy ginger, graying with age. It made her look like Medusa. She held out her hand. "I'm Gwyneth. Remember me?"

Megan shook her hand limply. "No—I'm sorry."

"I live at the house right at the neck of the valley. You might have seen it as you drove past? On the main road?"

Megan looked around, confused. "I…yes, I think so."

"My—you haven't changed at all!" Gwyneth held her hand to waist-height. "Except the last time I saw you, you were this big."

Megan smiled wanly. "How's my mother?"

The older woman's face took on a picture of concern. "Not good, I'm afraid. Not good at all. I think your dad's disappearance is taking its toll."

"My stepfather."

"What, love?"

"*Not* my father—my father left when I was a baby. Brian's my stepfather."

"Oh, right."

The silence was weighty. It was finally broken by Gwyneth. "Anyway, your mum's sleeping at the minute. The kettle's just boiled. You rest your feet and I'll make you a nice cup of tea."

Megan allowed herself to be ushered into a chair, enjoying the maternal fussing. She peered around the room as Gwyneth busied herself at the sink. It looked like it hadn't been redecorated since the late 80s. The open fire crackled and popped reassuringly. The flames were hypnotic. It made the gas-fire in her flat feel phony and unnatural.

Gwyneth's voice broke her reverie. "So, what was your journey like?"

Megan pursed her lips. "Horrible. It's so…remote out here."

"It is, it is—but us country folk prefer it remote." She laughed. "We tend to think city people are the ones who're mad, living on top of each other in all that hustle and bustle."

Megan said quietly, "Have they heard anything about Brian?"

The old woman didn't speak, just poured from the teapot until the two mugs were full. Then she brought them both to the table and took a seat opposite Megan.

"No, love. They've heard nothing at all yet."

Megan cupped her hands around the hot vessel.

"But it's only been ten days," Gwyneth said brightly. "There's no reason to lose hope. The police say he might have just hit his head and lost his memory or something. Perhaps he's wandering round Keswick with amnesia. Or he's just fallen down a rabbit hole like Alice in Wonderland."

Megan took a sip of tea. It was far too strong and sweet. The older woman's humour seemed awkwardly inappropriate. She became aware that Gwyneth was studying her from the corner of her eye. She bent her head in the pretence of drinking, allowing her hair to fall across her face, concealing it.

"Sorry about the dog. I forgot you were frightened of them. Your mum did tell me. I'm such a clutterhead sometimes."

Megan suppressed the discomfort that was in danger of colouring her cheeks. "That's okay." She turned her head self-consciously, as if she was surveying the room. "Might be best if I take Mother back to Leeds with me."

"Oh no," said Gwyneth sharply, "I don't think that would do her any good." She shook her head. "This is Sylvia's home. This is where she belongs. Brian's family have lived at this house for generations."

"I don't mean for good. Just for a while. Until we know what's happened to Brian."

The older woman shrugged disapprovingly and drank some of her tea. The clock on the wall ticked deafeningly. She said all of a sudden, "The story goes that years ago—early 40's, I reckon—some men were out on the moors lamping for rabbits when they came across a young boy wandering naked. They tried to speak to him, to find out what he was doing. But as they got close, he dropped down on all fours and changed into a fox. He escaped and they never caught him."

Megan nodded slowly, unsure of how else to respond.

"What I'm saying is that this area is a very *spiritual* place." The older woman's voice was insistent. "Witchcraft, magic—call it what you like. That feeling's built into Cumbrian folk. It's natural, like."

"But we're from Yorkshire," Megan pointed out. "We only came here after mother's divorce."

"Brian's from here."

"Brian's disappeared."

"Aye—he has." There was a sense of finality to her tone. As if Megan had been responsible for the vanishment. She glanced at the clock. "Anyway, I'd better get off home. My husband will be back soon. I'll come again tomorrow after tea." She stood and held up a piece of paper. "Here's my number. Just give me a call if you need anything." She added, almost as an afterthought, "I've made sure there's plenty of stuff in—from the shop, I mean."

Megan accepted the paper and thanked her. The woman put on her coat and nodded goodbye before disappearing out the door. Silence descended on the room. Megan drifted to the window, intending to draw the curtains in an effort to hold back the gathering darkness. She caught sight of Gwyneth loitering near the front door, and the older woman's behaviour looked curious enough to arrest Megan's movement.

Gwyneth was carefully picking something out of the ivy, her hands moving to her mouth in swift, fluid motion. It was fascinating to watch. She repeated this action several times. She licked her lips and swallowed as if she was devouring something from the centre of her cupped palm. The sight was so startling that Megan felt the hairs on her neck bristle. It looked almost as if the older woman was consuming the cuckoo spit from the ivy. Megan felt her stomach lurch at the thought. She yanked the curtains closed, recoiling at the old crackpot's bizarre behaviour.

*

Megan watched her mother as she slept. The old woman's eyes twitched beneath her closed lids, which were threaded with pale veins, and looked as fragile as a butterfly's wing. She hadn't changed much in the intervening years, other than time had sagged her skin and lined her features. She still carried the same dour expression. Despite speaking on the phone periodically—usually birthdays and Christmas—Megan had still pictured her as the hard-nosed individual that had been present in her childhood. She'd come to think of the woman not as her mother, but as an adult with whom she'd shared her home. Very much like Brian, in fact.

Clearly his disappearance had affected the woman; for the past couple of weeks she'd remained bedbound, relying on Gwyneth's assistance. Megan got the impression that the neighbour was relishing her recent supportive role.

Since Gwyneth had departed she'd prowled the house searching for telltale signs that revealed what kind of life her mother and Brian enjoyed. It was all rather depressing. The only photographs were of her mother and Brian in various coastal locations. Her old room was filled with junk, the drooping bed hidden beneath boxes of clutter and bric-a-brac. A faded Care-bear poster still adorned the wall; something she'd left hanging ironically as a remnant of her ripped childhood, well into her teens. Something precious from the former part of her life, before her self-image had been ravaged.

The presence of the dog unsettled Megan. She could hear it sniffing and whining in the parlour downstairs, its nails skittering on the parquet flooring. Her imagination conjured a slavering beast with fiery eyes that resembled the illustration from a childhood book—an abridged version of Doyle's *The Hound of the Baskervilles*. The cover alone had given her nightmares for weeks.

Gently, her mother opened her eyes. She shifted on the bed, turning slightly so she could see around the room. She blinked twice when she spotted Megan.

"Mother." Megan tried to keep her voice buoyant. "How're you feeling?"

"Hello, love." Sylvia swallowed with a wince. "Much better, thanks." She glanced towards the nearby table. "Is there any water left?"

Megan went to the bathroom and filled the glass. The room was clinical and chintzy and unambitious. She remembered how red the towels had been that morning as Brian pressed them against her face to stem the flow. She felt her cheek itch.

She returned with the water, handing it over without speaking.

"Thanks, love." The old woman drank eagerly. When she finished she looked up. "Thanks for coming. I wanted to see you before…the end."

Megan ignored the implications of the sentence. "No news about Brian then?"

The old woman shook her head once. "How are *you* anyway? Got yourself a nice boyfriend yet?"

She laughed hollowly. "It's too late for that now, at my age."

"Don't be daft—you're still young." The words felt flimsy, insubstantial. "You haven't changed a bit."

Megan smoothed out the creases in the quilt. "I think I might have missed that bus—*men*, I mean."

The world had disappeared outside, consumed by the darkness. The cottage lights made Megan feel isolated and vulnerable. She imagined countless eyes watching them, surrounding them, awaiting their move.

A low whine broke out from downstairs.

"Where's the dog?" Her mother's voice sounded stronger.

"Locked in the back room. You know how I hate dogs."

Sylvia held the empty glass out to Megan, then leaned back into her pillow with a contemptuous look. "Hmmm, you're more of a *cat-person*, aren't you?" The implied criticism was palpable.

"Well, I *do* have a cat, as a matter of fact." Megan put the glass down.

"Cats are sly and nasty," said her mother. "Whereas dogs are loyal and obedient and loving. You can rely on a dog. More than you can on a human, sometimes."

Megan snorted. "Well, you don't need to convince me of *that*."

"What's that supposed to mean, Meg?"

"It's *Megan*." She flared her nostrils. "You know what I mean. Where are the photos of *me*—your only child? Nowhere. But there's framed pictures of Trixie all over the place."

"I've got a stack of photo-albums in that wardrobe with you in them. Until you ran off."

"Can you blame me? Imagine how it felt to be brought up in a house where I came second place to a fucking dog." She enjoyed seeing her mother flinch at the bad language.

"Trixie was a loving pet; a member of the family. She was fifteen when she died. That's old for a dog."

Megan felt the tears surging in her throat, and fought to suppress them. "You let it rip my fucking face to ribbons. And did nothing about it."

The older woman sighed wearily. "How many times have we been through this? I told you not to play near her basket. You were too rough with her. She was only protecting herself."

"I was five years old. What five year old does as they're told?"

Her mother blinked smugly. "If you train them right, dogs will do as they're told. They'll do—"

"I needed *stitches*, mother. My lip and cheek was torn." Megan swallowed. "Anyone else would have had the dog put down. Anyone normal."

"You'd have loved that, wouldn't you?" The hysteria was evident now. "That'd have suited you down to the ground."

"Instead you made some feeble excuse. And Brian went along with it."

"It was a Friday night, the bank holiday weekend; all the vets were closed. We drove out to one in Penrith after we took you to A&E; Brian said we had no other option." Her mother sniffed indignantly. "But it was shut. And by the Tuesday, when it reopened, you seemed much better. The swelling had gone down. It wasn't as bad as it first looked."

Megan held back her hair to reveal the scar on her cheek. "It's faded but it still feels like everything changed from that day onwards."

Her mother glanced away. "Nonsense. You can't even see anything."

"I've spent the last 35 years trying to conceal it with my hair. Have you any idea how that makes you feel? Have you any idea what that does to your self-image?" She could contain the tears no more. She hurried from the bedroom before they broke, blindly rushing down the narrow stairs.

*

Megan ached even more when she awoke later. She'd lain tucked into a ball on the sofa. After she'd stormed downstairs in the wake of the argument, the inviting fire had stolen the final vestiges of her will and she'd felt herself succumbing to sleep.

She sat up and glanced at the clock, shocked. It was nearly eight. The smell of food was heavy in the air. There were dishes on the side and a pan on the cooker.

Megan went back up the stairs.

Her mother was still in bed, an empty bowl at her side. She glanced up as Megan entered. "You're awake."

"Yes, I'm awake. I've driven for several hours to get here, only to find you're not the invalid Gwyneth said you were. I see you managed to make yourself some soup?"

Her mother shrugged. "I did feel a bit better."

"Well I'm going back to Leeds first thing in the morning."

"That's fine. I don't know why you came anyway, pretending to care."

Megan stayed silent. The row was escalating again. This wasn't doing either of them any good. "What have the police said about Brian?"

Her mother blinked rapidly. "They've asked me loads of questions. They've been out with the helicopter. No one knows what's happened to him."

"What do *you* think happened to him?"

"If I knew that, don't you think I'd tell them?" She suddenly patted the bed next to her.

Megan felt a swell of emotion, thinking the old woman was inviting her to sit beside her. Then Sylvia made a clicking sound with her mouth. From the other side of the bed, the dog leapt up and lay down on the covers.

Megan took a step backwards, surprised by its sudden appearance. "I thought it was locked up."

"I let him out. This is his house now." The old woman stroked its head and flank. It was a small black greyhound with an angular head and watery eyes. It licked its lips in a disinterested manner.

"What's his name?" Megan felt her fear dissipate somewhat.

Her mother shrugged. "No idea. He's a stray. He was whining at the front door last week."

"A stray?" Megan sounded doubtful. "But there's no houses for miles."

"I know," she continued stroking the dog. "But it's been lovely having him for company this last week. I don't know what I'd have done without him."

Even this was a dig. Megan felt her resolution crumbling. "I think I'll go and have something to eat." She moved to go, then turned back. "Do you need anything?"

Sylvia shook her head and continued to watch the dog as she stroked it.

*

Megan made herself a ham sandwich. She ate it standing, browsing the books that lined the shelves. Most of them were non-fiction; natural history, British wildlife reference books, heaps of mystical mumbo-jumbo rubbish and Wiccan textbooks; magic and spiritual self-awareness. Even some occult titles.

She went out to the car to fetch her overnight bag in. On her way back, she set it down and peered closely at the ivy. Moonlight glistened on the dark leaves. She trailed her fingers along and was surprised how slimy the moisture of the cuckoo spit was. Almost on a whim, she held up her hand and sniffed. There was a sensuous organic scent to the dampness. It conjured vivid memories of her time at university…autumn afternoons spent in her room with Paul as rain patterned the glass and cast grey veins on the wall. Holding hands as they lay entwined on the sofa, watching films from the huge collection of VHS tapes that a previous housemate had left.

Megan blinked quickly and instinctively wiped her hand on the leg of her jeans as she realized what the fluid was. Human sperm. That subtle saltwater aroma vaguely mixed with bleach. She wrinkled her nose and hurried back inside with the bag.

It was late. She could hear the floorboards creaking as her mother moved around upstairs. It sounded like Megan would be able to return home tomorrow—with or without her.

Brian's belongings cluttered the house, silently gathering dust. Megan regarded them with a resentful gaze. She thought about his presence in her childhood; his awkward stance, their unspoken mutual disregard, the way in which he'd tried to drive a wedge between Megan and her mother. *But didn't all children feel that way about their step-parents?*

She lifted her hand and fingered the scar on her face. Sylvia was right—it *had* faded. But the emotional damage was invisible; had, in fact, remained raw and ugly within her for the past 35 years. Other than Paul—and the dynamic of that relationship had probably been driven by his sole enthusiasm—the other men in her life had been levered away by her self-perception. By her lack of confidence. By her sense of worthlessness. And all because her parents allowed the dog to maul her.

Megan went upstairs. She mentally told herself it was to check whether her mother needed anything before she retired to sleep, but she knew it was really to check the dog would be secured. The landing was narrow and in need of painting. As she made her way along the passage she heard the murmur of voices from her mother's room. She had almost reached the door when she realised that it was her mother's voice, not the sound of the radio or the television. She paused and listened.

It was frustrating. Her mother was definitely speaking—she could hear the distinct tone—but the words evaded her. And then—following a short pause that indicated conversation—a deeper male voice chimed up. Megan felt the back of her neck prickle. The voices continued, yet the actual words remained indiscernible. Curiously, she opened the door and peered into the room.

Her mother glanced up in surprise from the bed. The silence was edgy and compressed. The room was otherwise empty except for the dog that stood in the centre of the rug. It gazed at Megan, its head cocked. There was an eerie look in its eyes.

"Are you all right, love?" Her mother's voice was measured. Precise.

"Fine." Mega n continued to stare at the dog. "I thought…" She broke its gaze and turned to the woman in the bed. "I thought I heard voices, that's all."

"Ah—my age, probably. Talking to myself now."

Megan swallowed and hesitated. "It's weird. It sounded like Brian's voice."

Sylvia sighed and clutched her chest melodramatically. "If only it were, Meg. If only it were."

"Megan," corrected Megan absently. She turned back to the dog, which just stared back at her and twitched one of its ears. "Anyway, I just came up to see if you wanted anything. I'm going to turn in for the night."

"We're fine, thanks, love." Sylvia looked at the dog. "I've got my new bodyguard here."

Megan nodded and smiled thinly. She closed the door and walked back along the landing.

*

In her dream it took her ages to realise where she was. The embers of the fire had died down, transforming the room orange and one-dimensional and lacking in detail. Before she knew it she was moving towards the bottom of the stairs, instinctively feeling for the coolness of the wood as if testing whether she was awake.

Strange sounds trailed down the stairs. Megan slowly ascended, trying not to let the creaks betray her. As she reached the top she realised her imagination was in danger of conjuring something obscene from the wet, sucking noises and the murmur of low voices that came along the landing. She drifted through the darkness until her outstretched hand reached the door of her mother's room. Its slightly ajar position afforded her a glimpse through the crack.

Moonlight draped a wide square across the bed, silvering the room's contents, rendering them synthetic, almost unreal. She blinked once and her breath caught in her throat.

There was a woman in the bed, leaning forward from the pillow. It took Megan a few seconds to comprehend it was her mother. The older woman had unclipped her bun and her hair was hanging in a curtain, obscuring her face. On the duvet in front of her, the dog lay with its head resting against her torso, its mouth fastened around the woman's breast, lips drawn back. Sylvia was nursing it, stroking the dog's head as the animal lapped at her. Its tongue was frantic, flicking wildly between the teeth. The dog's snout was wet, its leg twitched. Milk had spilled onto the animal's pelt from the woman's erect nipple.

The notion that she was dreaming—*how else could she be witnessing such a bizarre and surreal image?*—occurred to her sharply. She turned from the sight, disturbed by the suggestion of pleasure in the dog's bulging eyes, troubled by the delicate angle of her mother's throat. The guttural animalistic gorging, the shallow sigh of her mother's breath. These noises chased her back downstairs.

When she awoke in the morning, the collapsed fire in the hearth resembled the one in her dream. Sunlight was crowding the edges of the curtain. The clock ticked a comforting heartbeat.

Timber was stretching within the structure of the building. The fridge began humming to itself, distracting her.

Megan winced as her feet touched the cold lino. It was eight o'clock. She wriggled into her dressing gown and switched on the kettle to boil.

The stairs felt narrower, as if it was a throat that was trying to swallow her. She drifted into the bathroom. She was sitting on the toilet when she realised things were not quite right; that there was a feeling of neglect gnawing the air. She finished, and hesitated before flushing the toilet, fearful of disturbing things. Resignedly, she did it anyway and paused, listening to the noise of the cistern refilling, enjoying the hiss as the water gushed through the pipes. Outside in the tree a bird was cawing. The cry sounded mournful and desolate, the loneliest noise she had ever heard.

She washed her hands and drew the cord of her dressing gown tighter around her waist. She went and stood outside her mother's room. The door was ajar, just as it had been in her dream. Nothing moved. The silence was oppressive, almost a solid energy that seemed to swathe her head and dull her senses. She peered through the crack. The tangled shape in the bedclothes looked unnatural.

Megan pushed open the door, forcing a despondent creak into the vacuum of the room. "Mother?"

As she drew close she could see that the figure in the bed was not her mother at all but a pale mannequin, staring sightlessly at the ceiling. The alabaster features were mottled with delicate threads of colour, the lips curled back in a parody of grimace. Megan carefully brushed her fingers against the figure's wrist, almost recoiling at the coldness of the touch.

Of course, her mother was dead.

There was a dull sheen to her eyes, a single jewel-like tear resting on the woman's upturned cheek. Megan gently touched the drop, allowing her fingers to absorb it.

She perched on the edge of the bed, trying to reconcile the impact of her mother's death. The air in the room felt viscous. Instinctively she fingered the scar on her face, an action that seemed somehow comforting. *How quickly the dead lose their spark*, she thought. *How lifeless the shell looks without the soul.* Absently she glanced around for the dog but its whereabouts was nowhere to be seen.

Megan felt the sudden need to escape. She stood and moved to the window. The morning sun was flexing its muscle; butterflies skimmed the grass, birds wheeled in the sky, clouds rode the very same breeze that combed the trees. And there, a movement on the hillock, twenty yards from the gate.

The greyhound stood staring back at the cottage, its coat rendered glossy by the sun. Beside it, a smaller dog also watched the window, this one a lighter colour than its mate. Its ears twitched, betraying the fact it was real, alive. For an age their eyes locked. Megan's chest wheezed with the grief that threatened to overwhelm her. The bigger dog turned and disappeared into the long grass that fringed the path, into the open moorland. For a few seconds the smaller dog maintained its position then it, too, turned and vanished from sight. It did not look back.

None So Blind

Novak found an apartment in one of the districts that had remained run-down. It was an unfortunate choice, overlooking the walls of a factory, the grounds heaped with discarded shop dummies. Countless lichen-coated limbs reached out from the rusting industrial bins that littered the yard. Dismembered torsos gathered dust in stacked piles, cobwebbed together like cocooned corpses. At times the smell of chemicals and burning machinery turned his stomach. The incessant clanging frayed his nerves. The squeal of gears haunted his dreams. Often he woke with raking coughs drawing strings of blood from his lungs. The damp patches on the ceiling of his apartment resembled scar tissue. But not once did he think about finding somewhere else; the apartment's location was too convenient.

At night, the city resembled the one from his memory—a cluster of grey buildings populated by threatening shadows and screaming sirens. A place where dark figures smoked in doorways and a footstep behind you might be the last sound you'd ever hear.

But everything appeared very different by daylight. The decade and a half since he'd fled the city had seen great change. Many of the floundering industrial areas had been redeveloped. There was a heavier police presence on the streets. People strolled casually, relaxing in the recreation areas that had been created. It felt almost like the dark underbelly of the city he'd abandoned had been varnished smooth, the cracks papered over. Yet peel back the veneer of respectability and the festering decay would be revealed. Of that he was sure.

For several weeks Novak had watched the woman from a distance, noting her routines and observing her as she went about her daily life. It was obvious she was a creature of habit. At precisely

10.30 every morning she'd venture out of the gates of her walled garden and make her way to the little café on the corner. There she would enjoy two cups of coffee and a pastry. On one occasion she plumped for a toasted teacake. The café owner was accustomed to her patronage, and welcomed her warmly each morning. She even had her own table near the window.

One spring morning fate drew them together once again.

From his table in the café, Novak heard the *tap-tap-tap* of her cane seconds before the woman stepped into view, walking past the window with assured movement. She entered the café and turned instinctively towards her usual table. The owner wiped his hands on his apron and greeted her.

Novak watched the woman from behind as she took a seat and folded her white cane, placing it on the chair beside her. The server came and took her order. They chatted for a few moments about the weather. The server went into the rear of the café and the woman was alone once more. She angled her face towards the window, as if enjoying the sunlight.

The first few times he'd seen her, Novak had been unnerved by the mask. It was virtually a full overhead covering, ending where her ears protruded and the remnants of her rutted skin smoothed out into her neck. There were small apertures for the eyes, but all they did were highlight the contrasting skin-colour and reveal the furrowed scars beneath.

He considered her. She appeared happy enough. She had her pleasant habits. He felt his chest rattling so he took out his handkerchief and coughed into it, observing the speckles of scarlet as he wiped his mouth.

The woman turned in her chair and spoke in his direction: "It's such a nice table here by the window. Why don't you join me?"

For a few stunned seconds he couldn't think of anything to say. His voice was gravelled by phlegm. "Thank you—that would be lovely." He pushed the hankie into his pocket and stood sharply, causing the chair to scrape on the tiled floor. The noise sounded crude.

Novak slid into the seat beside her. His hands shook.

"You're a regular—just like me, I think." Her voice sounded

breathy and soft beneath the mask.

"Regular?" He glanced towards the counter, where the manager was restocking the napkins.

She laughed. "I'm sorry—I recognized your cough. You really should get that checked out, you know." The blank expression of the mask was jarring. It was completely white, perfectly symmetrical features. When she moved her head it looked eerie, like she was a mannequin brought to life. He looked at her arms instead.

"I'm sorry, I hope the cough hasn't bothered you," he said. "I've been ill recently."

"My name's Lyssa," said the woman. She extended a slender arm, a fragile hand.

He shook it gently, tensing as his fingers touched her cool porcelain skin. "Nice to meet you. I'm Alex."

"Alex." She rolled the name around her mouth. It sounded like a different word because the mask muffled her voice.

He didn't know what to say. He stared at her, aware that her blindness protected him.

"I like it in here. They do the most delicious pecan slice." She moved her face towards him slightly and lowered her voice. "And the owner's friendly."

He made murmurs of assent. Out on the road, several cars drove past. Sunlight blinded him momentarily.

"So—you live nearby?"

The question caught him off-guard. He blinked quickly. "Just round the corner. Quite near."

"It's a nice area. Not everyone's cup of tea but I like it because it's quiet."

He studied her perfect arms. In the sunlight there were fine hairs visible on her skin. Her fingernails were neat.

For something to say, he told her, "I lived here years ago."

"Really? I've lived here all my life." He noticed how fragile her throat looked as she swallowed. She continued. "Do you live on your own?"

"Yes. I'm divorced."

"Oh." There was a pause. He detected a slight movement of her head. A moment passed between them. She said, finally, "I'm sorry…I made you feel uncomfortable."

"No, not at all, it's just—"

"You're wondering about *this*, aren't you? About my face?"

"No, not at all." He suppressed the urge to say *I never noticed.* "It's okay. Really."

"No, no." He closed his hands around hers. "Honestly, it doesn't matter."

She allowed him to clutch her hands within his. Made no move. Then she said softly: "Oh…your fingers."

Instinctively he pulled away.

She said quickly, "I'm sorry."

Now it was his turn. "That's okay." He returned his hands to hers. Everything was moving too quickly. He felt out of control.

"How did you lose the fingers? Were you in an accident?"

Most people never asked, but he usually noticed the looks. This woman's blindness had fooled him, buoyed him with misplaced confidence. He stared at her mask. For a long while he never spoke. Then he said quietly, "I knew your husband."

He saw her swallow, noticed a slight shift of her head. It was only the shallow fall of her chest that betrayed the fact she was still breathing. When her voice came again it was much more brittle. "Who are you?"

"My name is Alexander Novak. I used to own a bar down by the harbour." He could see her eyelids flickering through the sockets of the mask. The left one looked like it might be able to open; the skin of the right one seemed fused to the rest of the cheek.

The mask bored into his soul. Its flat indifference seemed harsh, cruel. "Did my husband do that to you? Your hand, I mean?"

"Yes. I owed him a great deal of money. Money I could never repay." Novak was wracked by a fit of coughs again, and reached for the handkerchief. His vision blurred. A pain throbbed in the back of his chest. When the coughs finally subsided he looked up, breathless.

At that moment the server brought her order. The woman waited until the cup and saucer and the pastry had been placed down in front of her. The server asked Novak if he'd like anything else. He declined, and the server left them. Novak paused. Lyssa did not speak for a while. When she finally did, her tone was different, less harsh.

"He was a very *persuasive* man, my husband." The shape of the mask's painted lips was seductive. Her words felt like thoughts because the mask gave the impression that she wasn't speaking. "What did he do to you?"

He glanced down at his left hand. It had been so long that it felt natural, like it had always been that way. His thumb and index finger were intact, but there was just a short knuckle of skin where the other three fingers had once been. He said, "Because I couldn't pay what I owed, my hand was crushed in a vice. I lost three fingers."

"I'm sorry," she said quietly.

He raised his eyebrows. "It's not your fault."

"I know." She swallowed. "But I'm sorry all the same."

"Honestly, it's fine. I can still function normally—it's my left one anyway." He displayed his hand, flexing it in a pincer movement. Then he remembered she was blind. He returned it below the table.

"He's dead, you know."

Novak stared at her. "I heard, yes."

She angled her face to the window again. "He got what he deserved in the end."

Novak remembered reading about it in the papers. He didn't reply.

"Someone kidnapped him and chopped him up into pieces." She sniffed. Novak detected defiance in it. "Someone with the same principles as him."

Behind them, steam burst in a fierce hiss from the stainless steel milk-frothing machine. Once the final gasps had died away, Lyssa said, "He took my face, you know."

Novak stared at her. The pale mask seemed to mock the gravity of the situation. He suddenly had the feeling that he was talking to one of the mannequins from the factory; that the conversation was just taking place in his head.

"My husband discovered I was having an affair with one of his drivers. He persuaded us it wasn't in our best interests for it to continue. He could be rather forthright sometimes."

"What did he do?" Novak tried to keep his voice level.

"Marcus disappeared off the face of the earth. I never found out what happened to him. I heard rumours over the years but…well, I just hope it was quick, whatever it was."

"Weren't you scared?"

"Before we realized he knew about us, he'd made his move." Her voice was emotionless, steely. "I was coming home from a shopping trip. I'd just stepped out of the car when a man appeared from nowhere. At first I thought he was carrying a collection box—you know, those containers of money for charity? Anyway it wasn't one of those, it was a jar of concentrated sulphuric acid."

Novak wiped at the hollows of his eyes. His skin was hot, his cheeks burned.

"At first I thought it was just water. My eyes felt blurry, I couldn't see a thing. I tried to rub my eyes. And all the time I could hear a loud hissing, and smell a horrible smell. And then I realized it was the skin on my face dissolving."

For a while Novak fought to control the weight of emotion that threatened to burst out of his chest. His throat felt constricted.

"My face was stolen that day. And with it, my sight, my hair—everything." She shook her head and shrugged.

He clutched her hand again. The skin on her neck was flushed now, the paleness banished. He could hear her breath rattling against the inside of the mask.

"My God," Novak said at last. "I can't imagine how you must have felt…" He remembered those long nights when his tortured mind could think of nothing else.

"My husband always called me his little bird." She laughed hollowly. "That day he caged me forever."

Novak closed his eyes. "I'm glad he ended up dying like he did, then."

"It was a long time ago. A lifetime ago, really." She sniffed delicately.

He could hear his own heartbeat pounding in his ears. He said, "And how did you feel about the man that actually did it, the one that threw the acid?"

She hesitated, her face angled away slightly. Then she said finally,

"I never saw who threw the acid. How did you know it wasn't my husband?"

Without missing a beat he said, "Men like your husband always have someone to do their dirty work, don't they?" He glanced down at his hand. "I can still remember the two men that kidnapped me—can't forget their faces, if truth be told." He began coughing again, this time mopping at the fluid that seeped into his mouth. The handkerchief was nearly sodden.

Once he'd regained control, he swallowed loudly. "I spent night after night hating them. Wishing they would die horrible, painful deaths."

"What's the point in that?" Her tone wasn't the least confrontational. It was placatory. "It's a waste of emotion. I realize he did it under the orders of my husband. He was probably as much a victim as I was."

Novak watched an old man through the window. He was walking his dog in the morning sun, his lips pursed in the act of whistling.

"My husband denied everything. I knew he'd arranged it, though. It was so like him. That was how he handed out punishments." Her delicate fingers absently traced the shape of the fork on the table. "From that day onwards, his little bird refused to sing—at least until his death. Those eight months were the most difficult."

Novak watched her, remembering the shine of her hair that day, imagining what remained of her face; a face that was once so beautiful. "I'm so sorry for what happened to you."

"Mr Novak, my life—since my husband's death, at least—has been pleasant enough. I have my little house, my belongings. I have my music. I can come and go as I please. My blindness hasn't stopped me doing things. On reflection, I can harbour no bitterness about what happened." She nodded firmly. "At least anymore." After a moment she added in a low voice, "I hope the men who did my husband's dirty work felt no guilt at what they were forced to do."

They sat in companionable silence for a while. Then Novak glanced at his watch and cleared his throat. "I'd better be going."

"I'm very grateful of the company this morning. Will you come here again?"

He glanced away from the mask that was angled at him expectantly. "I'm not sure. I don't know how much longer I'll be here." He stood up and took out his wallet, dropping some cash onto the table. "Like I said, I'm extremely ill. I just wanted to visit my old haunts one last time."

"Goodbye, Mr Novak. I hope everything works out."

"Goodbye, Lyssa." He noticed her coffee and pastry had remained untouched. A skin had formed on the surface of her coffee. "It was nice talking to you."

He left the café, throwing one final glance back. Her head was tilted at an angle as if she was listening to something that only she could hear. The perfect features of her mask seared their image into his mind.

Outside on the street, dark clouds gathered on the horizon. They looked like black wings about to envelop the blue sky. Gusts of wind tore at his coat. He zipped it up and hurried along the road. At the corner he took out the sodden handkerchief and dropped it in the bin. He could feel the blood in his lungs rattling. It wouldn't be long before he'd need the use of another handkerchief.

By the time he made it back to his apartment, the rain had started to pelt the dry, dusty ground.

Apports

They met at a café on the corner of Mulberry Street. It was a fairly nondescript place—greasy net curtains, laminated menus, chipped formica tables. Probably bustling with overweight truckers first thing in the morning, but at this hour it was almost deserted. Casual patrons had possibly been deterred by the rain. Or maybe the poor hygiene.

Cowan spotted Jimenez as soon as he stepped inside. He was sitting at a table in the corner, and he glanced up and waved at the sound of Cowan's entrance. The only other customer was an elderly man slurping noisily from a mug, a mangy dog lying at his feet. Despite the ban, the air was thick with cigarette smoke.

Cowan slid into the plastic chair opposite Jimenez. At first he thought the older man's hair was wet, but then realised the greying locks were actually slicked back with Brylcreem. Dandruff dusted his shoulders. The lines around his mouth were deeply ingrained with age, greying whiskers indicating several days' growth. He drew out a manila envelope from beneath the table and patted it with his nicotine-stained fingers. "Got what you wanted, Mr Campbell."

Cowan licked his lips. "Good." He squirmed inside his tight collar.

"Got the money?"

Cowan took an envelope from his pocket and passed it quickly across to Jimenez, who accepted it and transferred it into his own. There was a layer of dirt beneath the man's cracked fingernails, so ingrained it looked like wood-varnish.

"Five hundred—like you said." Cowan cleared his throat and glanced at the counter. The owner—an Asian woman in a stained apron—was wiping down the wall-tiles with a dishcloth. Behind her, a tinny speaker blared out the insipid blandness of local radio.

Jimenez began to speak. "I managed to locate him… Before I run through what I found, though, I need to ask you one question—why're you looking for Mark Fisk?"

Cowan continued to shift his gaze round the café. "I told you— we were at school together. He was a mate of mine. I just wanted to see him again. You know—catch up." His eyes were restless. "Old time's sake and all that."

"Ah yes, I remember now." He flexed his fingers and rubbed the back of his left hand. "Took quite an effort to find him. Our Mr Fisk did not want to be found."

"Really?"

"Hmmm. You see, he's going under an assumed name now— Peter Feltham. Been living under that name for several months, in fact." His eyes searched the younger man's face. "I had to call in some extra favours to discover this, believe me."

Cowan blinked. "I thought we'd agreed the fee—"

"We did, we did. Don't worry—no extra." Jiminez waved a hand. "No, I meant I know a few contacts in the criminal justice system, the legal profession. And the police, for that matter. Had to go to them to get the info. Quite interesting really."

"Oh?"

"Well you know the first part of the story—up till you left school, right? Well after that, Fisk got a job in the steelworks. Worked for a Sheffield company. He inherited his mothers' house when she died in 1994. Lived there for a couple of years. Then in '97 he married a Rosemary Willows. They sold his house and moved to Stannington. He was still at the steel company. She was a secretary at a firm of insurance brokers. They had a son, Alex, in 2002. This is where it takes a turn."

He leaned forward in his chair. "In 2006 they separated. The wife left him and got custody of the kid. He was pretty cut-up about it, apparently. As you would be. Had to move into a council flat. For a few months he was just getting access to the lad every other weekend. The missus starts seeing another bloke. Looks like Fisk then gets edgy –thinking he's going to lose the kid; reckons the lad's going to start calling another bloke '*Dad*'.

"Then in the summer of 2008 he picks little Alex up as usual.

Takes him to the top of the towerblock and they both jump off."

"Jump off?"

"Well, Fisk jumped and dragged the kid with him. Even left a suicide note for the ex, saying if *he* couldn't have his son, no one would."

Cowan swallowed and glanced away from the scrutiny of the older man's gaze. He watched the Asian woman browsing a magazine, licking her fingers as she turned the pages.

"I remember it in the news, actually," said Jimenez. "There was a public outcry. Front-page shit."

Cowan nodded noncommittally.

"But here's the best part—although the kid died, *Fisk survived.* Just snapped his fucking legs. The kid broke his fall."

Cowan looked out of the window. Mid-morning traffic crawled past, glistening in the rain. Pensioners shuffled along the pavement laden with carrier bags. He shook his head. "What a bastard."

"Bastard indeed." Jimenez pursed his lips. "He was charged with murder but the judge let him off—diminished responsibility. He got five years in a nut-house. The ex-wife killed herself a few months later. Overdose."

Cowan watched the older man remove a cigarette and light it, taking a deep drag and blowing the smoke out almost provocatively, his eyes narrowing. "The judge said Fisk *was* remorseful afterwards— he'd just cracked under the pressure of the divorce, that's all."

"So he's—what? Locked up still?"

Jimenez shook his head. "Got released after four years. Since last summer he's been living *here* under the name Peter Feltham." He opened the envelope and took out a folded sheet of A4 paper. His fingers hesitated on it for a second before he slid it across the table.

Cowan unfolded the paper and looked at the address. "Leeds?"

"Yeah. As part of the rehabilitation process he was given a new identity. That's why I asked why you were looking for him." Jimenez paused. "This info can't be traced back to my contact—it's now a matter of public record anyway, if you can be arsed to wade through enough paperwork—but I wanted to make sure you'd be...*discreet* with it."

Cowan forced himself to maintain eye-contact. "So you think—what? That I'll grass to the papers?"

"I don't know, son." His hand gripped Cowan's wrist. "But if you go through with what I think you're planning, I'd urge you to be careful."

Cowan released his hand, on the pretence of scratching his nose. "Mr Jimenez, I just wanted to see him—to talk. I won't mention it to anyone else."

Jimenez shrugged. "Look, I couldn't give a shit. Just don't bring my name into it if he gets itchy feet and scarpers. The authorities'll have your arse for an ashtray." His laughter sounded ugly and coarse.

"I just want to say hello—that's all. Maybe he'll be pleased to see an old face." Cowan slipped the address into his pocket.

Jimenez smiled wanly and began packing the envelope away. "Aye, Mr Campbell—or whatever your real name is—maybe he will."

*

The rain hadn't let up all week. Cowan tried to concentrate as he peered through the windscreen, the wipers doing their best to distract him. Rows of sagging shops blurred into one continuous line as he negotiated the ceaselessly spiralling roads. Leeds appeared to be a labyrinth of narrow streets choked by parked cars. The bricks of the buildings were a strange shade of ochre. It was quite unlike anything he'd seen before, certainly different to the houses in Sheffield.

He'd stumbled across a Tesco on the ring road. He'd been queuing at the checkout, clutching a Leeds A-Z, when the enormity of what he was about to do engulfed him. He quickly paid and rushed to the toilet, his legs almost buckling with nerves.

Outside, the cool air helped revive him. He waited in the car and browsed the A-Z, taking time to familiarise himself with his destination. He took a carrier-bag from the glove-box, gauging its weight in his hand. He drew back the plastic opening and admired the pistol inside, careful not to touch it with his fingers. The two-inch barrel looked deceptively harmless. It had been originally manufactured in Brazil; standard issue for the Singapore Police Force. The serial number had been filed down. This particular model—the Taurus 85—had an ornate pearl handgrip. He'd paid £600 for it from a man in his local, a transaction that had come with unspoken conditions attached: the weapon was untraceable—there would be no incriminating trail—*but Cowan better keep his mouth shut if things went wrong*. He swallowed and wrapped it back up.

Soon Cowan was back on the road, Fisk's address seared indelibly into his mind. He was headed for a tower-block in Gipton called Coldcote Heights. He pushed other thoughts away and tried to concentrate on driving.

Eventually he spotted an ugly, brooding building on the corner of Beech Lane—the Church of the Epiphany—and realised his destination was close by. He parked on the roadside and switched off the ignition, listening to the patter of rain on the roof as it synchronised with the ticks of the cooling engine. The wipers—frozen in the act of clearing the windscreen—helped to divert him as the raindrops obliterated his view.

He removed the carrier bag from the glove-box and tucked it into his jacket pocket. Then he paused for a few moments to gather his nerves before climbing out of the car and locking it.

A row of shops slouched to his left, rendered almost identical by the metal grilles obscuring their windows. Two elderly women in headscarves stood chatting outside the off-licence. An Asian man was talking loudly on his mobile phone, glaring through the window of the bookies. Cowan drew up his hood and set off across the grassy incline towards the kids' playground.

The squat, redbrick council houses surrounding the muddy expanse seemed to stare at him reproachfully. The play-area was in a poor state. Cowan stepped between used condoms and rusting syringes. The rungs of the slide's ladder were blackened with fire. Spray-painted obscenities adorned the side of the toddlers' climbing frame. Nearby, a heavily-muscled skinhead waited patiently as his Staffordshire Bull Terrier shivered a pale turd onto the grass. Cowan glanced away.

Ahead, his destination loomed like a beacon for the destitute. He hurried up the slope. Coldcote Heights towered broodingly above the roofs of the surrounding houses, seeming to watch over Gipton like a guardian. The cold impassive building almost made him shudder.

A chain-link fence at the top of the grassy square had been breached, its posts skewed by force. Empty cigarette packets and McDonald's cartons wilted in the rain. The sign on the Bangladeshi community centre had been vandalised, clearly by someone lacking the use of a spell-check. Youths loitered around the industrial bins at the rear.

Soon he had negotiated the warren of faceless tenements and found himself approaching the tower-block. He crossed the quadrangle of concrete, suddenly feeling exposed by the countless windows that watched his progress. A burnt-out car stood in the centre, rusting on four flat tyres. From somewhere nearby came the frantic barking of a dog. He pushed open the door of the building and entered the dark foyer.

The smell of piss was overpowering. To the left, a flight of concrete steps rose out of sight. A CCTV camera was positioned at a weird angle—possibly made ineffective by some wrong-doer. Signs on the walls promised direction but did nothing more than bewilder him. He scanned for the address that Jimenez had supplied, seeing that he needed to trek to the ninth floor.

The steel door of the lift was so scratched it looked as if ancient runes had been etched into its surface. Someone had smeared a foul-smelling substance over the call button. Wrinkling his nose, Cowan glanced down and spotted the neck of a broken beer-bottle discarded in the corner. He picked it up and used the lip of the glass to press the button. The noise of the lift's approach sounded ominous; as if the action had tripped some unseen signal.

Inside the lift, the smell of piss was just as strong. He used the glass shard to press the number 9 on the panel. A furry patch of mould stained the floor and a lower section of the compartment. Cowan stood as far away as possible from it as the lift bounced its ascent. The red LED above the panel flickered aggressively. Presently the door opened and he stepped out onto the ninth floor, taking time to carefully deposit the glass in the corner where he might later retrieve it.

A narrow corridor led into the heart of the building. Cowan wandered down it, glancing at the door numbers to check he was headed in the right direction. The light was meagre. Shadows scuttled in the corners. Windows at evenly-spaced intervals looked down into the quadrangle, accentuating his dizzying height. From further down the landing he heard the sound of someone singing in a foreign language, the staccato rhythm of the words suggesting a football chant. Cowan hurried along until he reached an intersection, heading to the left according to the door numbers.

He could feel his heart pounding as he drew close. The bag in his pocket felt like it was getting heavier. He stopped outside a door and stared at the plastic numbers screwed to the wood, licking his lips to alleviate the dryness. A quick glance both ways up the corridor eased his nerves. He pressed his ear to the door and listened.

Indistinct music was playing inside. Somewhere beyond the sound, a child was crying. Cowan considered the two bullets loaded in the pistol; for the first time worried that he ought to have requested more. The original intention had been for one bullet for Fisk and one for himself. The bloke in the pub had warned that it was difficult to silence this type of weapon; he'd need to make every shot count. He took a deep breath and tried the door handle.

He peered into a deserted hallway. The music was now recognisable—*The Style Council*—and he slipped inside the flat and closed the door.

From this angle he had a narrow vantage point into the living room. He could see the crown of someone's head as they sprawled on the sofa. The weeping child now sounded like it was coming from next door. He crept closer. As he drew near he could see that the prone figure was indeed Fisk. But not as he'd remembered him.

The man had his eyes closed tight, his face screwed up like a wrinkled cloth. His forehead looked unnaturally pock-marked. Sallow. The skin was pale and gaunt, stretched over the bones like tissue. His thinning hair barely covered the skull. His hands clutched the side of his head, accentuating the tendons in his rail-thin arms. He looked depleted.

Cowan swept a quick glance around, noting the signs of disarray. Empty beer bottles and cans littered the floor. Discarded pizza boxes and the misshapen trays from microwavable ready-meals. Boxes were stacked in the corners, filled with brightly-coloured objects. Light was pouring through the curtainless window. There was a powerful odour of stale sweat and booze. Relief surged. The pokey flat seemed otherwise empty. Cowan's fingers curled around the handle of the gun.

"Fisk." He stood over the emaciated wreck of a man, staring, daring him to look.

Fisk's eyes opened slowly. They looked blurred and bloodshot. He widened them, trying to focus, shuffling into an upright position.

"Remember me?" Cowan tried to keep his voice low and threatening, but he was afraid it just sounded weak.

Fisk blinked slowly. He appeared to be under the influence of something; probably drink, by the smell. He pulled a sour face.

"I've come to kill you," Cowan said quietly. He shuffled his feet.

Fisk smiled wanly and rolled onto his side, moved to a sitting position. "You were Rosie's bit on the side. I remember you." His voice sounded dead. Listless.

"I wasn't a *bit on the side*. I tried to help her after you two split up."

"So you say." Fisk laughed hollowly. "How'd you find me?"

Cowan made a fist. "I made a promise to Rose before she died."

Fisk shrugged. It was an unsightly gesture. Cowan marvelled again at the man's appearance. He looked ravaged. Close to death.

"Go on then." He sat up and put his head in his hands. "You'll be doing me a favour."

Cowan stared at him, clenching his teeth. He fought to suppress the rage that ached inside. "You piece of shit. He was six years old, for fuck's sake. A good kid."

"Should I tell you something…what's your name?"

"Cowan."

"Cowan, that's right. Cowan." He rolled the word around his mouth. "Let me tell you something—he's not a *good kid* any more."

"You selfish bastard. Why couldn't you just kill yourself and leave him with his mum."

"With *you* and Rosie, you mean? That would've been nice." His breath hitched. A change seemed to come over him. He looked detached. "Don't you think I'm sorry for what I done? Don't you think I wished I'd died that day? I'd end it tomorrow if I thought it would all stop."

"This place is a shit-hole. Why'd you move here?"

Fisk shrugged. "Why not? I lived round here as a kid. Till we moved to Sheffield when I left school."

Shit. Jimenez must have known about the lies. He must have known Fisk hadn't attended school in Sheffield.

Cowan glanced around. There was a cushion on the sofa. He could hold the gun against it and shoot through. It should muffle the shot. The crying kid next door might mask the noise. It could give him sufficient time to get away.

Fisk looked up, wrongly interpreting the pause. "*You* can hear him too, can't you?"

"That kid?"

Fisk nodded and grimaced, revealing yellow teeth. His next words chilled Cowan to the core. "That's Alex."

Cowan peered in the direction of the sound. He'd assumed it had been from the neighbouring flat, but he realised it was coming from the next room. Heart hammering in his throat, he approached the door and pushed it open.

The sound stopped instantly. He could see similar signs of disorder in the room—an unmade bed, clothes strewn on the floor, boxes of things stored in the corner.

"It's not so bad in the day," Fisk said. "The nights are worst. I can't get away. He's changed. He doesn't love his dad no more."

Cowan turned back.

"You should see his face at night. Fucking terrifying." Fisk stood with a groan and switched off the music. "That's why I have *that* on—drowns him out a bit." His foot knocked an empty can of Tennent's Super across the floor. He slumped back onto the sofa, the movement causing a hole in the upholstery to gape like a hungry mouth. He stared at a spot in the corner of the ceiling.

"Sometimes at night I see him watching me from up there." He motioned with his hand.

Despite himself, Cowan glanced into the empty, mildew-stained corner.

"He grows spindly legs like a spider. He creeps around quiet, daring me to watch. If I close my eyes, he'll pounce. It's just a game to him. Without the booze I can't sleep."

Cowan rolled his eyes. "Maybe the booze makes you imagine things."

"The fuck it does." He suddenly lifted the sleeve of his t-shirt, revealing a pattern of angry scabs. "Trouble is, I'm so out of it I can't feel him slashing me."

Cowan winced at the rawness of the wounds.

"Stanley knife," Fisk said. "Fucker likes to have his fun."

Cowan studied the boxes for the first time. They were stuffed with children's toys, videos, wooden jigsaws. "You need help."

Fisk laughed again, that horrible sound. "I'm past help." He slumped back onto the sofa. "I need to *drink*—that's what keeps me from seeing him. That or the gear." He ran his fingers through his hair and belched. Cowan could see the forearm was scarred with circular marks like burns. The man looked wrecked with exhaustion.

His anger was beginning to dissipate, replaced by a modicum of pity. It seemed like Fisk was existing in his own self-induced hell. Tormenting himself. The guilt must have tipped his mind. That or the booze.

"If I carry on drinking, I know I'll die. I've already seen signs. Liver's knackered. Be a blessing when it comes." He motioned with his hand. "Benny from over the way brought me a couple of bottles of absinthe back from his last trip. That's good stuff, let me tell you. Good stuff."

"Why do you keep these?" Cowan tapped the side of one of the cardboard boxes. "You should let it go. You're just torturing yourself."

Fisk shook his head. "You don't get it, do you? *He* brings them."

"You think Alex brought this stuff?"

"Uh-huh. He leaves me…little gifts. From the other side."

Cowan felt the skin on the back of his neck prickling. He lifted a soft toy out of the box. It was a cloth mouse wearing a gingham shirt—*something from Bagpuss?* Cowan's memory faltered. It looked old. Some of the stitching had come loose. One of its eyes looked wonky. As he held the object, a foul stench seemed to emanate from it. An intense feeling of revulsion struck. He tossed the toy back into the box, almost recoiling.

Little gifts. Cowan knew enough to understand the correct word even if Fisk didn't—*apports*. Fisk believed the toys were reminders from his dead son. Reminders of what damage he'd done. He had clearly lost his mind. The self-harming was just another symptom of the madness. Cowan supposed guilt could do that.

Fisk was speaking. "Remember that film with Bruce Willis's wife and the crazy black woman? And him—Lundgren?"

"Swayze."

"Yeah, that's it. Well that's what it's like. Twenty four hours a day. He's there taunting me, trying to hurt me. Reminding me that he's angry. At night he sometimes burns my skin." He rested his head back on the sofa. "And he set fire to my hair once. But it's no more than I deserve." His voice seemed stronger now, less slurred. Maybe he was sobering up.

Cowan became aware of the gun's weight again. He looked around the squalor, considering Fisk's situation. His physical condition was pathetic. Dishevelled. The mementoes, the cans of booze, the state of his mind. Ending Fisk's life would be doing him a favour, and that was the last thing he wanted to do.

"Why not kill yourself then? Proper this time though."

Fisk blinked slowly. "You a religious man?"

Cowan shook his head.

"Neither was I before all this shit." He swallowed. "But in hospital I was encouraged to find God. So I'm hedging my bets— this might be His test. I need to endure my punishment. Anything else would be to face eternal damnation. And—like I said—my liver's on its way out anyway."

Cowan shook his head. "You sick fuck. You committed a wicked act. For that you'll rot in hell when your time comes." He fought to keep his composure. "You ruined Rose's life—and mine. And you took poor Alex. But the judge was right—you're fucked-up in the head. That's no excuse for what you did, but I think you're suffering in your own hell."

He shook his head and left the flat, slamming the door behind him. Almost instantly the crying kid started up again. It really did sound like it was coming from inside Fisk's flat. The music recommenced straight away.

Cowan made his way back to the lift. Turning back, he glanced into the throat of the corridor. An indistinct shape loitered in the shadows. The singsong tone of a nursery rhyme echoed along the passage, followed by the sound of children's laughter.

"Hello?" Cowan's voice was taut. "Who's there?"

The laughter rang again, this time with a malevolent edge. Brittle.

Cowan turned back to the lift. He flared his nostrils at the panel and shouldered open the door to the stairs. The air was cool. He began his descent. Raindrops on the windows warped his view. Someone was kicking a football in the stairwell far below. A child's echoing voice recited *Baa Baa Black Sheep*. The noise felt like it was swirling around him. Monochrome colours of the décor matched his headache. He was gasping by the time he reached the ground floor, bursting from the foyer into the quadrangle. It had stopped raining.

He strode back to his car, feeling uncomfortably warm beneath his coat. Shafts of sunlight were fighting to break through the clouds. He uttered silent apologies to Rose as he crossed the playground, reminding himself that Fisk's suffering justified the broken promise. It made him feel no better.

As he drew near to the car, he clicked his remote control. The alarm squealed its short burst and unlocked the doors. He was desperate to get back to Sheffield. He was tired of this world of graffiti and decay, of litter and filth. He took off his coat and tossed it into the back. The key slid into the ignition and he turned it, firing the engine. And it was just as he was reaching over to fasten his seatbelt that he spotted the toy mouse on the dashboard.

He picked it up carefully and studied it. The faded gingham, the worn seams, the wonky eye—all identical to the one in Fisk's flat.

Cowan clicked the seatbelt in and released the handbrake.

*

He stopped in a lay-by several miles outside Leeds. A stone bridge spanned the road, under which flowed a deep waterway identified by a wooden sign as the River Aire. Cowan paused for a moment and peered at the brown water as it flowed languidly beneath. The road was deserted. He removed the plastic bag from his pocket and paused for a second before dropping it over the side. The splash was deep and satisfying. For several minutes he watched the ripples until they died away and the surface returned to its flat, constant motion. Then he walked back to the car.

Lord Of The Sand

Without Facebook, it never would have happened. We'd have all just continued living our lives, content to let the past remain the past. All of the bad feelings would have stayed deeply buried.

But Facebook allows you to assemble a ribbon of detritus from your life—a place where current friends mingle with barely-remembered school chums, former work colleagues mass like mementos from all the shit jobs you've ever had. I've even got a couple of ex-girlfriends on mine, just for old times' sake. What I'm saying is that I *realise* the past is a different country—and it certainly was in our case because we'd fought in it. So when the invitation to attend the reunion arrived, I should've just walked away. I should have let bygones be bygones. Looked forward instead of back. My God, how I wish I'd done just that.

By this time my army career felt like it had happened to someone else. Don't get me wrong—I'm grateful I experienced the things I did, grateful too for the training and qualifications I attained; achievements which—once my decade serving Queen and Country had ended—became the launch-pad into my new career as a telecommunications engineer. But as I'd grown older my political stance had shifted marginally. Operation Desert Storm had seemed an absolute necessity at the time. However, things had changed; I now felt uneasy about the way the West was dealing with the Middle-East. Twenty-five years had made one hell of a difference.

Christ, I'm starting to sound like my dad.

Anyway, the reunion of the Royal Regiment of Fusiliers 3rd Battalion was arranged for December 2nd in the function room of the Golden Plover, four miles outside Hastings. It had been chosen largely due to its accessibility from London and its close proximity to the home of the organiser, Shaun Adams.

I hadn't seen Shaun—or Beaky as we'd called him—since Fallujah in 1991. But his Facebook photos told me he'd barely changed other than a receding hairline and a few wrinkles. I was curious to catch up, to see what had happened to everyone during the intervening years. I'd initially joined the army with no clear idea of where I was going. Those qualifications that I mentioned earlier—they meant that I was now quite proud of what I'd ended up doing. The group messages suggested there would be quite an attendance if all those invited turned up.

I'd booked into a Travelodge that lay within walking distance of the pub. At the appointed time I nervously strolled into the function room, trying my best to look as slim as I'd been in the early nineties. The DJ was working overtime in recapturing the era—all Chesney Hawkes and Colour Me Badd and Jesus Jones. I allowed myself to be swept up into the slightly surreal experience of meeting people from my distant past; people I'd once entrusted with my life, but who now just looked vaguely familiar. The beer-bellies and slap-heads were in attendance everywhere. Within ten minutes I'd sunk three pints, all the better to steady my nerves. I'd been introduced to several wives (and managed to promptly forget their names), reminded of a dozen hilarious memories (which time had subsequently wiped), and raised sombre toasts to a couple of fallen comrades. And then, shortly before nine o'clock, Beaky made his entrance.

At this point I probably need to mention that Beaky had occupied a rather special position in our regiment. He'd been a thin, nervous lad; twitchy and unprepared for the horrors that awaited us in Iraq. Unfortunately he hadn't fared well. There were times when he'd skirted close to cracking. He'd been the butt of many of the pranks that had been played, borne the brunt of the majority of teasing. Not *bullying*, you understand, although I had felt a slight nervousness at seeing him again; a twinge of guilt that had manifested over the intervening years.

But I needn't have worried. Beaky was welcomed like a returning hero, his slight frame embraced by drunken ex-squaddies and surprised girlfriends. As organiser of the reunion, he was also congratulated as to its success, with slurred pledges to make it an annual event. Very soon he found himself at my table, occupying the empty seat beside me.

We made small-talk for a while. I offered to buy him a drink, but he advised me he was driving—something that puzzled me, given how close to the Plover he lived—surely he could afford the cost of a taxi. Nevertheless I returned from the bar with his coke and another pint for me.

I tried discretely to make light of his experience in the forces, quizzing him enthusiastically about his current life, overcompensating with the positives. Despite his Facebook pictures indicating otherwise, he appeared rather vacant; brittle and broken. There was a sallow, haunted sheen to his skin. His eyes constantly watched the door, restless and anxious. He admitted that he'd been prescribed powerful drugs for his insomnia. It seemed like he harboured the same debilitating lack of self-worth he'd displayed back then. I felt dreadfully sorry for him. At that point he excused himself and went to the toilet.

Beaky was obviously edgy as hell. And deep inside I knew why.

Brad Hoggard was conspicuous by his absence. Six-foot five, blond-haired Brad had served as our sergeant. He could handle himself, and by-God, did he know it. His biceps were so thick it must have used a gallon of ink just to tattoo the Celtic bands that encircled them. I was relieved that he hadn't shown up, even if it meant the central character from our regiment was missing. We all understood that it was Hoggard's mean streak which had fuelled the campaign of victimisation that Beaky had been forced to endure. He'd mentally bullied the kid as much as inflicting the physical damage on him. And I took no consolation in the fact that Hoggard had been the instigator of the bullying—every time I'd looked away or pretended not to hear, another part of my insides had withered. If I'm honest, I suspect that most of us had just felt relieved that the victim—Beaky, always Beaky—had been someone else instead of us.

Anyway, about half-nine I was chatting to a bloke who'd been airlifted out of Iraq early into our tour, when he swore under his breath and nodded towards the door. I glanced up and felt my heart sink.

The disco lights strobed against an imposing figure that was striding into the room. The silhouette was unmistakable. As he crossed the dance-floor I caught sight of Hoggard for the first time in decades. It seemed like nature had played a cruel hand; unlike the rest of us—all beer bellies, wrinkles, bald heads, jowls— Hoggard had apparently taken good care of himself. His hair was fashionably cut, the tight shirt accentuating his flat stomach and defined muscles. I noticed quite a few wives and girlfriend watching his progress as he strode over to our table. His skin looked like he'd been fucking airbrushed.

I stood and tried to spot Beaky at the bar. Several lads cautiously greeted Hoggard and he seemed to bask in the attention. I headed to the bar to distract Beaky, maybe even prepare him for the appearance of his nemesis. Someone turned and I heard him mutter, "Why the fuck has he been invited?" and someone replied, "Which dickhead invited him anyway?" I shrugged and in that moment decided to take on the role of peacemaker. But in the end it was all needless anyway.

The evening progressed not at all in the way I expected. Hoggard actually proved to be, whilst not exactly *likeable*, extremely more amiable than he'd been as our sergeant. His career hadn't progressed further than sergeant however (that may have had more to do with his overt sociopathic tendencies than any lack of ambition). And I was heartened to see that Beaky had let bygones be bygones. At one point I even saw them laughing together.

By the time last orders were called at the bar, the whole place had slipped into a merry state of inebriation. We'd all had a bloody good time. My ears were ringing with the music and I glanced about, intending to get in a final round of drinks. It was then that I spotted Hoggard slumped forward across a table nearby. I made some comment about how the big man obviously wasn't able to hold his beer any more. Beaky laughed and we went over to see if he was okay.

Hoggard was absolutely paralytic. We attempted to lift him up, his eyes rolling in their sockets. Someone suggested calling an ambulance, but that idea was quickly dismissed. I was just about to volunteer to let him stay in my room at the Travelodge, when Beaky piped up about how he knew Hoggard's address and—as he'd not been drinking—he'd drive him home. That was quickly agreed, and it took three of us to help him out to Beaky's Vectra and see them off, pleas to stay in touch echoing round the car park.

By the time I returned to the bar, the bell had gone so I missed the last drink. As a result, I began to sober-up slightly. That fact proved to be important later.

The crowd had thinned. People were drifting away, swapping phone numbers and drunkenly telling each other how much they'd enjoyed the evening. I felt a satisfied glow at how it had turned out. And then a passing comment tore my cosy world to shreds.

I remarked about how unfounded my concerns for Beaky had been; that Hoggard's appearance had failed to spoil the party. I received a puzzled glance, and was told that Beaky had *made contact* with Hoggard through Facebook and pretty much begged him to attend the reunion.

To clear my head, I went out to the car-park. I looked thoughtfully at the space that the Vectra had recently vacated, suddenly noticing the overflowing bin nearby, its top filled with discarded cigarette ends. There was an empty packet of tablets stuffed in among the rubbish, the prescription sticker torn off. I had to use my iPhone to google the word—Flunitrazepam—recognising the name *Rohypnol*, a powerful muscle-relaxant commonly prescribed for chronic insomnia.

The cogs were clicking in my brain. I ran back inside, babbling at the DJ that I needed to know Beaky's address. His blank face masked the concern he must have felt. I demanded to know the contact details of the bloke that had organised the evening. His reluctance crumbled when I told him I'd found Beaky's house keys in the car park. He looked it up in his notepad, and I wrote it down and called a taxi.

I was there in half an hour. There was a light burning in every window of Beaky's house. It was a rather shabby semi-detached property, with thin trees casting a shadow onto the bay window. I paid the taxi and fought to compose myself as I crept up the drive.

He took ages to come to the door. He looked surprised when

he saw me, but then I detected something shift in his eyes, and he held the door open and invited me in.

The house was silent. It looked like it hadn't been redecorated since John Major had been in power. He led me into the lounge and I sat down on a sagging sofa as its springs wheezed beneath me in protest.

"Drink?"

I shook my head. I'd had enough. Besides, I felt sick. "Where's Hog?"

He shrugged. "Sleeping like a baby, I imagine."

I felt relieved at his relaxed manner. Perhaps I was blowing this situation out of all proportion.

"He's still got his looks, hasn't he?" Beaky took a seat in the armchair opposite me. "Looked after himself."

I nodded. His house was cramped and cluttered. Bric-a-brac and cheap ornamental tat lined the shelves, entirely covering the surface of a scratched sideboard.

"Yeah, he looked well. How's life been since the army, Beak- err, Shaun?"

He shrugged. "Not bad, I suppose." He looked up sharply. "I enjoyed my time in the forces, you know—despite what happened."

"Good."

"Do you think about them days much?"

I shook my head. "Feels like it happened to someone else." The silence that descended then was bloated and dense. To break it, I said, "Do you?"

A thin smile played around his lips. The he said quietly, "I try not to."

To change the subject, I glanced around. "You've got a nice pad here."

He raised his eyebrows. "Suits me well enough. I've got everything I need here. I don't have many friends."

I nodded slowly. Something on a wooden cabinet in the corner caught my eye. "What's that?"

"Ah. My boys, my boys."

I stood and approached. It was a large glass tank. There was a metal lid on top, housing a heater. The interior of the container was dark, deliberately steeped in shadow. A stack of rocks lay half buried in a deep layer of sand. I bent and peered into the far recesses of the tank. "What you got in here?"

Beaky moved behind me. "I suppose they're my mementos from our time in Iraq. Did you bring anything back with you?—Any…trinkets?"

I looked at him sharply, studying his face. I was thinking of what I had hidden in my loft wrapped in a plastic bag—an automatic handgun, its serial number filed blank. I turned back to the tank. "My God—what is it?"

"Lords of the Sand." He moved his face close to the glass. "My two little babies." His voice had taken on a detached, dreamlike quality.

I stared into the tank, my eyes picking out the nest of threads that lined the shallow burrows of sand. I could make out the desiccated husks of several large crickets tucked into the niche. Slowly, expectantly, something scuttled out of the darkness. I could discern the fine hairs that coated the spider's pale legs. Its grotesque chelicerae twitched, lending it a monstrous image.

Camel spiders—or wind scorpions as they're sometimes called—are universally feared in the middle-east. Whilst not dangerously toxic, they possess powerful jaws which can inflect great damage on larger mammals. Some of the African lads referred to them as *beard-cutters* due to their reputation for clipping hair from sleeping men in order to line their burrows. I thought that was a load of old bollocks—but out in Iraq I had once seen one kill and devour a huge lizard. It was brutal and unforgettable. It was said their bite released an anaesthetic toxin which allowed it to chew away at the prey's numb flesh without detection. Several years ago I'd watched a documentary on the National Geographic channel where a camel spider had eaten the leg of a sleeping cat, stripping the flesh down to the bone. They were known as the Lords of the Sand.

"Christ, mate—why'd you want theses fuckers as pets?" I was caught halfway between repulsion and fascination.

Beaky smiled then, and I noticed his lidded eyes were cast low. "I became obsessed with them out in Fallujah. They seemed to represent something which struck a chord with me—they *can* actually attack camels, you know. I imported this pair a few years ago."

My eyes searched for the other one, the unseen partner. I was only vaguely aware of what Beaky was saying.

"I find them fascinating—how something of this size can be unafraid of taking on something as large as a camel…it's admirable, don't you think? The bigger they are, the harder they fall."

Something clicked in my brain. I turned to him. "Beaky, where's the other one? I can only see one here."

He laughed sharply. His face now looked reptilian, unreal. I felt the hairs on my forearms bristle.

"The other one's feeding."

I peered closely at the tank. "Where?"

"I've kept the other one isolated for a week or so." He turned away. "Just to get him nice and hungry."

In a second I was pushing past him, moving out of the lounge. The dining room was in darkness, but I could see the light spilling from the stairs. I bounded up them two at once.

"Hoggard!" My voice sounded deafening in the silence.

I reached the top of the stairs, feeling disorientated by the doors that faced me. Instinctively I moved to the left, barging the door with my shoulder.

It was the spare bedroom. A lamp illuminated the room from its place on the bedside cabinet. The next few seconds were difficult to comprehend because I experienced everything at once.

A shape was rising from the bed, sluggish and leaden. As I took in the sight of the figure, I stepped backwards. Vaguely I recognised Hoggard from his clothing, although at first I had the impression that he was wearing a mask.

The lower half of his face was a ruined mess. There was a gaping red hole where his nose should have been, pale strands of gristle protruding through the bloodstained remnants of his nose. His teeth were exposed in a fearsome grin. The skin around his lips was gone, revealing a slender jawbone. There was very little blood. His eyes blinked mechanically, betraying the fact that he was alive. *How could he be, when the lower half of his face had been stripped away, consumed?* His legs wobbled, and he stumbled back against the bed. I had a feeling the drug was wearing off. His wrecked face was rendering the cries unintelligible.

And then I spotted the huge spider on the duvet. It looked bloated and satisfied. Its legs trembled horribly. I flicked the material of the duvet and it fell to the floor, trying to scuttle away. My boot stamped quickly, squashing it against the carpet. Pale legs twitched. I swear I heard a sickening crunch.

I tried to grab my phone as Hoggard rolled around on the bed, shrieking frantically, fingering his destroyed face. He was mad with terror. It was a nightmarish scene.

And above the sound of his screams I could hear Beaky's unhinged laughter from downstairs.

Somewhere On Sebastian Street

Somewhere on Sebastian Street lies a place that isn't governed by the usual laws of nature; a place where the walls of reality are at their thinnest, and darkness occasionally bleeds through from beyond, tainting the people and objects it touches. Somewhere on Sebastian Street exists a portal between worlds.

The residents of Sebastian Street once dreamed of life and distance and time, bearing witness to sights that no one should ever see. Unspeakable acts. Their presence has long since faded from within the walls. But houses dream, too, and sometimes those dreams become nightmares.

*

I'm nearly finishing my second pint by the time I spot Gary enter the pub, threading his way between lunchtime workers and the ubiquitous assortment of regulars. He winks as he draws close to my table. He hasn't changed a bit in the five years since I last saw him; the sparkle in his eyes is still present, the brush of red hair lending his face a good-humoured appearance.

We shake hands and he asks what I'm drinking, then ventures to the bar. I watch his flirting fail to impress the barmaid. He returns a minute later with my pint and a Coke for him. I make some comment about how his drinking habits have *definitely* changed, and he laughs enthusiastically, pointing out that he's working. We deal with the pleasantries.

"So what're you doing back here? You said on the phone you needed help with access to a site?"

I nod. "The old Swinston estate."

He frowns. "There's nothing there now, mate. The last row of houses was knocked down last year."

"I know. I read about it on the internet. How come it took so long?"

Gary shrugs. "Some fuck-up between the council and the property developers. The demolition started back in the nineties when it was just used by rent-boys and junkies. The last row was delayed 'cause of some administrative cock-up—that's Leeds-fucking-Council for you. Anyway, finally the courts decided they could knock the lot down."

"Right. Well, I just need half an hour. Only to take some photos, soak up the atmosphere." I take a puff on my inhaler, feeling like my nerves are betraying me.

"There's nothing there no more—just rubble."

"That's okay. Just for old-times' sake. A final goodbye."

Gary eyes me strangely, as if he's just realised I've lost my mind. He's probably thinking about the woman that was killed there in the early 80s; those stories about how her body was mutilated and defiled.

"Please, Gaz. I won't cause a problem." I try to compose my best *trustworthy, old school-friend* face. I think I succeed.

He takes a drink of his Coke. I can hear the ice clinking against the glass. He wipes his mouth with the back of his sleeve. "I can give you twenty minutes."

*

His council van smells of stale sweat, hamburgers, and engine oil. The dashboard is littered with old newspapers and Post-it notes with addresses scrawled on them. As he drives, I can hear his toolboxes rattling in the back. He asks me what I'm doing back in town.

I explain about how my parents have just moved out of the family home into a smaller bungalow in Beeston, and how I've been helping them with the process. I mention how I've been sorting through some storage boxes from my old bedroom in an effort to thin out their belongings. I tell him it stirred up old memories from my childhood. This is all true. Needless to say, I don't tell him the entire truth.

I finger the plastic walkie-talkie in my pocket. Its rubber aerial pokes against my chest like a knife.

Soon we enter the industrial estate. Business offices and flimsy-looking warehouses stand conspicuously in the centre of deserted car-parks. All the company logos affixed to the buildings' walls look identical. Ahead, the road is barricaded by a framework of red and white plastic cordons. Behind it, a solid eight-foot wooden fence encircles the perimeter of the building site.

Gary pulls over and yanks on the handbrake. "Right." He unclips a Yale-key from the fob dangling from his ignition and passes it to me. "The entrance is over there. This is for the padlock." He looks at me strangely again. "I'll have to get back once I've had my dinner. That give you long enough?"

I nod and smile, climbing out of the car. The walkie-talkie in my pocket seems suddenly fragile and I cup it as I hurry over to the door that's cut into the roughly-erected fence. The metal of the padlock feels icy-cold and I'm relieved once it gives and I gain entry. I step through the door and close it behind me, pushing the swollen wood together with some effort.

It's difficult at first for me to reconcile what I'm seeing. The flat expanse of ground is broken up by piles of rubble—mainly heaped house-bricks, but also twisted metal struts, faded UPVC window frames and smashed paving slabs. Jewels of broken glass glisten in the afternoon sunlight. It resembles nothing of the place it was the last time I was here.

*

There was something about the empty houses that made them look sinister. It may have been the way their doors and windows had been barricaded up; as if the authorities were trying to prevent some obscene force from escaping. Perhaps local legends added to the sense of despair that attached itself to the deserted streets. Swinston estate had been left to rot many years ago; Leeds city council, it seemed, had thrown in the towel.

The boys were well aware of the stories. Everybody was. The

depravity that once went on in Sebastian Street was discussed in hushed tones, but still the kids heard about it. Lurid schoolyard stories kept the tale alive, passing it through generations as if it was part of the community, a fabric of local colour.

In 1982 a woman's mutilated corpse had been discovered inside one of the rows of terraced houses. Six different types of semen were found within her battered and abused body, as well as a length of bubble-wrap. Someone had slashed arcane symbols into her flesh. There was even a rumour that one sample of the semen had been equine.

The three boys stood on Sebastian Street and regarded the final row of terraced houses with something approaching reverence. Metal security shutters enclosed the doors; wooden boards were nailed across the windows. It symbolised all that was forbidden. Years before, heroin-addicts had frequented the houses. Ironically the only street to survive the estate's demolition had been the one with such notoriety.

"Why didn't they knock *these* ones down?" murmured Sam. Absently he fished out his asthma inhaler and took a blast.

Mal shrugged. "Which one was where it happened?"

Cameron poked the ground with a wooden stick. He glanced up and studied the row.

Sam tried to detect fear in the boy's expressionless face, but saw nothing. He glanced at the row himself. The security covers made the houses look like impassive faces staring back at them. Almost challenging.

"Not sure which one." Cameron's voice was indifferent. "They all look the same."

Several tiles were missing off the roof, which extended the length of the terrace. Only the individual chimney pots gave any indication of which house was which.

Sam took out the Spider Man walkie-talkies, handing one to Cameron. He accepted it silently.

"My brother told me that men sometimes bum other men inside there." Cameron blinked. "For money."

Mal grimaced, but said nothing. He knelt on the kerb. "You still up for this?"

Cameron nodded. "No problem."

Despite the younger kid's bravado, Sam noticed the damp patches under his arms. He considered again whether they were being fair—Cameron Glover was the school's misfit, seemingly friends with no one, a withdrawn introvert who took the butt of most of the pranks. Mal and Sam had offered him the opportunity to join their small circle of friends…at a price; first he'd need to prove his worthiness.

The sense of desolation that permeated the Swinston estate seemed a stern enough challenge. Its abandoned streets and silent, debris-stricken plots appeared to harbour darkness. Shadows gathered on the corners. Discarded rubbish thrived amongst the ruins, and overgrown weeds sprouted from the cracked tarmac. Parents warned their children not to venture onto the estate in the daylight, let alone during the hours of darkness. The place was synonymous with death and depravity.

Cameron studied the row of terraced houses and swallowed. He gripped the wooden stick tightly, almost brandishing it. Somewhere nearby, a plastic bag, half-buried by soil and bricks, flapped in the breeze like a frantic bird.

"How does this thing work?" The younger kid licked his lips and peered at the walkie-talkie.

"Just press the button and speak into the top. We'll hear you."

Cameron nodded slowly. Sam watched the younger boy walk towards the row of houses, clambering over the remnants of a fallen wall. Overgrown grass reached through the rubble like spindly fingers. Sam's eyes followed Cameron's progress until he disappeared round the back. He crouched on the kerb next to Mal. For a moment they listened.

Sam finally spoke into the walkie-talkie. "Can you see the hole in the board?"

There was a pause and then a short burst of static. "I'm in the kitchen already."

Mal pursed his lips and nodded approvingly.

"What can you see?" asked Sam.

"It's just a kitchen. It's dark, though. God, it stinks."

Sam smiled, detecting the faintest trace of fear in the younger lad's voice. "Go on."

"Nothing much. It's dusty. All the worktops are filthy."

"Go into some of the rooms."

There was silence for a few minutes. Then, "Right. I'm at the bottom of the stairs."

"What's it like?"

A tinny laugh. "Just stairs."

"I mean, is it dark?" Sam stared at the entranced Mal. "And scary?"

"No." But Cameron's voice sounded slender and taut.

"See what's upstairs."

"Okay."

For a few minutes there was just silence. Mal scratched his head. He said to Sam in a low voice, "Don't you think he's a weirdo? I'm not sure if we want him hanging around with us, anyway."

"What do you mean?"

"Seen his arms? He's got cuts all over them. He always wears that long-sleeved vest for PE but I saw it when he was washing his hands. I think he's into that *cutting-yourself* shit."

Sam searched for the word. "Self-harming?"

Mal nodded. "That's it."

Sam shrugged and stared at the row of houses. He didn't speak. His eyes tried to picture the kid inside, wandering around in the darkness.

A plaintive caw broke the silence. Sam watched a huge black crow land on the roof. It unfurled its wings slowly as if to catch the sun, making it look like it was wearing a cloak. Mal stood and threw a stone. It missed by a mile, striking the sagged guttering with a crack that echoed across the estate like a gunshot. The crow flapped into the air and flew languidly away.

There was a burst of static and the walkie-talkie crackled into life. "There's nothing up here. Just empty rooms."

Mal grabbed the handset from Sam. "Watch out for the ghost of the dead woman." He laughed exaggeratedly, maniacally.

Cameron's next words halted the laughter. "Hey—there's a hole in the wall. I can see something moving."

Sam stared at Mal's stunned face, listening intently. He reclaimed the walkie-talkie.

There was the sound of movement in the speaker. Bricks falling.

"Are you okay?" Sam cleared his throat and pressed the walkie-talkie to his ear.

"Just opening up a bigger gap."

Sam could hear him scrabbling around. When Cameron's voice returned, it was made gruff by his panting breath. "I can see into the bedroom. Looks like the house next door. There's something on the floor."

"What is it?"

"Hang on." Sounds of effort, a succession of knocks.

"Eugh. There's black stains on the floorboards. It looks like… dried blood."

"Shit, that must be where—"

"Hang on, what's that?"

The silence was unbearable. Mal stared at Sam expectantly, open-mouthed.

"What is it?" Mal prompted eventually. His breath was shallow.

"Stone steps. Going down."

Mal frowned.

Silence again for several moments. Then Cameron's voice returned: "God, they go on forever. I'm walking down them." He sounded breathless. "I'm on some kind of landing."

Sam continued to listen. He was aware that Mal was also holding his breath. "Is it still dark?"

No reply. When Cameron spoke again, his words chilled Sam to the bone: "I'm at the bottom. I can see something. It looks like…a lake."

Sam turned sharply, frowning at his companion. "I thought he said *lake*."

Mal's eyes were huge. "He did."

"Wow, it's lovely. There's…there's trees and a cornfield and… some massive dragonflies." He sounded awestruck.

Sam spoke slowly. "Cameron, are you okay? You sound a bit funny." He took a puff of his inhaler.

"Ah, they're not dragonflies. They're…what're they called?— hummingbirds?" His voice had taken on a dreamlike quality.

Sam yelled at him to stop being stupid, pleading with him to return. Mal's face was aghast. Pale. He stared dumbstruck as Sam shouted into the walkie-talkie, urging the younger boy to come back out. Cameron ignored him, instead continuing to describe impossible sights.

Sam stood with his head pressed against Mal's, listening to the younger boy speak. He was becoming detached from reality, carried away by Cameron's warped madness, the narration fuelling his fear and transporting his imagination. Sanity was being abandoned. Certainty was unravelling.

Eventually the walkie-talkie fell silent and Sam stared miserably at the row of houses, numb and broken. Nearby, Mal shivered, his hands laced together as if in silent prayer. Sam's chest felt constricted and wheezy. Fear deterred any notion of rescue; Cameron's words were lodged like barbs in his mind.

They turned to go, stunned and terrified. Their abandoned bikes seemed like they'd lain there for years, the frames coated with dust and grit. It was impossible to ride them because they had Cameron's spare bike to accommodate now. They hurried as best they could. Mal lived on the far side of town, so they separated at the boundary of the park, exchanging hushed farewells. Sam resisted the urge to ditch the bikes, instead negotiating the journey by clumsily pushing one on either side. By the time he arrived home and alerted his parents, he was aching and shivering.

Sam knew they'd never see Cameron again.

*

Much later—several weeks after the police had scoured the estate with forensic teams and assistance from a nearby force, weeks after Cameron's brother—whose arms also sported similar cuts and cigarette burns—was taken into care by social services, ages after Cameron's dad was arrested and the local press had reported the sickening catalogue of abuse—Sam returned to Sebastian Street and stared at the row of houses with eyes that had lost their innocence.

He'd learned things about the world that could never be unlearnt;

ugly truths that soured his trust and crumbled the foundations of his belief system. It had only been three weeks since Cameron's disappearance, yet it felt as if the world had changed; things had advanced.

It was early evening and the sun was descending beyond the rubble-strewn site, creating a black silhouette of the houses, rendering them flat and unreal. Sam had no idea why he'd brought the walkie-talkie. Maybe it felt like the single remaining link to Cameron; a fragile thread of contact. Perhaps it symbolised the final vestige of his own childhood.

He clicked on the button of the walkie-talkie and pressed it to his ear.

*

I take the walkie-talkie out with trembling hands and hold it for a moment, staring at the mountain of rubble that now approximates Sebastian Street. The silence is eerie. A breeze sweeps the site, combing through the overgrown weeds and sending dust rattling across the debris. Clouds race overhead. The sky presses me to the ground. I close my eyes.

I can remember how it felt to lie in bed at night, listening to the static's howl as I held the walkie-talkie to my ear. At first Cameron sounded frightened, his voice high-pitched and frantic, distorted by the swirls of interference. Sometimes I tried to answer him, but there was never any sign that he could hear, just the tortured warbles of sound. Eventually the noises faded and there was nothing but static; cold, black static. The batteries ran down and I never replaced them.

I examine the gaudy red and black plastic now, testing the weight in my hand. The new batteries seem to make it heavier than it once felt, even though I know that's impossible. I hold it up and carefully press the receive button.

It feels like I stand there forever holding my breath, listening to the crackling, whooshing white-noise. My imagination conjures swirls of vocals in the static but I dismiss that as lost hope. A cloud passes in front of the sun and it suddenly grows cold. Somewhere in the distance, a dog begins to bark. And then at once I hear a faint snatch of Cameron's voice—not words as such, just the murmur of his conversation. He's still a little boy, his pitch high and unbroken, but this time not by fear. He sounds excited and… *settled.* Comfortable. There is a squeal of interference and it all goes silent, but not before I make out a final, brief snatch of dialogue. *I'm okay.*

Satisfied, I return the walkie-talkie to my pocket and shuffle back to the door, sensing countless eyes watching my progress. I throw a final glance back to the rubble-strewn site before I step through the fence and padlock it behind me.

Gary looks relieved as he sees my approach. Across the city, I hear the low squeal of a police siren. Nothing much changes.

*

Somewhere on Sebastian Street lies a portal between two worlds; a place where salvation exists for those that seek it, an escape from the stark brutalities of life. Somewhere on Sebastian Street lurks a darkness that seems forbidding and threatening to some, yet welcoming and hospitable to others. This lost district provides refuge to those individuals whose despair is sufficient to enable passage into this realm of solitude. Somewhere on Sebastian Street, a boy chooses to remain young forever, electing to spend eternity alone rather than endure a tortured mortality. He inhabits the darkness alone…but he's never lonely.

Somewhere on Sebastian Street, that boy dreams of a life less real. Once his dreams were filled with love and hope and goodwill, but he always knew in his heart that these things would be denied him.

Somewhere on Sebastian Street lies a sanctuary for the forlorn, a haven for those beyond hope, and whatever dwells within its imaginary walls will never dwell alone.

For Gary McMahon

Bandersnatch

My sister has a very nice dog. He's exuberant and fussy, constantly nosing his way towards me to be stroked. If I'm honest, I'm a little surprised; back when we were kids my sister was always frightened of dogs. But I suppose people change over time. I wonder what else is different about her in the decade since we've last seen one other.

The party's great. If you like that kind of thing, I mean; full of handsome men and drop-dead gorgeous women, all reminiscing about their gap years or talking about their forthcoming Powerpoint presentations. I can see that Michelle is tense, despite her outward appearance. I've caught her throwing nervous glances my way, chewing her lip like she used to do when she was eight years old, and worried that Mum would return home and catch us.

This whole reunion thing wouldn't have happened without Mum, actually. Well what I mean is that it wouldn't have happened if Mum hadn't gotten cancer and died. I was spared the final agonising months, luckily, but it was Michelle's phone call in the wake of Mum's death that threw us both together again.

Roscoe nuzzles my hand and I stroke him, enjoying the softness of his fur, the velvety touch of his ears. The party is in full swing. I see people who were dignified earlier, now loosening, allowing us to view the real them. I don't recognise any of the music that's being played but everyone else seems to love it.

The partygoers have splintered into several factions. Ours happens to be in the garden. We sit around a table on the patio. It is a warm night and I can smell the honeysuckle clinging to the side of the garage.

Someone asks Michelle what she's going to do with the house, now Mum has gone. It was two months ago yet I'm surprised that anyone feels brave enough to broach the subject. Perhaps it's the alcohol.

Michelle announces that she intends to remain here. Obviously, she adds, catching my eye, she will need to remortgage to allow my share of Mum's inheritance to be distributed equally.

I smile back at her. Scott puts his arm around her and nuzzles the side of her neck, his shirt sleeves deliberately slim-fitting in an effort to make his biceps look bigger. The fact that he'll also continue to live here goes unspoken. So does the fact that the bank will require both their incomes to approve the remortgage. I see his tanned hand squeezing my sister's forearm, his meticulously manicured nails stroking the surface of her soft skin. In my mind I remember the scent of Nivea cream, of Radox bath soak. I wonder if she still uses that coconut shampoo.

"I expect the house is steeped in memories," says a freckled woman, the same one who earlier asked what my sister intended to do with the place. I can't remember her name, despite being introduced to her earlier. They're all the same anyway; just facades reflecting back implied success, all of them fighting to win my sister's attention.

"Yes," agrees my sister, "some nice memories." She glances towards me. "Agree, Lawrence?"

I smile and nod. I can see that this makes some of them uncomfortable. Until Mum's death, most of them were unaware of my existence. Obviously mother never mentioned me, and Michelle had been forbidden to speak about my existence, so I imagine I had become something of a spectre; a creature of legend, a figure to be erased from their life. The decade that followed must have been a time of exile for both of us.

Which reminds me of something from our childhood. "Remember when I used to read to you?"

She smiles shyly, though I know this is just an affectation she has cultured in the years since I was taken from her. "What was it again?" she asks. "*Alice In Wonderland?*"

"*Alice Through the Looking Glass*. You were terrified of the monster."

"Ah, yes," she murmurs. "The bandersnatch."

"You had trouble sleeping for weeks."

She laughs. I can see that Scott looks puzzled; she has obviously never spoken about it, and I am pleased by this fact. Michelle and I exchange another glance. Nothing more is required. I stirred the pool of memories and it's obvious that she's pleased with the result.

The rest of the evening passes interminably. I find myself at various intervals holding a glass of something whilst I nod and smile as someone talks to me, and all the time I'm watching Scott's hands. If they're not on my sister's knee they're on her shoulder or resting on her backside. At one point they interlace with Michelle's fingers during a story about how they met at university. I have a vague idea of what university life must be like, despite my rather sheltered schooling during the decade of my exile. But I'm pleased for Michelle and her degree. She must have worked hard to achieve success. As kids, I was always the bright one, the eldest child, the leader; but our mother cast all that aside when she elected to choose Michelle over me.

Scott seems okay, I suppose. He's good-looking; sporty, fond of the outdoors. I expect it was his idea to get the dog. And Roscoe is almost the canine version of him—pleasantly eye-catching, faithful, attentive.

Much later the freckled girl passes out. Someone has to take her to the toilet to be sick. She's totally out of it, almost comatose. I feel satisfied that the liquid I slipped into her vodka earlier must have been undetectable, just like the dealer said it was. Next time, though, I'll need to use a little more, just to be sure.

Around midnight I take a taxi back to the B&B where I've been living. I suppose I could have driven, seeing as how I haven't been drinking at the party but sometimes it's good to assume the allusion of vulnerability. In bed I think about Michelle for ages before I finally drop off, my sleep made deeper by the post-masturbatory slump.

*

A few days later we visit a stately home. Scott takes us in his BMW; driving sullenly, tutting at other cars on the road with thinly-veiled rage. Maybe he always drives like that. I sit in the back, watching his hands change gear, turning the steering wheel, clicking the indicator. I find myself wondering if those fingers give pleasure to my sister, imagining her gasping and shuddering at his touch.

I suggest that we wind the window down because I feel nauseous. That's the word I use—*nauseous*, not sick, because I know it will infuriate him. Scott grudgingly complies. I spend the rest of the journey in silence, stroking Roscoe who is sleeping beside me on the back seat. I notice that the dog's hind legs are roughly the same thickness as Scott's wrists.

Our visit to the stately home is enjoyable. It feels exhilarating to spend time with my sister in such decadent surroundings. The ornately decorated rooms accentuate my fantasy; just us two, isolated from the dregs of society, wrapped in our own private little world.

We have to leave Roscoe in the car while we tour the house, the window wound down a few inches to prevent him overheating. Scott tries to chip in with conversation during the tour but I manage to filter out his presence.

In the afternoon we release Roscoe from the car and take a stroll around the lake, basking in the sunshine. Roscoe runs ahead, barking at butterflies and fetching the stick that Scott throws. I reminisce with Michelle about our childhood. I can feel the bridge spanning our old life and the here and now strengthening. Scott holds hands with my sister at several points and I feel repulsed by the way his tapered fingers clutch at her.

Once we complete a full circuit of the lake we find a spot on the grass and pause for breath, sitting down with the sun warming our backs, watching Roscoe sniff at dandelions.

"I bet all manner of beasts live in those trees," I remark, nodding. "Something with a long neck and snapping jaws, something *frumious and swift*." I lean forward and tickle Michelle's waist. She collapses in a fit of giggles. Scott's hands claw the air where a moment before my sister's head had rested. I take pleasure in his scowl.

"What is this thing you keep going on about?" he asks.

"The bandersnatch," I tell him. "When Michelle was naughty it would come and get her, try to eat her up."

"What's a…a *bandersnatch*? Is it from a film?"

"We told you," says Michelle. "It's from a book."

"What is it? Like the Tasmanian Devil?"

Michelle giggles, looking at me directly. I return her grin. Scott seems frustrated by his own ignorance.

"It's long and thin and pale," I say. "And it has one eye."

"And it never tires. It never gives up." My sister collapses in an eruption of mirth. The laughter sounds wet in her throat.

Right now we could both be children again; it's almost as if the last ten years have disappeared in the blink of an eye. The obstacles that faced us—our mother's disapproval and the period of my exile—seem almost trivial now they're gone. Michelle's bent body accentuates the swell of her breast, the curve of her buttocks. I exhale slowly and try to give the impression that my squint is due to the sun. I can see Scott's clenched jaw, his petulant frown.

Roscoe, encouraged by my sister's expression of glee, runs over and noses his way into the fun.

*

I had no reservations about meeting Michelle again when she called to tell me about Mum. Maybe—it's fair to say—I was a little nervous about where the last decade had taken her. But that was allayed when I spotted her coming in through the door of the pub.

When she'd originally suggested that I meet her in the Mason's Arms I was a little bemused. The idea of her frequenting pubs seemed a strange one, given that she hadn't even reached her teenage years when I began my exile. And it got me wondering if there were other things that had changed in her life. But I needn't have worried. As we shared that first drink I could tell that our mutual feeling had lost none of its strength. We spoke about Mum—or rather Michelle's struggle to cope in the final months. I had always harboured resentment to Mum during my exile, but Michelle assured me that she had shouldered much of the blame for what had happened, despite Mum's assertion that I—as the eldest—was at fault.

And in the weeks that followed, our relationship developed

sufficiently, even though it wasn't in a physical sense the way it was before Mum betrayed us.

The only remaining obstacle was Scott. I watched those probing, constantly-moving hands of his as they clutched and touched at my sister's body like a pair of pale restless spiders. It was clear Michelle had fallen for his charm.

*

For the last ten years I had allowed myself to indulge in a little fantasy. Society had failed Michelle and me, driving a wedge between us that said more about its prejudices than it did about our own weakness. I had come to think of us both as star-crossed lovers, like Romeo and Juliet, separated from each other by an outside interference that possessed a distinct lack of understanding. During the period of my exile I never once considered taking my own life, despite having the opportunity on several occasions. I'm generally a positive person. I like to look on the bright side, wherever possible.

I've been staying at the B&B, just a stone's throw from Michelle's house. Despite Mum's death it still feels like I don't belong there, like her disapproving influence has remained within the house. It doesn't bother me. The landlady of the B&B is a widow, who allows me access to her late husband's tool-shed under the pretence that I have some DIY to attend to for my sister. I select an assortment of tools. There is even a wooden box that looks perfect. I empty out its contents—a Silverline hand plane which feels incredibly heavy—and take the box.

My sister's house backs onto a small area of woodland. It is relatively easy to approach through the trees, under cover of twilight, and wait until Michelle lets Roscoe out to do his business. It's simple to attract his attention; he is familiar with my scent, accustomed to seeing me. I manage to coax him under the fence. Seconds later we are hurrying away to my car, which is parked on the road at the end of the lane.

There is a picnic area just off the main road into town. It is suitably deserted at this hour of the day. A dilapidated public toilet stands to one side. Moss coats its felt roof; cobwebs line its grimy windows. It reeks of piss, so much so that for a moment I consider a different site, but then common sense kicks in and I concede this is the best spot.

I take Roscoe into the gents' side and let him sniff around the damp floor. There is half a house-brick propping open the door—which looks like it hasn't been closed in years—and I slide it to one side with my foot and shut the door. It feels ill-fitting and rusting on its hinges, the wooden panels greasy and etched with obscenities. I have brought my bag of tools with me so I place them down and lower myself down on my haunches. Roscoe looks confused, probably by the strange smells in the confines of the building or my furtive behaviour. I pat my thighs and he bounds over, his tongue lolling out of the side of his mouth like a fat pink ribbon. I grab him in a headlock and roll over onto my side quickly.

It's quite clear that this is going to be more difficult than I first imagined. There are plenty of yelps and barks, his claws scrabbling against my body. At one point he even bites my forearm but the adrenalin means it barely registers. I struggle for several minutes before I give up. In the end I resort to grabbing the house-brick and using it. Over and over again. The sudden silence feels obscene.

If I've learned one thing from this, it's that I need to use the liquid next time to subdue. It seemed to work well on the freckled girl.

I get out the piano wire and wind it around one of Roscoe's inert legs. I begin to adopt the sawing motion that I saw that girl use in that Korean film. At first it looks like it will work; it cuts through the skin as easily as anything. But once it reaches the bone I quickly realise that it's just not thick enough for the task. I have to use the bow-saw from my bag of tools. It's a good job I've come prepared. That seems to do the trick. There is still some unpleasantness however—the bones crack and split as the blade cuts through them, splinters of shard protruding from the stump. I study the paw and reflect on the finished article, feeling let down by the falsities of cinema once again. It has taken far longer than I expected, there is considerably more blood that I imagined. Now I have Roscoe's paw in my hand I can study it closely. I fear I might have been wrong; maybe it is a little thinner than Scott's wrist. That's certainly something to consider.

I put the dog in the boot of my car, together with the bag of tools. My clothes are covered in blood so I use them to mop up as much of the puddle as I can from the floor of the toilet. I flush the remainder away with my own urine, directing the flow towards the grate in the corner. I remember to prop open the door with the brick before I leave. I don't think anyone will notice the stains on it.

On my way back into town I pass a disused factory that looks like it closed its doors not long after the recession hit. There is a large industrial skip in the yard. I slide the dog's remains down into it, where is will be hidden by rusting metal frames and discarded MDF shelves. I drive back to the B&B to attend to my clothing.

*

The next day is a strange one. Michelle rings me early in the morning, crying because Roscoe has escaped. I drive over straight away. I leave the wooden box and my bag of tools on the back seat.

Even though she's spent most of the night in a frantic state, she still looks breathtaking. Scott is there, all fuzzy-haired and bleary eyed. He's called in sick at work. Apparently he's been out combing the surrounding area, shouting Roscoe's name into the darkness.

I try to calm them down, making a cup of sweet tea for them both. Adopting the stoic mantle. Scott seems to be constantly wringing his hands. Cracking his knuckles nervously.

I talk about going out for a walk, searching for Roscoe in the neighbouring woodland. I suggest Michelle jumps in the shower, tries to relax while Scott and I go looking. She nods. Desperate to believe that we'll find him. They finish their tea and I feel satisfied with how things are progressing. My sister disappears upstairs and Scott puts on his jacket and we head out the door. By the time we reach the garden gate his speech is slurred, he needs to lean against me for support. I guide him towards my car.

Fear Of The Music

I don't dance so much these days. Whether that's not wanting to be reminded or fear of the music itself, I'm not sure. Part of it's knowing I'll never be as good as James. It was less than a year ago that we first met. I remember I'd just gone into a nightclub. I hadn't even bought a drink. He was standing at one of the dark tables in front of the dance floor. A tall man, quite thin, dressed in a black t-shirt and jeans. He remained absolutely still for about ten minutes, watching the dancers. There was something angry in his stillness, a tense feeling. Suddenly he emptied his glass and slipped onto the dance floor. The music shivered through his limbs; he was caught up in it like a floating candle on a river. I knew I had to speak to him.

At the bar he drank slowly, the neon painting pink beads of sweat onto his face. He put down his empty glass and I caught the bartender's eye and asked for it to be refilled. He turned and for a few moments he just peered at me with those intense eyes before finally nodding. 'I'm James.'

The club was stifling so we stood near the fire-door and made small-talk. Though the conversation was two-way, I could tell he was half-distracted, his eyes never leaving the dance floor, like he was searching for someone amongst the strobing figures and lurching shapes. I studied his face as I talked, admiring the angular features, sensing something potent concealed in the hollows of his eyes. He began to blink and sigh. It felt like he was drifting away from me so I suggested going for a dance. He hesitated for a second, and at that exact moment the opening guitar from The Cure's 'A Forest' came throbbing through the speakers. We were off.

He was just as energetic as before, especially towards the climax of the song, his limbs pulsing and spasming like he was possessed.

His technique reminded me of how Ian Curtis danced in the 'Transmission' video, only James seemed more fluid, more naturally gifted, his movement totally in tune with the rhythm of the music. I couldn't take my eyes off him. The image was mesmerising. I tried to emulate his performance and he flashed a smile at me, seemingly pleased with my effort. By the time the song ended and the next one came on I was breathless and spent, and we stumbled back to the fire-door. Not long after, we left.

He had a flat in Digbeth in the shadow of a railway bridge, on the corner of Moseley Street and Pickford Street. The brickwork adjacent to the building was decorated with graffiti, lending the place a contemporary, cartoonish quality, at odds with the remnants of industry that remained visible beneath the modern veneer. The flat was as cold as the grave. Its walls were cluttered with album covers and posters of films by Jean-Luc Godard. Scrawled in paint on the wall above the bed were the words: *And those who were seen dancing were thought to be insane by those who could not hear the music.*

Within minutes we were fucking on the bed. He had a pale, hairless body, muscular at the shoulders and biceps, toned thighs; the physique of someone naturally athletic rather than one acquired at the gym. When he came he shuddered violently, his breath rattling through my eardrum like a train. He clung to me and exhaled a deep sigh. It sounded desolate, fractured. We lay under the covers and slept until dawn.

James cooked us breakfast the next morning. I felt oddly awkward, quite unsure why. I'd had plenty of one-night stands. But with James it felt like I was on the brink of something *life-changing*. He wasn't even my type really. But there was an intensity to him I found alluring.

I was just finishing my coffee when I nodded towards the words scrawled above the bed. 'You can't half bust some moves on the dance floor, yourself.'

He glanced at the quotation and smiled. 'Nietzsche.'

'More original than the one about gazing into the abyss.'

He didn't speak for a moment. I could hear the traffic out on the road, the gurgling of the radiators in the flat, a squeak of floorboards from upstairs.

'How you dance says a lot about how you view life. You can tell a lot about someone by watching them dance.'

I pursed my lips. 'But they just might like a song more than another.'

He frowned. 'No, it's more than that. Most people dance exactly the way they live their life. Or, in most cases, they don't *live*—they just exist.'

I thought about the way most dance-floors looked; people shuffling like zombies, hopping and moving around in time to the music. I thought about how James had danced the night before; the enthusiasm, the passion, the sheer unadulterated enjoyment of his own body gyrating in time to the beats of the music. It felt vivid and pure.

I knew then that I wanted to spend all my time with him.

*

We saw a lot of each other in the next few weeks. Most times I stayed at his place. Often we walked miles along the banks of the canal, stopping for a drink in some of the pubs scattered along its route. We talked about anything and everything. It felt like the more I discovered about him, the further I felt myself spiralling down into his personality. He told me about how he'd survived childhood leukaemia and the impact the disease had made on his life. During the early stages of its diagnosis, his father had walked out on them. James had never seen him again. He spoke about all the time he'd spent in hospital, separated from the rest of his friends, in the end almost forgotten. He seemed to feel embarrassed by his survival, as if he had invented the whole story, bitter and apologetic.

By the end of the summer James and I were constantly morose. The weather had changed. Autumn came with a bite. Frost glittered the dead leaves underfoot, mist hung low over the canal. Afternoon darkness seemed to descend with a vengeance. The news was filled with reports of students being attacked in the area, one of whom nearly lost an eye after having acid thrown in his face. Streetlamps were dimmed by the fog that choked the streets. By the time winter arrived I had started to feel dislocated by the weather. Christmas came and went in a warm rainy haze. To counter the melancholy mood, James started messing around with drugs. One night he brought home some pink tablets in a plastic bag. He'd bought them off a lorry driver in the pub, imported from Eastern Europe apparently. We took a couple on the last Friday in February. When we came to, it was early March.

Even now I can remember how quickly the rush came on. I felt an intense tingling sensation in my legs. I could feel my heart racing, hear a roaring in my ears. My vision was flecked with sparkles of light. We both collapsed on the bed in a tangle of limbs.

I woke after a few hours, nauseous and shivering. I sat up on the bed. James was gone. I could hear voices outside the room, indistinct and monotone. There was a hum within my chest, like a deep bass that I could not hear, only feel.

I stood and opened the door. Instead of seeing the living room I was expecting, I was faced with a long corridor which ended at another door. It was freezing cold. I could see my breath in front of me, tiny ghosts of thought escaping the confines of my head. There was music coming from beyond the door. I walked the length of the corridor and opened it.

The room was dimly lit. It had a high ceiling and arched windows covered by blinds. People were dancing in the centre, the sight of which was startling. There must have been about thirty of them, gyrating in time to the music, which was loud and upbeat. I was confused by the whole situation. I asked someone where James was but he just looked at me and shook his head. I negotiated my way through the melee to the back of the room where a closed coffin was propped up on some trestles. There was a framed photograph of James on top of it. At that moment it dawned on me that this must be a dream. Although—thinking about it now—surely that means that it must just have been a hallucinogenic vision brought on by the drugs, because when you're having a dream you never realise you're dreaming, do you?

I grabbed hold of a girl near me and shouted to be heard over the music. I felt dislocated, puzzled by the fact that there was a coffin in the room. She wiped the sweat from her face and explained that this was James's wake. She told me that he had been killed walking home from the pub one night, stabbed in the neck. I felt sick. My vision was lurching. Maybe it was the lighting and music. I looked at the dancing people, desperate to recognise someone but all the faces appeared identical, waxy and featureless. It was awkward because I was the only one not dancing but my limbs were like weights. No matter how much I wanted to join in, my body wouldn't let me. I sat down at a table in the corner. It was covered by a starchy white tablecloth and I fingered some dark stains around its edge. I watched the coffin for a while, wondering if I should open the lid and check that James was inside.

Just then I felt something in the pocket of my trousers. I pulled out a short-bladed knife, instantly noticing the dried blood caked on the serrations. I knew then I would never be able to dance the way that James wanted me to.

*

The next few weeks passed in a blur. It was suddenly May, the month of the general election. Opinion polls were suggesting that the hung parliament would be over, that reports indicated Labour could be heading for a majority. James was excited at the prospect of the coalition government's demise. He spent the evening of Thursday 7th May in a maelstrom of nerves. I fell asleep at 11:45, just as the initial results were coming in. James woke me at 7:30 the next morning, ashen-faced and bleary-eyed. He looked like he'd aged ten years overnight. The election results were devastating—a Conservative majority.

James took it really hard. In the following days he became more and more bitter. His eyes took on a dull, dampened hue, his chin grizzled with stubble. It was almost as if he had become disillusioned with society.

'It's the apathy that gets to me,' he said. 'Not the ones voting for the Tories but those that can't even be bothered to turn up at the polling stations or fill in the postal votes.' There was anger beneath his tone. He told me that people were more likely to vote in the final of a pop music reality show than a general election. By then his cheekbones were prominent.

His mood had not improved. He told me he had been taking more and more of those pills from the Latvian. He was wracked with visions, usually of his own death. In the majority of these he had been murdered by people who professed to love him. I sensed a degree of paranoia creeping in to his behaviour. He began going out on his own, not telling me what he had been up to, not caring that he was alienating me with his secrecy. He told me that I was part of the problem, he'd known it from the very night we had met. He could see it in the way I danced. I was as listless and dead as the rest. I wondered how much of it had been brought on by the drugs he was taking. One day I came to his flat and found him sitting at his kitchen table, scrawling notes into a writing pad about how the media was influencing the public, how Labour's plans to break up the stranglehold the banks enjoyed, and how imposing energy price-caps, would have been good for the country. The walls of his flat had been plastered with newspaper headlines illustrating how they were scaremongering the public into hating certain races and cultures.

Meanwhile the attacks in Digbeth had escalated. A Muslim student had been abducted and had had his hands mutilated in what newspapers called 'a tit-for-tat crime', A travellers' camp on the outskirts of Aston had been the victim of calculated arson attacks. The newspapers screamed about IS suicide bombers and the dangers of allowing Syrian refugees into the country, while on page four they'd spread celebrity gossip about Kanye West and Kim Kardashian. It seemed like there was no longer any middle ground for news.

One night at the end of May I went for a walk and found myself on a bridge that spanned the old railway tracks. It was a warm humid evening so I sat on the railings and drank a can of Fosters, watching the light from James's window, wondering what his fevered brain would be working on now. It was almost as if his efforts in life were to compensate for the apathy and ennui of others. Everything he did, he did with enthusiasm, spirit, purpose.

An hour later I wandered over, all the more brave for having consumed the four-pack of lager. He opened the door and peered at me for a moment, as if trying to place me. This hurt, but I managed to mask it. His eyes had that dull glassy look that only downers give. Once his brain had allowed him to recognise me, he invited me in.

His computer was on, the screen displaying text in a language I had never seen before. On the table beside it was a map. None of the place names meant anything to me. It was a confusion of gradients and crisscrossed streets. In the centre was the symbol for a church, surrounded by labyrinthine pathways that seemed too randomly confusing. The word REVERENCE was written on it in James's spidery style.

He offered me a drink but looked relieved when I declined. I asked how he was. He seemed to consider for a moment before saying, 'Getting better.' Even though he was only in his thirties, I could see grey flecks of whiskers on his chin. His eyes were hollow and distant, like gems I could vaguely remember owning.

He talked about the area's random attacks, how the newspapers were selective in their reporting; manipulative fuel for the fire. He told me how three days ago an elderly woman had been found dead in her flat. She had ingested almost a litre of bleach. James held up a copy of yesterday's paper which showed the photograph of an Asian man whose shop had been targeted by vandals. It made great pains to point out that the man was originally from Leeds, the same city as one of the London 7/7 bombers.

'It's in their interest to join the dots for us,' he said. 'Feed us the news so we understand their message. It doesn't matter if it's true or not, all that matters is we accept it.'

There was a pile of leaflets on the table next to the map, most of them glossy and colourful, some of them hand-printed and mono.

I asked what he'd been up to. He ran his fingers through his hair and glanced around as if trying to remember.

'I'm sick of people making no effort,' he said at last. 'I didn't survive my blood cancer to just sit on the sofa and watch television. There has to be a purpose to things, otherwise life is meaningless. We all have our roles to play.'

I tried to tell him to relax, tried to make arrangements to go out with him at the weekend. He shook his head. 'You're just like the rest. Happy to remain in the flock, content to do as you're told.'

He wouldn't calm down. I asked if he was till taking the pills from the Latvian. He laughed and said they were the doorway to his new church. He could only get there when he took them. He spoke about a friend of his who ran the church. 'Simon's full of ideas, tired of being passive instead of active. He has a vision of how life should be and he needs everyone to follow it.'

I pointed out that one man's ideology was another man's oppression. At this he grew angry. He told me to leave. As he was ushering me out, I managed to nab one of the flyers off the top of the pile whilst his back was turned. He stood on the threshold and hesitated before closing the door. 'You should try another pill, Gary. The last one didn't suit you but the next one might.' I didn't want to antagonise him further so I accepted the plastic bag. I said goodbye and turned into the warm night.

*

The flyer had the word REVERENCE stencilled at the top. Beneath it was a black and white photograph of a church, followed by another of those strange maps of a district I didn't recognise. It detailed nearby landmarks as a museum and something called a camera obscura.

I returned home, morose and regretful. Seeing him like this had made me feel weak, ineffective. I yearned for him to like me. It was only then that I realised how much I admired his sense of verve. I envied him for possessing the thing that I truly lacked—*life*. For half an hour I prowled my flat, flicking through the TV channels, ejecting every CD that I tried to listen to. Eventually I gave in and fished the pill out of the plastic bag. I washed it down with a shot of vodka.

At first nothing happened. I sat on the sofa in silence, staring at my reflection in the blank television screen. I took out the flyer. After a few minutes I realised that I knew the location of the church. I recalled the lost places on the map, wondering if I had ever really forgotten. My legs felt wobbly but I managed to stand and leave the house.

It was raining, the dampness darkening the bricks of the buildings, creating glistening Rorschach patterns on the walls. Each step hurt the balls of my feet. I walked onwards, following my memory as I hurried towards the church. The streets were deserted. As I saw each landmark, my memories of them formed. Soon I was at the gates, looking up at the ancient stone edifice, daunted by its imposing spire. I had the most intense sense of deja-vu. I could hear music coming from its walls.

The path was overgrown with briars and thorns. I fought my way through the thicket with little to show other than a few tears in my jeans. The door was made of solid oak, weathered and pale with age. I rattled the iron handle but the door was locked. I knocked on it but the sound was deafened by the music from within. Frustrated, I wondered around the side of the church to where an iron bench was positioned just against the wall. I managed to stand on its sagging wooden seat and peer in through the mullioned window. My view was obscured by what seemed like centuries of dust and grime but I could just make out the parishioners inside. An overwhelming sense of dread crept over me then for all the people inside looked as if they were pale figures moving around, like wax mannequins come to life. Even their clothes were as milky as their skin. I watched, fascinated. They were lifelike enough to be real. The church was devoid of pews, the floor had been cleared to make way for its congregation. The music was still very loud and the figures were dancing violently, just as James had done on the night we'd met. My eyes searched the crowd. I spotted him on the far side, moving in that unmistakable dance-style I had so admired. I stared for a moment, hypnotised by the spasming bodies, absently disturbed by their waxy appearance.

Just then my attention was seized by a flickering from the front of the church. I saw the orange bloom of flames around the altar. It resembled the wavering petals of some monstrous flower. The congregation seemed to form a line, still gyrating. The rhythm was haphazard and random, as if each person was moving to a different beat, but the animation was shared by all. One by one they moved towards the fire, stepping into the flames, the heat bending their limbs, destroying their bodies. I could not tear my eyes away. They disappeared into the orange blaze. I blinked the image away but even as I closed my eyes I could see the waxy figures in my mind, dancing, forever dancing, while I did nothing but stand and watch them burn.

*

I came to on my sofa. It was day. My muscles ached as if I too had spent the night dancing. But I knew this could not be true because I didn't have James's skill. I was not able to hear the same tune as he heard.

I hurried to his flat. As I drew near I saw the crowd loitering behind the police tape, noticed the reporters speaking gravely into the pointed television cameras. Lighting rigs had been erected behind them, bathing his apartment block in stark pale definition. I eavesdropped on the reporters' conversations: a man in his thirties had been found dead in his flat. A post-mortem had revealed the strange circumstances surrounding the death. It appeared that the man had died sometime around a week ago. Forensics had confirmed that a fire had occurred, originating within the body of the deceased, apparently without any external sources of ignition.

I turned away. My head was pounding. I felt the warm sun on my arms. I knew I would never meet anyone like James again. His passion for life, his utter determination to make the most of things meant that I would probably always feel inadequate in comparison.

There has to be a purpose to things, otherwise life is meaningless. We all have our roles to play. I think about this every day and wonder if I'll ever meet anyone that will revere me in the same way I loved James. I very much doubt it.

The Summer of Bradbury

I must have told this story a hundred times over the years, and still I don't fully understand what happened that day. Yet I can still recall with absolute clarity every detail of it, despite the passage of time.

That summer seemed endless. The heatwave lasted throughout all of June, July and August, turning the grass brown and brittle, warping the felt roof of our play-den, fraying the tempers of the townsfolk. To us kids it was a dream come true. The previous winter I'd discovered Ray Bradbury. My mind had been filled with cupolas and orchards, of lightning rods and Dust Witches. Bradbury offered me an escape from the humdrum monotony of the Yorkshire mining village in which I lived. I'd spent rainy school holidays in my bedroom, reading *Dandelion Wine* and *The Illustrated Man* and *Something Wicked This Way Comes*, imagining that I too lived that carefree life of small-town America.

And that summer Renfield actually felt like it could be Green Town, Illinois. It hadn't rained since May. Britain sweltered under record temperatures. A constant aroma of melting road-tar seemed to permeate the air. Brown arid fields surrounded Renfield, transforming the usually-patchwork Yorkshire scenery into a desert-like vista. Zealous newsreaders took great delight in reporting the widespread hosepipe ban. One of our neighbours' dogs had been driven crazy by the merciless heat, and the RSPCA were called into action. Renfield enjoyed a steady whir of lawnmower engines, basked in the heady smell of freshly-cut grass. There was even talk of some towns having to resort to standpipes due to the water shortage.

On the day it happened I was in my room, writing in my notepad with a fountain-pen—a birthday gift from my parents.

It was 11 am, a Tuesday; the fifth week of the summer holidays. I could hear the radio playing downstairs. The window had been flung open. Blue skies stretched forever. I happened to look up and see Fiona, the twelve year old girl from further up the street, sitting on the kerb opposite, chalking on the pavement. I stood and leaned out of the window, shouted her name. She just glanced up and smiled but her eyes looked cheerless.

Dad was at work. Mum was hanging out the washing in the back garden. There was absolutely nothing to indicate this day would be unlike any other.

A few weeks previously, my Uncle Terry had been diagnosed with late-stage emphysema; he wasn't expected to make it beyond Christmas. Since then Mum had shuffled around like she was in a trance. A few times I'd noticed her staring into space; I imagined she was reliving the childhood she'd enjoyed with her only brother. His imminent death felt like a black cloud looming on the horizon. I decided to go outside and talk to Fiona.

She glanced up as I approached, tucking a stray piece of hair behind her ear, wrinkling her nose like she did when one of us was teasing her. But her face looked pale. I thought at first she was outlining a hopscotch grid with the chalk but it was obvious she was just doodling on the pavement.

I sat down beside her. The kerb felt hot through the fabric of my shorts. There wasn't the slightest breeze to disturb the air. An aeroplane droned overhead, its cotton-wool contrail marking a line across the brilliant azure sky.

"Heyup, how's it going?"

She smiled an empty smile. "Not bad." She continued to chalk on the pavement.

This was weird. Fiona was one of our gang. She hung out with us, climbed the same trees as us; sometimes even slept out in the club den we'd built by the reservoir. To see her as listless as this was unsettling. "Owt wrong?" I asked.

She shrugged. "Just belly ache."

I nodded. It was the heat. It sapped the energy, killed your hunger. There wasn't a cloud in the sky. I couldn't imagine it ever raining again.

"Seen the others?"

"Errm—yeah, earlier. They're up at the den. I think Lee's got a new glider."

This brightened my mood. A glider was always a great source of fun. Lee had broken his last one when it had overshot the park fence and landed on the road. Balsa was no match for a car's wheel.

"Wanna head up there?"

She nodded. "Not on bikes, though." She clutched her stomach to illustrate why.

We set off along the track that threaded between the houses. There was an area of waste-ground beyond the estate that extended about a quarter of a mile up the slope towards the reservoir. Our feet raised dust from the dry ground. Lately I'd been mocked for referring to my trainers as sneakers, for calling the stream that ran through the middle of the woods as a creek—Bradbury's words, which romanticised them beyond their mundane normality. I'd even come to think of the woods as a *jungle*, but had known better than to vocalise that thought. Well that morning I noticed that my *sneakers* were coated in dust. But I trusted it wouldn't slow me down.

We walked in companionable silence for a while. I tried to throw sidelong glances at Fiona. Recently I'd begun to notice aspects of her to which I'd previously been oblivious: her tanned legs seemed that little bit longer, there was shape and definition to her upper body. She looked nice. A small part of me felt embarrassed for harbouring such thoughts, but it was an exhilarating feeling nonetheless.

The walk took about ten minutes, though usually we made the trek on bikes. Whilst I wanted the journey to go slow so I could savour my time alone with Fiona, I was eager to see the state of the reservoir.

All that summer we'd taken great delight in walking up to the peak of the hill and gazing down at the ever-diminishing water level; marvelling as, week by week, more and more of the reservoir's shale bank had been exposed. The valley in which the reservoir was built had originally been a neighbouring village—Bowerton—and had, in the '40s, been purposefully *drowned*, once the council had transferred the inhabitants to a newly-built housing estate in Renfield. The reservoir's expansion had been a necessity, to serve the vast growth that post-war Sheffield had undergone. My grandfather told the story of how the villagers had all gathered one cold morning in March 1946, and watched the dam gates being opened further up the valley, allowing the water to flow into the lower section of the reservoir. By then most of the original buildings had been demolished—except for the church, the primary school, and the majority of the central structure that made up the pub. Apparently the image of the water rising above them was an unforgettable sight.

Sometimes I thought about what lay beneath the water, my imagination conjuring sunken buildings and creepy, weed-filled rooms. The idea that people once lived their lives in a place that was now submerged felt evocative, fertile, terrifying.

I was breathless by the time we reached the brow of the valley. We'd been up three days previously and the level had been lower than I'd ever seen it; the clock-tower of the crumbling church just visible above the water. Now there was more shale exposed as the reservoir's volume had receded even further. The concrete wall at the head of the valley looked ridiculously high. I squinted against the sun and stared out across the reservoir, my eyes drawn instantly to the crumbling structures that protruded above the waterline. As well as the church's clock tower, a section of the school's hall had now been revealed, like the exposed skeleton of some fantastical beast. It looked surreal.

For a few minutes we surveyed the view. I felt infinitely sad, my thoughts turning inexplicably to my Uncle Terry. Fiona's breathing was heavy next to me. Somehow I had the impression she wasn't just breathless from the walk up here. I was conscious of her nearness. I could smell the feminine aroma of her deodorant.

She turned to me, breaking the reverie. "C'mon, let's find the others."

Our den was built further along the ridge, in a copse of trees that overlooked the reservoir. It had originally been an abandoned shed which we'd appropriated for our personal use. Its single glass window was still intact. We'd carefully constructed a screen of bushes around the den in an effort to conceal it from curious eyes. Not many kids played up here. The wire fence that ran around the perimeter of the reservoir was adorned with numerous signs warning of the dangers of deep water.

I tried to make small talk. "Seems a long way up here when we don't have us bikes."

Fiona nodded. She seemed distracted.

I continued. "They're on about riding over to old man Wilson's orchard on Saturday."

She pursed her lips. "I might give it a miss. Apples'll only give me a worse gut-rot."

"Yeah, I s'pose." I hoped she couldn't hear the disappointment in my voice.

"To be honest, I'm thinking of giving the club a miss for a while..." She glanced at me sharply. "Sometimes them lot can be...a bit *immature*."

I nodded slowly. Maybe she'd looked more grown-up lately because of those telltale signs of her distancing herself purposefully from us—her jeans had been less grass-stained, she'd sustained fewer cuts and scabs to her legs. It occurred to me that her body-language had become awkward, like she felt self-conscious hanging around with us. Another piece of my heart crumbled.

We'd reached the den, ducking beneath overhanging branches as we approached the door. The dry grass crackled underfoot. Flies buzzed at the periphery of my view. There were two wooden steps leading up to the door and I noticed the padlock fastened across the handle and locking-sash. I reached under the top step and fished the key out from its hiding place. As I gripped the padlock to insert the key I experienced a huge static shock from the metal. My tongue tingled and I felt the tiny hairs on my forearms bristling. The air seemed heavy and damp. I unlocked the door and we entered the den.

It was stifling hot in there. There was a smell of body-odour and stale farts. Lee's glider was lying on the floor next to a stack of Dandy and Beano comics. There was a pack of Top Trump cards already dealt out into four neat piles.

Fiona dropped down onto one of the beanbags. "Wonder where

they are?"

I shrugged, and propped open the door to allow fresh air to circulate with the warmer air inside. "Sure you're all right? You look a bit funny."

"Remember that talk we had at school?" Fiona exhaled loudly. "About...puberty and stuff? Well soon we'll all start going our separate ways probably. It's just part of growing up."

I didn't know how to reply. This was the last thing I wanted to hear. Our gang felt incredibly important to me. We were a strong unit. As an only child, the gang were the brothers and sister I never had. I loved each member like a sibling. Unconditionally. So to hear Fiona voicing such thoughts left me dismayed.

She continued. "Mum says it happens to lasses earlier than lads so you lot'll probably start to get fed up with the gang next year anyway."

I felt puzzled. Comic-books and bikes and climbing trees and playing soldiers on the field—that was my life. It was inconceivable that I'd ever get fed up with it. When I wasn't physically participating in those tasks, I was still thinking about doing them. I felt sure she was wrong.

Just then I heard a frantic chattering of birdsong from outside. I stood at the door and watched as a flock of starlings swarmed into the branches. Their behaviour seemed unnatural. Fiona must have seen my expression because she said, "What's up?"

"Don't know." I moved down the steps onto the ground. The birds had fallen silent once more. I could hear from somewhere distant the jangling chime of an ice-cream van. I guessed it was down by the picnic-area that backed onto the reservoir. The air felt muted, like we were insects trapped in a killing jar. I stared at the blistered trees and inhaled the breath of summer, all sweet fruit and dry grass, my view waved on by buzzing flies and skipping butterflies. The contrast between the trees' shadows and the shafts of sunlight filtering through them was startling. I could hear someone swishing through the long grass nearby.

"Sean's here," called Fiona from inside.

He appeared a few seconds later through the bushes, red-faced and panting. His eyebrows rose as he spotted us. "I need the torch.

Quick."

He pushed past me and blundered into the den. I felt the heat radiating from him. He began rummaging through the contents of a cardboard box.

"Where's everyone?" I asked.

He looked up as if noticing us for the first time. "Guess what?—we've found a tunnel down there. I need the torch."

Fiona leaned forward on the beanbag. She finally looked enthusiastic. "Where?"

He waved generally in one direction. "The reservoir." He threw a few Action Man figures aside and held up a torch. He flicked it on to test the batteries. "C'mon, I'll show you."

A boy-shaped maelstrom had entered our lives, disrupting the calm fabric of our certainty. I glanced at Fiona. The sunlight limned her shape. For the first time I saw the figure of a young woman instead of the tomboy she had been.

We headed out of the den, pausing only to look the padlock and secrete the key beneath the step. There was a faint breeze stirring the surrounding bushes, giving the impression of something unseen moving through the trees. Sean led the way, explaining as he shuffled ahead. "The water's even lower now. We noticed, soon as we got here." He pointed across the reservoir to the distant bank. "Dec spotted summat. Remember that ladder we saw going into the water? Well it ends at a tunnel in the wall."

We hurried after him. This high in the valley you could see for miles. In the distance I spotted the unmistakeable outline of the Renfield Colliery winding wheel, and the discoloured slag heap beyond it. Until recently my Uncle Terry had worked there. The structure was an imposing sight. Black clouds seemed to be massing in the sky over towards Doncaster. I shivered instinctively, despite the heat.

"There's summat in the tunnel," said Sean. He spoke at the same moment I shivered so I wasn't sure whether it was the environment or his words which had the effect. Fiona blew her hair away from her face like she hadn't heard.

He explained as we walked. They'd gone up to the den to hang out; maybe play cards, throw the glider, read some comics. One of the lads, Dec, had noticed the freshly-exposed tunnel as he'd been messing about with the binoculars. Curious, they'd ventured out to investigate. Mikey had been the first to dare to climb down to the tunnel. The others had waited at the top. Eventually they'd grown impatient and had climbed down, one by one, until only Sean remained. He too had resisted for as long as he could, gathering his courage in the baking sun. He was just about to head on down there himself when he remembered the torch back at the den. That was where we came in.

He told the story through panting breaths, gasps of exertion as we hurried. Yet there was something unspoken beneath the actual words. Maybe I just picked up on the fact that his behaviour suggested fear rather than excitement or anticipation. I think he was relieved to have stumbled across us.

We had reached the part of the fence that had been breached. Sean lifted up a section of the chain-link and we all ducked under. We crossed the grassy bank to where he indicated. As we drew close, I could see the metal frame enclosing the ladder. We'd examined it many times and speculated as to its presence. Now the water level had dropped, it seemed obvious. The ladder descended the reservoir's vertical wall for about thirty feet before ending at the base of a circular tunnel. I suppose it was the service channel, used in the event of a fault. We stood at the top and peered down. I tried to ignore the flat surface of black water lying ten feet below the gaping throat of the tunnel.

"I'll go first," said Sean. He glanced at me. "Then Fiona, then you. There's not enough room for us all together." I nodded.

He clicked on the torch and held it between his teeth. His face was flushed. He gripped the metal handrail and began his descent. I peered over the side and watched him carefully negotiate the slippery rungs until he reached the tunnel. He swung his leg over, beyond my angle of sight, and drew his body across. It appeared the tunnel wasn't that wide.

I glanced at Fiona. "Ready?"

She seemed to hesitate for a second. I could see the indecision in her face, torn between the desire to explore the tunnel and the stomach-ache that was troubling her. On this occasion curiosity won. She stepped over the wall, onto the ladder.

"Fiona." I placed my hand on the railing next to hers. "Be careful."

She nodded and began to move down the ladder. I watched her until she reached the mouth of the tunnel. She stared across at something I couldn't see, then gingerly stepped over to join Sean.

I could hear the birdsong again, the gentle lapping of water against the reservoir's wall, the soughing of wind through the trees. I turned and lowered down onto my haunches, pressing my back against the wall. The heat burned through my T-shirt.

Abruptly I felt like an outsider. Abandoned. I could hear nothing from the tunnel, yet my friends' sudden absence seemed unsettling. Maybe I was just jittery from becoming attuned to Sean's mood, almost as if the nerves had been passed on to me like a virus. I tried to think about something else but my mind wouldn't allow it.

The air was heavy with moisture. I could taste it. I could feel it on my face, on the tingling hairs on my forearms. The light was strange. Everything had a rather sallow tinge. Those dark clouds were closing in.

Just then I heard the clang of footsteps on the ladder. I spun round and saw Fiona climbing over the wall. There was a look of distaste on her face. She was clutching her stomach. "I don't feel well."

"What's down there?"

She looked at me absently, as if I had just asked her what the currency of Kenya was. Her face was pale, her eyes glazed. "Just dark." She hugged herself. The gesture looked odd in the heat. "I didn't like it."

For a second I wasn't sure what she was going to do. If she had started to walk away then, I think I'd have followed her. Instead she lowered herself to the ground and leaned back against the wall, resting her head on her bent knees.

"I'll just see if they're okay." I waited for her to nod vaguely, then stepped over the wall onto the ladder. My *sneakers* squeaked on the metal rungs. As I climbed down, I was aware of the water lapping below. It sounded like a hungry mouth. The birdsong had fallen silent. Despite the frame encircling the ladder, I felt isolated and vulnerable. My legs shook. My palms were damp.

I reached the tunnel pretty quickly. The air had changed. It was more enclosed. There was a dank aroma that seemed to have attached itself to the ladder. I angled my head and peered into the tunnel. It was only about six feet across, with a flat base coated in silt and mud. The sunlight reached barely more than a few paces inside. I could hear nothing at all, and the darkness was made all the more solid by the bright sunshine that bathed the wall.

"Sean?" The echo of my voice sounded strange. I hesitated, leaning into the tunnel with my feet on the ladder. I could see dead leaves and weeds trapped in the carpet of sludge. My chest felt tight. The skin on the back of my neck prickled. I stepped across into the tunnel, opening my eyes wide to try to become accustomed to the dark. I could just make out the edge of Sean's torch lying half-submerged in the mud. I bent to pick it up. It was so cold it made me recoil. I clicked it on and shone it into the darkness.

Something was standing about 10 feet away. The torch's unsteady beam picked out a pale featureless blur, and I jumped in surprise. In the split-second it took me to realign the beam, my mind conjured a tooth-filled gaping mouth, spindly limbs, matted hair. But my steadying of the beam revealed nothing more than a young boy flinching in the light.

I held my breath and peered at him. He was dressed in short trousers and a woollen jumper. I could see the knot of a necktie above the V of his shirt. His dark hair was styled in an old-fashioned side-parting. He looked a year or so younger than us. There was some feature of his timid stance that suggested apprehension, and I took a step forward, buoyed by his non-threatening body language.

The torch made his face as pale as marble. He blinked at the glare, and I angled the beam away.

"Hello?" My voice sounded unsteady in the confines of the tunnel. "Where're me mates?"

He didn't speak, just remained peering at me, hunched in that peculiar-looking jumper like he was uncomfortable inside his own skin, let alone his clothes.

What occurred in the next few minutes is difficult for me to explain—not because I don't remember what happened, but rather because a great deal of it took place internally. What I mean is, at that precise moment my head became flooded by thoughts, like a cascade of photographs. I experienced a powerful feeling of elation. I felt my throat tighten. I was on the verge of tears. Everything seemed comfortable and warm and fuzzy. I couldn't see much because of the darkness, yet somehow I knew that beyond the tunnel's bend lay something I desperately wanted. My mind fogged with desire. I thought of comic books and *Victor* annuals, of *Action Man* figures and football cards. I knew this without question. I was giddy. Elated. I simply *had to* go further into the tunnel.

The boy's expressionless face continued to stare back at me. It was all so unassuming. I was just about to head further into the tunnel when something made me hesitate.

In those days my Dad worked at Sheffield Forgemasters, at their Stocksbridge foundry seven miles away. He'd make the journey by motorbike. Occasionally I'd be getting dressed for school as he was returning from his nightshift; I'd hug him as he'd fight to shake off his exhaustion and help Mum get me breakfasted and ready for school before he retired to bed. There was always a distinct smell to his work clothes; a mixture of oil and sweat and his usual Brut aftershave. I remember how comfortable that smell was, how safe it made me feel.

But there was always something lying beneath that smell. Some alien aspect to it that unsettled me. I suppose it must have been from the chemicals that Dad used during the steel manufacturing process, or maybe just the near-toxic industrial air that clung to his clothes whilst he worked. It was certainly not present at other times. But it was mildly unpleasant, like it was doing its best to taint my Dad.

And in that split second as I hesitated in the tunnel, this thought came to me: there was something about the boy that was at odds with his innocent appearance.

I peered a little closer. His black eyes glittered in the beam, he grinned his passive grin. I angled the beam directly at him. There was a green shade to his teeth, up around the gums. His fingernails looked too pointed. Too clean. I studied his clothes, deciding that his appearance looked deliberate, like a book cover or an illustration from a magazine. I thought I could see things squirming in his hair. Insects, earthworms, maybe spiders. I felt suddenly afraid.

It occurred to me then that he had not yet spoken a single word, even though he'd given me the impression that something desirable awaited me further along the tunnel. Had I made this assumption myself? There was no visible indication that this boy would do me harm. Just then I heard laughter and voices in the distant.

"Sean?" I listened but there was no reply, although the voices continued. "Dec!"

I hesitated again, trying to rationalise my thoughts, trying to decide why I shouldn't go and join my friends further along the tunnel. They sounded excited, like they were all having fun, and I yearned to join them.

But this was the summer of Bradbury; a time when the fabric of everyday life was being torn back to reveal dark curiosities beneath; a time when my imagination was being fuelled by a power beyond my childhood comprehension. Recently acquired knowledge had altered the way I'd looked at things. For the first time in my short life I understood that mortality was as fragile as a dew-coated spider's web in October—slender and precious—and that it could be broken at any time. Ray Bradbury's stories had shown me that things were not always as they first appeared. There must always be questions. I had begun to see the world through the eyes of a man who told life's truths through the art of fiction. Uncle Terry's illness had been reflected in the faces of my parents; for the first time it made me realise that they too would one day die. And I'd come to realise that, even though life coursed through our bodies like oxygen in blood, death was waiting to pounce at any minute.

I took a step backwards and gripped the torch like it was a weapon. Now my mind was made up I felt suddenly afraid, that the figure would know my intention and make its move. I kept the beam trained on its grinning face as I edged back through the sludge towards the ladder.

"Listen, I'm going to head back and get Fiona." My voice was soft and placatory, as if I was trying to reassure a snarling dog. I noticed that I'd moved into the arc of sunlight and I reached across and grabbed the metal of the ladder, suddenly fearful of turning my back against the thing that watched in the dark. I clicked off the torch and slid it into the back pocket of my jeans. At the last moment I had the impression of that tall spindly-limbed figure again, but then the darkness rushed in to steal it.

The handrail was hot in the sunlight, such a sharp contrast to the cool interior of the tunnel. For a second I was momentarily blinded, but I scrambled up the ladder, my sneakers making deft clunks on each rung.

At the top, I stepped over the low wall, noting the black water far below. It felt incredibly good to be standing on firm ground. My sneakers were clogged with sludge. I realised my hands were trembling.

Fiona glanced up from where she sat. Her face was pale. She looked startled when she saw my expression. "Where are they?"

I shook my head. The relief at being out of the tunnel suddenly hit me, and I bent and vomited onto the grass. I was aware of Fiona's hand on my back and her nearness brought tears to my eyes. I clutched her desperately, not caring about how pathetic I must have looked.

Lightning flickered in the sky and there was a growl of thunder from across the valley. The breeze was increasing; it flapped the sleeves of my t-shirt, made the trees shudder impatiently behind us.

"C'mon, let's get home," said Fiona. Her hand lingered on my back and I was scared to say anything, to break the spell. "It's gunna rain."

The light had gone weird. A strange sickly colour had tainted the sky, like a yellow caul sealing the valley. I felt dizzy. The lightning strobed again, adding a dimension of melodrama to the proceedings that was not required.

It started to rain then, just sporadic drops at first, but soon they were huge splodges that darkened our t-shirts. We began to hurry. I noticed a weird mark on the back Fiona's jeans and I pointed it out. She stopped and rubbed at it self-consciously, angling her body so that it was hidden. "Are you okay?" I said, studying her face. "Looks like blood."

"I'm fine," she said quickly. "It's nothing."

The rain was heavy now. I could hear it pounding the dry ground around us, shivering the trees into movement. The surface of the reservoir looked like it was being struck by mini-explosions as the rain pelted it. Heavy black clouds had stolen away the blue sky that had been constant for the past three months.

As we hurried along the brow of the reservoir I gazed down upon Renfield, spotting the church spire, a jagged scar of dry-stone walls bordering the school on the far hill, the pub at the central crossroads that bisected our town. The slate roofs of the houses looked drab and grey, glistening in the rain, and I felt my chest ache at the sight. The drab ordinariness of it looked suddenly welcoming, desirable now. My yearning for a life more exotic had been dampened. I longed to be in my bedroom, reading a book and watching the storm through my window.

As if to illustrate a point, lightning flickered in the sky and thunder cracked overhead. It was deafening. We hunched our shoulders and began to hurry.

By the time we arrived home we were dripping wet, our hair plastered flat to our heads by the torrent. Water gushed from overflowing drainpipes, a vast puddle spanned the full length of the main road, its surface peppered by raindrops. My shirt clung to my body as I squelched along our road. I mumbled a hasty goodbye to Fiona, who waved a vague hand and hurried up her drive.

My summer of Bradbury was over.

*

No one ever found out what happened to our friends. Their bodies were never recovered. For a while the story was featured in many of the papers, a tragic tale of four young boys drowned whilst playing in the reservoir. I told my version of what happened but the police dismissed it, instead believing that they'd simply become lost in the service tunnel and had perished as the water level had risen. They ignored what I told them about the strange boy, insisting that I must have been confused in the darkness.

We had a school assembly in memory of Declan, Sean, Mikey

and Lee. For a few days Fiona and I were elevated to the status of minor celebrities. I'm ashamed to say there was a small part of me that relished the attention. But I told myself that it was just part of the coping mechanism. For a while afterwards my dreams were stalked by loping creatures with black eyes and mouths of razor teeth. To this day I have a fear of tunnels, not because of the confinement, but rather from what might lurk in the darkness. Fiona seemed to deal with what had happened by dismissing it as kids' stuff, just a dreadful accident. Her family moved to Barnsley a few months later. I never saw her again.

In the intervening years I've had time to consider that day. I don't mean *understand* what happened—age has allowed me to reconcile what I believed at the time with the rational thought of an adult–but to reflect on how Fiona and I managed to escape. I think there was more than luck involved.

It's clear to me now that Fiona had outgrown our gang. She had changed mentally as well as physically. Perhaps the idea of exploring a filthy, dark tunnel wasn't that appealing to a young girl on the cusp of womanhood.

And in my case, I was saved by Ray Bradbury, whose fiction taught me that death waits nearby for those foolish enough to wander close; a notion fairly alien to most 12 year-old boys, whose feelings of immortality gradually lessen as they grew older. And poor old Uncle Terry's illness reiterated that fact. He died a few months later, just after Mum's birthday in November. I don't think our family was ever the same after that.

*

A few years ago I was in Sheffield on business, and I came across a heritage museum on the outskirts of the city centre. It was housed in a building that had once been used as a corn mill on the banks of the River Don. There were sections covering the history of South Yorkshire's industry—a room dedicated to coal-mining, one to the city's steel manufacturing plants and so on—and hundreds of photographs showing how the area had changed since the Victorian times. There were even a few pictures of Renfield from the late 70s, images which evoked powerful memories in me. But it was a section in the corner that I found the most interesting; black and white photographs of Bowerton, the village that was drowned to make way for the reservoir. One in particular caught my eye, dated 1938—taken outside the primary school, three rows of children starting sullenly at the camera like they were suspicious of what was happening. In particular I noticed their clothes—the short trousers, the woollen pullovers, the neckties of their school uniform. They all had the same short back and sides, the neat parting to one side. Those dark monochrome features offering nothing but a simple reminder of what was now long dead. I shivered as my eyes searched their faces one by one but there was nobody there I recognised.

The Devil's Only Friend

The walk from the train station was exhausting. By the time Nolan had reached the B&B his lips were chapped, his face stung by the wind. He paid by cash and was directed to a room on the third floor: a sparse hovel, barely larger than the box he'd occupied for the past six years. At least the threadbare carpet was marginally more comfortable than those cold tiles.

He sat on the sagging bed and stared through the net curtains. The building opposite lurked sullenly, a hulking silhouette that blocked the glare of the town's neon. At some point, part of its roof had collapsed, though Nolan could see shadows flitting through the broken windows, movement beneath the exposed eaves. Probably just roosting gulls. Scaffolding and polythene sheets did their best to conceal the building's ruined state. A wooden fence surrounded the perimeter of the grounds, plastered with warning signs prohibiting entry.

It was getting late. The window was draughty, and Nolan could hear the pulse of techno music from the bar, two streets away. He felt his heart race instinctively. He was out of practice but he knew he couldn't resist the lure.

Six years was six years.

*

Afterwards they lay in silence on the bed, allowing the mood to slip away. Nolan's arm was under the boy's side and he tried not to imagine he was trapped. It had been so long since he'd done this he wasn't quite sure of the correct etiquette. But the boy twisted his spray-tanned torso and turned to Nolan. "This a smoking room?"

Nolan knew it wasn't but he was afraid of losing the boy so

he said, "You'll be all right." He fought the urge to glance at the ceiling's smoke detector.

The boy—*Brett, wasn't it?*—leaned out of bed and fished around in the pocket of his jeans. He lit a cigarette and lay back against the pillow, exhaling a slender coil of smoke.

Nolan watched the process with his stomach in knots. Every time the boy sucked on the cigarette the tip glowed, burning with an intensity that matched his own accelerated heartbeat. He tried to remember the relaxation techniques he'd been taught in his therapy sessions but they seemed so distant it almost felt like they'd happened to someone else. Although didn't everything? They'd told him this was all part of the coping mechanism.

The boy finished his cigarette and climbed out of bed. He was skinny and hairless, well-defined arms and stomach. A nice tattoo extended from his left shoulder to the tops of his buttocks. He opened the window and tossed the cigarette-butt out. For a few seconds he remained staring through the net curtains. "Bout time they knocked that place down." He turned and looked at Nolan, smiling provocatively.

Nolan returned his gaze through the smokey veil. He could feel the tension in his chest. The smell of smoke and his memory of the cigarette stirred excitement. Vibrant. Untethered.

The boy misinterpreted Nolan's pause. "That place over the road, I mean."

"Yeah," said Nolan expressionlessly.

But the boy continued. "Fucking place burned down years ago. Arson—so they said. Rumoured it's gonna be an Aldi, once they sort out the insurance."

Nolan shrugged. Aldi left him feeling detached, just like Ikea and all those trendy coffee-shops. In the week since his release he'd noticed them littering the high street; replacements for the shops that had closed during the period of his detainment—Woolworths, Comet, Clinton Cards, Jessops—names that now sounded like relics of his old life, back when his desire felt more like compulsion than just a yearning.

His thoughts were interrupted by the boy. "So you used to live round here then?"

"Years ago." Nolan nodded. "Came here after I dropped out of Uni."

The boy walked back and threw himself on to the bed. "Too bad you weren't here in the summer. We'd've had some fun."

Nolan smiled absently and leaned forward.

*

The park was almost empty. Nolan had been there for almost an hour. Now the kids had gone back to school it was populated by dog-walkers and red-faced joggers, pensioners wearing thick anoraks who used the park as a short-cut to the community centre. He could hear the caw of gulls from up on the shopping arcade's roof, its glass cracked and speckled with dirt. Traffic sounds did their best to mask the distant sussuration of the sea. It was as if the seaside part of the town was slowly been overtaken by shops and car-parks.

The wrought-iron bench was rusting and uncomfortable, its wooden seat warped by the elements. Nolan nursed a plastic carrier-bag, watching the house for any sign of life. Earlier he'd spotted the outline of a figure through the frosted glass of the front door, thirty seconds after the postman had departed. It was a vague watercolour-hazed blur of browns and greys. Nolan had been staring at the house for so long it felt like he was looking at a photograph. He was just about to give up and return to the B&B when he saw a man come out of the front door and shuffle along the garden path, looking directly at him from across the road. He was dressed in a beige anorak and a pair of dark trousers.

Nolan shifted in his seat and waited while the man trudged slowly across the zebra-crossing. As he drew close, Nolan could see Mark's strong resemblance in the old man's tired face. This caused a spike of regret to lance through him. He swallowed and tried to prevent his hands from shaking.

The man sat down wearily next to him. He must have only been in his mid-fifties, yet he appeared much older. He smelt vaguely of stale, enclosed rooms, like the interior of caravans or a musty attic; nothing too unpleasant, but somehow infinitely sad. His breathing was ragged. When the man finally spoke he sounded frail: "You win. Thought I'd better come out—seeing as you don't look like you're about to give up anytime soon."

Nolan cleared his throat. "Thanks for coming, Mr Wheeler." He watched a woman and a toddler feeding some ducks on the edge of the pond. "Sorry to keep ringing you like that, only-"

"Mabel thinks I've popped out to buy some milk, so I can only spare a few minutes." The man half-turned so that he was looking at Nolan. "If you've come to say you're sorry, you can save your breath. There's nothing you can say that'll make it right."

Nolan patted the bag on his lap. "I've just come to return some of Mark's things, that's all."

"When d'you get out?"

"Friday."

The man whistled between his teeth. "Wasted no time in coming back then."

Nolan ignored this, and handed the bag over. "Just some of Mark's CDs, a couple of photos, stuff like that."

For a few moments neither of them spoke. The old man took a linen handkerchief from his pocket and wiped his nose. "Mabel thinks it was just an accident. A housefire. I managed to shield her. She's never been the same since, but if she'd known the truth it would've killed her."

"Mr Wheeler—for what it's worth—I'm very sorry."

The man laughed hollowly. "Well—it's worth nothing, lad. Nothing at all."

The woman and the toddler had exited the park through the gates. There was a flurry of activity from the pond, flapping wings and squawks of protest. A typhoon of feathers.

Nolan sensed the man was about to stand up, but instead he said, "So you've learned your lesson? You're reformed?"

"I had therapy sessions in prison, Mr Wheeler. Three times a week. Mark's death was a horrible accident. But...I've been addicted to starting fires since I was eight. It's just what I did. I never meant to hurt anyone."

"Aye—they said that at the trial. But locking you up as a young 'un still hadn't cured you, had it?"

"No. Juvenile detention... just *toughened* me more."

"The judge said you were selfish and weak. In denial."

"I know. But the doctors managed to help me—shown me how to control it."

"So why'd you do it? That's something that no one was able to answer."

Nolan shook his head once. "Apparently it stems from when I was a kid. My upbringing. No friends. A lack of control." He shrugged.

The old man pursed his lips. "I didn't even know Mark was... *that way out*. He'd had girlfriends when he was a teenager."

"Me and Mark got on well. We had a lot in common."

"You're nothing like him," said the old man vehemently. He was grimacing. Nolan could feel the contempt in his voice.

"What I mean is, we enjoyed the same things–music, films, books, bands."

Neither spoke for a long time. Overhead the gulls wheeled, a car horn blasted from the promenade. Nolan could hear random electronic melodies from an amusement arcade.

"So what now—you move on, whilst we have to live with what you did?" There was a tremor in the man's voice that wasn't there before.

Nolan shrugged. "Too much has changed. There's a war being fought on these streets. I'm just another casualty of it."

"Poor you."

"Not just me. I know Mark felt disconnected from society as well. I saw men in prison who don't know anything except what it's like to commit crime. Career criminals, they call 'em. I saw a man who lost an eye in Helmand reduced to dealing drugs on the streets. There was one bloke in therapy who'd lain on the railway tracks 'cause he was being forced to work or they'd stop his benefits. He thought losing the other leg might make his disability more real, might prevent him going through the assessment."

"None of this has anything to do with Mark. He was happy at home. We had a lovely family."

"Yes." Nolan ran a hand across his stubbled chin. "So happy he was scared to tell you what he really was."

As soon as the words were out he regretted it. He was here to make his peace, not antagonise anyone. God knew he'd caused enough suffering already.

"You young people think the world owes you everything, don't you? Won't get out of bed unless you're getting forty grand a year. You want to be famous but you can't be arsed to learn a craft. Well it's not just you that's fighting this war—I was made redundant a few years back. Can't get another job. No one wants to employ a 57 year-old. Now we've got to pay more rent 'cause we've got an unused bedroom. The council don't care. So we either move to a one-bedroom place miles away from here, or rent out the room to a lodger. Can you imagine how hard it is to tell your wife she'll have to pack away all your dead son's stuff and let a stranger move into his old room? So spare me the victim card, because I'm all out of sympathy." He blew his nose with the handkerchief. He seemed to have been invigourated by Nolan's presence. "And all the while the bloody energy companies are making more money than ever. The gulf's widening. The bankers are sitting on million-pound pensions and the government's moving the goalposts for me to draw my state pension. I always imagined pushing the grand-kids on them swings once I'd finished work but now that's never gonna happen.

"Sometimes I wish it'd been me in that bloody hotel, not Mark."

A brittle silence descended on them. For ages they sat without moving. The man wiped his eyes again. "I can't bare to walk down that road where it happened. They keep talking about turning it into a supermarket. I wish they bloody well would. Once it's gone I might be able to move on."

"Look—I just came to bring you his things and tell you I'm sorry. I never meant to hurt anyone. I was messing about—just like I always did. The fire got out of hand. I managed to get out, Mark wasn't so lucky. There isn't a day that goes by that I don't regret what happened. I think about it all the time..."

The man laughed. It sounded ugly. "You'll get a job and in a few years this'll all be behind you. Well, it's not right. It's not right, I tell you. I hope this bloody-well haunts you till the day you die."

Nolan stood and zipped up his coat. "It has, Mr Wheeler. It

definitely has."

*

In the afternoon he walked along the seafront, staring at the grey churning tide. It felt like he was teetering on the brink of another world. The briny air whipped his face. Overhead, gulls soared like unteathered kites. Two dogs raced across the wet sand as the wind did its best to snatch away their barks. There was a wooden hut on the promenade, from which he bought an ice-cream. Faded postcards rattled in the metal rack next to the window, threatening to leap to freedom on the breeze. He sat on a bench facing the sea, licking his ice-cream. About twenty feet away, three teenagers huddled together, isolated from one another by the attention their mobile phones demanded. Nolan watched them swiping photos across their screens, playing games, listening to music. One of them laughed at something on a pop video.

Nolan finished his cornet and took out his battered Nokia. He scrolled through the contacts list and deleted Mark's number from its memory. Instinctively he held up the phone and sniffed it. The antiseptic stench of prison still clung to its plastic case. Another relic from his old life. He stood and threw the phone as far as he could onto the beach. It landed on a stretch of pebbles and smashed, bouncing into several parts. The teenagers eyed him warily.

The six years separating the old him and the here and now felt like a chasm too wide to span. Everything had altered. Society had changed. Its features were still recognisable but there was a minute difference, an imperceptible shift that was so subtle it was hard to pinpoint. Like a waxwork dummy that so closely resembled a human it was uncanny.

In prison he'd been shielded from the full effects of the change. Of course he'd had access to television and newspapers, but this week had shown him that the old enemies had just taken on a different appearance. Bankers and multi globalised companies had rushed to fill the void that politicians and footballers had once occupied. Family-friendly faces from his past seemed to be arrested on an almost daily basis; further evidence that the foundations of his childhood were collapsing. His memories felt like they were fabricated. Synthetic.

He stood quickly, anxious that his manner might betray the emotion that threatened to consume him. He turned and hurried along the promenade towards his B&B, the teenagers' mocking laughter ringing in his ears.

*

Nolan woke during the night. The digital clock told him it was 3:22. He turned over and faced the wall, trying to allow sleep to reclaim him. Almost at once he became aware of the smell of smoke. He sat upright and blinked his eyes in the dim light. He reached over and switched on the lamp. The room was clear, there was nothing visible in the air. The smoke detector on the ceiling continued its silent red blink every thirty seconds. He inhaled deeply, wondering if the smell was just a fragment of a swiftly-forgotten dream. He closed his eyes. The acrid stench of ash and charred wood was distinct—he had smelled it enough times for it to be unmistakable.

He stood and padded to the window. The building opposite loitered in the darkness, its scaffolding masking the desolate ruination. But he couldn't be fooled. The product of his disorder was still recognisable.

He wondered if unseen eyes watched him from the shadows. He thought about what he'd endured for the past six years. How could all those court appearances, therapy sessions, countless days spent locked in his room—how could all those endless nights have passed while the destroyed building remained in its state of suspended animation? It felt as if the hotel had been awaiting his return.

He stepped away from the window, but just as he did so he noticed movement in the street below. From this angle he was afforded a view inside the wooden perimeter that cordoned the site off to the public. Things squirmed in the shadows, reaching up with indistinct limbs. As if in supplication. Nolan could hear a dull roaring in his ears, like static or the endless churn of the tide.

Darkness rippled beyond the fence. Yet the streetlights bathed the road beyond the fence in an orange glow, creating fine detail and sharp definition to everything. Once again it occurred to him that the contrast between the two impressions was acute, that he was viewing both worlds from the threshold of a doorway. *The gulf is widening.*

Nolan closed his eyes against the writhing darkness. He stumbled to the bed and climbed beneath the covers. He clicked off the lamp and lay for ages until the odour of ash returned. He knew this was just his guilt manifesting itself into something physical so he turned over. In the wake of the light's absence, the darkness in the room was claustrophobic. He opened his eyes. Someone was standing against the far wall. He could make out its shape as his eyes grew accumstomed to the dark.

"Mark?"

There was no reply. Nolan held his breath. The hairs on the back of his neck bristled. He recognised the hunched slope of the figure's shoulders. The smell of burning was stronger. Nolan's eyes were adjusting to the gloom. The figure slowly lowered until it was lying on the floor. It curled into a foetal position, arms enclosed over its head. It looked helpless. Frightened. Nolan sat up and clicked on the lamp but there was nobody there.

*

Sunlight had bleached colour from the cheaply framed print that hung on the wall opposite the window. It looked like it been there for decades. Nolan glanced at the clock, stretching until his joints popped. It was 7.47 AM.

The room was bright. The air was clear. No smoke, no ash. No signs to indicate last night's smell of burning had been anything physical. He rolled out of bed and walked to the window. There was a weird atmosphere, difficult to pinpoint. He exhaled, enjoying the hiss of release. After a few seconds he realised what it was: there was no noise from the street.

He peered through the window. It was a bright morning. Sunlight glinted off cars parked along the road. A languid cat prowled between two wheely-bins positioned near the kerb. But there was no sound of traffic from the main road. Nolan angled his head and peered up the road to the seafront. There was nobody about. Stranger still, it was silent. The only thing he could hear was the occasional cawing of a gull from somewhere nearby. It was a plaintive, desolate cry.

Nolan dressed absently, listening for sounds of life. He let himself out of the room and descended the stairs. The reception was deserted. Sunlight poured through the window, dazzling him momentarily as he paused at the desk.

"Hello?" His voice sounded alien in the muscular silence.

Nothing.

He crossed the reception and shouldered open the door. The first thing he spotted was a hanging basket suspended from a backet. Its flowers were scorched, the petals withered and charred. The sight was disturbing.

Nolan staggered to the edge of the pavement, squinting against the sun, peering in both directions in an effort to spot someone. Anyone. He felt a surge of giddiness. Silence and the apparent lack of people created a sense of dislocation in him. Random thoughts and memories flooded his mind. He recalled an old episode of *The Twilight Zone*, the one where everyone had vanished, but this made him wonder if he was still asleep. *Surely if he could reason such things he couldn't be dreaming?*

He loped up the deserted road. Newspapers and discarded burger cartons huddled against the kerb. He paused outside a squat building, staring in puzzlement at its frontage. It was an old-fashioned tea-room boasting a sign written in a fancy Edwardian font, and a 'specials' chalkboard attached to the wall. Nolan shook his head slowly, frowning. He'd passed this very same building on his way to the B&B yesterday and had noticed the hastily-constructed vinyl cover declaring that it was the area's *Food Bank*. A local charity's name and web address had been plastered all over the sign, and covering every inch of its windows. But that was gone.

Quite suddenly he became aware of a figure standing at the top of the road, on the corner of the promenade. From this angle it looked like the figure was watching him. He squinted but the image broke up, and when he blinked there was no one there. He began to jog towards the end of the road.

By the time he reached the seafront he was sweating. The silence was eerie. Oppressive. He glanced up and down the promenade but there was no one to be seen. He was struck by an abrupt feeling of confusion. At first he couldn't put his finger on it. His eyes searched for detail in the scene, noticing the odd bird in the sky, registering that the breeze that had been present earlier had now dropped. Then he realised what it was: the sea had vanished.

He stared out across the expanse of pebbles and sand, expecting to see the ceaselessly churning tide but instead it looked like his view had been replaced with a desert scene. Brown. Brittle. Parched. A tableau of orange. Endless sand extended for several miles, running at a gentle decline before becoming more disjointed as the terrain plunged lower. There were black gaps between angled tors of similar height, gaping chasms between the plateaus. He suddenly felt like he was about to overbalance, and he readjusted his feet to counter it.

The expanse of sand quivered and broke up in the distance. Nolan understood he was seeing a heat haze. Warm air ruffled his hair, bringing with it a stench of fire and ash. It promised salvation. It beckoned him home.

He blinked at the tiny figure, stark against the lighter background beyond. *Mark.* A long way away. He was waiting. Nolan began to head towards the figure.

He hurried across the road onto the promenade. His footsteps were deafening. He was glad when he reached the beach, and the sand smothered the sound. He could see the shimmering figure, distant. The pull was immense. He began to hasten, tripping over his feet as he hurried to reach his destination. Sand stretched on forever. He remained focused on the figure ahead as he jogged, his breath the only sound in his ears. Soon he was lost to the rhythm of his movement; urgent, determined, relentless, a blur of indistinct brown swallowing him.

He thought about those nights in prison, seeing his cellmate's ridiculed face in the aftermath of suddenly waking, the threads of a nightmare still clinging to him. How sometimes he heard

Mark's voice in his head, or turned over in the night to see a figure standing in the corner of the room. Nolan realised that Mark was the one thing that had accompanied him on his journey from *then* to *now*. He was the doorway.

The prison therapist had preached to him that his obsession for setting fires stemmed from childhood boredom. *The Devil finds work for idle hands.* Nolan had never understood that dogma. He remembered his step-father's behaviour in the aftermath of Nolan's mother's death; it had left him no time for boredom. He'd yearned for someone with whom he could share the suffering, but his lack of friends had left him confined. Isolated.

The gulf is widening.

His thoughts were interrupted. The light felt wrong. Nolan stopped and turned. The distant strip of hotels, amusement arcades, food outlets, looked thin and fragile and insignificant. Diminished. Nothing moved. He felt like an actor on stage.

His eyes couldn't make out any detail but somehow he knew that the town was the version from six years ago—the one with fewer boarded-up shops, the one whose streets were patrolled by a higher number of police officers, whose hospitals were staffed by nurses who felt less disillusioned by government cuts and enforced changes to their jobs. From a time when the idea of a food bank would have been archaic and absurd. Nolan guessed that *this* town's library wouldn't yet be closed, that the community centres and NHS walk-in clinics would still exist. The town he was seeing was as distant to him now as the sun.

He was reminded of heat and flame and ash, and he glanced upward. A strange hue had flooded the sky. Ominous and crepuscular. He blinked at the unnatural light, frowning as a series of ragged shadows pattened the floor. He turned again, to glance at the distant shoreline but it was gone. There was just a rocky slope leading away, tongues of black seaweed carpeting the ground.

And in that instant he understood that he'd crossed the threshold and the door had closed.

Silence was silence, but it had taken on a transformed quality. Like after it had snowed. Muffled. Enclosed. He glanced down at his feet. Eely fronds of weed clutched at his boots. He had the sudden feeling that he was being watched, and he turned and took a step back. His breath caught in his throat.

A sheer wall of water towered above him, so high it was impossible to see the peak. It held firm, but was liquid enough to ripple and undulate like it was a living organism.

As a child he'd owned an encyclopaedia, and had spent hours poring over its contents. There'd been one picture that had remained unforgettable: a dramatic illustration of Moses parting the Red Sea. The insignificance of those humans cowering in the vast trench had left Nolan breathless.

Now he stared up at the mountainous wall of water with a smiliar expression of awe and fear as those fleeing Israelites. He watched absently, fascinated at the way the sides of the water trembled. It was as if there was an invisible membrane of glass holding back the tide, hundreds of feet high. He blinked his eyes, hearing a crackling and popping in his head. It sounded like burning.

The top gave way first, appearing to teeter for a second before starting its fall. It seemed to happen in slow motion, and he turned and began to stagger. There was a futile roaring in his ears which he registered was his own voice.

The water pushed him into the ground mercilessly, forcing the oxygen from his lungs. His broken limbs became numb. He was dragged this way and that. The cold harsh weight of the sea held him in its grip. Grey darkness enveloped him, confusing him with bubbles and murk, freezing his chest. He fought to remain upright in the water. Pain tore through his nostrils and throat. In the confusion of light and sound he spotted faces in the water, too brief and infrequent to identify. The faces were formed by smoke, their features malevolent. Nolan was in so much agony he could barely register the pain. Fear clouded his mind as the smoke figures circled him in the water. It was so dark he couldn't see the surface of the sea. The cold was immeasurable. But then his desperate fingers reached the comfort they sought as a hand, welcoming and warm, found his own flailing hand and led him away.

Pennyroyal

Only after the old man's belongings have been packed away in cardboard boxes—a lifetime's accumulation of bric-a-brac condensed into just the scant few allowed by the nursing home—and the furniture has been taken away in a van to be sold, leaving the rooms unfamiliar, filled with echoes—only then does the old man shuffle into the kitchen and stare through the window with eyes left moist by more than just age and rheum. The bare worktops accentuate what is no longer there. Now the heating has been switched off, the radiators have ceased their sighed eulogies.

"One more thing," says the old man. "We need to dig in the garden."

"Granddad," says Richard, "Sarah'll have the tea ready soon. We need to go." He feels bad for saying it.

The old man continues as if he hasn't heard, "Should've done this a few years ago when your grandmother died."

Richard glances at his watch. He can hear his son in the living room, busy on his Nintendo DS. He looks at the old man standing forlorn, staring through the window as if seeing ghosts in the back garden.

The old man takes a cotton handkerchief out of his pocket and wipes his nose. He turns to his grandson. "Have we got time, Richard, for me to tell you a little story?"

*

He was confused when he got home from work and found the house deserted. The oven wasn't on, Elspeth wasn't there. It didn't even seem like the evening tea had begun to be prepared. But Ernest was a pragmatic man so he tried to push the worrisome thoughts away and instead have a bath. His afternoon shift had been particularly tiring, and he was keen to wash away the smell of oil and sweat, so he promptly went upstairs. It was over half an hour later, once he had finally ventured back down, that he spotted Elspeth's note.

It was propped up against the carriage clock, written in his wife's familiar script but with an element of brevity to suggest it had been scribbled in haste. Just five words—*Ernie, gone to Maureen's, El.*

He frowned. There was nothing at all unusual about his wife visiting their neighbours' house; it was just the timing of it that was strange. Maureen's husband, Frank, would also be in from work at this hour, and it seemed odd to think that Elspeth might still be there.

Ernest sat at the kitchen table and began to read the newspaper. He decided against switching on the wireless. The refrigerator hummed impatiently, the wall clock ticked; every few minutes the tap dripped into the sink.

The sound of footsteps echoed along the ginnel separating their house from the next, and a moment later the back door opened. It was his son, Alan. "Dad, Mum said you've got to come to the Vincents'. Kath is poorly and her dad's drunk."

Ernest paused long enough to shrug on his work coat and follow his son out of the house, up towards the terrace on the end belonging to Frank and Maureen.

Once they had reached the back yard Alan seemed satisfied that he had accomplished his task so he drifted away to a loitering group of boys who were impatiently bouncing a football. Ernest knocked once on the back door and entered.

He had been inside the Vincents' house on several occasions, the most recent being the previous New Year's Eve. The kitchen's layout was identical to their own except the units and worktops were very modern. He watched the tap for a moment but detected no drips. There were, however, raised voices from upstairs. He hesitated for a moment, unsure of what to do. He walked to the bottom of the stairs, throwing an admiring glance into the living room at the Goldstar television that stood in the corner. The shop in the high street rented them out, and Ernest had promised himself they would get one if he managed to win that Charge-hand promotion that was coming up at the factory.

Finally he decided that he could postpone it no longer. He called up the stairs, as quietly as he could, "Elspeth."

The raised voices continued, but a second later his wife appeared and hurried down the stairs, wiping her hands on her pinafore. She swept past him and he followed her into the kitchen.

"Ernie, thank God you're here. " She sounded anxious, her voice hushed.

"What's up, love?"

"It's Kath. She's—" She threw a furtive glance towards the stairs and mouthed, rather than spoke, the next part, "—she's…*with child*."

"What? How come?" Ernest stared. "She's nowt but a kid."

"She's fifteen." Elspeth removed a packet of cigarettes from her pocket and lit one, exhaling a plume of smoke from the corner of her mouth. "Frank's doing his nut up there."

"I'll bet he is."

"Maureen's been giving her herbal tea for two days."

"Tea?"

"Herbal tea—pennyroyal." Elspeth took another long drag on the cigarette. "Nature's way of sorting things out."

"How far gone is she?"

Elspeth shrugged. "Far enough, I think. She's got a proper bump, though she's kept it hidden. This next bit's not going to be nice, put it that way."

"Does she need the hospital?"

"Shouldn't think so. We'll be able to get it sorted here. I reckon the pennyroyal she's had, and all the poking around up there, will have done the trick." Elspeth motioned with her head upstairs. "Maureen found out yesterday when she noticed Kath's monthlies had stopped. Can you talk to Frank while we see to it? He's been on the sauce."

Ernest felt relief soar in his chest. Best leave it to the womenfolk, this kind of thing. They were the real experts, the ones who knew what they were doing. Pregnancies seemed to rally them in a way little else did. Women had been helping other women have babies—or, where necessary, getting rid of them—for centuries. If all he was required to do was entertain a disgruntled father during his daughter's hour of discomfort, that was all right, wasn't it?

Elspeth finished her cigarette and ground the butt into an ashtray. Ernest pulled out a chair from the table and sat down. From the floor above rose Kath's panicked cries. Elspeth hastily washed her hands at the sink and hurried upstairs.

Ernest took out his own cigarettes and lit one, contemplating what to say to Frank. The Vincents seemed like such a nice well-to-do family it was difficult to know what had gone wrong. He smoked thoughtfully, anticipating Frank's mood. Presently he heard the squeak of floorboards and the sound of someone descending the stairs.

"Hey up, Frank." He tried to inject some cheer into his voice.

The man looked wretched. His cheeks were flushed, his hair—usually so neatly parted with Brylcreem—unkempt and in disarray. There was a blue tinge to his lips. His eyes looked watery and bloodshot.

"Come on, have a sit down." Frank drew out a chair so the other man could slump down onto it. "Cuppa tea?"

A shake of the head. He rubbed his slack jaw. He swallowed a few times, seeming to get a hold of himself. "There's a bottle on that sideboard. D'you mind?"

Ernest fetched the bottle and poured a few inches into one of the glasses from the draining-board. Frank necked it straight down and held his glass out again. Ernest poured out a second measure, then took one for himself. He sipped, wincing at the taste.

Frank stared straight ahead. His face was haggard, yet flushed. Now he was closer, Ernest could smell the booze on him. He'd probably been in the pub since leaving work at 2 o'clock, as his seniority allowed him the benefit of a more favourable shift. His flushed cheeks were no doubt the result of the pale ales he'd sunk. At last he spoke. "Ernie, where've we gone wrong, eh?"

Ernest smiled wryly and with a little sadness, unsure of whether the question was rhetorical.

But Frank continued. "She's not even got a boyfriend, for God's sake." His voice sounded bitter. His eyes searched out Ernest's face.

"You've got it easy—you've got a lad; you don't have to bloody worry about that with lads."

"No."

"But…I can't understand it; she's been doing well at school. How could she be so damn stupid?"

"Has she said who the…?" Ernest flinched away from voicing the word *father*.

"I blame them bloody school-friends of hers. Arty-farty types, they are," said Frank. "Filling her head with soddin' books and poetry." He rubbed his grizzled chin. "She says she hasn't… *been* with anyone; says she can't be in the family way because she's never even been with *anyone*."

"Could it be that she isn't?"

Frank shrugged. "Well, she says her monthly cycle's stopped, so God knows." He banged his hand on the table, rattling the glasses. "It's bloody shameful, I tell yer, Ernie. Shameful."

"Look, I think Maureen and Elspeth'll sort this out. No one else needs know."

Frank's eyes searched Ernest's face again, like he was seeing him in a new light. "She's a good woman, your Elspeth. You look after her, Ernie."

"I will."

He finished the second glass. "She swears she's never done it, just had dreams about doing it."

"Dreams?"

"A man dressed in white, she says. He comes into her dreams and she can't help herself. She says a few of her friends have dreamt about the same fella. He's…—she couldn't say no to him." He laughed without mirth, his eyes blazing. "This is what bloody happens when you let kids read books written by these hippy-trippy types. What a load of bull."

There was another muted yell from upstairs. From outside came the shouts of boys playing football on the street, the bounce of a ball against the wall.

Ernest remembered the birth of his own son, how he'd ridden his bike home from the factory as soon as he'd heard the news that Elspeth had gone into labour. Pacing the back-garden after the midwife had ushered him outside. He'd ended up re-potting his tomato plants in the greenhouse in an effort to take his mind off it. Frank here didn't look nervous; he just seemed angry and upset. Ernest wasn't sure what else he could say to him.

The screams upstairs were increasing. Floorboards creaked, implying movement from the two older women. This went on for a few moments, interspersed by the raised voices of Maureen and Elspeth, their words made indistinguishable by the context of their speech and the floor separating them.

"I don't know what'll happen now," said Frank. He sounded bewildered.

Ernest hesitated. "I think Elspeth said her…Kath's body, I mean…will probably… stop it going any further. Naturally, like."

"Stop it?"

"What I mean is…the body will reject it now."

Frank glanced down at his empty glass. "Like a miscarriage, you mean?"

"I suppose so, yes."

After a while Frank nodded. "It's for the best, I reckon."

"It is."

Things were reaching a head upstairs. The intensity of the noise was frightening. And, quite abruptly, it changed. Kath's screams subsided; now came the tears, her sobs and plaintive cries almost as unsettling as the screams. She sounded like a terrified little girl.

Frank wiped his hands across his face. He now looked sober, the redness from his cheeks gone, replaced by a ghastly pale colour. Tiny globules of spittle beaded the corner of his mouth. His eyes were bloodshot.

"Frank," Ernie said, "it'll be all right, you just see."

Frank swallowed and nodded. Kath was still crying upstairs. They could hear Maureen's voice, trying to comfort her daughter.

The sound of footsteps coming down the stairs. Both men turned to look as Elspeth appeared at the kitchen door. "Frank, I think you should go up."

He peered at her, studying her face for the slightest trace. "Is everything…all right?"

She nodded. "It's all done with now, love. It's all over."

Frank sighed. It was the most desolate sound Ernest had ever heard.

"Go up to them," urged Elspeth again. "They both need you."

Frank nodded and stood up. He paused for a moment as if he was trying to remember how to move. Then he hurried past her and went up the stairs.

Ernest blew out his cheeks. "How'd it go?"

"Not good." Elspeth grimaced. "Looks like she would've lost it anyway—wasn't right."

"How do you mean?"

She shrugged. "Disabled, I reckon. Not properly developing."

"Oh hell."

"It's all right now anyway." She lifted a Woolworth's carrier-bag that she'd been clutching by her side. "Listen, love, would you do me a favour and get rid of this?" Her face looked distasteful.

He nodded.

She handed it over. "Everything's in there, even the little placenta. Throw it on the fire, will you?"

He was surprised at the substantial weight of the bag, felt alarmed at the significance of it.

"Poor Kath's tired out. I'll go and run her a bath while her mam and dad are in with her." She kissed Ernest on the cheek. "See you later."

"Bye, love." He heard his wife go back upstairs. For a few moments he waited, listening to the faint murmur of voices from above. The tears were still there but now there were reconciliatory tones, a soothing emphasis of pitch. Part of him felt cowardly for enjoying the relief, now that it was all over. He opened the bag and peered inside. A bloated black sac, bulging with veins, took up most of the space. He angled the bag and revealed the smaller item beside it, glistening in blood, the sight of which caused him to flinch. The thing looked barely human. A grotesque misshapen head twisted at an impossible angle, a distended torso from which sprouted two vague limbs. Even the poor thing's feet looked badly malformed; each foot was split down the centre, making it appear almost cloven. He closed the bag and looked away. There was no doubt this little mite would have faced a battle to live anyway, what with these deformities.

He let himself out of the back door. Frantic birdsong filled the air from the sparrows that roosted in the trees nearby. He walked down the road towards his own house. He passed through the ginnel to the back of his property. The evening was so warm the idea of lighting a fire in the hearth seemed absurd. He hesitated in the garden, afraid to carry the bag over the threshold. Somehow he felt that he would be inviting bad luck on them if he brought this inside their house. Maybe Kath would experience complications later on, and this would be needed as medical evidence? Instinctively he knew that burning it might not be a good idea. Not yet, at least. Then he remembered that patch of ground near the garage. He went to fetch a shovel from the coalhouse.

*

Ernest finished the last dregs of Double Diamond and went to throw the bottle in the bin. For a moment he watched the kids squabbling over a paper plate stacked with sausage-rolls. The tables had been lined up together in the centre of the street, covered with Union Jack tablecloths and festooned with plastic silver crowns. Red, white and blue bunting stretched between the guttering of the houses, spanning the road like a monstrous spider-web. The June sun was beating down on them. Ernest found himself constantly mopping his brow with a handkerchief. Someone had brought out a transistor radio and had perched it on the edge of the table; *Angelo* by Brotherhood of Man crackled from its speaker. Alan was with a couple of his friends at the head of the table, surreptitiously swigging from a bottle of cider every time he thought his father wasn't looking. Ernest didn't mind; his son was almost seventeen. He smiled at the kids' excited chatter, waved at Maureen who was busy dishing out a fresh batch of cheese sandwiches, and decided it was time for another beer.

He walked along the ginnel and into the back garden. He was just about to duck inside and grab a bottle from the fridge when he spotted a figure leaning against the coalhouse.

"Hello, Mr Barber."

Ernest nodded soberly. It had been years since he'd set eyes on Kath; seeing her in his own back garden now seemed disconcerting. "How're doing, love?"

"Good." She smiled coyly and hitched herself onto the wall of the coalhouse, crossing her tanned legs.

Ernest felt himself colouring, glanced away from the sight. "How's college?"

"Oh, it's all right, I s'pose," she sighed, pulling a face. "Most of them are childish though."

Ernest nodded, unsure of what to say. There was a faint smell in the air, a sharply sweet aroma. *Had she been smoking something?*

"It's difficult being surrounded by boys when what you really want is a man." She shuffled on the coalhouse and her skirt rode up, revealing a flash of underwear.

He hesitated. "Shouldn't you be out there with the others at the party?"

She shrugged, glowering. "It's boring." She looked up. "Where's Alan, anyway?"

He felt suddenly alarmed by her presence. Words faltered on his lips. He could feel the trickle of sweat as it ran from his brow onto his neck. "Alan's only sixteen, you know. You're—what—twenty-one?"

"Twenty." She smiled a sad smile. Her dark eyes looked limitless. The pupils were dilated. *She had been smoking something.*

"How's your mam and dad?"

"They're okay," she said. "But you'll know that—you see them more than I do."

"Yes, probably." He gave a little laugh to alleviate the awkwardness.

She threw her head back and stifled a yawn with the back of her hand, a movement that accentuated the swell of her breasts.

"You look tired."

Her hair had fallen over her face. She peered at him through it as if it was a veil. "I'm not sleeping well."

"Oh. Sorry to hear that. What're you studying at college anyway?"

She stared at him, her mouth slightly parted. He could see the glistening pink of her tongue. At last she spoke. "Have you ever had the same dream over and over again, every night, until you know what's coming? A dream that's so vivid you'd swear that it's real?"

He shook his head, all at once uncertain of everything.

"Dreams that at first were so pleasurable you looked forward to them? With such force that you wished your waking hours and your dreams would switch? But even pleasure becomes routine after a while, so much so that you begin to loathe the feeling." Her eyes had narrowed, her lips became flat. "Mr Barber, I'm…*plagued* by this dream; it's consumed my life." Her breath hitched in her throat. "There's no escape from him…"

"From…him?"

Her face looked frozen. Confused. She was staring at something in the middle distance, unguarded and vulnerable. For a split-second he had a glimpse of her as a little girl once more, playing hopscotch on the street.

Ernest realised it wasn't confusion on her face; the poor girl looked haunted, like she was fighting to escape the shell of her own skin. He cleared his throat. "Look, I'll have to get back."

The spell was broken like that. She blinked and glanced down, rubbing the back of her neck.

"Goodbye, Kath," said Ernest, opening the back door with his damp hands.

"Bye, Mr Barber."

He stepped into the cool relief of the house, eager to escape the afternoon's heat. He didn't look back.

*

The area that the old man indicates is a patch about two feet square, close to the side of the garage. There is nothing there but a ragged plot of dry soil, cracked by the warm weather. The old man sits on his wooden bench and smokes a cigarette. "Nothing's ever grown there." He stares at the patch, sullen, resentful. "We tried, over the years, but everything died. Even the grass just turned yellow. It's like the ground was poisoned."

Despite the dry earth, Richard finds the digging easy enough. The first few feet comprises of just black soil, even bereft of earthworms. As the hole gets deeper he begins to adopt a more cautious manner. Soon his spade comes into contact with something firmer, an obstruction. He bends and claws away some of the soil with his hands, revealing a plastic bag the colour of bone. He carefully loosens it from the earth and lifts it out.

The old man finishes his cigarette, glances nonchalantly at the bird-table at the end of the garden. He doesn't want to give the object in the bag any prominence. He stands with some effort. "Do me a favour—get rid of that in the furnace at work?"

Richard nods. "No problem."

The old man takes a final look around the garden while Richard refills the hole. He's remembering the barbecues they've enjoyed out here during those countless summers, recalls the fireworks he's lit on those Bonfire Nights when Alan was a boy. He's thinking about football they played on the lawn when Richard eventually came along. The seasons of his life, contrasts. Evidence of a life lived. He sniffs, rubbing his whiskered chin. "I don't think she was ever the same after that…"

"Who?"

"Kath." The old man takes out a handkerchief and blows his nose. "She went to college, ended up getting into drugs. Died of an overdose at some music festival I think."

Richard stands on the topsoil, flattening it, suddenly feeling an overwhelming sense of sadness. Perhaps he's only now understanding the enormity of what his grandfather is leaving behind; all those times; years of memories accrued in one place. Somehow it feels like the beginning of the end. He smiles at the old man. "C'mon, Sarah'll be wondering where we've got to."

He leads his grandfather and son around to the front of the house. He helps the old man into the passenger seat and fastens Josh into the back. He takes the house keys and checks both front and back doors are locked. He returns the spade to the garden shed and turns to go, suddenly remembering the yellowed plastic bag lying on the grass. He picks it up. Despite its size the bag feels fragile, insubstantial. He can see several twig-like protrusions against the side of the bag. He bends on his haunches and peers inside.

The smell is sickening, and he winces at the intensity of the stench. It's as if the miasma has been trapped within the plastic bag for years, and is now released. He examines the crumbling bones in the bag. They are black and stained, with some kind of oily fungus coating the plastic. Not all of the flash has decomposed; brown sinew and pale brittle tendons bind the skeleton almost intact, most probably preserved by its plastic shroud. The tiny skull is elongated and cracked, revealing a series of pointed teeth set into its upper jaw. The bones of the limbs look slender and fragile, the extended paws misshapen. There is a flat canine spine ending in a short tail.

He closes the bag in distaste. For a few moments he considers what he's just seen. Then a faint smile crosses his mouth as he realises his grandfather has been playing a little joke on him. He always was good at spinning a yarn. This is obviously the remains of a family pet; a dog if he's not mistaken.

He transports the bag carefully around to the front of the house. As he reaches the gate he tries to shield the bag with the angle of his body before opening the car's boot and laying it inside. He climbs into the driver's seat and clicks the key into the ignition. "Ready?"

His grandfather is looking at the house, staring unblinking at the net curtains and the wooden trellis and the wind-chime that dangles off the fascia above the ground floor window. In the back seat, Josh's Nintendo DS beeps and whistles as he defeats pixellated enemies. The old man smiles faintly. "We were happy here. There was goodness in this house. I hope the next owners are just as happy as we were." He nods and smiles faintly. "Come on then, let's go."

The car pulls away. Richard notices his grandfather craning his neck to see the house for the final few seconds before they turn the corner.

Husks

When he made the inevitable decision to return to the cottage, he realised that he'd have to make the journey itself without the booze.

The memories almost suffocated Haddon as he drove south, staring through the windscreen with eyes that felt too big for their sockets.

The incident at the service station was a mistake; he'd taken the photograph from his wallet for the first time in years, believing he could handle the act of seeing them. For a few moments he'd felt an overwhelming surge of love as he'd stared at the picture of his wife and daughter. Then all at once the sense of regret bit like a snake, and it became imperative that he reach the cottage as soon as possible.

The motorway felt perilous; cars roared past with scant care, oblivious to his fragile state. Haddon gripped the wheel with focused intent.

The aviaries are busy with exotic birds, shrill cries, fanned-tails and jerky movements. Eager to spot the exhibits, they crowd the cage, entranced by the strange kookaburras.

It's feeding time and the birds are restless. The gloved keeper is inside the aviary, distributing limp, fluffy bundles—dead chicks.

The natural brutality of the kookaburras is mesmerising; how they grip the chicks in their razored bills, pounding the tiny bodies against rocks or branches until they become limp. Then they tip their heads and swallow the carcasses inch by inch until every part of the chick is consumed.

Cerys is disturbed by the sight and Jill quickly moves to comfort her. They hurry away, aghast, the insane mocking laughter of the kookaburras ringing in their ears.

It was evening before he left the A338 and began his final approach to Christchurch. The Dorset scenery was vaguely familiar even after all these years, redolent of late summer. The images evoked memories of happier times, languid holidays at the cottage before the darkness swept in.

He almost missed the turn-off from the B-road; it was only the presence of the pub opposite that alerted him to the proximity of the lane, virtually obscured by overgrown grass and shrubs that had sprouted in the intervening years. He drove slowly along the bumpy track, switching on his lights to banish the shadows created by the canopy of trees. The cottage waited at the end of the track, made ghost-like and malevolent by the car's light.

Once he'd switched off the ignition, the ticking of the cooling engine crowded his senses. The windows of the cottage stared back, challenging his gaze. It looked exactly as it had in his dreams.

Weeds had cracked the paving stones, as if nature was trying to consume the building. Ivy clung to the roof, smothering the chimney.

Haddon gripped the brass key and turned it with some effort, sensing the resistance of the lock. He pushed it open with a squeal of hinges and stepped inside.

Mildew and stale air conspired to mask the scents familiar from Haddon's previous visits. He clicked the switch and light flooded the entrance, prompting a vague recollection of him agreeing to pay the electric bill by direct debit. He might have been thankful of this, but the truth was he couldn't have cared less. He'd brought a battery-powered lantern, nevertheless.

Dust motes trembled in the air as he moved inside. Everything looked *almost* the same. The table and chairs had been moved against the opposite wall, presumably to allow the paramedics easier access. He entered the kitchen. A spike of regret: the chipped coffee mugs had been hung on the mug-tree instead of stored in the cupboard like Jill would have preferred, probably by some well-meaning police officer who'd felt the need to wash-up in the aftermath. The worktop looked bleached of colour. Cerys's old toys had been thrown together into a cardboard box.

He paused at the foot of the stairs, staring up into the waiting darkness. A click of the switch revealed magnolia walls, faded watercolours, yellowed skirting. He thought about that final visit, how they'd arrived as a living, breathing family, and left as lifeless husks. Even he—who'd been stretchered out hooked up to drips and a portable ventilator—had spent the last five years in his own alcohol-induced stasis.

He climbed the stairs. Both of the bedroom doors were closed but he could see into the bathroom, noticing the remains of several insects on the white lino. Dust had coated everything. The air felt grimy and stagnant. Too fragile to face his daughter's room, Haddon drifted into the main bedroom and collapsed onto the bed.

The sheets were chilled and starched, smelling of damp. And in the room in which, five years before, his wife had died, Haddon fell into a deep sleep.

Cerys is drinking her hot chocolate. He knows the sweetness of it will mask the bitterness. Jill waits downstairs. He can hear her weeping from up here in Cerys's room. He watches his daughter for several moments, still astonished by the volume of love he feels. She finishes the drink and he wipes the final remnants from her upper lip. He dims the nightlight and tucks her into bed. She's puzzled by the fact that he hasn't made her brush her teeth.

"It doesn't matter, love," he whispers to her. "Nothing matters now."

She lies down and he strokes her forehead, watching her eyes flutter closed, noticing her breath deepening. His hands trace the dome of her skull, where wisps of hair still cling resolutely to the sallow skin.

Soon it's time to leave her. Jill will be coming up to say her final goodbyes, before they'll embark on their own journey. He can hear the chink as she stirs the mugs downstairs.

At the door he turns suddenly, hearing a light flapping sound from the direction of the window. There is nothing there. Maybe it's an owl, nesting in the eaves. He clicks off the light and his daughter becomes a frail shape in the bedclothes.

Haddon awoke, instinctively throwing a glance towards the window.

The thin curtains were still drawn, sunlight seeping around the ill-fitting fabric. Of course there was nothing there. In fact, his dream that night had been of a bird perched on *Cerys's* window-sill, not his own. But in dreams there is no logic.

He was still dressed. His limbs ached to a degree he'd never experienced before. Opening the curtains, he allowed the light to enter the room. The view into the trees accentuated his isolation. His eyes traced the line of a path through the woods. They'd imagined one day strolling along it with their future grandchildren, picnic basket in hand. They'd bought the cottage several years before Jill fell pregnant. He swallowed and turned away from the window.

In the bathroom cupboard there was a toothbrush with stiff bristles. He ran cold water over it before squeezing a centimetre of dried toothpaste onto it and brushing his teeth. It felt alien and obscene in his mouth.

Once he'd washed, he went downstairs and made a cup of black tea with bags that were orange and brittle. It tasted even worse than it looked.

Someone had propped the fridge door open and switched it off at the plug. A newspaper, curling at the edges, lay on the worktop, imparting news from five years before. He opened the cupboard that housed the boiler and flicked the switch. Vague knockings and a hiss from the pipes brought to mind veins coursing with blood; it was as if the house had been woken from its slumber.

The morning progressed at glacial speed. Haddon investigated the woodland surrounding the cottage, surprised by how far the vegetation had encroached. Remnants of yellow police tape remained tied to the spindles of the veranda; the words *DO NOT CROSS* almost obliterated by the elements. He found two curious objects on the wooden steps. They were small desiccated bundles of some unknown material. He held them close and examined their consistency. The husks resembled owl pellets—cracked, brown, oblong casts that crumbled as he touched them. Strangely there were no tiny bones contained within, merely brittle lumps of dried tissue. The remnants disintegrated between his fingers and were dispersed on the breeze.

He supposed he should have been double-checking that all his affairs were in place, but the simple fact was he couldn't be bothered. It was pointless. He had no other family except for a cousin he hadn't seen in twenty-odd years; Jill's family had shown him nothing but fury and contempt since her death. At the inquest they'd seemed angrier about Haddon surviving than they had about Cerys and Jill's deaths, as if it was further proof of his inadequacies; he hadn't even succeeded in taking his own life.

The overnight bag in the boot of his car crackled as he carried it into the cottage. He opened it on the bed, removing the packets of tablets that he'd been stockpiling over the past few months. This time there would be no—*backing out*—mistakes; he'd swallow enough to ensure there was no coming back.

The wall clock reminded him that it was lunchtime, even if his body was oblivious to the fact. He wasn't hungry, but felt his bedtime cocktail might sit better on a stomach already lined. He'd learned that in the suicide group-therapy sessions he'd been forced to attend. He was now a fount of knowledge where it came to taking your own life; he knew the best knot to tie in a hanging, how to slit correctly one's wrists in the bath, what kind of hose would be the most effective when attached to an exhaust. To use any method other than an overdose, however, would be cheating.

Haddon walked to the pub on the main road. The lane was frantic with bird calls and movement in the trees. At one point he thought he heard something laughing, but he reasoned it was probably just a chaffinch.

The pub was relatively empty. An elderly couple sat in the window pecking at their shepherd's pie, and a man who was obviously a sales rep was wolfing down a ploughman's lunch. Haddon ordered a small lasagne and chips and a pint of lager, and chose a table in the darkest recess of the room. While he waited, he tried to ignore the plastic climbing frame that was visible through the window.

When the meal arrived he ate slowly.

As he was leaving, he caught sight of a reflection in the chrome trim that edged the bar; something with an impossibly bloated head appeared frozen on four spindly limbs behind him, the pale, domed skull balancing on a frame of bones.

He gasped and turned. A dog-shaped plastic collection box for the RSPCA stared back, the eyes of the Golden Retriever rendered deliberately mournful. Its sentiment matched his own.

Soon, my love. Soon.

The walk back to the cottage was languid and considered. He'd purchased a bottle of whiskey from the bar, fighting the urge to moan about the price. He tucked the bottle under his arm as he walked. To shake the image of Cerys in her final days—the loss of hair, dark hollow eyes, the misshapen bulge of her head—he removed the photograph from his wallet and braved a glance. The picture had been taken at some theme park, as Jill pressed close to Cerys, laughing at something out of shot. A month later the tumour had been diagnosed.

At first he and Jill had resolved to remain strong. They'd certainly never let Cerys become aware of her own impending death, despite the doctors' advice. After months of avoiding the issue, Haddon had finally realised that they both shared the same belief; life beyond Cerys was inconceivable. They'd refused to contemplate such an existence. So they'd hatched the suicide pact one drunken night, lost in their own sorrow at news that the cancer had spread.

Haddon's hands have now stopped shaking. He is lying in the bed, his arms wrapped round Jill. She is not moving; her breathing is shallow. He reminds himself that this is the only option. Cerys is already at peace. There is no going back now. He forces open one of his eyes and glances at his wife. Her skin is losing its colour. Her lips look darker, though her face appears unreal, synthetic. In the woods outside, a fox cries sharply. It sounds like a child.

For several minutes he lies still, eyes closed, willing his body to drift into the abyss. His mind is dimming, his brain becoming detached from its surroundings. He can imagine looking down on himself from above, sounds fading as he settles into the realms of sleep.

But what is that? A sharp cackle of laughter from his daughter's room. He is moving there instantly, propelled by fear. From above he watches as Cerys lies motionless on the bed. The laughter rings out again and Haddon's attention is drawn to a small hunched shape on the window-ledge. A flutter of wings and he realises that it is the kookaburra they saw at the zoo. Its jerky movement looks mechanical. The bird hops onto the bed and edges upwards with a shake of its feathers. It pauses as it reaches Cerys's pillow and cocks its head.

Haddon watches aghast as the bird leans in near to her skull and pecks sharply at a point above the ear. It repeats this action several times. Haddon screams silently in frustration as he is forced to watch. Soon he can see the blood creeping across the pillow, the wound black and glistening. The bird continues working away at his daughter's head until it has opened a gaping cavity. The alabaster bone is stark against the scarlet. Then, in one precise fluid movement, the kookaburra reaches its pointed beak into the hole and plucks out a soft mass of black tissue. It tugs on the jellied flesh, stretching it in an effort to remove the quivering lump. Finally it is free of the skull. The bird flutters onto the post of the headboard, trailing spots of blood across the duvet. It shifts the lump of flesh until it is gripped tightly, then cracks the mass against the wood several times. Finally satisfied, it tips its head and the lump disappears down the bird's throat.

Suddenly he is back in his own room, images of his daughter's head still raw in his mind. He opens his eyes in alarm and flips off the side of the bed, landing heavily on the floor. He crawls across the carpet towards the door. He reaches for his coat, which was hanging on the back of the chair, feeling for the mobile phone in his pocket. The effort is exhausting and he drops back onto the floor, the phone almost jolting free of his fingers. He tries to look at the handset but his eyes are unfocused and watering. The number-pad feels too small, but he jabs frantically at the 9 three times. There is a burning sensation in his chest and he turns to his left and vomits onto the floor.

From the handset he hears the shrill static of a voice answering. He wipes the vomit from his mouth, clamps the phone to his ear and says "Ambulance, please. I need an ambulance."

Upon his return, the cottage had an air of expectancy about it. The late summer sun cast long shadows across the ground. The air was warm and still. Haddon wandered the house, searching for something profound to do with the time remaining. He came away feeling unsatisfied, instead having to content himself with drinking the whiskey and looking at the photograph of Jill and Cerys.

The booze was as welcome as a long-lost friend. He relaxed into its embrace, sensing the edges of reality being smoothed, feeling the grip of oblivion tighten. The shadows slid across the bedroom wall as evening advanced. Soon the sounds of birdsong filled the air, pushing away all other noise. The shrill melodies and rhythmic calls were like a lullaby. Presently he realised he would have to swallow the tablets.

The meagre light was enough for him to see as he pressed the pills free of the foil wrappers, collecting them together in the folds of the sheets. Soon there was a small pile of red capsules. He topped up the whiskey and began pushing the pills into his mouth, washing them down with a forceful swig. Haddon could feel them lodging in his gullet. The whiskey was helping. He felt a mild tingling sensation in his stomach. His body was becoming bloated and sluggish.

He rolled onto his side and rested his head on the pillow. Earlier, he'd thought about leaving a note but decided it was needless.

The sky was losing its final vestiges of light. The bird had fallen silent. His legs seemed to be vibrating. Eyes closed, he allowed his mind to settle, slowing his breathing to an absolute minimum.

And then he heard the sound of the front door opening; footsteps in the hallway, the creak of the stairs as someone ascended.

Haddon closed his eyes and tried to become invisible in the tangle of sheets. The bedroom door opened and then he heard a voice:

"Daddy, where have you been?"

He opened his eyes and stared at Cerys in the doorway. She was wearing her favourite jeans—the ones with the pink piping—and her *Dora the Explorer* t-shirt. Her hair was tied into two neat bunches at either side of her head. She was smiling and her face radiated delight.

Haddon tried to sit up. He stared back.

She was still there. "Mummy and me have been waiting for you."

He swallowed and shook his head slowly. "Where is Mummy?"

"She's outside." She blinked. "We've missed you, Daddy."

He stood gingerly and limped over to the little girl. She took his hand. The window was still open. He looked out, seeing a dark figure waiting in the long grass. The figure seemed to hesitate and then waved. He returned the gesture.

"Daddy, are you all right?"

He turned to see Cerys's beautiful face. "I'm fine, sweetheart. I just had a bad dream, that's all."

She hugged his legs. "Well—everything's okay, isn't it?"

"It is." He put his hand on her shoulder. "C'mon, let's go and see Mummy."

At the top of the stairs he paused and threw a final glance back into the bedroom, doing his best to ignore the crumpled shape that lay tangled in the bedclothes.

His daughter capered ahead, skipping down the stairs. By the time Haddon reached the bottom, Jill had appeared at the door. They embraced and he breathed in the familiar scent of her hair, and then the Haddons drifted out into the darkness.

The Children Of Medea

Saxton stood on the quayside, squinting against the shimmering sea. He could just make out the island across the flat expanse of water. It looked fragile and insignificant. He closed his eyes for a minute, enjoying the sunshine that prickled his face. Birds wheeled overhead, occasionally cawing as they squabbled for food. The gentle lapping of water against the harbour-side was hypnotic. He opened one eye to glance at his watch. The ferry was due any minute.

Three young boys sat cross-legged on the quay, chattering amongst themselves. Saxton watched them for a while, trying to pick out the odd word. They were leaning over something. One of them laughed, tossed his head back, and Saxton saw their attention was fixed on an object moving on the cobblestones. He stepped closer for a better view. A grey fish flapped languidly between them, opening and closing its mouth, its eyes bulging. One of the boys was carefully stabbing a penknife into the creature's side. They laughed, examining the bloodstained scales that adhered to the blade. One of them caught sight of Saxton watching but continued to pierce the fish, unmindful of Saxton's withering glare.

A rattling noise rang out from behind and Saxton turned. The ferry was approaching. His heart sank at the vessel's crude construction—it was little more than a raft, barely able to hold a handful of passengers. This didn't bode well for the island's appeal. He walked back to the quayside and watched as it glided into dock. The driver tied a length of rope to the jetty and stepped onto the wooden platform. Saxton called, "Kyriabos?"

The man nodded sullenly. He was bare-chested, wearing a pair of white three-quarter length jeans and sandals. Saxton stepped over the chain and walked along the platform until he reached the ferry. The driver unclipped his gate and allowed Saxton to board. A transistor radio dangled from a hook, playing what sounded like Greek pop music. The driver grabbed a bottle of water and took a swig, surveying the harbour with heavily-lidded eyes. He didn't seem surprised that Saxton was the only passenger. The air was thick with the greasy stench of diesel. Saxton felt the throbbing engine shudder through his legs, accentuating the nausea.

Presently the driver fastened the gate across the entryway. He moved assuredly, almost casually. He flicked a switch on the wheel's console and the engine roared. Saxton gripped the railing as the ferry backed away from the jetty in a churn of frothy waves. In no time at all they were juddering across the bay towards the island.

Saxton shielded his eyes as he studied their destination. It looked to be barely more than a rock, with several house crowding the western edge and a series of larger buildings further up the slope. Sporadic patches of green appeared stark against the otherwise grey shale. A couple of boats bobbed about in what served as the island's harbour.

Kyriabos was further away than it looked. By the time they had reached it Saxton felt sick to his stomach. It took the driver an extremely long time to dock the ferry and secure the gateway. Saxton wasted no time in crossing the jetty and hurrying up the quayside, which consisted of a rectangle of decking stretching the short length of the harbour. A middle-aged man sat on a bench at the corner, a folded newspaper resting on his lap. He stood as Saxton approached, tucking the paper beneath his arm.

"Mr Saxton?" He offered his hand. "I'm Kiron Laskaris, the school's principal." His English was precise. He wore a thick beard.

Saxton suppressed a wince at the man's iron grip. His skin was rough and tanned. Keen eyes peered out from beneath a pair of bushy eyebrows. His hair was a mass of grey coils.

"Nice to meet you," said Saxton, relieved there was someone there to meet him.

Laskaris glanced down at Saxton's empty hands. "No bags?"

Saxton tutted loudly. "Delayed at Athens. Apparently on route to Latvia by now." He shook his head. "The airline company have assured me they'll get them here within 48 hours."

Laskaris shrugged. "Nevertheless—welcome to Kyriabos. We're extremely grateful to you for stepping in at such short notice."

"Not at all."

They walked up the incline. A row of clay-built single-storey houses stood to the left, their brilliant whiteness accentuated by sunlight and the azure sky beyond. Saxton could hear crickets in the scrub grass.

"I'll take you to your apartment," Laskaris said. "No doubt you'll want to freshen up."

There was an asphalt track at the top, which meandered along the length of the coast like a black ribbon. Two bicycles were leaning against the low wall. A bored-looking teenager glanced up from the saddle of his own bicycle, attached to which was a rickety metal trolley.

"It's fine—go, go," Laskaris said to the boy, waving his hands in a shooing motion. "Mr Saxton's bags haven't arrived yet."

The boy shrugged and slowly pedalled away.

"The school is on the north side of the island, down by the waterfront." Laskaris pointed. "You can't see from here but it's just past that hill. Your apartment's only a few hundred yards from it." He tucked the newspaper into his back pocket and mounted one of the bikes. "Please make use of the bicycle—the island's too small to accommodate cars so we find these are the best method of transportation."

Saxton awkwardly picked up his bike. It had been many years since he'd ridden one. There was a part of him that felt ridiculous. Nevertheless, he pushed with his toe and set off. Laskaris led the way.

The track took a rather wandering route along the elevated shoreline. They didn't go fast, but Saxton felt a thrill of exhilaration as the breeze combed through his hair. Every so often he caught a glimpse of rocks protruding through the waterline to his right. Black stone and white sand created an alternately patterned backdrop. The narrow track was pot-holed and random, and Saxton had to concentrate in an effort to avoid serious injury. A grove of fruit trees stretched further up the slope to the left; the citrus smell was engaging. Saxton experienced a brief flash from his old life—a memory of being in Body Shop with Joanne; her spraying some overpriced tester onto her neck whilst he did his best to look enthusiastic… Saxton pushed the thought away and concentrated on his driving.

There were several cottages on the incline, and an ivy-smothered structure built from crumbling stone perched on the lip of a craggy ledge. Outside one of the residences—a decrepit cottage by the water's edge—a barnacled fishing boat lay upside down in its dry-dock. A bare-chested man was working on the hull and he glanced up in surprise as they passed.

Eventually Laskaris drew to a halt and climbed off the bike, resting it against the stump of a felled Mimosa tree. "We're on foot from here." He led the way down a narrow track that descended steeply across the incline in a jagged path. Just visible was a small white-stone building nestling in a hollow, almost as if it was taking shelter. Sunlight glinted off the roof's skylight, blinding him momentarily.

Saxton parked his bike next to the other and carefully made his way down the uneven path. He could feel the sting of sea-spray on his face. The building was a double-storey cottage with ocean-facing windows and a tired, weather-eroded facade. Laskaris unlocked the peeling door and pushed it open, handing the key to Saxton. "The school's just up there on the ridge."

Saxton nodded. "*That's* a commute I can handle." He stepped inside the cottage, wrinkling his nose at the unfamiliar smell— something distinctly feminine, with a rather pleasant allure, mixed with polish and disinfectant.

Laskaris gave him a brief tour. The cottage consisted of just a ground-floor living section and kitchen, with a single bedroom and bathroom upstairs. At least there was a flush toilet. They'd even installed a boiler so a hot shower shouldn't be a problem. The bedroom's skylight allowed a rectangle of sunshine to bathe the floor. Saxton noticed some of the corners cluttered with filled boxes and a stack of bulging cases.

"I'm afraid they're Miss Hemsworth's things," explained Laskaris. "They'll need to be stored here until her family can make arrangements to have them shipped back to England."

Saxton nodded. "Still no news?"

"I'm afraid not." Laskaris shrugged gravely. "The police think she just took off. There were no signs of anything…*untoward*."

"Why would she do that?"

He shrugged again. "Who knows? She seemed a little… preoccupied just before she disappeared." He blinked soberly and tipped his head. "It can get a little lonely out here sometimes. You know—claustrophobic."

Saxton glanced round the room, nodding. "I'll be fine." He puffed out his cheeks. "To be honest I think the change of scenery will do me good."

Laskaris's eyes clouded. "They did mention your…*tragedy*. I'm very sorry."

Saxton waved his hand dismissively, his head angled away as he peered around the cottage. He remained like that for a few moments. When he turned back he swallowed, making firm eye-contact with the other man. "Thanks." He shook Laskaris's hand, breaking the moment of discomfort. "I needed to get away, to be honest—leave the ghosts back in England."

Laskaris nodded again. He pursed his lips, as if unsure how to continue. Then he blinked and shrugged. "Well, I'm sure the children will keep you busy, keep your mind occupied." He wrote something on a piece of paper. "This is my number. I live on the north side of the island. If you need anything, just give me a ring." He thought for a second. "There's a little shop down by the beach where you can get milk and bread and stuff."

"I'll find it."

Laskaris shook his hand again. "I hope you'll be very happy here, Mr Saxton." And with that he was gone.

Saxton stood alone in the cottage, suddenly aware of the abrupt silence that had descended.

*

The next few days felt never-ending. Saxton did his best to settle into the cottage, but with the air-company still failing to deliver his luggage it just felt like he was an interloper, a listless holidaymaker.

He visited the island's only general store and managed to stock up on provisions. From time to time he stared at his mobile phone's display. The absence of a signal seemed to increase his desire to call Anya, but he knew that was not a temptation he could ever act on; too much had been said, too many tears had been shed; too much time had passed.

He explored the island. There looked to be about several hundred people living on Kyriabos. The majority of the menfolk seemed to be fishermen. He'd hear the boats setting off in the early hours of the morning, listening to their owners' shouts from the harbour as he huddled beneath the starched sheets of his bed. Then in the afternoon he'd watch them streaming back into the quay, their nets laden with shimmering fish. Most of the island's women seemed to attend constantly to their laundry; nearly everywhere you looked, clotheslines billowed with garments. They resembled restless ghosts.

The bicycle was useful for traversing the island. There was, ostensibly, just one main road, which skirted the coastline around Kyriabos, managing to link the houses that were clustered together in sporadic communities. But thin tracks crisscrossed the land-mass like veins, rising up into the hills and weaving through the scrub. The highest point of Kyriabos was its geographic centre, a narrow plateau of rock marked by several Date-plum trees. One afternoon Saxton biked up there and sat in the shade, breathing in the scent of persimmon while he caught his breath and rested his aching legs. This vantage point afforded him a perfect view of the entire island. He took out his binoculars and surveyed his new home.

The primary school stood prominently down by the water's edge, adjacent to a hamlet of adobe cottages. Its windows reflected the sunlight like the faceted eyes of an insect. Further around the shoreline he could make out the home of a local artist; clay pots and vases stood drying on a plinth. The island's only taverna, Cristo's, lay close to the harbour, conspicuous by its colourful display of outdoor parasols. Saxton angled his view to the west and it was then, as he turned the focus-wheel in an effort to make out some detail, that he caught sight of the ruined building barely visible through an overgrown canopy of olive trees. Its crumbling dome was adorned with gilt-edged depictions of the sun, although it looked to be in a rather poor state of repair. Several arched windows had been smashed. Curious, Saxton stood and peered with renewed interest.

*

"So, how are you settling in?"

Saxton took a sip of his juice and nodded. "Very well, Mr Laskaris. It's a beautiful island, and very peaceful—just what I'd imagined." He smiled and added, as if it wasn't at all an afterthought, "And I'm looking forward to meeting the children."

Laskaris smiled across the desk from him. They were in the principal's office. It was a poorly-ventilated room, filled with shelves weighed down with box-files and textbooks. There was an overflowing ashtray on the desk, next to a manila folder. Laskaris took out some papers and read them for a moment. "All the children speak English, so language shouldn't be a problem. I believe they discussed the syllabus requirements at your interview in Athens?" Saxton nodded and the principle continued. "These papers will give you an insight. I don't think the remaining term will be too difficult. Once we break for the summer, the education authority will be able to recruit someone permanent. We're very grateful for you coming at such short notice."

"It'll be good to get back to work," said Saxton. "To move on."

"Precisely." Laskaris put the papers back into the manila folder. Saxton noticed how large his knuckles were, how much hair there was on his forearms and the backs of his hands.

"Any news on Miss Hemsworth?"

Laskaris looked confused for a second, then understanding seemed to dawn. He shook his head. "Still nothing, I'm afraid. Like I said, her personal effects shouldn't be in your way for too much longer; her next of kin are arranging to move them."

Saxton made conciliatory noises, suddenly feeling awkward for implying her belongings were troublesome. To change the subject he said, "I notice the gravestones share just a few names." He added quickly, "I took a stroll through the cemetery the other day."

Laskaris shrugged. "Kyriabos is a close-knit community. Most of the residents have family stretching back several generations, myself included. We like to bury our dead close by. As a child, I attended this very school before moving to the secondary one on the mainland."

"Really?"

"Yes, it's a real honour for me to work here." Laskaris stood and offered his hand. "Well, good luck with everything, Mr Saxton."

*

The first few days were less taxing than Saxton had anticipated. His class of nine year-olds—all 17 of them—appeared rather more attentive than the group he'd previously taught back in England. They seemed more studious and mature than any nine year-olds he had previously come into contact with. He put this down to nerves; after all, their usual teacher had disappeared partway through the academic year, and it was only natural they might appear reticent. There also seemed to be very little interaction between them. Each child sat at their own desk, staring ahead with wide expressionless faces. Saxton was reminded of that film, *The Village of the Damned*, but did his best to suppress such inappropriate humour. He tried hard to engage them, telling of his experiences in teaching back home, describing the cultural differences between their two countries. At one point he had to leave them unattended whilst he went to fetch a new pack of paper, fully expecting, upon his return, for mayhem to have broken out. But as he re-entered the classroom he was surprised to find them just how he'd left them. Uncannily identical, almost as if they'd frozen the minute he'd departed the room.

There was one pupil that was rather more curious that the others. Her name was Taryn. She sat on the second row and spoke very little English, preferring to murmur occasionally in Greek. When Saxton addressed her directly she responded in a polite, if rather taciturn, manner. Her eye-contact was never maintained for more than a second.

By the end of the first week Saxton was feeling positive about his current employment. He sat on a wicker chair on the paved area outside his cottage, sipping wine as he watched the sun descend. The ceaseless crashing of the tide was relaxing. Nearby, insects chirruped in the grass. He could smell food cooking as it wafted across from the taverna; luscious garlic and wood-smoked chicken. Saxton felt his stomach growl. He watched gulls wheeling overhead, buffeted by the warm breeze. He closed his eyes and tried not to think of Joanne.

The air company had delivered his luggage several days ago. He'd unpacked it with a degree of guilt, feeling like he was erasing all trace of his predecessor. But time moved on. Things progressed. It was impossible to halt the inevitable.

Feeling mildly drunk, he took out his phone and reread the texts from Anya. It felt unreal, as if the whole thing had happened to someone else. The signal drifted in and out intermittently. At the present time there was a bar indicating network coverage. His fingers hesitated over Anya's speedial number. His mind wrestled with uncertainty. *What good would calling her do? The past was the past.*

Instead he scrolled through the photos. There were several of Anya, mostly taken in busy pubs or swanky cocktail bars. His heart lurched as he stared at her image. That vivacious smile, those limitless eyes. He blinked and began flicking through his stored pictures, finally coming across one of Joanne taken several years before. They'd gone out to celebrate her birthday. He'd ended up getting drunk and they'd argued. Another night spent on the sofa. The ones of Charlie were stored in a different folder, but he still felt too raw to view them.

He powered off the phone, tossed it into his lap. Then he downed the rest of the wine and watched the final vestiges of sunlight disappear.

*

On the Sunday he rode his bike up the trail to the summit of Kyriabos again. He'd been thinking about that ruined building.

There was something about the derelict nature of the place that had intrigued him: that copper dome, the gilt-edged icons, the ornate windows—it had resembled a church, yet the air of neglect suggested it might be worth exploring.

Saxton caught his breath on the wooded slope, enjoying the sense of isolation. The birdsong reminded him of his childhood back in England. He leaned his bike against a tussock and stood for a few minutes, taking advantage of the respite from the blazing sun. Up ahead, the dome of the church protruded through a canopy of trees. He walked up the incline, feeling dry leaves crunch underfoot. As he approached, he caught a view of the ruined church through the trees. A stone path had been constructed in front of the building. The church's doorway lay in deep shadow. There was a smashed window to the right. Lichen and moss coated the exterior walls.

The wooden door was ajar. He pushed it wide and there was a squeal of hinges and a sudden aroma of brackish soil, earthy and organic. Saxton wrinkled his nose and stepped inside.

The dimness blinded him for a second. He paused until his vision returned. Discarded cans and food wrappers littered the dusty floor. Several rows of chairs stood in angled lines along the length of the church. The stone walls were decorated by a series of etchings, now rendered faint by mildew and age. Saxton approached the illustrations and peered at them through their patina of grime.

In the first one a robed woman with a knife stood over a pair of cowering infants. Blood flowed freely from their wounds. The next one depicted the woman riding in a chariot. Her face was grotesque, insane. The third illustration showed a man standing by a graveside, drowning in his own tears. The final image was of the robed woman ascending skyward in the chariot. Despite the aged state of the pictures, there was a chilling aspect to them: a bold fluency to the artwork that unnerved Saxton.

He turned abruptly. Something had startled him. The interior of the church was dim, shadows motionless. Yet there was a low hum, like the murmur of voices, too indistinct to hear. Barely audible. Just beyond reach. Saxton felt the hairs on his forearms bristle.

A ruined altar lay at the end of the aisle. Rotting wood protruded through its ancient structure, like the ribcage of a dead animal. Airborn dust tickled his nose. He suddenly had the feeling that he was being watched. He backed out of the church and escaped into the sunlight. There was no fear in his movement. The murmuring had been not at all threatening; if anything, there was a compelling aspect to the tone. Almost welcoming.

*

One day he quizzed the children about the island's history. He knew very little of it personally, so it was as much for his own curiosity as it was for the benefit of the class. A pale-faced boy on the back row raised his hand. "Sir, our families have lived on Kyriabos for years. My great-grandparents are buried in the cemetery." He glanced around the class. "All our grandparents are."

Saxton had tried countless times to get them to address him as *Mr Saxton* so he ignored the overtly formal version the boy had used. "I see. So your families have lived on the island for many generations?"

A series of nodding heads. The original boy continued, "Even during the war we were left alone. The Nazis didn't bother us."

Saxton pursed his lips and frowned. "But I thought Greece was occupied by the Germans in World War Two, so surely—"

"They were afraid of the island," said a girl sitting further back. "Of what the island was."

"*What the island was?*" Saxton struggled to comprehend the words. Maybe the meaning was lost in translation.

Taryn caught his eye, a strange smile playing around her thin lips. "Kyriabos is tainted island—bad history." Her voice was guttural and sharp.

"Tainted?"

There was silence for a moment. Then the boy on the back row spoke up again. "It is diseased island. A colony. For hundreds of years the people here suffer from bad disease—disease of Hansen? It make skin go scaly and...*deformities?*"

Saxton scratched his head. "Hansen? You mean leprosy, don't

you? Hansen's disease is leprosy."

"Leprosy, yes."

"The soldiers are afraid of us." Taryn smiled serenely. "They leave us alone. Just send food to us."

Sazton was still puzzled. "But if leprosy was still here in the forties, there would be signs today, surely?"

Someone shrugged. "It is gone. We prey. Our God stops the suffering."

At that moment the bell rang, signalling the end of the lesson. Saxton, distracted, stood and gathered together some textbooks. The children filed out of the room, eager to escape into the playground. But an air of disquiet lingered in the room with Saxton.

*

At night, the island seemed different. Brooding. Vigilant. Gone was the birdsong and the restless surf and the daytime sounds of everyday life, replaced by an eerie silence, broken only by the odd returning fishing-boat. Even the tide sounded different at night, the darkness lending it an unnaturally hesitant quality, a suggestion of activity that existed just beyond Saxton's perception. Like whispers in an empty room.

He had become used to the cottage's air of unreality. The sudden aroma of perfume, sometimes a sense of being watched, occasionally the sound of faint breathing in the bedroom at night. The skylight created a silvered, moonlit square which crept imperceptibly around the tiled floor. Something scratched and scampered behind the walls. Water gurgled through subterranean pipes. Distant, yet close-by.

Sometimes at night, the urge to call Anya became an obsession. He imagined her back in England, cuddled up with her husband. He wondered if she had deleted his number and the photos from her phone. Always he resisted the temptation to call. That wound was healing over, the last thing he wanted to do was pick the scab and expose it again.

His dead son's face swirled in the darkness so he stared at the skylight instead. Yet Charlie's voice broke the silence within his head. Saxton tried to busy his mind with life instead of death.

He thought about his job. These past few months had seen little progress in his relationship with the children. They remained impassive, unreachable almost. He'd finally begun to question his own teaching skills.

One night he woke in a fever, tangled in the damp sheets. A dull ache throbbed the back of his head. He tried to mop his brow. As he turned he noticed a silhouette at the skylight, limned by the moon, peering in at him through the glass. It was a face, too dark to discern feature, yet somehow he knew it was watching him. For several minutes he remained frozen, holding his breath as he stared back at the shape. There was a shimmering quality to the image, as if he was viewing it through a heat-haze. It undulated and wavered. Like its mass and the surrounding shadows were merging. Then, sickeningly, it lurched in a solid gathering movement, as if it had poured through the glass and reformed itself inside the room. Saxton felt his throat click as he struggled to speak. The black shape slowly crept across the angle of the ceiling. He could make out rail-thin limbs, a slender torso, clutching childlike hands. He watched in horror as it made its way to the corner, where it paused in the shadows, waiting.

A rushing noise in Saxton's ears made him swallow. He was still in bed, too frightened to move, yet conversely the sound was comforting. Harmonious. There was a rhythm to the noise that calmed Saxton's terror. It rose in volume and he recognised it as the murmuring he'd heard in the church. The layers separated until he could identify individual voices for a second, then they harmonised again to become one. Although what he was staring at was horrific, the sense of acceptance he took from the voices overrode any feelings of disquiet. It was angelic and sweet. Joyous. He closed his eyes and lay back on the pillow, allowing himself to be embraced by the choir.

*

Saxton gave the signal and the children began peeling back the foil from the lid of their milk cartons. They were usually eager to drink their milk, an event that occurred daily at 10.30 am. It was a quaint habit. Saxton enjoyed it, the sight of their milk-moustaches reminding him of his own childhood back in England, years before the government ended the practice.

Once they had finished, he walked round the room with the bin-bag and collected the empty cartons. The class began to take out their books. Saxton returned to his desk. "Does anyone know anything about the old building up on the slope?"

A boy on the front row raised his hand and waited for Saxton to point to him. "Yes, sir, it's the church."

"I took a trip up there. It hasn't been used in years."

The boy shared a glance with his classmate to the left. "Our church is no longer needed. The Lady's presence is everywhere."

"The lady?"

Saxton felt troubled by the profound silence. The kids looked cagey. He pressed again. "What do you mean—the lady?"

"It is the church of Medea, our mother." The boy stared at Saxton. Challenging. Defiant. "We are *all* her children."

Saxton could feel a tic twitching at his left eye. He blinked. There was something familiar about the kid's words. His memory struggled with the English literature he'd studied at Uni. "Medea? Wasn't that a play?"

The pale boy on the back row chipped in. "The church is in honour of Medea, who murdered her own children to hurt her adulterous husband, Jason."

Saxton frowned. There was a sour taste in his mouth. "Why would you worship someone like *that*?" He could hear how unsteady his voice sounded.

A girl spoke from the second row. Saxton felt his heart lurch as he realised it was Taryn.

"Jason rejects Medea for another woman called Glauce." Taryn's voice was emotionless. "Medea cannot contain his love. So she kills Glauce. Then, when this revenge does not hurt Jason enough, she murders their children with a knife."

Saxton was furious. "Who taught you such things?"

"It is our culture," said the boy from the back row. He shrugged. "Euripides wrote of the poor children—Mermerus and Pheres—

and their innocence in a cruel world. Kyriabos for centuries has been island of disease. We are all children, living in a cruel world. Sometimes innocence is punished."

"What did Miss Hemsworth make of it?" Saxton rubbed his forehead. The room was stifling.

A few of the children giggled. "She did not like it."

"I really must talk to Mr Laskaris about this. I mean, it's not as if you're old enough—"

"Your wife killed *your* children, did she not?"

Saxton stared at Taryn. The question was stark. Unreal. He couldn't believe he'd heard correctly. "*What did you say?*"

She met his glare and returned it with equal measure. "Your wife—Joanne. She murdered your children. She was vengeance herself."

His vision felt like it might lurch at any moment. He began to stammer. "My wife died in a car crash. She didn't—she didn't kill anyone. I mean, well, she was killed in the crash with my young son." He could barely swallow. Stars were blooming in his vision. "It was just a horrible accident…"

"She knew about you and the other woman." Taryn's voice had taken on a dreamlike quality, as if she was talking in her sleep. "She did it to punish you."

"Shut up." He was close to hysteria now. The entire class was watching him. "Shut up!"

"Your other son was growing inside her. She murdered him, too."

His eyelids flickered uncontrollably. He reached to the desk to steady himself. He could taste bile in his mouth. And slowly, in such a way that at first he couldn't be sure he was hearing it, he became aware of the susurration in his head. That serene murmur of harmonies. A chorus that spoke a language he could understand. It rose in volume until it overwhelmed the sound of Taryn's voice.

*

"I'm sorry, Mr Laskaris, I really don't know what happened." Saxton shrugged. "I admit—I've been struggling lately."

The principle scratched his beard and rearranged some papers in front of him. "Mr Saxton, I'll be entirely honest with you—the education authority has arranged a permanent teacher for next term. Your contract won't be renewed."

They were in the principal's office. The air was thick with cigarette smoke. The overflowing ashtray gave off a stale aroma. Somewhere close by, someone was practising chords on a piano.

Saxton sighed. "Listen—I think they just got under my skin. There's no need to go and—"

"I don't need to remind you of your behaviour these past few weeks? It's been observed that you've been under increased pressure." As he spoke, spittle flew from the principal's mouth. "The children seem rather disturbed by your erratic conduct."

Saxton hesitated, licking his lips. His hands shook. He closed his eyes. "They're not like the children I'm used to dealing with." He could hear the disappointment in his own voice. "What I mean is—they're cruel. Callous, actually."

"Mr Saxton, children are very selfish by nature. It's down to us as adults to teach them the right way to—"

"They talk about wartime atrocities. They speak about things that children shouldn't know. I've even seen them torturing insects in the yard."

Laskaris wrote something on the notepad. He looked up. "How's your health been lately? Sleeping okay?"

"What?"

"The owner of the grocery store mentioned that you were troubled by rats." Laskaris raised an eyebrow. "He said you'd ordered a canister of rat poison. He had to get it from the mainland especially."

Saxton nodded. "I can hear them at night, running around the cottage. It keeps me awake."

"Kyriabos has never had a rat problem before. It's strange that it should happen now."

Saxton blinked. He felt confused. Detached by the events of the past few weeks. "It's eerie at night." He laced his hands together, as if supplication. "I've seen things. Heard things."

Laskaris blew out his cheeks. "It's been a very difficult eighteen months for you—the loss of your wife and son, the upheaval in relocating here. We're very appreciative of your help, of course, but you're only human—it's understandable that things might catch up with you."

"They knew about the child," Saxton said quietly, staring at the desk.

"The child?"

"They knew—that my wife was pregnant when she died."

Laskaris tutted and shook his head. "I've recommended that you take some time off. You've been through hell this past year."

"They mentioned names." He stared at Laskaris. "I never mentioned names to them, yet they knew…"

An awkward silence. Laskaris cleared his throat, unsure of what to say.

Saxton ran his hands through his hair. "There's an old church. Horrible artwork. They said it was in honour of a woman who killed her sons to avenge her husband's infidelity."

"Medea? The church was built in the 18th century to celebrate a wonderful piece of Greek culture—Europides' ancient tragedy. We're proud of the play. It's performed annually in the open-air theatre on the mainland."

Saxton closed his eyes tight. "I can hear singing wherever I go on the island…"

"It can get claustrophobic—I think I said that when you arrived. Island life's not for everyone, unfortunately." The principal smiled a sad smile. He waited a few beats. "I'll need you to put together a report, I'm afraid. So I can brief your replacement for next term." He cocked his head. "I'm sure you understand."

Saxton nodded, feeling resigned.

"I'm sorry things didn't work out." Laskaris stood and offered his hand. "Good luck with everything."

*

It is the final day of term. An unusually overcast morning. Clouds steal away shadows, usually ever-present. A warm breeze shivers the trees in the playground, rolls footballs into corners. The grey sea is flat and subdued. Saxton has spent his final day on Kyriabos with a strong sense of purpose.

The children appear sad to be saying goodbye. There is an air of finality about the classroom. Saxton waits while they file in from the playground and take their seats. He watches them examining the cartons on their desks, some of them sharing quizzical glances because for the first time the foil has already been removed from the lids of their cartons. Saxton nods at them. *It's okay, it's okay—I took it off this time.* Reassured, they begin to drink their milk. He watches their faces carefully but none of the children seem to detect a difference in the taste.

Saxton studies the handmade good-luck cards the children have presented him with. They cover his entire desk. Declarations of affection, wishes of good fortune. The children drink their milk in typically quiet fashion. He waits until they have all finished. During this time, he thinks about those he has lost. He remembers Joanne's anger when she discovered his affair. Maybe there is a small part of him that can understand Medea's desire for revenge. He adjusts the position of his feet under the desk, careful not to knock over the canister.

Now the children have finished their milk. He looks up at those innocent expressionless faces, and waits for things to start happening.

What Grief Can Do

When her stepfather opened the door, Tina's first thought was, *he looks almost dead himself.*

But a faint spark flared in his face when he saw her, enough to banish the sallow colour and the gaunt emaciation. *Grief can do that*, she thought. *Grief can allow death to touch those nearby.*

"Oh, Tina, love!" Edgar clutched her so tightly she could feel his heart fluttering beneath the layers of bobbled cardigan. His unshaven chin scratched her cheek. The moment seemed to last forever. Perhaps he sensed her discomfort, because he stepped back into the hallway timidly, almost apologetic. "Come in, love, come in." His voice sounded frail.

Shadows moved in the far reaches of the hallway. As she entered the sitting room she could hear her stepfather's frantic breathing behind her. The air was stale and compressed. She perched on the cushion of a drooping armchair, its springs groaning mournfully. The tightly-shut curtains denied the room daylight. Tina watched her stepfather's listless movement, partly wanting to give in to the emotion that threatened to consume her. She mentally asserted herself.

"It's good to see you. I've been beside myself with worry." The poor light caused his wrinkles to appear more defined. He slumped onto the sofa opposite her. "And Michael's been worried about you. He says you won't answer any of his calls either." He swallowed audibly. "It must have been hell for you—finding her like that…"

She fought to keep her breathing level. "It was…horrible."

"I haven't heard from you since the funeral. Michael thinks you should see a doctor, love—just till you're back on your feet."

"It's been a month now. I'm fine."

"Tina, love, we're all still coming to terms with it. But you…

finding her like that on the bed…God knows how you must have felt."

She glanced round the room at the signs of disarray. Dust motes swirled in the meagre light. There was an empty plate balanced on the chair-arm, stained with dried food. The handbag in her lap felt like a dead weight.

"You and Michael are all I've got now. He's done what he can… but he's got his own family, hasn't he? He's been worried sick."

"I know, I've been avoiding him." Tina blinked slowly. She hesitated. "I've seen her—*Mum*, I mean. She's been to my house."

Edgar sagged visibly. It looked like he was deflating. A sorrowful sigh escaped his lips. "It's just the shock, love. You haven't really seen her. She's *gone*, love."

"No." The word felt strong. Muscular. "I have seen her."

He sighed again and wiped his mouth. She could hear the grizzle of whiskers. "Let me make you a cup of tea."

She nodded, suppressing the urge to seize control and do it for them. Reminding herself that she was here to complete a task.

He stood and moved to the door, pausing with his hand on the back of her chair. "I've got some of your Mum's things for you to take with you—some bits of jewellery and whatnot. And her perfume. You know she always loved Anais-Anais. You must have bought her tons of bottles over the years."

Tina nodded curtly, leaning forward in the chair. Beyond his reach. He left the room and she could hear him pottering around in the kitchen. Her agitation stepped down a gear.

The fish-tank in the corner drew her attention. How she envied the languid movement of its occupant. The room hadn't been decorated in years. It felt deliberate; as if its appearance mocked her childhood memories, reminding her of what had been altered by her mother's death. The coffee table in the centre was littered with discarded newspapers, each one bearing a circular teacup stain. She thought about her stepfather's life, now he'd retired. Didn't he miss work? Had old-age changed him at all? Was he content to spend the rest of his days as listless as the goldfish?

She noticed the sympathy cards that cluttered the surfaces of the sideboard. Perhaps there were others on the windowsill, hiding behind the closed curtains. She suddenly became aware of a presence behind her, sensing a breath of movement against her neck. She turned sharply.

The room was empty. Somewhere close-by she heard a rasping breath, growing louder.

The door opened and her stepfather shuffled in. She realised the sound was just his slippers on the carpet. He handed her a mug of tea. She gripped it tightly, enjoying the heat against her hands. It made her feel real, alive. Tiny wraiths danced from the surface of the tea.

Her stepfather lowered himself onto the sofa, staring into space, sipping his own drink. For a few moments she watched him out of the corner of her eye—this old man, now a grandfather. How many different roles had he played in his lifetime?—son, husband, stepfather, grandfather. All those years he'd worked hard, determined to provide for the family. All those nights he'd spent away from home, sleeping in the cab of his HGV lorry—had he missed them in the same way as they'd missed him?

As if he could read her thoughts, he said, "I miss her terribly, you know. I always will."

She nodded. "I imagined I could still see her in the bedroom as I walked up the hill. She always used to wave to me."

"Aye." He took another sip. "God knows why she did it. She seemed happy enough."

Tina didn't speak. The carriage clock on the mantelpiece ticked out a calming rhythm. She thought she could hear her name whispered beneath the layers of oppressive silence, or was that just her imagination? "When's Michael coming again?" she said.

"At the weekend, with Ben and Charlotte."

Tina was being lulled by the low hiss of the gas fire. It was a warm day; there was no need for it to be on.

Her stepfather's rheumy eyes looked too moist, like they were a parody of sorrow. Tina said quietly, "She was in my bathroom last night—Mum, I mean."

Edgar ran his hand through his thinning hair. "Tina… sweetheart. Your mum's gone, love. She took her own life." For a second it looked like he was about to place his hand on her knee, and she recoiled slightly. "If only we knew why. If only she'd *said* something, left a note…"

"She did leave a note." Her words stabbed the air like a knife.

Edgar blinked twice, his face a cold mask of uncertainty.

She continued to speak, staring at her mug of tea. "I called that morning on the off-chance that she was in. The door was locked so I had to use my key." Her voice was like that of a machine. Precise, rehearsed. "I knew something wasn't right—the bedroom curtains were closed. I thought perhaps she was ill. The house was freezing. I realised you'd be down at the allotment." Now she raised her eyes and looked at him fiercely. "Somehow I knew things weren't right. I came up the stairs and stood on the landing for ages. I called out but there was no reply. My stomach was in knots. Somehow I *knew*—I was frightened to look. Finally I opened the door and went into the bedroom.

"She was there on top of the covers. At first I thought she was asleep, but even in the poor light I could see she was dead. There was a weird colour to her skin—nothing like it is on TV or in films.

"The note was on the bedside table. And laid out on the bed around her were these."

She reached into her bag and took out a manila envelope.

Her stepfather's eyes bulged. He seemed to be holding his breath.

She continued, "I read the note over and over but it didn't register. There was too much to take in—Mum's death, the note, these pictures." She thought she saw his left eye twitching furiously. He wiped his mouth with a grubby handkerchief.

And then, as if she was revealing her winning hand, she emptied the photos onto the coffee-table. It was a jumble of faded colours and tatty, dog-eared images. Pale skin, flared collars, bushy side-burned men, spindly-limbed youths. She'd only glimpsed the pictures briefly as she'd gathered them from around her dead mother that morning, but the depravity and wickedness depicted in them had been permanently seared into her brain.

Her stepfather's expression of surprise broke. He dropped his mug onto the carpet and it rolled away, the puddle of tea creeping across the carpet towards her. He looked ruptured, depleted.

For the past month she'd tried to imagine what his real face was like; what salacious appearance had he concealed beneath his mask all these years; how had he looked when he'd browsed these depraved pictures? She and Michael had never seen anything other than the warm face of a loving man. But now his mask had slipped and a new expression had been revealed.

His features were distorted, tears pushing from between his closed eyes. He buried his head in his hands. His shoulders shook violently. The scalp of his blotchy head was visible beneath the canopy of wispy grey hair. He looked pathetic.

If she'd harboured any doubt about the photos, they were dispelled the instant she saw his reaction. He rocked to and fro, repeating *No* in a sorrowful gasp. It sounded like he was choking.

Tina felt bile sour in her mouth. She stood abruptly and hurried out of the room. The hallway was cooler. She gripped the smooth handrail as she ascended the stairs. Her legs threatened to buckle. She clenched her teeth in an effort to prevent the rawness from spilling out.

The bathroom was stifling. A towel was folded over the rim of the bath. It looked starched and rough. She slammed the door and threw the bolt. Condensation fogged the mirror, making the room insubstantial and dreamlike. She closed the lid of the toilet and sat down. Her body was thrumming with adrenaline. She could hear her stepfather's anguished wails from downstairs. It sounded feral. Even at the funeral he'd managed to keep his emotion under control. Part of her wanted to escape, to flee from this insane idea she'd formulated in the weeks since her Mum's suicide. But she knew that wasn't possible; the shapes that writhed in the darkness at night would not let her. The thought that she'd betray her Mum by not having the courage to follow this through…that was too much to bear.

She gritted her teeth and stood, wiping her eyes on the towel. Her reflection shifted in the mirror but the condensation made her face look indistinct and ethereal. Her features seemed undefined, like she was wearing a shroud. She drifted out.

On the landing, the floorboards creaked in encouragement. She hesitated at the top of the stairs, staring at the closed door of the bedroom. Limitless sorrow engulfed her and she almost collapsed. But suddenly, as she flailed in the memories of her childhood, she became aware of the faint scent of Anais-Anais. It was subtle—maybe only conjured by her imagination—but it was reminder enough of what was at stake. She went downstairs.

Her stepfather was crying. It was the worst sound she had ever heard. He looked up as she entered the room.

"Tina, love, I swear I'd forgotten they were there. I only kept them because I didn't know what else to do with them." A bubble of snot emerged from his left nostril.

"She must have found them by accident—your little hidey-hole under the floorboards is well hidden." Tina paused. The dust coating the envelope corroborated the fact that it hadn't been taken out in years. But that wasn't the point.

"Let's burn them together then," he said. "Forget they ever exist-"

"So I tried to protect you—I put them back and destroyed Mum's note." She enjoyed seeing him wince at this. He looked pitiful. "But Mum's still angry. She's been to see me."

"Tina, she hasn't. You're imagining it. Grief can do that."

"How could you have these *things* in your possession?"

He sighed, resigned. "Curiosity, I suppose." His voice was growing in strength. Recovering. "But it didn't interest me. For god's sake, I was married to your Mum for over thirty years."

"I loved you like you were my real dad. How could you have had these…*this filth*…in the house?" Her loathing was becoming evident now; she could feel it twisting her mouth and furrowing her brow, altering her voice.

His eyes had lost their moisture. They were sparkling faintly. "I'd forgotten they were there, to be honest."

"Is that so?" Tina's words were precise. She wielded them like a weapon. Her tone lowered, quelling the anger that edged it. "There was one picture that seemed…newer than the rest."

"Newer?" He looked puzzled, frowning, the mask of uncertainty back. "Like I said, I haven't seen them properly. Someone I used to work with gave them to me ages ago." He shrugged.

"Oh, I think you'd recognise the one I mean," Tina heard herself say, surprised at how confident she sounded. Like she was an actor delivering lines. "The one with the young lad tied to the chair." He was holding his breath; staring at her like he knew what was coming. "It looks at lot like the inside of your lorry."

The twitch was definitely there now, flickering around his eye like a panicked moth. He laughed delicately, hollowly. "What do you mean?" He licked his lips. She could detect the frantic swarm of thoughts firing round his head.

She said quietly, "You know what I mean."

A few seconds of uncomfortable silence passed between them. Tina opened her handbag and took out a small plastic bottle.

"What's that?"

She ignored him and placed it on the coffee-table. "You see, I also recognised that young lad in the photo. I remembered his face from the news." Her voice was quiet still, threatening. "He's naked in the photo but you can see his scout uniform on the floor behind him. I googled it. He was abducted in 1986, on his way home from cubs. His body was never found."

Her stepfather frowned dismissively. He swallowed, shaking his head.

"You used to deliver up round Middlesbrough, didn't you?"

A strange wheeze began to issue from him. He raised a trembling hand to his chest. His colour was mottled.

"I'll leave the photographs for you to look at. Remind you of what you really are." Her throat tightened, altering her voice. "I hope you rot in hell for what you've done—to Mum and to all these other kids." Tears fragmented her view. She fought to keep her voice from breaking. "These tablets'll do the trick. Wash 'em all down with something from the drinks cabinet. You'll drop off to sleep—that'll be it. Painless."

She sniffed. "I'll call round in the morning and tidy everything up. Burn everything. Nobody else'll know. Everyone will assume you've just done it because of Mum." Her voice hardened. "Grief can do that."

"Tina, love—" There was a pleading tone. "I can't. I'm frightened."

She stared directly into his eyes. "Or I'll give the other photos to the police. Think about what it'll do to Michael and the kids."

He glanced down at the floor. He seemed limp and depleted, like the bones had been removed from his body. She moved to the door.

"Do this and you'll be remembered as a grieving husband." Her chin trembled. "Instead of the monster you actually are." She hurried into the hallway. Once again the faintest breath whispered against her neck, the shadows embraced her. Just before she stepped through the front door and slammed it behind her, she heard the distant rattle of pills from the bottle.

Her lungs clawed at fresh air. She hurried towards the bus stop, clutching her handbag tightly. When she was halfway down the hill she turned and glanced back at the house. The net curtains in the bedroom window were bunched together like cobwebbed dreams. If she was expecting a vague movement of shadows approximating a wave, she was disappointed. The glass reflected the slate-grey buildings opposite. She turned and continued down the hill.

The Ivory Teat

Often, in the heat of summer, when the windows of the apartment block were flung open in hope of channelling the slightest breeze, the music would rise, unbidden, and flow through the building like a liquid, seeping into the furthest reaches of the rooms, altering the mood of the residents like an emotional trigger. The fluid, melancholy piano became a backdrop to the events that went on, almost a soundtrack to the lives of the tenants. But rather than just a noise to accompany the daily rigours of life, the music had become something more; almost a tenant itself, its near-constant presence exerting a morose influence upon those that dwelt within the grey walls of Balzac Towers.

Metzler had noticed the music within days of moving into his apartment. At first it had seemed a curious inconvenience, but over the years he had become immune to its intrusion. Indeed, on windless days when the panicked shrieks of animals were carried effortlessly across the heath from the nearby abattoir, its sudden commencement was a blessing. In the first few weeks following his arrival, Metzler had tried to discover the source of the wonderful music. It seemed to come from both everywhere and nowhere. Quizzing a surly neighbour on the stairs one day, he'd managed to determine that the tenant in room 313 was responsible, although no one ever saw him. He appeared to come and go like a wraith. But the reclusive pianist's influence had suffused the building until it was as much a part of the structure's fabric as the bricks and mortar.

Sometimes at night Metzler would stare out of his window, watching couples frolicking in the dense bushes that fringed the heath, and the music seemed to render the physical acts of carnality infinitely sad. He'd been told that the composition was by

Chopin—his *Nocturnes* series—but it was played in a remarkably original interpretation.

Metzler had tried to locate room 313 but it seemed an impossible task; none of the apartment doors possessed identifying numbers, and the labyrinth of identical stairways and landings left him puzzled and frustrated. He only recognised the door to his own apartment by memory and force of habit—the landlord had directed him and provided a key when he'd moved in. And the omnipresent nature of the music meant that tracking the sound down was like an enigma with no clear resolution—he was left thwarted every time.

On the wintry mornings when Metzler had to trudge to the university laden with books, he physically had to force himself to leave the bosom of the music, as if the notes themselves were sustaining him. Many years before, he'd discussed the situation with an elderly neighbour, who'd informed him that a previous tenant had also been obsessed with the same composition. She, too, had played the *Nocturnes* endlessly, until her depression had gathered such weight that it had dragged her into the abyss: she'd been discovered dead in her room, after drinking a cocktail of bleach and oven-cleaner. They said the corrosive liquids had ravaged gaping holes in her mouth and throat. Some suggested the melody had been passed on like a virus to the tenant in room 313, almost as if the sound itself was a powerful drug. Metzler could indeed sympathise with that school of thought.

One Saturday morning he ventured out for a breath of fresh air, prowling the bushes at the edge of the heath. The sky was hazy and grey. People hurried by, made mannequin-like by thick coats and oversized gloves. Woollen scarves couldn't prevent the ghosts of their breath escaping. He completed a circuit of the duck-pond, marvelling at the mirror-like surface of the water. Frozen reeds protruded from the pond like exclamation marks. As he drew close to his apartment block, he sensed someone watching him from the doorway of a building opposite. A woman dressed in a red coat smiled and waved awkwardly as he glanced over. He hesitated then returned the gesture. She detached herself from the doorway and drifted across to him.

"Hi." Her voice was low and diffident. She glanced down at the ground.

"Hello." Metzler smiled, uncertain of what else to do.

"You live in there." She motioned vaguely to Balzac Towers. He wasn't sure whether it was a statement or a question. "I've seen you." Her eyes widened. "At night, in your room."

"Oh."

"I live opposite." The silence was oppressive.

He looked back towards the doorway of his building, and said, on a whim, "Would you like to come up for a drink?"

She nodded and they set off walking. It was only as they were entering the foyer that he realised that he'd never taken anyone back to his apartment before. He struggled with the weight of expectancy.

He felt embarrassed by the crude graffiti that adorned the walls. The staircase seemed endless, and it occurred to Metzler for the first time that perhaps he'd be able to find a more suitable apartment for what he paid in rent. A cold breeze swirled around them.

The woman looked sideways at him. "I'm Martha."

"Pleased to meet you, Martha. My name's John." He swallowed, suddenly nervous.

From upstairs, a door slammed and there was the sound of banging. "You've got till tomorrow, you hear? Then I cut the power. No rent—no electricity!"

A heavyset man barged past them on his way downstairs, the echoes of his footsteps creating an impression of unseen followers.

"The landlord," Metzler whispered, once he was out of earshot. "Bit of a nutcase." They continued on their trek.

As he unlocked the door, Metzler tied to remember what he drinks he had on offer inside the apartment. She took off her coat and glanced around the room.

"Tea? Coffee?" He hung her coat on the peg. "Or something stronger?"

"Coffee's fine, thanks." She went to the full-length window and looked out, pointing across the courtyard. "There's my flat—the one with the red curtains."

He made some coffee in the kitchen, listening to the silence as she studied the contents of his room. Soon he carried the mugs out.

"Thanks." She cupped her hands around the warm vessel. She was leaning back on his sofa, her legs arched at an attractive angle. Her shoes were nice.

To allay his nerves, Metzler sipped his drink, burning his lips and tongue with the hot liquid. He mentally urged the piano to begin, desperate for its release. He needed the melody as a crutch.

"Sometimes at night I watch you at the window, looking down on the world." Martha's voice was hypnotic. Dreamlike. He felt himself blushing. Half her face was hidden, where she clutched the mug to her mouth. "You look very…noble. But lost, somehow."

He nodded and glanced down at his drink, watching the steam that writhed and squirmed and undulated.

She peered round the room. He was expecting her to compliment him on his décor, but instead she said, "It smells of tears in here."

He looked at the salty stains on the arm of his sofa. "I get lonely sometimes."

She seemed to consider this, staring at him as she sipped her tea. Eventually she said, "You keep yourself busy. Or—at least—you seem to." She turned away and he sensed her guilt. "This place could do with a woman's touch."

Metzler slammed his mug down on the table, slopping the tea. "What's all this about you knowing my business? What I get up to is nothing to do with anyone else."

Martha nodded quickly and stood, holding her mug at arm's length as if it were poison, placing it down. "I should go."

He nodded, turning to the window. The sky was still as formless as before. He could hear her sliding into the sleeves of her coat, zipping it up. There was a pause, and he guessed she was trying to think of something to say. He parted his lips in anticipation but she had opened the door and was leaving. "Goodbye, John." She closed the door behind her. Her gentle voice and the lingering scent of her perfume were like abandoned children. He could hear his heart thumping, imprisoned behind his ribs—mocking, tormenting him with his own inadequacies.

Metzler stood and went to the window. Eventually he saw

her figure emerge from the shadow of the building and cross the courtyard to her own. When he turned back to his tea, he felt confused by the identical mugs standing so close to one another. He examined them both and spotted the trace of lipstick on the rim of one. He drank the rest of his tea, staring at the other one accusingly.

The remainder of the day was brittle and unforgiving. He prowled his room, waiting for the piano to begin, but the prevailing silence seemed to suck the oxygen from the air. His textbooks lay unopened on one side. Outside the sky changed from dull grey to a blackness that was absolute. The heath was a dark apron stretched across the town, smothering the humanity. Grey lights twinkled from the upper windows of the abattoir. The animals were silent.

At some point during the night he became aware of the reassuring melody of the *Nocturnes* playing from somewhere far below—the tranquil, assured notes perfectly formed to evoke feelings of relaxation and slumber, the moodiness of after-dark. Sleep held him tight in its grip, but the music's near presence was enough to soothe away the frustration he'd felt earlier in the day.

In the morning he awoke late. The electric clock on his bedside table was blinking. He rose and dressed quickly. Sundays were usually so languid; the murmur of voices and banging doors downstairs teased a mild disquiet in his stomach. On the pretence of fetching a newspaper, he left his flat and wandered downstairs.

There was a throng of people outside one of the rooms. Yellow police tape cordoned off the doorway. Angled heads were bent in an attempt to see into the room, and the silence was punctured by reverential whispers. Metzler asked one of them what was going on. A wide-eyed middle-aged man told him that the occupant had been threatened with having their power cut off, and had taken drastic steps to avoid being evicted: *he'd fallen into a drunken stupor with the blade of an electric chain-saw resting on his neck. The timer had already been set so at the allotted minute the machine had roared into action and...* the result was illustrated by the sawing action of the neighbour's hand. Apparently the building's power had been fused by the effort of the blade chewing through bone and gristle.

An ambulance was parked in the courtyard outside. Metzler

loitered in a nearby doorway until the crew emerged pushing a covered stretcher. The colour of their faces matched the concrete towers that crowded them. He overheard someone call out the room number to the one of the paramedics who was tasked with completing the paperwork. The words *three-one-three* were as inevitable as birth preceding death.

The next few days all bled into one other. Metzler spent the time shivering in his room, leaving his bed only for the calls of nature. He retched oatmeal-coloured vomit into the toilet's porcelain bowl. Spasms ravaged his bones. His tongue felt bloated and slimy. Time seemed to distort and contract, throwing his temporal awareness out of alignment. It felt like the hours of darkness and daylight were entwining like ribbons, alternating at a terrifying frequency. Invisible teeth gnawed at joists beneath the floorboards, the sounds amplified by the dusty gap; rats probably. And all the while, throughout the whole of this process, Metzler endured his illness without the melody of the *Nocturnes* to ease the discomfort.

When he finally emerged from the fugue of sickness, his body felt like a withered husk, devoid of all feeling. A powerful sensation ached at his stomach. He struggled with an almost physical need to hear the piano's melody, to be carried by the music, to allow himself to be transported by the notes. Instead he remained bereft, without nourishment. Dark shadows lingered in the hollows of his eyes. His hair felt greasy and lank. When he glanced around the interior of his apartment it seemed like something had changed imperceptibly. He slumped on the sofa and began going through the pile of letters that had been delivered during the time of his illness. They lay heaped in front of his door like antique snow. He was slightly bemused to find a handwritten note from one of the senior lecturers telling him not to bother returning to the university. The scribbled date at the top looked odd so he checked the dial of his watch, realising with a jolt that several weeks had passed since he'd last attended. He tore the note into pieces and let them to drift to the floor.

That night he returned to the window, watching the figures on the heath scuttle and throb and pulse like they were feeding on the shadows. Just before he managed to peel himself away from the glass he caught sight of a silhouette in one of the windows opposite—the red curtains identified it.

He slept fitfully. Something scurried behind the skirting boards, scratching unseen at the other side of the plaster. At some point during the night he became aware of a furious banging on his door, the landlord's insistent threats tempered by a detectible weariness in his voice. Certain words bled through Metzler's filter of sleep, enough for him to understand that he'd neglected to pay his rent for quite a while. He shivered beneath the covers and turned over.

In the morning he forced himself to eat. His stomach looked collapsed, the curve of ribs visible through his mottled skin. He resembled a death-camp refugee. He dressed and ventured outside throwing furtive glances about, his head cocked for the landlord's approach.

The breeze flapped at his baggy clothes, emphasising his recent weight loss. Late winter air carried a welcome scent of grass and warmth: spring was on its way.

There was a grocery shop nearby. Gaudy banners obscured the window, rendering the interior illicit and exciting, yet the spot-lit blandness within left him disappointed. The stock on the shelves made him feel nauseous. He inquired about rat-poison. The shopkeeper brought up a canister from beneath the counter, explaining with grisly relish how the liquid worked—*It's an anti-coagulant. Breaks down the vermin's ability to clot blood*. He licked his glistening lips as he said it—*They bleed to death internally*. Metzler handed over the money while the shopkeeper placed the canister into a plastic bag. It looked tear-shaped.

He was halfway across the courtyard when he spotted Martha out of the corner of his eye. Her red coat seemed more vivid than before. She smiled as she approached from the direction of her own building. He could hear the gravel crunch underfoot. His heart felt the same way.

"John—how've you been?"

"Good, thanks." He nodded as if to prove it. "And you?"

She shrugged. "Have you been ill? I haven't…seen you out much for a while."

"Actually, I have. Feeling better now, though."

Her eyes drifted restlessly. It felt like she was about to say something. She looked back towards her own building. "Do you fancy coming up for a cup of tea?"

He glanced at the block that housed his own apartment. Through the stairwell windows could see a figure descending. "Yeah, why not?" He accompanied Martha back to her building.

It was very different to Balzac Towers. The foyer confused him with its mirrored ceiling and polished-tiled floor. It felt like the reflections were mimicking his movement. There was a smell of camomile and lavender. An old black bakelite telephone stood on one side like a monstrous crab. Metzler fought the urge to see if it was real or just a prop. They took the elevator up to the sixth floor. The landing carpets looked immaculate, as if they'd never been walked upon. A brass plaque proudly identified the number of her apartment. As she unlocked the door he suddenly felt ashamed of his own flat, regretful that she'd seen it in such a state. She welcomed him inside and waved him to a chair.

It was an impressive home. She went into the kitchen and switched on the kettle, then came over to the window and pointed out. "That's your place there."

Metzler was surprised how clear the view was into his room, although it looked very different from this angle. He suddenly felt vulnerable.

"You look like you haven't eaten in weeks," Martha said. "Want me to make you a sandwich? I've got some turkey in the fridge."

"No, I'm fine, thanks."

Martha disappeared into the kitchen, leaving him alone with his sense of isolation. He felt mildly disconcerted by the difference of comfort between her apartment and his own. She returned abruptly with the tea. He took it from her and sipped without drinking any.

"What's in there?" She motioned to the bag at his feet.

"Rat poison."

"You've got rats?"

"Sounds like it." He raised his eyebrows. "I can hear them in the walls. Under the floor."

"Eugh! Horrible. Can't the landlord see to them?"

"Possibly. I've only just noticed it. Since the music stopped, it's amazing how much more noise there is."

A silence descended between them. She said quietly, "Sometimes I watch you at night…"

He felt uncomfortable, glancing away to avoid her eye contact.

She continued. "You look so lonely—up there on your own."

He smiled thinly.

She brushed a curl of hair from her face. "Sometimes I wake in the middle of the night and watch you for ages, playing that thing…"

"What?"

She looked startled at the sharpness of his tone. "The piano—sometimes I watch you play the piano. I like to imagine what tunes you might be—"

"I haven't got a piano."

She studied him, confused, murmuring, "But I've *seen* you…"

Metzler put the tea down and stood, grabbing the bag. "I need to go." He hurriedly left, sensing Martha's unasked questions boring into the back of his head.

The elevator bounced gently, the speakers emitting jaunty, insipid muzak as it descended. He clutched the canister of poison like a baby. In the foyer, shadows fled ahead, wading alongside him through the reflections. The silence and tranquillity of this building reminded him of a morgue. As he emerged outside he was blasted by a gust of wind, tugging at his sallow skin and combing through his filthy hair.

The familiarity of his own apartment block was reassuring. The smell of piss had never been more comforting. Only the commanding silence probed a knot of uneasiness within. He carefully trudged up the stairs, breathless by the time he reached his floor. Sweat tried to blind him, his gasping chest conspired to mask the landlord's approach.

There was a note pinned to his door. *You're rents still due. 1 more week then the power gets cut. Final warning.*

Metzler hurried inside, locked the door and threw the bolts, leaning against the wood, breathing heavy. Now he felt secure.

The window was the only remaining point of exposure. He stared at the opposite building, imagining eyes peering back between the parted folds of red curtain. He tried not to think about how it resembled female genitalia.

He could hear things chewing and scuttling inside the cavity of the walls. With a languid finality he yanked across his own drapes, dulling the light, softening the shadows, transforming the apartment. Now he could not be disturbed.

Something crouched in the corner of the room, shrouded by a heavy dust sheet. He stared at it for ages, considering its presence. He carefully approached and lowered himself onto the stool in front. His hands gripped the cover and he lifted it, uncovering the tarnished lid beneath. There was a resigned inevitability to his movement. He opened the lid and his fingers automatically began to caress the black and white keys, birthing the notes with a remarkable purity. This felt overwhelmingly familiar. He closed his eyes and feasted on the melody. He could no longer hear the gnawing of the rats. There was something irrevocable to his actions, a fluency that couldn't be denied. He played and allowed himself to be swept away by the music, watching the shadows creep around the walls. The curtains filtered day and night into one solitary moment. How long he sat there he couldn't be sure.

At some point he noticed the mug. Furred semi-liquid coated the interior. The rim still bore the traces of Martha's lipstick. He smelt the porcelain, unsure whether the faint aroma of skin-cream was due entirely to his imagination. He filled the mug with the rat poison and sipped from it at intervals, his other hand drawing assured notes from the keys.

The music was a comforting blend of melancholia and tranquil contemplation. Its melody transported Metzler away, masking the sound of the rats' movement and the landlord's ceaseless hammering. He continued to play, even as his insides wept scarlet tears, and blood seeped freely from the valves of his heart.

Double Helix

Claire was accustomed to the air-conditioned luxury of her husband's Lexus so Pete's battered Ford Focus seemed primitive and quaint by comparison. The heat was stifling. Within minutes they were trundling away from Sheffield train station, heading out towards the motorway and the A1 beyond. Pete wound down the windows to catch the June breeze.

She noticed him studying her reflection in the wing mirror. Glancing at her lap, she let her thinning hair fall across her face.

"You look well," he said brightly. "All things considered."

She grimaced. "Don't feel it." It was as if she was teetering on the brink of an abyss.

I shouldn't have come.

The silence was punctuated by cars zipping past in the opposite direction. She pretended she was interested in the traffic, stealing a glance out of the corner of her eye. Appraising him. When she'd first climbed into the battered Ford she'd been surprised by how lined his face had looked. Aged. The wrinkles around his eyes were pronounced, a visible indication that he'd spent much of the last twenty years smiling. This disappointed her, and she forced the unkind thought away.

I shouldn't have come. It's been too long.

Pete took an old cassette from the dashboard's console and pushed it into the player. The familiar strains of Morrissey filled the car. *There Is a Light That Never Goes Out.* Abruptly, distant memories surfaced from their time at Uni—drunken nights in student bars, chilly day-trips to the seaside, afternoons huddled together in bed listening to The Smiths.

"Oh, Pete..." Her voice sounded exasperated, so she added a laugh to soften it.

"What?—Nothing wrong with reliving the good times." He shrugged, smiling. "I still listen to this stuff. It's timeless."

She considered her husband's in-car CD-changer and wireless iPod connection, and how the elaborate speaker system did nothing but bathe the Lexus in bland, insipid noise. And yet the warbled music from this old tape sounded fresher, more exciting, exhilarating.

"So, what did you tell your husband?"

She raised a weary eyebrow. "That I was visiting my sister in Sunderland. I'll have to ring him later."

"We might not get a signal where we're going," he warned. "It's patchy up there, you know?—in the middle of nowhere."

For the first time she felt a mild sense of unease at what they were doing. Why had she agreed to come? Surely there was more to this trip than old times' sake?

They drove in silence for a while. She closed her eyes, enjoying the wind against her face. Maybe the medication was starting to take its toll; she felt exhausted. Yet her earlier nerves had dissipated. Quite out of the blue she admitted, her eyes still closed, "Pete, I'm sorry. For what happened. Well—I mean—sorry for cheating on you."

She opened her eyes, puzzled by his silence. He was looking at her, a sad smile playing around his mouth. "Don't worry. That's all water under the bridge now."

"No, I mean it." Tears brimmed in her eyes. "I need to tell you. You're a good man, you deserved better."

He nodded slowly, angling his head. "Is he…Does he treat you…well?"

She glanced out of the window, watching the scenery fly past. "He does. He's worked really hard over the years, building up his business. Putting the hours in. We've a huge house. Holiday in the Bahamas every year. I want for nothing."

He smiled thinly. "Sounds like a great life."

"It is." Now she swallowed to prevent the tears from flowing. For several minutes she didn't speak. He allowed her time to compose herself, and she was grateful. He always was good at understanding her.

"You know," he said, "sometimes I wonder how things might've turned out if we'd adopted—I'm sure things would have been different…"

She shrugged. "Who knows? Bernard made it clear from the start that he never wanted kids. I expect my infertility seemed like a bonus…" She added, "Sometimes I can't believe I treated you so badly." She pondered things for a long time. "We *did* have some laughs though, didn't we?"

"Remember that time we went to Oxford for the weekend? You ended up getting us thrown out of the theatre for giggling."

She smiled. "All that blossom caught in my hair as we ran through the park. You said it looked like confetti."

He nodded, laughing. "I stole that from Marillion…"

"I know, I know." Buoyed by his good humour, she asked, "So, this trip up north—where're we going exactly?"

He hesitated. "Scotland."

"*Scotland?*"

"Just overnight. We'll be back tomorrow." His face looked flushed. Excited. "Remember I told you once about an old family friend that lived near Aberdeen? We're going to see him."

She nodded vaguely. "I always wanted to visit Scotland."

"You always wanted to go to Australia," Pete said. "Did you ever manage it?"

She shook her head. The sorrow was palpable.

"Remember I told you once I had meningitis as a toddler?"

She blinked her morose thoughts away, glad to have changed the subject. "Yes."

"Well, it caused my brain to swell. The doctors thought I'd be severely disabled. Permanently, like." He glanced at her. "I was in intensive care for weeks. Eventually they released me, but I couldn't walk or talk. I lost my sight, everything."

"That's awful. I can't believe you never told me this before."

"I know." He paused. "Anyway my parents took me up to see an old family friend—Archie. Dad was an evacuee at his farm during the war."

"Ah, yeah, I remember you mentioned *that* once."

"Well, Archie had…something that helped me recover."

The car crossed the slip-road onto the exit for the A1. Claire watched the sheep in the fields grazing indifferently. The sky was azure, bluer than she had ever seen it. Maybe the bluest she would ever see.

"Pete, I appreciate the effort but I doubt anybody can—"

"No, Claire—I mean he'll be able to help *you*."

"Pete—no one can! The doctors say I've got between six and nine months left." Her voice was sharp. "Christmas is likely, but I probably won't see my next birthday. I've had dozens of tests, hundreds of tablets, more biopsies than I care to remember. Bernard's spent a fortune on the best advice Harley Street can give—they all say six to nine months." She regretted the outburst as soon as it subsided. Regretted how bitter she sounded.

He laid a gentle hand on her arm. "Listen, sorry. But you mustn't give up. Let's just see, shall we?"

Silence descended upon them. She angled her body to the left and watched the world pass by. Lush fields shimmered in the heat. It was vibrant, hypnotic. The patchwork countryside reminded her of an eiderdown she'd had as a child. Comforting. Recollections from a happier time. Soon she was dozing, head lolling against the window, *The Queen Is Dead* bridging the gap between her distant memories and their middle-aged bodies.

*

They stopped at a service station. Grease and diesel and heat made Claire's stomach spasm. Pete went to order them a coffee and she wandered around in search of the toilets.

Afterwards she studied herself in the mirror. Her sallow skin looked frail and thin, accentuated by unnatural light. The pores of her cheeks seemed magnified. Perhaps she was trying to expel her sickness through them.

The coffee burned her tongue, which was just as well because it was tasteless, despite the cost. She cupped her hands around the polystyrene cup as if she was cold, enjoying the pain of the heat. It made her feel alive. They chatted idly for some time, watching people come and go. Everybody moved with such purpose. Hurried and precise. They all seemed to be living their perfect lives. The plastic chair was stiff, but it was a relief to be out of the car for a while. Once the drink had cooled, Claire took out her pills and swallowed them with a grimace.

Soon they were back on the road. She closed her eyes again, not quite pretending to sleep but allowing herself time to think. She could hear the *swish-swish-swish* of tyres on the carriageway, lulling her mind, allowing her to imagine they were abandoning her illness back in Sheffield. Yet every time she drew breath she could still feel that black sourness rattling inside her chest, reminding her there was no escape.

Sometimes she was gripped by an overwhelming fear about wasting whatever time she had remaining. Queuing at the ATM felt melodramatic by its triviality. Minutes spent waiting at traffic-lights could leave her shaking. Sleep seemed an extravagance she could no longer afford, despite the fact that her medication induced it.

She thought about the last twenty years and tried to conjure some highlights. The time blurred, her memories felt inert and apologetic. Maybe it was the medication. She knew she owed Pete this trip. Remembered how she'd shattered him back then. Allowing him these 48 hours wasn't an idle indulgence on her part; it was almost a shot at redemption.

"Claire, to think what would've happened if I'd not bumped into your brother last week…" He shook his head. "It might have been too late."

She didn't speak. *So this was just for old times' sake. A sentimental goodbye.* But then his next sentence confused her.

"If I'd heard about the cancer after you'd died, it'd have been too late. Archie wouldn't have been able to help then."

She was surprised by his words. The old Pete—the Pete she'd once loved with all her heart—used to believe in science before religion, fact over faith. Maybe he'd also changed in the intervening years. God knew she had. It sounded like this old Scottish guy had set himself up as some kind of faith-healer. She quelled the argument that trembled on her lips. Decided to go through with whatever Pete suggested. She mentally calculated the cash in her purse, hoping it would be enough.

"You said on the phone you'd never married?" She was surprised by how nonchalant she sounded.

"No." He shrugged. "Never met the right girl, I suppose."

She sensed something unspoken lurking in the silence. It felt wedged between them. Unsure of how to breach the hush she concentrated on the road ahead. The distant tarmac shimmered in the heat, ethereal and undefined. Cattle drifted by in the fields, like black and white boats in an ocean of green. She tried once again to doze.

They were on the A68, rising through the Northumberland National Park, when Claire woke. The increased altitude had caused her ears to pop. She sat up suddenly. "I feel sick."

Pete glanced over. "Want me to pull—"

She covered her mouth with her hand and nodded urgently.

Luckily they were on a quiet stretch of road. Pete braked sharply and pulled over, gravel spluttering against the underside of the car. Claire leapt out and stumbled into the overgrown grass, almost bent double. Her stomach hitched several times and she expelled a gush of dark bile onto the ground. The cramps felt like a dagger twisting. She could hear Pete climbing out of the car and hurrying to her. He laid a comforting hand on her back, holding her hair out of the way. Absently she felt embarrassed by how straw-like it was, cringing at Pete seeing her in this state. For a minute or two they remained in that position. Once the sickness had subsided she wiped a string of saliva from her chin and stood upright.

"Okay?" he asked. "You look white as a ghost."

She nodded. "Medication's side-effects." She swallowed. "It's fine." He helped her back to the car. Her limbs shook violently but she fought to suppress them. His face was etched with concern. Once he was satisfied she was safely belted up, he climbed in the driver's seat and set off.

Suddenly she despised her illness more than ever. It wasn't just the way it ravaged her body, it was the sickening way it touched those she loved. Her ghastly pallor had become mirrored in the faces of her family and friends. She closed her eyes again in an effort to shut out the truth. Her chin trembled at the thought of what little time she had remaining. Bitterly, she hoped the end would arrive soon.

*

It was late evening by the time they embarked on their final leg of the journey. They'd left the towns and cities far behind, turning off the A90 onto a side track which meandered through the countryside like a scar, an aberration of life, a contradiction of nature. The car stereo had long since fallen silent. In the distance the Cairngorms glowered sullenly. Dusk ignited the heather-flecked hills that crowded around them as they negotiated the narrow road. They hadn't seen another car for nearly an hour. Shadows gathered beneath the rocky tors protruding from the earth like monstrous black teeth. Clumps of thistles shied away from them as they passed. The car's tired engine rattled ominously. Pete looked exhausted as he gripped the wheel and stared through the windscreen, his face a determined mask.

The moorland was desolate and bleak, seemingly untouched by humanity. It was easy to imagine creatures prowling the shadows. The sky still retained some vestiges of light, and this birthed movement on the ground and echoed the sense of spirituality that permeated the area.

Pete finally spoke, his voice throaty: "We're here."

Claire sat up, peering ahead. Across the expanse of dark she saw a glimmering light. A house crouched in the hollow of the valley, sheltered by an adjacent hill. A thin coil of smoke rose from its chimney. The car drew to a halt outside and Pete switched off the ignition. The cooling engine ticked in relief. She could make out the dark silhouette of a 4x4 parked nearby.

Claire's joints ached so much she struggled to clamber out of the car. A warm breeze fluttered her hair. The silence was claustrophobic, the darkness oppressive. Pete hurried around from his side and helped her out. She leaned on his arm for support as they ascended the wooden steps. The house looked like it might collapse at any minute, the flimsy construction suggesting it couldn't possibly fare well against the weather. Yet its timber walls must have withstood decades of battering by the harsh Scottish elements.

The door opened and an old man nodded at them in dour acknowledgement. He held the door open while they entered. The room consisted of both kitchen and sitting areas, divided in the centre by a plasterboard arch. A portable TV was perched on a nest of tables in front of the window. Mismatched chairs had been arranged around the room. The sparse furniture was cluttered with bric-a-brac. Claire took a seat on the low couch and stretched her limbs until they popped.

Pete and the old man talked for a minute on the porch. Then they came into the house. Pete was carrying a battered holdall which he passed to the old man, who took it and nodded to Claire. "Thisser?"

"Yes, this is Claire," said Pete. "Claire, meet Archie—an old friend."

The old man nodded again, just the once. He was much younger than she was expecting. His eyes were heavily-lidded, almost reptilian. Dark bags pulled down the skin beneath his eyes. Despite the warm day, he was dressed in a knitted polo-neck sweater, denim jeans and sturdy boots. Even in the meagre light she could see the dirt under his fingernails, the calloused roughness of his hands. She prayed he'd be using gloves when he attempted his faith-healing stunt.

Pete was waved into a nearby chair.

"Wannadrink?" asked Archie.

"Not for me, thanks," said Pete. Claire replied in the same manner.

She glanced round the room. "Nice place you have here." The small-talk sounded clumsy. Awkward.

"Aye. Bit lonely sometimes…" He laughed. "But I like that, yer ken?"

She smiled faintly. Looked to Pete for help.

"How's yon lassie feelin?" Archie peered at her inquisitively.

She understood this one. "Not so bad, thanks."

He nodded sagely. "We'll have yer sorted, by God we will."

She nodded once and averted her eyes. The sleep she'd managed to grab in the car had recharged her physically, but she wasn't sure if she was mentally prepared for the forthcoming events. She looked at Pete, nervous. He just nodded and smiled back at her.

Archie lowered himself into the sagging sofa, the springs squeaking in protest. From somewhere out in the glen, a weird sound rose abruptly, echoing out across the valley. It sounded childlike and insane. Mocking almost. Claire held her breath expectantly, then exhaled, reasoning it had to be some kind of bird.

Archie scratched his chin and continued like he hadn't heard it. "Yer ready for it, hin?"

Claire shrugged and smiled. "Hope so." Suddenly she felt frightened.

"Young Pete says yer have the cancer?"

She just nodded. Her throat felt tight. She was so used to being described as *ill* or *sick* or *poorly*, it was jarring to hear the C word. Even the doctors used alternatives—tumour or carcinoma or malignant neoplasm. Hearing it spoken out loud made it stark and final, inevitable. Real.

"She slept a great deal in the car, Archie." Pete said. "I think she'll be okay. She's stronger than she looks."

"Good." The old man rubbed his hands together. "It's a warm neet at least—might not be tae bad."

"How long should it take?" Pete ran his fingers through his hair. "I think I'll try to get some shut-eye while you're up there."

Archie shrugged. "Couple o' hours, prolly."

"Fine." Pete glanced at Claire. "Why don't you get cleaned up and we'll get this show on the road?"

∗

The sky was totally dark now. It was after midnight. Seated in the front of Archie's Land Rover, looking into the formless black void beyond the windscreen, she could almost believe she'd gone blind; only the faint glow from the dashboard told her otherwise. She chewed her nails and struggled with the panic that threatened to overwhelm her.

Earlier, back at the house, she'd freshened herself up in Archie's tiny bathroom. The cold water had stung her face. She'd been desperate to have a quiet word with Pete; she felt out of control, like things were spiralling away from her. But there'd never been a point when she could get him alone, and the moment had passed.

Now she was in the Land Rover with Archie, heading towards God-knew where. It was late. He'd helped her into the car and loaded a few things into the back. She'd asked where they were going but his terse reply told her nothing. Her further attempts at conversation were batted away verbally.

She pressed her temple and rubbed her eyes. It felt like her migraine was returning. Some of the medication left her feeling sicker than the illness did, ravaging her organs in its futile attempt to slow the spread. Her body was on the verge of collapse.

The track threaded out along the valley, rising between the tight incline that bordered the glen. Moths swarmed in the headlights. The car's engine sounded deafening in the silence of the night. Impenetrable darkness pressed against the side of the car, seemingly stealing the oxygen from within. Claire took deep breaths and tried to relax. She checked her phone several times but the lack of reception made the display as blank as Archie's face. She was afraid to ask where they were going. It felt like they had been driving for almost half an hour when Archie started to slow the car. She leaned forward in the seat, searching for something visible in the night. He pulled over and killed the engine.

Claire looked at him. "What're we doing?"

He pointed out the window. "There's a building over there. Will yer be able tae manage walkin' tae it?"

She swallowed and nodded. A plea trembled on her lips. "Will I be okay?"

He glanced at her strangely. Now, more than ever, she needed his reassurance, needed him to become more than the surly old man he'd been so far. But he just nodded and said, "Aye, lass."

He handed her an electric torch. She brandished it like a weapon as they climbed out of the vehicle. The welcome breeze combed through her hair, flapped her clothes. It smelt clear and pure. Safe. She tried to discern the building but its shape was lost among the shadows.

Archie also had a torch, and he'd taken a sports bag from the boot of the car and hoisted it over his shoulder. "This way, hin." His torch lit their path across the heath.

She followed closely, swishing through the long bracken. Insects chirruped around them. The ground was hard and uneven. She directed the beam ahead, picking out a corrugated hut sheltering on a gravelled plateau. Its walls and roof were streaked orange with rust. As they drew close she could make out a square window, obscured by cobwebs, reflecting back the light. It resembled a winking face.

Archie dragged the door open with a squeal of hinges. A damp brackish smell greeted them. Claire wrinkled her nose and shone the torch inside.

It was little more than a garden shed. Wooden shelves lined the walls, cluttered with dusty tools and cobwebbed-swathed jars. A chair stood in the centre. Archie took down an old paraffin lantern from the wall and used a match to light the wick. Its glass bulb threw out a softly pulsing glow, accentuating the shadows. Archie motioned to the chair. "Sit down, lassie. Might tek me a wee bit o' time tae dig, what wi' the ground being so hard."

Claire perched nervously on the rickety chair. Questions flooded her mind, but she was too weak to give voice to them. Her limbs ached. Archie wandered outside, carrying the bag. She fumbled her phone out of her pocket. The reception was still non-existent but she took comfort in seeing the names and numbers, reminders that she still had a life hundreds of miles south—albeit one that was slipping away far too quickly.

She heard the rattle of Archie's bag being tossed to the ground. He came back inside and picked up a spade from the corner. "What *is* this place?" she asked.

He looked around as if seeing it for the first time. "Just ma shed."

"You leave it unlocked?"

He shrugged. "There's nae one round here but me."

She blinked and watched him go outside again. The open doorway framed him in the light that spilled from the lamp. He began to dig.

As soon as he'd turned over several spadefuls of soil, the organic smell hit her. It was earthy and invigorating. She watched him for a long time. It felt wrong somehow, allowing an elderly man to endure such tough physical labour, but her own body was so weak she could contribute nothing but weary interest. She wondered if he was searching for some natural element to rub onto her skin. Would he soon embark on his crazy attempt at faith-healing? She pondered the inextinguishable allure of religion in these days of cutting-edge science. The futility of the situation was absurd.

She must have drifted off at some point because when she looked up she realised Archie had lost the bottom section of his body; he was still busy with the spade but the hole was now sufficient to conceal his legs below the knee. She stood and stretched, enjoying the popping sound in her joints.

He looked up at her. "Good timing. Here we are."

She frowned and stepped out of the hut. It was cooler outside, more energising. She could almost taste the electricity in the air. Archie stepped backwards out of the hole, shaking the soil from his boots. The pile of earth beyond him looked pale and significant. Even in the moonlight, the sheen of sweat was visible on his face. She was scared, filled with the fear that he'd dug a shallow grave in which to bury her, and she hesitated, staring at him with wide eyes.

He glanced up at her, but his face held no malice. "Ready?"

She could feel her heart pounding. It was so powerful she could almost hear it. She slowly approached the hole and looked down.

It was several feet deep. The smell was even stronger outside. Damp and unpleasant. Just visible below the top layers of soil she could discern a lighter material, stark against the darker earth. She glanced quizzically at Archie.

He nodded slowly. "It's okay, it's okay."

"What is it?"

He turned and looked towards the car parked on the roadside, then back to her. "You'll have tae dee this on yer own. I'll wait in the car."

She almost yelled. "What am I supposed to do?" Tension hardened her voice.

He moved back into the grass. "Take it in the shed. Close the door. Don't open it out here. Shout if yer need me." With that he was off, striding back to the car. She resisted the urge to chase after him. Instead she looked back into the hole.

It was certainly curious. But the speed with which Archie had departed frightened her. She swallowed audibly and tucked a loose strand of hair behind her ear. Carefully she stepped down into the pit.

Despite the dry weather, her feet sank into the soil. Hesitantly she poked her toe against the half-buried object, examining what Archie had uncovered. She brushed the earth away with the sole of her shoe.

It looked like a hessian sack. She could see narrow lines of soil caught in the coarse weave of the material. It was fastened at the top with a thick plastic cable-tie. She gripped the gathered bunch and pulled. Its considerable load caught her off-guard and she stumbled back, the edge of the pit connecting with the back of her thighs. She tried again, this time managing to drag the sack loose from the earth surrounding it. It dropped back as her strength ebbed. She took a deep breath and yanked it once more, scrabbling around for purchase. This time she managed to haul it against the side of the hole. It was a dead weight. She studied the bumps and protrusions in the sides of the bag.

She stepped up onto the level ground and bent to grasp it again. Her arms and shoulders were in agony. This time she straightened her back and lugged the thing clumsily out of the hole, dragging it against the edge and over. For an agonising second it teetered momentarily before dropping flat onto the grass. She exhaled loudly and looked up towards the car. Archie wasn't visible in the darkness.

For a few moments she regarded the sack. It looked faintly sinister in the moonlight. Instinctively she felt she shouldn't open it. She wrestled her fear—the real possibility that she'd be unable to resist doing just that—and felt her stomach lurch and her pulse quicken when she realised she might never see Pete again. She searched the moonlit heath as if he might materialise suddenly.

Swallowing, she grasped the neck of the bag and tested its weight. The coarse material implied strength and robustness. She dragged it towards the hut. The cumbersome thing flattened a wide trail of grass in its wake. She was breathless by the time she'd pulled it over the threshold. It slid marginally better on the dusty wooden boards. She kicked the chair aside to make room. She closed the door and regarded the sack while she caught her breath.

The dimness of the hut rendered the thing even more sinister. Claire noticed a second paraffin lantern hanging on the hook, and she moved to lift it down. And it was then, as she was caught in the act of reaching across the dusty bench to take it down, that something inside the sack wriggled.

She yelped in surprise and recoiled. The movement had been swift and unnerving. Like a jerk or a slither. She held her breath and stared at the sack, daring it to move again, half-telling herself that she'd imagined it.

Nothing. Everything was silent and still.

She lit the paraffin lamp and allowed its flame to settle, banishing the lurking shadows. Then slowly she approached the sack and began to tug the plastic cable-tie off the bunched top. Something shifted again inside, this time more subtly. Her hands trembled and the cable-tie almost slipped through her fingers, but she managed it somehow. Her heart was thundering. She allowed the top to fall back, revealing its contents.

It felt almost as if she were undergoing an out-of-the-body experience. She cocked her head and stared at the naked woman emerging from the sack, unable to comprehend what she was seeing. The woman shook off the cover, and the lamp illuminated her perfectly.

Claire stared in awe at the perfect image of herself. The woman in the sack was identical in appearance. A carbon copy. She gazed back serenely, unblinking, almost expectant. Claire pressed a hand to her own mouth, rocked back on her haunches. It was uncanny. The woman even shared the same thin scar on her chin; a souvenir from when Claire was 11 years old and her brother's cricket bat had accidentally struck her.

It was difficult to take in. The woman certainly *looked* real, but that couldn't be possible. There was something about her appearance—some barely perceptible element—that indicated things were not quite right. Claire studied the woman, marvelling at the physical detail that matched her own. However, it occurred to her that this strange figure looked perfectly healthy—how she might have looked without the cancer. She had the uncanny sensation that she was seeing a version of herself that had never cheated on Pete all those years ago, but had instead remained faithful and constant and happy. Uneasiness prickled her scalp. She brushed the thought away. Claire's eyes traced the familiar contours of flesh, and it was only then that it dawned on her that the woman's chest was not moving. She was not breathing.

Yet this did not disturb Claire. It just added to her sense of dislocation. She felt as if she was staring into a strange mirror. In fact, it seemed almost as she could see the present cancer-ridden version through the eyes of the *other* her, like a mirror reflecting another mirror until the image became lost to infinity.

The naked woman's eyes sparkled in the lamplight. *My eyes*, Claire insisted, blinking the grittiness away. *My eyes are sparkling.*

Claire reached out a trembling hand. Her arm was a lead weight. She hesitated for a split-second before making the final tentative movement to brush her fingers against the woman's cheek. It was cold. Unnaturally so. She shivered and fought the urge to withdraw.

The other woman lifted her arms and they embraced. Tears filled Claire's eyes, feeling hot and fierce. She allowed herself to be cradled. It was comforting, despite the coldness of the woman's skin. Her chest heaved. She drew in several lungfuls, feeling stronger with each breath. A sensation of vigour flowed through her body, gathering momentum as it swept into her limbs. She flexed her fingers. It was reassuring here in the woman's arms, but Claire finally looked up at the woman and nodded once. A tear spilled down her cheek.

Now the naked woman looked gaunt. Shadows pooled beneath dull eyes. Her hair had lost its shine. Sharp collarbones protruded through her sallow skin, making her resemble just a slender frame covered by a length of taut hide. She looked depleted. Unreal.

Claire stood and backed away. She felt the door behind her. The woman lay down on the sack, continuing to stare ahead, unblinking. Claire turned away, unable to look at the woman any longer. She opened the door and slipped outside.

The hole had been filled in. Now the loose soil resembled a freshly-dug grave. Someone—presumably Archie—had stacked a low pile of wood nearby, its gaps stuffed with kindling and rolled-up balls of newspaper. It looked like a funeral pyre. She was dizzy with uncertainty.

Archie approached across the grass, carrying a heavy axe. He drew close and studied her. "Aye." There was an air of satisfaction in his tone.

"What are you going to do?" she said.

He nodded to the right. "Pete's waiting up there. I'll take care o' the rest." He lifted the axe, pushed past her and went into the hut, closing the door behind him.

She glanced up to the right, feeling confused. Everything now seemed visible. The darkness had lessened. In the moonlight she could make out Pete's Focus parked on the highest ridge of the hill. It looked distant and small, yet its presence exerted a powerful force on her. A beacon of light in a vast desert of blackness. Her eyes traced the path that led upwards to the car. It would take her a long time, but she felt strong enough to make it.

*

She made her way up. Pete awoke with a jolt as she opened the door, rubbing sleep from his eyes. He blinked rapidly, staring at her in the meagre light. Scrutinising her.

"It's worked, hasn't it?" He licked his lips. "I can tell. You look different already."

She took a deep breath and watched Pete's cheeks bloom in excitement. He studied her closely. Her chest did seem strangely *unhindered*; clearer than it had felt in a long time. She turned and examined herself in the rear-view mirror. Her eyes were bright; the skin of her face looked healthier. The dry gauntness had been replaced by a warmer tone. Energy tingled her fingers. The aches had gone from her bones, replaced by strength and energy.

Life.

Pete took her hand. "Come on, let's get you home."

She thought, *I am home*, but she didn't say anything. Instead she leaned across so that her head was resting on Pete's chest. She could feel the warmth of his body, listening to the steady thrum of his heart. The position felt natural and welcoming. She reached out and switched on the cassette player.

And they sat together like that for a very long time, enjoying The Smiths, watching the first rays of sun creep over the distant horizon, burning through the morning dew that glistened the fields and jewelled the heather. It was going to be another beautiful day.

The Cambion

They were three hours south of the Tibesti Mountains when the storm hit. Cocooned within the shell of their Toyota land-cruiser, the first sign of its arrival was the shrill moan of wind against the vehicle's bodywork. Tiny particles of sand whirled in anticipation, gathering momentum as the storm began to flex its muscle. On the shimmering horizon to the west, where the endless arid plains gave way to Nigeria, the wind massed in purple clouds like a bruise.

They had crossed the border from Sudan to the northeast, cutting through the lower foothills of the Ennedi plateau in an effort to skirt the most inhospitable sections of the Sahara. The three Troop Carriers—formidable to behold—were rugged and lightweight despite their twin fuel tanks and cargo of personnel. Body-bags, aid equipment and government paperwork were stowed carefully in the interior. Flags fluttered from the vehicles' wings: their colour conferring status, promising safety. But this did little to reassure the occupants.

From the back window, Kate watched the sand spiralling in mini-funnels, moving like they were a living organism. The air was becoming hazy and red. Wind moaned around the windows and wing-mirrors, hurling sand against the bodywork in constantly ticking surges. They sounded like tuts of disapproval.

They'd traversed the eastern fringe of Chad, avoiding the countless Sudanese refugee camps that lay scattered along its border, maintaining a constant vigil for hijackers and militiamen. Their UN identification offered scant protection against the rife lawlessness that plagued the northern part of Chad. Political violence was as commonplace and indiscriminate as financial piracy.

Kate could see their destination on her map: an insignificant township lying just above the more fertile lowlands to the south.

The convoy was careful to stick closely together. Kate's driver had pinned a Koranic inscription to the back of his sun-visor—*Allah, the merciful, the compassionate, protect us from the bullets*—and he touched it at intervals and muttered the words like a mantra. They'd passed countless burnt-out villages and abandoned farms on their journey. It was obvious why Chad was sometimes referred to as the *Dead Heart of Africa.*

Their car rocked suddenly, and the female aid-worker in the passenger seat cried out in surprise. Fierce gusts of wind buffeted the vehicle. Simultaneously a hail of sand rained down on the windscreen, filling the gaps around the wipers until sections of the glass were obscured. The driver switched on the wipers but it did little to clear their view. Instead, the mechanism's discordant grind made Kate wince. They braked and coasted at a much slower speed. A babble of static burst from the radio. The driver grabbed it and answered in Arabic.

The woman in the passenger seat turned to Kate. She was the guide and translator, Kasifah. "We've hit the storm. We must slow for a while. It's too dangerous to continue at this speed."

Kate nodded and turned to look through the back window. The other vehicles had also slowed, still maintaining their close proximity but fanning out to avoid billowing dust from the wheels in front. She turned back to Kasifah. "We've enough fuel?"

The black-skinned woman nodded. "Easily. We can do a thousand kilometres on full tanks."

Kate sat back, satisfied. This would delay them, but it was too dangerous to continue as they were. She opened a manila folder and began reading her paperwork, allowing herself to become lulled by the uneven ground and the assailing wind. Her eyelids drooped.

*

It was dusk by the time they reached the village. The storm had taken an hour to pass through, an experience which made Kate nauseous. Constant bombardment by the sand and gales left her with ringing ears and a feeling of claustrophobia.

They'd been allotted rooms in a cinder-block building overlooking the main square. Dry sunlight had baked the town relentlessly all day. Now that darkness had swept in, the streets exuded heat. Thank God for the electricity generators. Kate lay on the modest bunk and did her best to unwind. The ceiling fan rocked rhythmically, trying valiantly to disperse the radiated heat. Through the shuttered window she could hear the distant chanting of Arabic scripture. It was usually a soothing sound, but this time the hysterical tone of the woman's voice seemed alien. Kate stood and walked to the window, unfastening the shutters. A string of coloured lanterns spanned each junction of the square, incongruous by their presence. Several townsfolk hurried along the street. The aftermath of the storm was visible everywhere — thick layers of dust coated everything; sand lay in drifts against the walls of buildings, making it look like they were half-buried. A row of empty market-stalls stood forlornly in the square, their canopies throwing angled shadows onto the ground. Several goats were tethered to a post in the corner. They constantly flicked their tails in an effort to discourage feeding insects from their bodies. One of them emitted a plaintive bleat; it sounded desolate, almost mournful.

Beyond the limits of the village, an impenetrable blackness seemed to lurk malevolently, smothering them in its grip. It felt like the rest of the world had been consumed. Kate had been in North Africa long enough to understand the patterns and rhythms of the weather; realizing the night was viewed as a welcome respite, allowing the land to gather its strength in readiness for the coming day. Nonetheless, it felt oppressive.

She decided to reread the notes from the manila folder. Just as she was drawing the shutters, she hesitated, catching sight of a figure emerging from the shadows of a doorway. It was clear he'd been observing her. He glanced away self-consciously and withdrew into the darkness, but not before she caught a glimpse of the furrowed scar distorting one side of his face and felt the penetrating weight of his stare.

*

Kasifah met her at the arranged time the following morning. Kate had spent a restless night, tossing and turning beneath the mosquito-net as the wooden slats of the bed creaked in protest. She felt irritable, in no mood for today's games. Kasifah handed her a cup of coffee, which she gladly accepted. It tasted earthy and organic.

"Qadim speaks English so I won't be allowed within his quarters", said Kasifah, sipping from her own terracotta cup. "But I'll accompany you in my official capacity." Despite the early hour, beads of sweat jewelled her brow.

They were sitting in a sparsely-decorated billet, adjacent to the building in which they'd slept. An electric fan whirred impatiently on the table. The room was dim. Beyond the shutters, sunlight bleached the colour from the world.

Kate took another gulp of coffee. "What do we know of him? The notes were vague."

Kasifah shrugged. "He's the town's Elder. Little is known of his background. It's rumoured that he was educated in England. He fought in Chad's civil war in the late 80s. This actual settlement's been established for nearly two decades. The Libyans razed the previous site—this present one grew from its ashes. In the last few years the population has swelled due of the Sudanese refugees. They're a mixed bunch—diverse languages, different backgrounds. It's quite unlike anywhere else."

"Religion?"

She shrugged again. "Difficult to say. Neither Islamic nor Christianity—I suppose because of the Arabic-French history. Despite the fact that their country teeters on the brink of an abyss, they remain strong. I don't need to remind you of the UN warnings of instability, of the threat of genocide, of further humanitarian requirements…"

Kate nodded absently. "That's not my concern today, though."

"I know." Her eyes met Kate's. They burned intently. "But please be careful. Qadim may not show a woman the same respect he'd show a man. I've heard him described as *al-ankabut*—the spider."

Kate finished her coffee. She grimaced. The dregs were teeming with gritty sediment. "Well let's see what he has to say, should we?"

The UN vehicle threaded slowly through the crowds lining the narrow streets. Sand billowed around them. The stark contrast between sunlight and shadow was disconcerting as the car negotiated the warren of alleys. The townsfolk stared at them as they passed, squinting against the dusty breeze. Kate felt like she was a specimen under their microscope.

In truth, Qadim's residence was quite within walking distance. Kate supposed the transfer by car afforded them a status of formality, a warning of officialdom. At one point they passed a wide plaza, bordered on three sides by crumbling buildings. A canopy of sheets had been erected across the yard—crude attempts at creating shelter from the sun. In the centre, a handful of men toiled in manual labour, their bare chests glistening with sweat. It appeared they were digging a hole. A huge pile of rocks was forming to one side. Two men wearing pale djellabas waved canes and barked orders. Just before the car passed beyond view, Kate caught sight of the scarred man from the previous night wiping his face on a towel. The muscles in his arms and his heavily-defined stomach seemed to mock her sense of modesty.

The car turned left at the junction and drove along a dusty back-street. They turned into a walled courtyard and drew to a halt outside a two-storey stucco building. The driver opened the door for Kate and Kasifah, who entered the building with a brisk step. Kate was carrying a sturdy attaché-case.

It was comfortably cooler inside. Their footsteps echoed on the terracotta tiles. A flight of steps rose to the left. The reception smelled of sandalwood and camomile. A large potted plant stood in one corner. Here was a visible sense of refinement that appeared to be lacking elsewhere in the village.

They were met by a smartly-dressed man who bowed and ushered them upstairs. They found themselves on a wide mezzanine.

He waved Kasifah to a chair and approached a door in the furthest wall, where he knocked once and popped his head round. He emitted a few staccato sentences in Arabic. Kate recognised one of the words as her name.

He turned and motioned for her to enter.

The room was dim. Shutters at the window allowed shafts of light to fall obliquely against the tiled floor. A swathe of patterned fabrics covered the rear wall. There was a huge table in the centre of the room, behind which sat a wrinkled man. He rose to greet Kate, motioning for her to take a seat. She flashed her identification card but he paid little interest. She declined his offer of a drink. He dealt with the pleasantries in a rather detached manner.

"Mr Qadim, I take it you understand why the UN have instructed me to visit you today?"

His eyes were heavily-lidded, almost reptilian. "The correspondence said it concerned my report on Khaleda Mahal's suicide."

"Among other things, yes."

"Then I'll cooperate however I can."

"Thank you." She took a breath and removed a manila folder from the attaché-case. "What can you tell me about Khaleda's personal history?—information that's not in the report, I mean."

He shrugged. "The woman admitted harbouring *impure* thoughts. Carnal lusts dogged her waking hours. At night her dreams were plagued by desire and immorality. She was weak—in a spiritual sense. Eventually she gave birth to a *cambion*."

"A…what?"

"Cambion—the product of a coupling between a woman and a demon."

Kate blinked several times, considering her next question carefully. "And what evidence do you have to suggest the child was…unnatural?—that it was born outside the marriage realm?"

He laughed dryly. "It's obvious that the woman's poor husband did not sire the cambion. Its physical appearance betrayed it."

"Wasn't it true that the woman admitted to an adulterous affair with a Norwegian aid-worker?"

He shrugged. "I know nothing about the woman's alleged unfaithfulness. All I know is that she confessed that an incubus visited her at night and they…cavorted several times."

"What happened to her?"

"Don't patronise me with your feigned ignorance, Miss

Walters—you've read the report."

"But I'd like to hear it from you. Off the record."

He performed a dismissive gesture. "The cambion was removed from the woman. She felt a great deal of shame once the truth emerged—understandably so. It's my belief that in the end she succumbed to a mental disorder."

"Why was the child taken from the woman?"

"To protect her. The creature is unearthly. Since its removal, we've kept its human contact to an absolute minimum."

"Your report said that the woman committed suicide?"

"I'm afraid so. Her mental state had deteriorated to the extent that she was being cared for by some women from the village. One night she gouged out her own eyes. Unfortunately by the time we discovered her, she'd died. We had her body transported to N'Djamena where the post-mortem was conducted independently."

"Wasn't there other signs of mutilation?"

"Yes, she'd scored something into the flesh of her body—the Arabic word for *whore*."

"The report said this mutilation was extensive."

"Indeed. It was scratched into her skin in many places."

"Thirty eight places, the report said."

"Possibly." He shrugged. "Clearly her guilt was overwhelming."

"But some of the words were scored into her back and on her shoulders—wouldn't that have been incredibly difficult to achieve by herself?"

He shrugged again. "I think it shows the depths of her despair. And the degree of mental instability we were faced with."

"You haven't answered my question—how could she physically manage to score that word into her back?"

"Miss Walters, mental illness can make those afflicted extremely resourceful."

The silence was impenetrable. Kate finally broke it. "Can you categorically confirm that she did this to herself?—That no one from the village committed this act of violence against her? She must've been viewed as a pariah."

"Miss Walters, we're a deeply religious community. Our society doesn't shun those in genuine need of support. But she yielded to a carnal weakness that allowed evil to take advantage. Her death was an unfortunate by-product of that flaw."

Kate said slowly, "Could it be that the truth was too ugly to face? That instead, superstition was used as a weapon?"

"There are ancient things out here in the desert, Miss Walters. Things your western mind wouldn't comprehend…"

"And what of the boy?"

"The cambion is being cared for in our orphanage."

"In solitary confinement, from what I hear."

"Only to protect the women who dedicate themselves to its care. Our orphanage houses many children whose parents have been victims of the atrocities that have occurred in the last few years. Miss Walters, this country is an unruly place. We've seen vast displacement of people from the surrounding countries. We've seen lawlessness and disease ravaging our communities. We've experienced the harsh reality of civil war. The life-expectancy here is forty-five years. We do what we can in these difficult times…"

"And is it true that the child has been condemned to death?"

Qadim stared at her in silence for a long time. "We cannot allow evil to flourish."

"What will happen to him?"

"It hasn't yet been decided."

"We've heard that he's scheduled to be stoned."

Qadim clicked his tongue. "Hearsay and supposition. I wish the UN would resist getting involved with hysterical rumour-mongering."

"We take this very seriously, sir. Lapidation is an extremely brutal way to die. We're talking about an eight year-old child."

"We're talking about a cambion—an *evil* being. It's not human. Its father was a demon. It exists to spread death and wreak madness."

"The UN is viewing this as a matter of huge significance. We warn you to proceed with the greatest care. Stoning is a horrific method of execution. It's unlawful in Chad. Amnesty International considers it particularly barbaric. I realise that Sharia Law dictates—"

"Miss Walters, I don't think you quite understand the nature of our religion. We are not Muslims, we're not Jews, neither are we

Roman Catholics. We follow the teachings of the Book of Kh'lei Rushnan—a prophet from the 14th century. Perhaps you should have studied our background a little better before coming here and interfering with our internal—"

"Sir, with respect, your religion is of no concern—though I am extremely mindful of it. But what does fall into my jurisdiction is the law of this country, and—"

"My people cower twice a day as the Antonov bombers fly overhead. They pray every time we're visited by the warlords that control this area. The wadi is half a mile east of here, and the women have to go out daily to fetch the water. We're used to the harsh realities of life. So don't pretend to take an interest in our welfare."

"That brings me to my next point. It could be advantageous for you to comply with the UN's request. We've arranged for a huge shipment of drinking water to be delivered—as long as the child is handed over to us."

He shrugged again. "Don't try to bribe me. We're already in the process of digging a well. Our religion's integrity cannot be bought."

"Mr Qadim, I just need to be sure that the community's religious beliefs operate within the boundaries of the law."

He blinked slowly, staring at an invisible spot on the table. "And we need to be sure that our faith isn't compromised by your western frailties. Because… in the absence of good, evil will find a way in."

*

The orphanage was a crumbling building on the outskirts of the village. It looked like it had once been used as a school. Now it was populated by a handful of nuns, several dour-faced local women and an army of children. They all wore pale, uncertain looks.

Kasifah and Kate had been shown to a sparse room on the first floor of the main building. The window was filthy, coated in dust and streaked with grime, allowing meagre light through. They sat at a scarred table and chatted, awaiting the arrival of the orphanage's head, Sister Josette.

Kate felt unnerved by the building's silence. She'd been expecting riotous noise, if any of the schools or orphanages she'd experienced back home had been anything to go by. But here it was more like a nursing-home or a hospital psychiatric ward; the footfalls were hushed, the air was tranquil and muted, punctuated by occasionally unhinged laughter or cries of despair from somewhere nearby. It was hardly a comforting place.

Sister Josette entered and greeted them briskly. They got straight to business.

"Abdul Malik has been with us since he was born, eight years ago. I believe his mother recently took her own life." Sister Josette's eyes were limitless, sad.

"We spoke to Mr Qadim. He seemed to suggest there was something…*unnatural* about the child?"

Sister Josette looked from Kate to Kasifah. She nodded uncertainly. "It's true he has a rather strange physical appearance. When he was born he had no breath, no pulse—he was cold as marble. They thought he was stillborn. He was placed in our care within days. He's been here ever since."

"Why? What about his parents?"

She pursed her lips. "His mother's mental state deteriorated. She was looked after too."

"Where?"

"By some of the local women."

"Were you aware of the woman's physical mutilation?"

"Yes, I heard about that. Bless her soul, she must have been under immense strain."

"What triggered it—after all these years, I mean?"

"I'm afraid I do not know."

"Could it be that she'd discovered her child had been condemned to death?"

Sister Josette cocked her head. "I don't think so."

"So he *has* been condemned to death?"

"Miss Walters, I try not to get involved with the running of the village. Our orphanage survives only because of the generous gifts that Mr Qadim bestows on us."

"There's no need to be afraid. We can offer protection from

him…"

"We're *all* afraid, Miss Walters. That *haboob* yesterday—the dust-storm—was an omen of your arrival. Yet our faith remains strong."

Kate studied the woman's face for a long time. Then she said at last, "May we see the boy?"

Sister Josette stood and moved to the window. Kate and Kasifah followed, glancing down into the courtyard.

It was empty except for a young boy sitting on a bench. He was playing with a toy train. He had pale skin and incredibly bright blond hair. It looked almost white. His face was placid and composed, reminiscent of the surface of a stagnant pool.

Kate shivered and rubbed her own forearm.

"Okay?" Kasifah looked concerned.

Kate nodded absently. "Think I'm coming down with a fever."

They turned from the window. Kate had the absurd sensation of being watched. As if the boy was aware of her presence and was looking up at the window, a smile touching his lips. "I think I'll head back and have an early night," she said. "I don't feel well."

*

The room is in darkness. Bedsheets cling to her skin, entwining her in their warm grip. The mosquito net hovers above her like a ghost. Even though it is night-time, the room is damp and unyielding. Kate's eyes are closed. Sweat coats her face, tickling the nape of her neck. The ceiling fan ticks out a rhythmic beat. She is naked beneath the covers. She is aware of the midnight sounds of the town—hushed voices on the street, a distant sudden barking, the occasional chirp of insects, muted laughter from somewhere nearby. She can hear the heavy tread of footsteps on the stairs. It feels like the noise is swelling, growing in stature as well as volume.

Through the haze of fever she opens her eyes and peers at the door. The handle slowly turns and a dark silhouette looms through the gap, filling the opening with a blackness that is insubstantial, ethereal. The figure closes the door and drifts towards the bed. She recognises it as the man with the scar. He looks as he did earlier, bare-chested and glistening. In the dim light she can see the harshly furrowed skin of his face.

A low gasp issues from her lips. She is not the least bit frightened. His eyes glitter in the darkness. She can see his biceps flex as he lifts the netting and ducks beneath it. He undresses and moves onto the bed. It squeaks under his weight. She can feel the heat radiating from his body. There is a faint aroma of sweat but it is not at all unpleasant; instead rather alluring. He moves up towards her.

Eager lips brush her cheek. She enjoys the feel of his stubble, a symbol of masculinity that causes her body to tingle in anticipation. The hot dampness is sensual and thrilling. Her skin almost erupts at his touch. Their bodies come together. She feels the molten tip of his heat against her thigh. She trembles, eagerly opening her knees to engage him in her wetness. Her legs are bathed in sweat. His tongue enters her mouth, probing her, tasting her. Her breasts feel like they might explode. And then he is inside her, and it's simultaneously the most pleasurable and most agonising sensation she has ever felt. Her groin feels like it has been soaked in gasoline and set on fire. She can see the steady rise and fall of his buttocks, his tanned back glistening with sweat. She clutches him as the tempo increases. She closes her eyes and arches her back. His thrusting is growing in rhythm, pushing into her deeper and deeper until it feels like they are becoming one and the same, physically conjoined almost. She grips the damp sheets. Frantic gasps escape her lips. Her stomach is in spasm, tensing as the waves of pleasure begin to build, pushing out from her groin to shudder through her body. She bucks involuntarily, biting her lower lip to prevent a moan. His thrusting is overriding any physical control she has for her own body. The most intense sensation of pleasure ripples through every single fibre and cell as she arches her back until the bones of her spine pop. And then, as she is almost completely overwhelmed by the power of her climax, she glances at him and sees not the muscular, dark-haired worker from the village, but a white-haired child. He glances down at her, smiling that thin-lipped smile, squinting that blue-eyed gaze.

She screams in horror and repulsion. The boy vanishes from her body. Out of her body. She pants in an effort to regain her breath.

Something moves in the corner of the ceiling. Kate peers up into the darkness. A monstrous spider crouches vigilant, almost a metre in

Kate woke suddenly, a shrill cry trembling on her lips. Her heart was thundering in her chest. She sat up in bed and glanced round the room. It was silent. She was alone. Her body was bathed in perspiration. She lay back against the pillow and closed her eyes, fighting the urge to look up at the corner of the ceiling. Sleep eventually came.

*

The ringing bell woke her. She'd spent a restless night, made uncomfortable by the vibration of the ceiling fan that seemed to mock her nightmare.

Instantly she sensed something wasn't right. She glanced at the clock, blinking away the threads of her dream. It was midmorning. She hurriedly dressed, throwing open the shutters. The square was deserted, but from somewhere nearby she could hear the clamour of voices. She rushed downstairs, her body aching, her limbs heavy. She blinked in the harsh sunlight, temporarily blinded. The voices were strident, growing in volume. She peered around the square. Directly ahead, a crowd was flowing into one of the numerous alleyways that criss-crossed the village. They were animated, moving with great purpose. Many of them were dressed in lightly-coloured djellabas, accentuating the sense of ritualistic ceremony. The blur of material was bewildering. Like a tide of sand. Some of the robed women chattered loudly to one other. This was very different behaviour to what Kate had seen thus far. The men— several of them bare-chested and dripping with sweat—bellowed and gesticulated, fighting to be heard over the clamour of voices. A gaggle of children capered around their legs, equally as lively. The focussed movement of the crowd seemed threatening.

Kate plunged into the horde, swimming against the current.

She was barged and knocked by bony shoulders and stray hips but she pushed her way through. The chatter was menacing in its intensity. She noticed that not everyone was full of life however, that a few people looked pale and unsettled. A woman stood to one side, retching onto the ground. Kate noticed tears in the eyes of several that passed. Absently she continued to barge her way through, eliciting yells and looks of disdain. Eventually she made it to the top of the alley. To her left the street rose at an incline as the buildings crowded together nearer the square. Sheets billowed on washing lines in every direction she looked, as if countless ghosts were closing in on her. The air was heavy with the smell of cooking food. She blundered along the narrow streets, unaware of her actual destination, knowing simply that the ringing bell signified something of great importance. She felt disorientated by the labyrinthine streets. Her chest burned. It seemed almost as if she were trapped in an ochre maze whose walls were trying to swallow her. Almost at once, just as she was beginning to feel the first moments of panic, she turned a corner and emerged into a dusty clearing. A low hill extended into the distance as far as she could see. And there, lying conspicuously on the ground, surrounded by piles of rocks and discarded stones, was what looked like a black ball.

Kate's heart thudded in her chest. She stepped forward absently. Despite the scorching heat, a piercing chill shivered down her spine. As she drew close she could hear the buzzing of flies, could smell a sickeningly organic odour. She dropped to her knees. A wail escaped her mouth. The silence was weighty, now she was detached from the village and the clamouring horde.

They'd buried him up to his neck. Blood stained the sand where it had gushed from the wounds. His features were so streaked with gore it was impossible to make out the individual components of his face. Most of the skin had been scoured away by the impact of the stones. The boy's neck was visible, tendons and cords stretched taut in his final efforts to evade attack. The sand around had been scuffed by him threshing. Stray clumps of hair and strips of flesh clung to many of the stones. Flies and ants were swarming all over the head but it was still possible to make out strands of white-blond hair beneath the teeming multitude.

Kate felt bile rise in her throat. She turned abruptly, shutting her eyes in an effort to purge the sight from her mind. Vaguely she was aware of cells dividing deep inside her aching body.

And from somewhere in the village came the joyous chime of the bell, and the jubilant tremor of voices raised in exultation.

Happy Sands

They'd said on the radio that Bruce Springsteen had died so Fallen was in a foul mood by the time he reached Morecambe. He was desperate to escape the confines of the car. Springsteen's music had been streaming on every station, and a morose feeling had accompanied him on his journey north.

He parked on an area of waste-ground and stared out across the bay, watching gulls soar in a sky the colour of a fresh bruise. Grey mudflats stretched away towards the sea; an expanse of sand that appeared deceptively benign, yet Fallon remembered how as a child he'd heard about those Chinese cockle-pickers that had drowned by a swiftly incoming tide.

The view from the headland had barely changed since he'd stood there as a boy, his dad trying valiantly to fly their kite in the gales that buffeted the bay. It felt timeless, constant, undeviating.

Fallon made his way down the incline towards the rendezvous, where a sagging chain-link fence ran the perimeter of the site. As he drew near to the corner he could make out a thin figure sucking fiercely on a cigarette. The man had a shaven head and eyes that were so hollow it looked like they were retreating into his skull. He tossed the cigarette down and crushed it underfoot. He made Fallon stand against the fence while he frisked him in belligerent silence. Once he was satisfied that Fallon was clean, he at last spoke. "You're late." He rubbed his nose. He was a real twitchy fucker, the kind Fallon had encountered many times before. His skin was sallow and pock-marked. The few teeth he had were brown.

"They said that Bruce Springsteen's dead," said Fallon quietly. "Heart failure."

The man shrugged. Fallon wasn't sure whether the gesture meant he didn't know who Springsteen was or he just didn't care.

Either way Fallon wanted to punch him until his eyes bled.

They ducked beneath a breach in the fence and made their way across the overgrown field. A large wooden sign faced what would once have been the entrance driveway, now just a narrow track stretching between a jungle of waist-high grass. The lettering had been obliterated by time and decades of harsh weather but Fallon knew the sign had once welcomed guests to *Happy Sands Holiday Camp*. His childhood memories felt intrusively odd, given the reason for this particular visit.

"I used to come here as a kid." He studied a dilapidated line of chalets, their smashed windows gaping like a row of hungry mouths.

"It's a shit-hole."

"It is now, yes."

A bell-shaped swimming pool lay ahead of them. Decades' worth of rainfall had accumulated inside it, the shallow black water choked with rotting weeds and stagnant sludge. Moss had obscured its tiles. A tennis court stood to their left, now just a fence-enclosed rectangle, its net obscured by overgrown grass. It looked like an abandoned zoo enclosure. Wind soughed across the valley, buffeting the unkempt bushes, swaying the limbs of the trees. Fallon spotted the crumbling shell of the concert hall ahead. It was originally built to resemble a luxurious ocean liner but little of its grandeur remained. The level of degradation was shocking. Once an ambitious and striking building, it now looked ugly and forlorn. Sections of the felt roofing had peeled back to reveal damp grey concrete beneath. The guttering had cracked and broken in two, trailing detritus down the walls like a bloodstain. Wrought-iron railings were streaked with rust and moss. Rows of port-hole windows looked out onto different levels, the few that remained intact now coated in filth, cobwebbed and grimy.

Fallon followed the man down the crumbling steps towards the building. The glass door had been boarded with metal panels, standing ajar like a primed trap.

As soon as they passed through into the reception Fallon wrinkled his nose at the overpowering smell. Decay and neglect. Decades of abandonment. Puddles on the floor reflected the nicotine-coated ceiling. Sodden cardboard boxes were strewn across the reception area, their contents long-removed. Fallon could see wan daylight spilling through the plywood panels of the interior door.

They stepped through into the main concert hall. A stage had been built at the far end. Thick sheets obscured the windows, blocking the outside world. Despite the size of the room Fallen felt mildly claustrophobic. A frail balcony extended two-thirds of the way around the first-floor level. Fallon tried to see what was at the back of the stage but the darkness there was impenetrable. A pair of lighting rigs had been erected at each side. Instinctively he noted the location of the emergency exits.

The hall was smaller than Fallon had remembered, although back then it had been crammed to the rafters with sweaty holidaymakers and cola-guzzling kids. Someone had thrown the windows open in a futile effort to channel the warm August breeze. The air had been hazy with cigarette smoke. In the expectant hush before the show was due to commence, the tidal sounds from the nearby beach had been reassuring, tranquil, constant.

"Wait here." The thin man walked across the chipped floor to the stage, and disappeared behind the curtains.

Patches of mildew coated the sagging ceiling tiles, several of which were missing. The hall reeked with neglect.

One of the lights buzzed into life, followed a split-second later by the other. It lent everything a pallid hue.

"Brought the money, Mr Fisher?"

Fallon turned. A figure stood on the balcony, above where they'd entered. He was dressed in a grey pinstripe suit. He began walking to the stairs with an exaggerated air of confidence. It was clear he fancied himself as some sort of wide-boy businessman; a Bond villain or a member of the Mafia. To Fallon he just looked like a middle-aged accountant—sad and impotent, unused to dealing with the grim realities of life.

"Of course." Fallon patted his jacket pocket.

The man reached the bottom of the stairs and languidly crossed the floor. There seemed to be little point to the manner of his entrance; it was as clichéd as his dress sense, an effect.

"Mr Dimitri, I take it?" said Fallon.

"Glad to make your acquaintance, Mr Fisher. Charlie here will unburden you."

The thin man had reappeared from behind the stage.

"After I see the goods."

Dimitri tutted. He studied his nails. "Come, come—we're all professionals here, Mr Fisher. This isn't some market in Marrakesh, you know."

Fallon nodded. He supposed it was all irrelevant anyway.

The thin man approached and Fallon handed him the plastic bag from his pocket. He retreated a few steps and peered inside it for a few moments before nodding at his boss. "It's all there."

"Excellent," said Dimitri. "My employer's always happy to do business with like-minded individuals, Mr Fisher."

"He took a while to set this up."

"Nevertheless you're here now." Dimitri smiled. "But before we proceed, I hope you don't mind if we dispose of the falsities and allow me to address you by your real name—*Mr Robert Kent?*"

Fallon smiled wryly. "You got me." The fake driving licence in his wallet supported this Kent identity but it was there solely as protection.

"Now that we find ourselves on an equal footing, what say we show you the merchandise?" Dimitri nodded to Charlie, who disappeared behind the stage again.

"I've taken the liberty of bringing our tech guy," said Dimitri. "Just in case you have any questions."

A chubby man in his mid-twenties stepped onto the stage. He was dressed in brown cords, a satin waistcoat and a pair of training shoes. "Hi there."

Fallon raised an eyebrow in response. So, three men at least; probably only one of them armed. It was unlikely Dimitri and the geek would be carrying, but the bulge around Charlie's hip suggested a semi-automatic; un-holstered by the angle and shape. Fallon had laid his trail of online breadcrumbs to perfection; he was confident their suspicions wouldn't be high.

"Go ahead then," said Dimitri.

"Okay." The tech guy cleared his throat. "I mean, like, most of this technology started back in the early twenties. There were, like, a few companies out in San Jose working on AI back at the turn of the century but—err—it's really only the last ten years that we've seen it reach this level. Hmmm…the version we've got here is, like, a CP209FL, originally developed by ComCorp in—"

"Look, let's cut the lecture," said Dimitri, with a sharpness to his voice. "He can download all this if he wants to. All he cares about is how realistic it is."

"Fine." He turned to one side, looking past the stage, beyond Fallon's line of sight. "Here, here. C'mon."

Fallon held his breath and watched as a young girl stepped out from behind the curtain. She appeared to be about 10 or 11 years old. Dirty blonde hair framed an ashen face, lit up by a pair of blue eyes. She was wearing faded denim jeans, a white shirt with a sports logo on the front and a pair of leather shoes.

Fallon released his breath through his nose. It wasn't her. The relief gave way to thinly-veiled rage. "Can I see?"

"Of course, of course," said Dimitri. "Charlie." He made a gesture with his hand.

The skinny man grabbed the girl by the arm and almost pulled her down the steps of the stage. He stood her in front of Fallon. This close, he could see her blue eyes were flecked with green. The skin on her face was freckled. There was a tiny mole on her left earlobe. She peered at Fallon, blinking at the lighting rig behind him.

"It's perfect, isn't it?" said Dimitri. "It looks real."

Fallon didn't speak. He could see the natural tangle of hair on her head, watched her chest rise and fall as if she was drawing breath.

"There's a regulator inside that will alter the depth of its respiration, depending on movement. During synthesised sleep its breath will be very deep. It can even snore, should you require it." Dimitri addressed Charlie again: "Show him what else."

Charlie lifted his right hand and slapped the girl's face. She let out a gasp, her head snapping back with force. The area of impact bloomed red, her breath hitched and sobbed. There appeared to be tears in her eyes. She blinked more rapidly. She raised a hand to her cheek.

"Of course the emotional response can be regulated to accommodate your requirements." Dimitri stepped close to Fallon. "It can be as compliant…or as *resistant*…as you like."

"You can pretty much do what you like," the fat guy chimed in. "The skin can be replaced, the alloy skeleton inside can be reattached if it gets damaged."

"For a small fee, of course," Dimitri said. "Although membership of The Acolytes allows you unlimited servicing for up to one year free of charge. You'll also have admission to The Acolytes' secure hub with 24 hour access, and be able to download all material at no extra cost."

Fallon watched as a tear brimmed on the girl's lower eyelid then dropped onto her cheek. She brushed it away with the back of her hand.

"Incredible, isn't it?" Dimitri's feigned admiration was sickening.

Fallon glanced away from the girl and addressed Dimitri. "Any chance I can get another one?"

"What's wrong with-?"

"Not a different one—I mean another one. A second one." Fallon shrugged. "Twins."

Dimitri absently scratched the back of his own head. "That's going to take some time to sort. These things aren't lying around all over the place, you know."

"I'll make it worth your while."

Dimitri pursed his lips. "Let me see what I can do. I'll make a call. Back soon." He walked to the rear of the hall and went out into the reception.

Fallon returned his attention to the girl. She was blinking naturally, her movement far more realistic than he'd ever imagined. This was a far more advanced model. He lifted his hand and felt the back of her head, a gesture which caused her to flinch. He could feel the indentation at the base of her skull where the microboard was installed. Her neck felt cool due to the synthetic skin.

The fat guy spoke up. "Err—we permanently wiped the rootcode chips so it's untraceable. There's no signal router so as long as you keep it private, it'll stay private—no WiFi snare will detect it."

"Where'd you get her from?"

Fat guy shrugged. "Does it matter?"

"S'pose not." Fallon turned back to the girl but took advantage of the angle to study the skinny man again out of the corner of his eye. The handgun was definitely tucked into his waistband. Fallon memorised which side. He ran through the imagined scenario in his head several times, mentally rehearsing the manoeuvre until he was confident he could perform it.

"It passes the Turing Test," said the fat guy, "if that's what you're thinking?"

Fallon nodded. "Does she know she's a machine?"

"Nope. Not that advanced. It's programmed to be a little girl so it'll behave like a little girl."

"Ain't she purty?" The skinny fuck drawled the line in a mock hillbilly accent.

Fallon was just about to retort when the sound of Dimitri's return silenced him. The suited man strode across the hall, tucking his phone into his pocket. "I just spoke with my employer and we could probably let you have another model to go with this one. The…errr…price would be significantly higher for a second though."

"Fine."

"And you'll need to allow us time to acquire and modify it."

"Yeah."

Now Dimitri had made the call Fallon felt his composure changing. The *softly-softly* part was over; it was time to wrap things up. He could feel his heart thudding. His mouth was dry. He spoke deliberately low: "When exactly will the other be ready?"

Dimitri came closer in an effort to hear. "A month or so."

"Okay." Fallon stared in silence at the girl for a moment, steeling himself.

"Do you have any further questions before you leave? Kai here can wipe the system clean before you take it, just so you'll start with a fresh slate, so to speak?"

Fallon glanced at the men. "You shouldn't really be formatting her behavioural chips. They're not designed for that. It'll cause malfunction."

"I assure you, Mr Kent, it's in perfect working order. Besides, the terms of your Acolytes membership means you're guaranteed whilst your service agreement is in place."

"She'll have to continually relearn stuff—people's names, where she's living, what she likes—even her own name. It's damaging to keep resetting her."

"You don't *have* to reset it. Keep the chips active," said Dimitri. "But believe me, it's probably kinder if the chips *are* reset. Some of these machines experience some pretty extreme activity. I know— I've seen some of the videos."

"It just seems fucked-up, that's all…"

"Mr Kent, our clients benefit from the freedom of role-play without the consequences of criminal prosecution. This is not a living person. It's not a real child. Some of our members just want to experience how it feels to totally dominate another human being. Others have rather more…carnal desires, should we say." Dimitri clicked his fingers. "But then the button can be pressed— to undo what's been done. No lasting damage to the subject, guilt-free pleasure for the owner."

"The AI chips in these things are meant to aid personality evolution," said Fallon. "There's a circuit in there that stores everything. She'll remember things that have happened, and her behaviour will alter accordingly. It's not something you can just reset so your conscience can be erased."

"Mr Kent, that's exactly what makes it all the more realistic." Dimitri sounded like he was unveiling his winning hand. "It's just like a real child. You can do whatever you want with it, without breaking the law. And who are we to judge those that have a need for this? If no law is being broken, where's the harm—"

"Well technically the law *is* being broken." Fallon realised he was squaring his jaw. "These machines were built to replicate childlike behaviour in an effort to help grieving parents deal with loss. They're a short-term bereavement aid."

"Mr Kent, can I ask why you've gone to the trouble of coming here if you have a problem with the ethics of it? I would've thought that someone with a predilection such as yours wouldn't be troubled by outside concerns. This is a matter for nobody but the two parties involved. One of those parties is a real person, the other a mere machine."

Fallon slipped his hand into his pocket and gripped the car key in his palm, allowing the shaft of the key to protrude between his fingers. He took a deep breath and made a sudden twist to his left, throwing a punch at the skinny man. The key pierced his windpipe with a spray of blood, knocking him back onto the floor. He rolled around, screaming and clutching at his throat as blood bubbled between his fingers. With his other hand he frantically pulled the gun from the waistband of his trousers but Fallon kicked it away and picked it up himself. He turned and shot the skinny man in the stomach. The noise was deafening. The man stopped moving, blood continuing to seep from his neck. Fallon's ears rang with a low hum. There was an overpowering smell of cordite.

The girl was crouched with her hands over her ears. Fallon turned on his haunches and surveyed the hall. The fat guy had vanished. Dimitri was running towards the back entrance. Fallon aimed the red laser sight at him and fired twice, wincing at the weapon's recoil. The fleeing man dropped like a sack of bricks.

Fallon stood. The little girl was whimpering now. He turned and hopped up on to the stage, diving behind the curtain. It was dark backstage, and confined. Further along the passage a fluorescent light flickered madly, creating a nightmarish pattern of strobing images. Some distant part of his brain wondered where the electricity was coming from. He stepped forward, knocking against boxes, the edge of a table, a stack of chairs. His finger tensed on the trigger for the slightest movement as he reached the corridor.

The stretch of green lino was blistered and cracked. The once-white ceiling tiles were coated in cobwebs and mildew. A red fire-door stood closed at the far end. The door to the left had a tarnished plaque declaring it a *dressing room*, whilst the door opposite was open, revealing a cramped kitchen area smelling of sour milk and stagnant water.

Fallon kicked the door of the dressing room open and leaned in, his gun pointing the way. The room was empty. Just a solitary chair and a dressing table, the wall-mirror blotched and cracked. He caught his breath and thought for a moment. Then in the silence he heard a ragged breathing from the kitchen. He went to investigate.

The fat man was crouched beneath the counter next to a rusting fridge. He stared up at Fallon and closed his eyes, wincing, awaiting the inevitable with a resigned look of defeat. Fallon turned his face away and pulled the trigger. The shot echoed in his ears for a long time.

By the time he had made it back to the hall, Dimitri had gone. The little girl was still crying. Fallon leapt down off the stage and ran towards the door. There was a bloodstain leading all the way through to the reception. He followed it.

Dimitri had managed to drag himself out of the building and up the steps. Fallon found him close to the derelict swimming pool, face-down, motionless but breathing shallowly. The back of his jacket glistened with blood. His eyes had taken on a milky glaze. Froth bubbled at the corners of his mouth.

Fallon reached down and searched Dimitri's pocket for his mobile phone. It was still powered up. The older man's breath wheezed in his chest. "Fucker."

"Who's your boss?"

Several sighs and shudders. A spasm in the man's chest.

"Who's your boss?"

Dimitri smiled sickly and closed his eyes. Fallon looked up towards the hill where he had parked his car. His eyes traced the outline of the landscape. It was nearly dark. He could taste the salty tang of the sea on his lips. He placed the gun against Dimitri's temple and pulled the trigger, spraying the paving stones with its contents.

Fallon scrolled through the call log of the phone. The most recent entry displayed a number which he punched into his own phone. He rolled Dimitri's body with his foot, tipping it into the pool with a muddy splash. The black water was not quite deep enough to cover it entirely.

He strode back down to fetch the little girl. He tears had stopped, but her face was streaked with dirt, her eyes bloodshot and red.

"What's your name?"

She shrugged, blinking. "Ella." She looked confused.

"Come on, Ella." He held out his hand and she took it. They walked back to his car. He watched her movement, noting how she appeared to calm down after being outside for a few minutes. Her breathing increased as they made their way up the incline. She reacted naturally to the sudden caw of nesting gulls from somewhere nearby.

Once they were in the car Fallon synced Dimitri's phone with an app on his own. The final number from the call log began flicking through the search engine. While they waited, Fallon switched on the radio, remembering the news about Bruce Springsteen, feeling the crush of misery settle back onto his shoulders. He suddenly felt exhausted.

"Are we going?" asked Ella. She was in the back.

"In a bit."

"What is your name?"

He hesitated for a moment, checking the rapidly scrolling display of his phone. "It doesn't matter." He sounded distracted.

He turned and looked at the girl again. After a moment he began flicking through the images on his phone until he found a particular one. He studied the photo for a minute and then compared it with the girl.

"Is that your wife and daughter?"

He blinked. "No. We had a daughter but she died a long time ago."

"Oh."

"This was the…we were given this girl for a while, to help us come to terms with what had happened."

"A replacement?"

"Not really. Just to help us let go."

"I see."

"But she was stolen, sold into the black market. I'm looking for her. Been looking for her for ages."

"Will it make you happy if you find her?"

His eyes never left the phone's screen. "I suppose so. I won't bring my daughter back… but it's the next best thing."

"Is your wife helping to look, too?"

He frowned, then looked up. "My wife always blamed herself for what'd happened. She died last year."

They were both silent for a while, listening to the music. Moths swirled in the car's headlights. He could see her reflection in the windscreen, could almost convince himself she was the one he was looking for. Almost, but not quite.

The phone chimed. Fallon picked it up and stared at the display. The number he'd punched in was highlighted; beneath it a set of coordinates and an address in Middlesbrough.

He started the car. "Sit back, we've got quite a drive." He checked the handgun. The clip was nearly empty so he replaced it with a fresh one. It felt good in his hand, comfortable. He turned up the music, tapping the steering wheel in time to *Thunder Road*.

In no time at all he was cruising purposefully along the A683, heading east.

Rapid Eye Movement

Lochran is two hours into his night-shift when the news breaks. The radio channel he usually tunes to—a local station with thirty songs on its play-list and a carousel of cheaply-made ads—interrupts the nightly phone-in with a hastily constructed newsflash. Lochran listens to the newsreader's taut voice with a growing sense of unease.

He pats the pockets of his boiler-suit. *Damn.* He's left his phone back in the office. He stands still for a minute, listening; absorbing the report. Once it's finished he kills the radio and stares blankly round the deserted factory floor. Just the usual mechanical stutter from one of the pistons, an occasional grind of gears from the motors. But above the typical work-noise is something quite alien: a hubbub of voices.

Lochran walks out through the double doors into the storage yard. It is a warm Tuesday night in July. An almost-full moon is suspended in the cloudless sky. Normally he would expect to hear traffic from the main road, even at 10 o'clock. But tonight the roads are quiet. He can hear a cacophony of voices from further down the street, too animated for him to pick out individual words.

He hurries back to the office to fetch his phone. He presses the speed-dial for HOME but the number won't connect. He listens to an automated voice telling him the network is currently unavailable. He picks up the handset of the office landline, but there is no dialling tone.

He locks the factory door and hurries to his car. Now the radio has stopped. They are just broadcasting a looped automated message advising that transmission has been interrupted due to circumstances beyond their control.

Shit.

His home is twelve miles away; roughly a 20 minute drive

through the city at this time of night. He floors the accelerator and squeals out of the yard.

The streets are just as empty as he first thought. But lights burn in every window. People wearing worried masks huddle together on the pavement. He sees some of them weeping.

By the time he draws close to home, things start to change: screaming sirens come at him from all sides, the Doppler-effect confusing him with its randomness. Countless windows reflect the flashing blue lights as ambulances strobe past. Figures are streaming along the pavement, looking for answers but finding nothing. Lochran's radio is still not broadcasting. The phone network remains out of action. Traffic is beginning to choke the roads, driven by dazed-looking ghosts. A crowd of people stand outside the corner-shop, passing armfuls of energy drinks through the broken window. Wide eyes, furrowed brows, tear-streaked faces. The car's headlights pick out broken glass littering the ground.

He skids to a halt outside his own house. Lights burn upstairs and down. Lochran's stomach is molten liquid. Their elderly next-door neighbour stands on her doorstep, furiously smoking a cigarette. She is wearing a pink dressing-gown. He hurries along his garden path but she doesn't seem to notice him. He can hear her muttering passages from the Bible.

It is silent inside his house. He pauses in the hallway, staring up the stairs. "Simone!"

"Here." The relief in her voice makes it almost unrecognisable. He pushes open the living-room door and enters.

Simone is standing in the centre of the rug. She is wringing her hands, moving from one slippered foot to the other. Her eyes are huge, her movement frantic. She looks like she has been stricken with Bell's palsy; the skin on her face is slack. "Dean. Dean. Dean."

He hugs her. Over her shoulder he can see that the television is switched on, displaying the static test-card. He feels a surreal sense of dislocation—it's the version from his childhood, the one with the girl and the strange puppet playing noughts and crosses. The colours in its border look vivid and garish.

"What can we do?" He feels her shivering against him. She is wearing those pyjamas he bought her for Christmas.

"What's happened?" He studies her face. "Have you seen the news?"

She nods silently. Her lower lip trembles. When she speaks, her voice is husky and monotone. "It was on the ten o'clock news. People have been dying in their sleep. Thousands of them. In Australia. They say this might be the end."

Lochran swallows audibly. "The radio said not to go to sleep. Try to stay awake."

She nods, her movement dreamlike, ethereal. "I've just had some black coffee. Don't know what else to do..." She steps back and stares at Lochran. A single tear glistens on her cheek. "I don't want to go to sleep."

"Don't be silly," he says, "we'll stay here together until they sort it out."

"Who?"

He shrugs. "The government. They'll be working on something."

She angles her head and blinks slowly. Like she is addressing a child. "Dean, you don't get it—they said on the news that once you go to sleep, you don't wake up."

He thinks about what he heard on the radio. The grave tone of the newsreader, his voice tinged with hysteria. An estimated death-toll so large its number sounded meaningless. He also thinks about the fact that he woke up at 6pm—his regular routine when he's on nights—and still feels fresh. He notices Simone's bloodshot eyes. He knows she's normally in bed by eleven. "The radio said it happens if you fall into a certain stage of sleep—REM sleep, they said. We'll try to keep each other awake until they come up with something."

A faint spark lights in her face. "We could just have short naps, wake each other up before we go too deep. That might be okay."

He nods at her, but he knows that it won't work. They are too tired. The newsreader said that the REM state occurs sooner than normal if the patient is tired.

Music suddenly starts up from somewhere several houses away. The walls almost vibrate with the deafening volume.

"Jesus Christ!"

"Simone, leave it. They're probably just trying to stay awake."

She looks crestfallen. "Oh. Yeah." As if the noise had jolted her out of a bad dream. Just as it dawns on her that she *isn't* dreaming. *This is real.*

"Come on, let's have some tea." Lochran walks into the kitchen. The main lights are on. The worktops are cluttered, in disarray. He switches on the kettle to boil, and busies himself with preparing the tea. A dog is barking somewhere outside. He notices the radio next to the toaster, and tries it but it is just broadcasting static.

Simone looms in the doorway. "Maggie'll be asleep now..."

Lochran pours the milk into the cups, carefully measuring out the correct amount. He's been dreading the mention of her sister; he's already thought about the fact that Tokyo is nine hours ahead of them.

"Listen, love, we don't know that." His voice is gentle. "The news will've broke all over the world so they'll know–"

"But it was only after Australia didn't wake up that they realised there was a problem—that's too late for Japan. It'll be morning now."

He puts the milk away and drops two teabags into the cups, unsure of what to say.

"I don't want her to... die in another country." Simone's voice cracks and she bows her head. He hugs her, rubbing her shoulders.

"Love... Sim, love, if... if they *are* asleep... at least she'll be with Neil." He thinks about his brother-in-law, suddenly coming to terms with what is happening. He likes Neil. They had some laughs.

"I wish she was here, instead of a foreign country." Her breath is hitching.

"I know, love. I know." He holds her for a few minutes while the sobs subside.

The dog is still at it; a plaintive soundtrack to the last hours of their world.

*

Lochran is watching the digital clock, counting the seconds in his head as the minutes change, trying to synchronise his internal beat with that of the machine. He wonders how long the power will continue, once everyone is gone.

"Another coffee?" Simone has just had her second shower. It is 2.19am. Normally he would be on his break at this time, probably reading the paper. Maybe eating his crisps. He nods at her.

The main road is visible from the window. Traffic is gridlocked. About half an hour ago a fight broke out. It was finished quickly. Now people are stepping over something lying on the pavement.

Lochran has given up all hope of getting help. Everything, the radio, television, phone networks, the internet, they are all still down. He realises the last Facebook status he posted was on Saturday—a photograph of his lunch. He'd laugh if it wasn't so pathetic.

The dog fell silent an hour ago. Lochran blinks slowly. He can hear the sound of Simone making coffee in the kitchen. Those noises, which before seemed so mundane, now feel important. He imagines how a candle must look when it's burnt down to its end.

Simone brings the drinks up to the bedroom. He smiles as she enters, tries not to let his expression betray what lies in his heart. Her face looks drawn and depleted. Her skin is sallow, black hollows shade her eyes. They sit together on the bed, nursing the warm mugs in their hands. She rests her head on his shoulder. He can feel her warm breath on his chest. Abruptly, they hear a woman wailing from next door. It is Edith, one of their elderly neighbours. She is crying her husband's name over and over. *Frank, Frank, Frank, Frank, Frank.* It goes on for an interminably long time.

Lochran closes his eyes for as long as he dares, stroking Simone's hair.

*

Simone is switching between periods of nausea and intense bursts of energy. Her mood is almost giddy. Perversely, it's the most upbeat she's been in years. She bounces on the bed, laughing when he warns her that she'll ruin the springs. She's playing her favourite CD. She sings in her tuneless voice, something that Lochran once found so endearing. He realises he hasn't heard it in ages.

"Do you wish we'd had kids earlier, rather than waiting?" He is suddenly conscious he may have broken her mood.

She stops and considers the question soberly. "Not really. I don't think I could cope with... this."

He nods slowly. "I know what you mean."

"Kids would just make this a hundred times worse."

"Yeah, I suppose." He recognises a sense of melancholy has crept in again. It was last here about two hours ago. "I keep thinking about things I've done, things I shouldn't have done."

She looks sharply. "What I *do* regret is not going to Florida this year. We should have just fucking gone anyway."

"You wanted the new kitchen." He feels a total shit for saying it.

"For all the good it'll do us now..." She shakes her head.

"But what good would a holiday have done us? It'll still be the same in the end." Lochran pictures their kitchen, the layout of the house downstairs. He decides he will stay here now, spend what time he has left upstairs.

She says the next thing very carefully. "But isn't that the case anyway? Otherwise what's life for? I can see that now." She sniffs. "Now it's too late."

The digital clock says 4.43.

*

They can hear a commotion from the back garden. Lochran stands, feeling the pins and needles flexing through his calf muscle. They hurry into the back bedroom—the one they always referred to as the spare room, but which they both hoped would one day be the baby's room—and peer out of the window.

There is a figure in the garden that backs onto theirs. The sun has risen. The sky has that unnaturally bright distance, like it does in films. The land is still dark. Lochran sometimes sees this effect when he's on nightshift. The new day emerging.

The figure is the middle-aged man from the house across the way. They don't know his name. The only contact they've ever had was several years ago. It involved a rather bitter argument over land boundaries, and whose responsibility it was to replace some fence panels that had blown down. Lochran ended up seeing to it out of sheer frustration.

The man is shouting at the sky. *Fuck you. Bastards. Fucking bastards.* He is carrying a red canister. He is shaking it in the air, all around his chest and shoulders. He holds it above his head and it is only then, as they see his wet hair and the glistening dampness on his shirt and the spreading darkness of his jeans, that they realise what he is doing. Simone gasps and covers her mouth with a hand. The man tosses the canister away and fumbles for a moment as he removes something from his pocket. He takes out a match and strikes it on the box and there is a roar which they hear from up in the bedroom. The man's upper body is engulfed in a bright ball of flames. Simone turns away quickly. Lochran hugs her, but he cannot tear his eyes away from the sight. The burning man flails his arms, staggering around in a tight circle like he's drunk. He shouts something again—this time unintelligible—and drops to his knees. Lochran squints. The fire is so intense in the pre-dawn light that it sears an image into his retinas. The man continues to pump his arms around hysterically. Eventually he falls face-forward onto the grass and lies there, still twitching as the fire ravages what's left of him. Lochran watches until the man stops moving.

*

Simone is just finishing her third shower when Lochran notices the burst blood-vessels in her eye. She is drying herself in the bathroom. He pops his head round the door to see if she wants anything to eat. She looks at him, shaking her head. He notices the white of her left eye spoiled by the dotted fragments of red. It makes her look different.

He is eating some toast in the bedroom when she comes in. She is wearing the dressing-gown, and carrying a towel.

"Why do you think he did that?" She motions with her head to the back of the house.

Lochran shrugs. "I don't know. Frustration? Raging against the hopelessness of it all, I suppose."

She is drying her hair. "What good did that do? Nothing—

that's what."

Lochran doesn't know what to say.

She continues. "Impotent, that's what we are. Just waiting for the inevitable. Killing yourself won't do any good."

"Inevitable means we'll die eventually anyway. But that's life. We know that."

She nods once.

He looks at her. "Aren't we supposed to do something...*profound.* Like make love or something?"

She laughs, and it cheers him incredibly to hear it. A thin smile touches her lips. She sneers theatrically. "Nah—to be honest I'd rather just watch a film. Coen Brothers. Or a Hitchcock."

He returns her smile and reaches out for her hand. "I love you."

They close the curtains and lie on the bed. Lochan goes to fetch a DVD.

*

Someone is yelling outside.

Lochran stands and opens the curtains. He can see a commotion on the main road. It looks like the traffic has ground to a halt; abandoned cars have blocked the street.

Three men and a woman are shouting and gesturing. People are streaming around them like they are stones in a brook. One of the men in the central group is holding something aloft. A book. He calls out for sinners to repent, for the End of Days is upon them all.

Somebody yells something in response, and this prompts a furious exchange between them. A woman begins crying. She approaches the leader of the group, tries to slap his face.

Two of the religious followers restrain her but this does nothing but trigger the crowd into movement. There is a surge of bodies and the dialogue erupts into screaming and furious reaction. Punches are thrown. Some of the people on the periphery do nothing but watch. They shuffle past like zombies.

Lochran wonders where the hell everyone is going. Why aren't they spending their final moments with the ones they love?

In the distance he can see black smoke billowing into the sky.

Something huge is on fire. Maybe a house.

Simone looks up from the bed. "What's happening?"

"Some religious nuts have been set on by a group. They're getting a bit of a kicking, to be honest."

"Religious nuts?"

"Well—you know." He shrugs. "Street preachers. Shouting about the end of the world. *Repent and you'll be saved. It's not too late.*"

She sighs. "Don't you wish you believed in God?"

He considers her question carefully. "Not really. What good would that do now?"

"It might make it less scary. If you believed you were going to Heaven."

For a while he doesn't speak, just stares into space. Then he says, "I don't really fear death like that." He looks directly at her. "Death is scary when others die, when you're forced to continue living without the presence of those that you love. Or—if you're the one dying—feeling sadness for those that'll have to go on without you. And missing out on the times that are yet to come—your kids' lives, family moments..."

Tears glint in her eyes. She blinks them away.

Lochran continues. "But none of that will happen. We'll all be gone by tomorrow anyway."

"Dean, don't say that."

He sees the fear in her face. Hates himself for his honesty. He closes the curtains and lies back down on the bed next to her, holding her hand. On the TV Frances McDormand is questioning William H Macy. Their quaint singsong accent warms Lochran's heart, just as it always does.

"Is the phone still dead?" Simone asks.

He nods. "And the TV. The radio's still on loop." He angles his head so he can peer at her face. "Are you okay?"

She is panting, her chest rising and falling as she struggles to breathe. "Feel sick." She gasps, pulling a sour face. The next minute she is up, hurrying to the bathroom. He can hear her vomiting into the toilet. He gives her a moment to compose herself, then follows her. He performs the task of holding her hair and rubbing her back until the sickness subsides. When she finishes, she spins on her bottom and sits with her legs drawn up.

"I can't hold out much longer, Dean." She wipes her mouth with the back of her hand.

He knows. It's visible in her body; the broken blood vessel in her eye, the sallow complexion of her skin. Maybe it's the caffeine overload. Or possibly just stress at dealing with what's happening. He closes his hand over hers.

She laughs hollowly. "I always thought the end of the world would be more...I don't know—*dramatic* than this."

"How do you mean?"

"I don't know. I thought there'd be more to it than just going to sleep and never waking up."

"Hmmm. You were expecting zombies? Or superbug viruses?" He's joking and she knows it. She smiles at him. He looks her directly in the eye. "At least we're together..."

She nods. "What's so special about today?" she asks abruptly. "Is there a significance to the date?"

"No. Just a random day, that's all."

He helps her to her feet and they go back to the bedroom. She glances at the clock on the bedside table. It is 10.43am.

They lie on the bed. Lochran can feel the warmth of her body next to his. He kisses her on the mouth, ignoring the fact that she's just been violently sick. She smiles a sad smile. Infinite. "Dean, I think I'm gonna go to sleep."

He nods, stroking her hair. He can smell the familiar scent of her shampoo. She is just as beautiful to him now as she was the first time he saw her, despite the lack of sleep and the intense stress of what is happening. "Sim, I love you."

"I love you, too." She stares directly into his eyes. "Will you cuddle me till I'm asleep?"

His throat is tight. He just nods because it is impossible for him to speak.

He continues to stroke her hair as she closes her eyes and relaxes. Her breathing becomes regular. He whispers gently against her ear, not words, just reassuring murmurs to remind her he's here. After a few minutes her chest rises and falls in a steady rhythm.

He mentally counts her breaths, losing himself in the numbers. He thinks about their life together, deciding that overall they've had no reason to complain. He focusses his mind on happy times. He reminds himself that there is nothing to be afraid of; what will shortly happen will be happening all over the world. He pictures a graph illustrating the location of the deaths, a red wave sweeping from east to west across the globe. He finds comfort in the multitude. He wouldn't want to be a survivor, should that even be a possibility. And then he suddenly notices that Simone is still, her chest now motionless.

He lays his head back on the pillow. He can still smell her hair. He closes his eyes. The haunting music of Carter Burwell plays in the background as the DVD reaches its end.

Lochran tries to control his own breathing, concentrating on relaxing. He pushes away all other thoughts that fight to distract him. He wants this to happen fast. He allows memories to flood his mind as he embraces his wife. Images, random snapshots, both of them laughing together, holidays they'd been on, parties they'd attended, films they'd enjoyed. He feels his body slipping towards sleep, and then all at once—like the television testcard from his childhood—the image of her face becomes frozen in his mind and a second later he's aware of nothing else but their love, her nearness, those beautiful eyes. These things accompany his final descent as sleep overcomes him.

It Came From The Ground

1

We'd been in Rwanda for only a few days before we saw the child with the machete. In the grand scheme of things, he came to represent the human form of horror that greeted us, unlike the things we encountered later. Sometimes at night I wake shuddering, desperate to escape my own glimpse through that border of sanity. The child with the machete was our motivation for going to Kigali, but the creature we witnessed in the sprawling farmland of Rwanda is the reason I will never return.

This was in the winter of 1994, when Rwanda was infested with death and madness. Karen, Joel and I had flown in from Johannesburg, my camera and dictaphone hidden deep in the bottom of my rucksack. I'd been listening constantly to *In Utero*, the raw vocals of Kurt Cobain throbbing in my head like a mantra. It was the only CD I had in my Discman. Nirvana's fury definitely eased my mood.

The airport was balanced on the summit of a rocky mountain. We caught a cab down into the city, feeling a sense of relief when we escaped the baking exposure of the airport.

We'd bummed around for the first twenty four hours. I tried to ignore the atmosphere between us, occasionally throwing surreptitious glances in the direction of Joel and Karen. To her credit, she never once betrayed her true feelings, although my own imagination taunted me mercilessly.

The heat was less oppressive than in the hills so the narrow roads encircling the western quarter offered welcome shelter from the sun. Tucked inside my wallet was a piece of paper bearing a single name—*David Kirenga*. Next to it was a hastily scribbled phone number, given to me by our contact in Burundi, who'd recently fled the country to escape the civil war. In the back room of a sweaty café we had examined the photographs he'd shown us; six blurred polaroids of a child running through the street wielding a bloodstained machete. Apparently the kid—an orphan, who looked to be no older than twelve—was an influential Hutu warlord, who'd allegedly seized power by escaping the orphanage after the atrocities had begun. He he'd lost his left arm in the conflicts, and this added to the grotesque image. Our contact—a jittery Tutsi farmer who constantly mopped his brow with a foul-smelling handkerchief—gave the information with an air of near-hysteria. He described an area of farmland, many miles outside Kigali, where the kid had set up a kind of commune.

I'd stared entranced at the polaroids. They were poor quality but I could imagine the potential they promised. My Nikon was capable of doing the hard work—all I needed was to get close enough to catch the opportunity. The photos, grainy and blurred as they were, offered enough to suggest that we'd not come on some fool's errand. My journalistic instinct had been right.

Ask any reporter and you'll get one of a few different answers about why we do what we do. Some will say the desire for honesty and truth, the need to tell the news. Some will cite noble ventures like integrity and morality. For me it was the Pulitzer.

For years I had dreamed of achieving the highest recognition in my field. It was what kept me warm on those days when I shook cold rain from my hair. It was what kept me alert on those nights when boredom tugged at my eyelids. If I'd thought about it long enough I might have actually realised that the possibility was *beyond* hope, but it was all I had to keep me focused. Images from a time of war were the way to reach the Pulitzer—think of Nick Ut's photo of the little Vietnamese girl running naked along the road, or Joe Rosenthal's shot of the flag being raised on Iwo Jima—absolutely breathtaking images that have resonated with the public ever since. I wanted my name to be spoken of with such esteem. Recognition was the only reward that would impress my father; his own millions bought him whatever he wanted. Even a minor journalistic award would be the ultimate way of ramming his disapproval of my career as far down his throat as possible.

We rented a room in a cheap hotel on the outskirts of the city, more out of necessity to remain low-profile than for financial reasons. Karen and I took one room, Joel the one next door.

I lay on the bed watching the ceiling-fan rotate. Karen was taking a shower. Somewhere nearby an argument raged in staccato French. Upstairs a television blared out a programme in Swahili. I wondered what Joel was doing, imagining his movement in the room next door.

Karen hadn't brought her journal on this trip, just her notepad. I'd checked it for entries while she showered but it was just filled with background on Rwanda and the civil war. Joel wasn't even mentioned.

At nine o'clock I went down to the payphone in the foyer. I dropped several centime coins into the slot and dialled the number from the scrap of paper in my wallet.

David Kirenga's voice was quiet and distinct. We agreed a fee for his trouble, and made arrangements for the following morning. I returned to the room.

Karen was in a weird mood. She tried to entice me into bed, but I resisted. She's a noisy lover and I was afraid Joel would hear us.

The car drew up outside at the allotted time the following morning. The trunk of the vehicle smelled of sour milk so I was careful where to stow our rucksacks. Joel took the front, Karen and I jumped in the back.

David talked as he drove. I had to lean forward to hear, which left me nauseous and disorientated. His English, though accented with the soft intonation of French, was near perfect. The initial journey through the streets of Kigali was tense and jerky and I was relieved when we finally reached the outskirts of the city.

2

Rwanda isn't called *The Land of a Thousand Hills* for nothing, and the grasslands and countryside that extended beyond the capital were far more verdant than I'd expected. David explained that armed guerrillas frequently patrolled the hills. An anxious glance passed between us, even though our research had prepared us for such facts.

David's voice was captivating and he told a compelling tale as we travelled the dirt roads that encircled the city, rising high into the hills.

The kid with the machete was called Fabrice Kambanda. Little was known about him prior to his escape from the Kigali orphanage in April. David pointed across the valley to a black scorch, stark against the green hillside.

"Our president's plane was shot down in April." He swallowed. "The fire is still burning in our hearts."

I could hear the scratch of Karen's pencil as she wrote in her pad. I remembered the report of the president's death; several days later the news was eclipsed by the suicide of Kurt Cobain. To the Western world, the immortalisation of a rock star takes precedence over the death of the leader of an African nation. What a fucked-up place we live in.

"Fabrice has become a legend in less than two months. People talk about him like he's the Devil. Maybe he is, but he's still a twelve year-old boy."

"How'd he lose the arm?" Joel asked.

"In the skirmishes." David shrugged. I could see the reflection of his dark eyes in the mirror. "Many bad things have happened. It's like the world has gone mad."

"Not the world." Joel raised a cynical eyebrow. "Just Rwanda."

We drove through the countryside for about an hour. It was difficult to gauge the distance because of the undulating terrain. At one point we had to pull over to the side of the road and let the car rest behind a screen of bushes. We waited anxiously as the vehicle ticked and creaked in the heat, silently awaiting the approach of the jeep that David had spotted across the far side of the valley. The armoured truck was carrying three passengers—all members of the Hutu militia—brandishing rifles and knives. As we watched through the trees I felt the weight of Karen's stare and understood the message; *David's fee had been worth every penny, given his knowledge of what we were dealing with.*

Soon we were on our way, slowly climbing into the foothills.

David continued to talk as he drove and we were lulled by his narration.

He spoke of the way the atrocities had affected the people he knew. Karen was frantically transcribing these personal accounts, but I was impatient for us to reach the kid. The endless stories of mutilation and massacre were hard to absorb, and I felt my mind hardening against the reality of what was happening here.

There were several signs of horror on the road. We saw a burned-out car, blackened and twisted like a grotesque metal beetle. The shattered glass glittered in the sunlight as we passed. Several feet away, a body lay in the shrub-grass. I could have been wrong but it looked like the figure was missing its head. I fired off some shots through the window, convincing myself that I was mistaken—that it was instead a bundle of rags or some remnants thrown from the fire-stricken car.

The ache in my back was starting to become an acute pain when David suddenly announced that we were a few miles from our destination. Fatigue that had just begun to settle into my limbs was now dispelled by the news, and I licked my lips and glanced out of the window, suddenly alert.

Our car pulled over. A dried mud-track bisected the grass that edged the asphalt road and threaded into the trees thirty feet away. Our passage was blocked by a tree trunk that had been deliberately placed to prevent vehicles from driving along the dirt road. We climbed out.

"From here we're on foot." David opened the trunk of the car and we grabbed the rucksacks. He took a bottle from his own bag and gulped down a long swig of water. "It's too dangerous to go any further by road. The militia is active along there."

I noticed a lingering glance pass between Joel and Karen at this point, as I was fastening the rucksack's strap across my chest.

David was attending to our equipment, checking to ensure we were ready for the hike. He stood and peered at me. "There's a convent about four miles east. We'll be staying there for the night; Fabrice has taken over a farm close to the convent. That should enable us to be near enough for you to get what you want."

His intent may have been lost in translation, but I thought I detected a hint of distaste in his voice. For the first time I wondered what these people must think of us; taking photographs and writing reports while their own people massacred each other. I glanced away.

We began walking, led by David. All around us the long grass whispered in the gentle breeze, creating movement and confusion. The ground underfoot was soft. I tried to concentrate on covering the distance with minimal damage to my body. My gym days were long behind me, and I was a little worried that I might become a liability.

Karen suddenly took my hand and I turned and smiled at her. Instinctively I glanced towards Joel, who was peering into the trees. The mid afternoon sun was beginning to descend, shadows encroaching across the grassland.

We walked for about 45 minutes. The going was tough because the track was overgrown. Once or twice we crossed chain-link fences that ran into the distance as far as we could see. Their gates were padlocked so we had no option but to climb them. We stopped for a break in the shade of a small grove. David passed around some crumbling flatbread, very sweet to taste. He urged us to eat to maintain energy levels.

We set off again shortly, and I noticed Joel's face was flushed with exertion. I felt a sense of satisfaction that I appeared to be managing better physically.

Our terrain was changing; the gently rolling hills were giving way to denser vegetation. Clumps of trees were springing up at increasing intervals, adding to my feeling of claustrophobia. I moved carefully. Darkness settled around us, though the sky still retained the final vestiges of daylight.

We were about to cross a narrow stream when, from somewhere nearby, a volley of gunshots rang out.

3

Instinctively we hit the ground. My ragged breath sounded deafening in the still air. A flurry of yells rose from the trees ahead.

We remained as we were for almost ten minutes as the voices seemed to diminish. There was one further gunshot, sounding quite distant, before we relaxed enough to stand again. We negotiated the stream with increased nervousness before hurrying after David.

Within twenty minutes we emerged from the woods into a clearing. The outline of a large two-storey building stood in silhouette against the sky. An adobe wall encircled the perimeter of the ridge.

"We're here."

I felt a surge of relief at David's words. We dragged our feet up the incline towards a wooden gate that stood proud of the wall.

"It's more like a prison than a convent," Joel remarked.

There was an electric bell on the outside of the gate. David pushed it twice. I noticed relief in Karen and Joel's faces, even in the darkness. Presently a small hatch in the door opened, and a wrinkled face appeared. David explained why we were there. The door swung open to allow us entry.

The poor light hid detail from the building but we walked towards it nevertheless. Lights burned in several of the windows.

We let David do the talking. The old man who'd admitted us—a shuffling Rwandan—ushered us into a sparsely decorated hallway. Various religious paintings adorned the walls. A rickety staircase rose into the darkness to our right. He led us along a dimly-lit corridor towards a room at the rear of the building.

A woman stood as we entered. Grey hair peeped out from beneath her blue wimple. Her face was lined with kindness and she greeted us warmly.

"My name is Sister Claudine." She spoke English with a gentle accent. "Welcome to the convent of the Sisters of Saint Francis."

She gave us a brief tour of the place. Unused to the practices of organised religion, I was impressed by the atmosphere of reverence that surrounded the convent. That may sound strange, given the fact that we were taking refuge within the confines of a religious order, but the horrors that were occurring elsewhere in Rwanda seemed distant. We were shown to our rooms on the first floor, both containing a pair of single beds. David and Joel took one room, allowing Karen and me to take the other.

After unpacking our meagre belongings and washing in the basin that seemed to deliver only cold water, we returned downstairs. There was a smaller room, separate from that of the nuns, and we ate a simple meal of soup and cold meat with vegetables. Sister Claudine accompanied us. Our conversation touched on the reason for our visit to Kigali, and I was again struck by how shallow and mercenary our motives seemed. Sister Claudine's eyes clouded when she spoke of what she'd heard about Fabrice.

"Like all false gods, he is surrounded by people who wish to commit sin." She dabbed at the corner of her mouth with a napkin. "I find it hard to believe that you have come all this way, for what?—Just to take a *photograph*?"

I nodded. "To take a photograph…with extreme prejudice." Either she didn't get the reference or she didn't find it funny. An uncomfortable silence fell upon us.

David bowed his head politely. "Sister Claudine, we are very grateful for your hospitality, but we must impose no more upon you. I think my friends have—"

"The boy's *tribe* attacked a family several weeks ago." The words sounded harsh in the silence of the dining room. Her eyes locked on mine. "The family had been fleeing from their home. They killed the children and raped the mother."

I heard Karen inhale sharply.

"They tortured the father for several days but he managed to escape. He came here. We did our best to help him but the madness had…*infected* him. He left us. Several days later I heard he had consulted a sorcerer, someone from the hills. He chose a dark path instead of the one we offered."

"My God." Karen held her hand across her mouth. I wasn't sure whether this was because of the story, or her blasphemy. "What happened to them?"

"A man comes here every two weeks to deliver supplies. He told me, according to the reports, that a *jinn* has been invoked. People are afraid."

"What happened to the family?"

Sister Claudine blinked. "His wife and children had been killed. These people are very superstitious. They believe that a great sacrifice is required to summon a jinn. The man slit his own throat—as instructed by the sorcerer—to unleash the jinn in a fit of vengeance."

I have no idea how, but the conversation shifted quite suddenly onto something lighter. By the time we finished the meal and retired to our room we had managed to repair the feeling of awkwardness that had festered between us and Sister Claudine. I felt we had reconciled our Westerners' lack of understanding with their country's beliefs.

Our room seemed dimmer than it had before the meal. We were both tired from the hike across the fields, so it wasn't long before we were asleep. My dreams were troubled; creatures made of black smoke walked through the grass, their eyes glowing with fiery intent. I awoke disturbed, a faint shriek trembling on the edge of my lips. With relief I realised where I was, and in an effort to shake the remnants of the vision from my mind I climbed out of bed and approached the sink. I splashed cold water onto my face, its bite invigorating me.

I became aware of a noise from the bed. Karen, too, was dreaming. Her face was twitching and her breath came in sobs. She was writhing slightly, and from the moonlight that poured in through the window, I could see the sweat on her body. A murmur escaped her lips.

Frowning, I approached, tilting my head to one side. Had I heard correctly? Did she just say *Joel?* I watched her for a second. Maybe she had said no. Her movement under the covers suggested arousal rather than fear. I gently shook her by the shoulder.

"Hmmm? What—Jason?" She opened her eyes, wide in surprise. "What's wrong?"

"Nothing. You were having a dream, that's all."

"Oh." She closed her eyes, turned over and returned to sleep. I settled down next to her but it was quite a while before my mind allowed me back to sleep. When at last it did come, it was restless, made uncomfortable by the wedge of resentment that had been driven between us.

The room was unbearably hot the following morning. The window was a shimmering haze of light and I sat up in surprise.

I was alone in the room. Dressing and washing quickly, I went downstairs. There was an unbelievably lovely aroma of cooking food. At the foot of the stairs I caught a glimpse directly into the small dining room in which we'd been entertained the previous evening. Karen and Joel were sitting at the table, laughing at something that Joel had just said. Their mirth abated somewhat as I entered the room.

"Morning, Jason," said Karen. "Thought you'd never get up."

"It's not *that* late." I glanced at my watch.

"Sit down, buddy." Joel stood. "I'll tell the cook you're up now."

"Where's David?" I took a seat next to Karen as Joel left the room.

"He's gone to organise some supplies. He thinks we might be able to get our shots today, and be back here for nightfall."

I felt disgruntled, as if they'd all been organising things while I'd slept. David entered, followed by a young lad carrying a plate of food. I began to eat enthusiastically, as David and Karen drifted out into the corridor. Joel joined them. I could hear their conversation as I ate, and this added to my feeling of dislocation. Maybe I was just tired, but the paranoia was beginning to get to me.

After I'd gulped down my breakfast I joined them out in the yard. The nuns had created a modest vegetable patch in the land adjoining the building. Rows of sprouting vegetation ran the length of the furrows like leafy markers.

We double-checked our rucksacks. I sat in the shade of a moringa tree and took out my Nikon, making sure the batteries were still okay, looking over the light meter and checking the hot-shoe contacts were free of dust and moisture. Karen helped David refill our water canisters and stow them in the rucksacks.

I felt suddenly, as we crouched there in the sun, an overwhelming sense of inevitability, a dark cloud on our horizon. I stood and urged my friends together, arms outstretched so they could join me. Offering my camera to David, I posed on the veranda, Joel and Karen either side, smiling uncertainly at the lens. Just last week I was looking at the photo in my apartment, realising that it captured the final time we were all together before death swept in.

We said our goodbyes to Sister Claudine. I discreetly slipped a wad of francs into the collection box in the hallway. Soon we were out in the fields. Just as we topped a low hill, I sneaked a final glimpse back towards the convent. It was almost as if I needed reassurance that polite society still existed out here in the wilderness.

As we walked, I brought up the subject of the jinn.

David seemed to consider his words carefully. "This is a country with an ancient history. Some people have beliefs that stretch back many generations."

I threw a bemused glance at him. "But a sorcerer conjuring *jinns*?"

He shrugged. "Is that any less realistic than those of western faiths? Would you believe a man could return from the dead any more than you'd believe a monster could be conjured using black magic?"

"Fair point." I looked at him. "You don't believe then?"

He was staring ahead into the trees. For ages he didn't speak. "As a child I was brought up in the faith of Catholicism."

"And now?"

His eyes seemed to darken. "I have seen a great deal recently to test what I previously believed to be right and wrong."

We walked on for a while in silence. I chewed over his words, trying to prevent his thoughts from unnerving me. Joel and Karen chatted brightly alongside us.

After about an hour of walking, I suddenly spotted a looping coil of black smoke in the sky some distance ahead. I looked at David, but he shook his head gravely.

"We're some way distant yet—this isn't Fabrice's place."

We continued carefully, Karen and Joel falling to the rear. We entered a small copse of trees, peering through the branches towards the clearing that angled upwards at a gentle slope.

4

A ramshackle hut stood desolate and conspicuous in a ripped clearing. A clutch of chickens pecked the ground. Smoke was rising gently behind the dwelling, creating a dark cloud.

"Wait here." David walked cautiously into the clearing. I followed close by, noticing his right hand move slowly towards a Velcro strap on the side of his rucksack.

The earth around the door of the hut was scuffed and bleached. David tried to peer in through the small window, but the grime and the interior netting conspired to obscure the view. He gently tried the handle of the door. Part of me wanted it to be locked, but I felt a surge of adrenaline when it opened and he slowly pushed the door.

The hut—which looked like it was usually home to several people—was empty. Two chairs were overturned, and the sheets had been dragged off the ramshackle bed that crouched in the corner. Broken pieces of earthenware pottery were scattered across the floor. David suddenly touched the edge of the table and held his hand up to the light that struggled to filter through the window. "Blood."

We went back outside and walked round the back of the building. A grain store was propped against the hut, blackened and smouldering, its wooden struts protruding from the chassis of the frame. The fire had been doused by something—possibly the damp air that had descended upon us quite suddenly—and I felt myself looking toward the perimeter of the clearing, where the trees seemed to intrude.

David picked up a thick tarpaulin from the back of the adjacent shed and covered the remaining flames, dampening the smoke. Soon he drew it back and we gazed at the dying embers. "Let's go on."

We moved back to where Karen and Joel anxiously waited. I fired off some photos of the dwelling. Together we continued. My mind was preoccupied with the scenes at the abandoned hut and, not for the first time, I wondered if we understood the full implication of what we were taking on.

Within minutes the dark clouds had gathered and I could sense the electricity in the air. We plodded onward, our conversation light and positive. We talked about things from back home, the familiar details that reminded us of our normal lives. I found myself missing my office. We'd only left home four days earlier but already it felt like an eternity.

Underfoot, the terrain was grassy and rutted. No sooner had we reached the summit of a low hill than we faced countless others beyond. I noticed the vegetation was altering as we progressed, becoming more leafy and tree-like. I'd been surprised by how rural the country appeared when we'd first arrived in Rwanda; now we were going to experience something that my ignorant mind realised was jungle.

Drips of perspiration tickled my body. Flies buzzed ahead of us in the heat. The sky was darkening, closing its grey wings over the diminishing amber light. Objects shimmered in the distance, the heat-haze twisting things unfamiliar. We broke for a rest in the shade of a rocky tor. A stream bubbled between the rocks, plunging underground several feet away. David directed us to refill our flasks. I, for one, was grateful for the break. Joel and Karen had been silent for quite a while and I was starting to feel that their moods were synchronised, something that irritated me intensely. The welcoming chill of the water burned my throat.

I sat next to Karen for a few moments. She was red-faced, her features slick with perspiration. She nodded at me reassuringly, but I sensed a slight crumbling beneath the exterior, a tiny erosion of her confidence. I squeezed her knee and reminded her that we'd be home in a couple of days. While we talked I watched Joel prowling the perimeter of the clearing, looking into the dense trees that fringed the clearing, twitchy with nerves. Occasional snaps of branches or bird cries from the forest elicited wide-eyed responses from him. I'd be lying if I said his behaviour didn't please me.

Eventually David turned from where he'd been peering across the valley through a set of brass binoculars. "We're getting close." He hitched his backpack onto his shoulder and smiled at us.

We set off once again. I fell into pace next to David, feeling satisfied that my moment with Karen had helped repair our relationship. I allowed myself to ignore that they were following together. Instead I enjoyed the trek, relaxing in the prospect of us attaining our target, focusing on not missing our opportunity to get the photo that would make us famous.

I was comfortable in David's company; the more time I spent

with the man the deeper I appreciated his acceptance of our proposal, even though it was at odds with his own beliefs and concerns. I asked him if he was nervous of encountering Fabrice.

He shrugged. "It's true he commands a great deal of influence. Yet he is still a boy. Maybe power is something that should only be bestowed on those mature enough to handle responsibility."

I stared out across the valley. "Power seems to attract people, whatever their age."

Soon we were descending the slope, wading through the tall grass. Flies hovered ahead, frantic in their movement. A narrow track encircled the valley, winding down towards a building that stood isolated in the foot of the basin. We stepped onto the track, suddenly feeling exposed and vulnerable. I stared at the silent house that awaited us, relieved as we plunged again into the cover of the overgrown grassland. It seemed like the building drifted towards us on a sea of green, as my senses went into overdrive, alert for any sense of danger. It felt like we were trapped inside a glass jar; the darkening clouds had smothered the breeze. I could almost taste the moisture in the air.

The house was dark and silent. As we drew close I became aware of a low moan coming from further around the veranda. We froze for a second. The sound came again. David crept up the steps, peering round the corner of the building. From my vantage point on the bottom stair I could see a black man sprawled on the decking, arms outstretched, low moans coming from him. David quickly knelt down and examined him. The man's prone state inspired a little courage in me; I followed and peered inquisitively.

His eyes were closed, tears flowing down his dark, weathered cheeks. His body was wracked by spasms, causing his limbs to judder. David loosened the man's shirt at the neck and leaned in close to examine him. White foam bubbled at the man's lips as he murmured incoherently.

David frowned. "He's delirious." He lifted one of the man's eyelids. "Looks like he's been poisoned." I recoiled slightly at the man's white bulging eye rolling in its socket.

"Will he be all right?" My voice sounded lost in the panic.

David shrugged. Behind us I heard the swing door open and

then close; I listened to Karen and Joel moving inside the house. There was a huge tear in the man's clothing, revealing a glistening wound in his shoulder. The screen door banged again and Karen appeared holding a cloth.

"It's empty." She handed the cloth to David, who pressed it against the man's shoulder. He grimaced and thrashed his head from side to side. Again I could see his eyeballs rolling beneath the lids. After a few moments he grew still.

"I think he's unconscious." David stood. "We should move him inside."

"What's happened to him?" Joel nodded from the top of the porch steps.

David shrugged. "He has a wound to his shoulder. Looks like something ripped into him, though his symptoms suggest poison."

"Machete?"

David looked at me. "Maybe."

We lifted the man and heaved his body into the house, taking care not to jolt him. I was struck by how smothered the atmosphere felt inside. Dry shadows scuttled in the corners.

We laid the man on a wicker sofa in the centre of the room. Joel drew a bowl of water and Karen bathed the gash on the man's shoulder with some towels from the kitchen. David took me to one side.

"Jason, we need to think about finding the boy. It'll be getting dark before we know it."

I nodded towards the unconscious man. "What about him?"

"Two people are just as effective as four. I thought you and I might leave Karen and Joel here with him, and we'll go and get your photographs."

I nodded slowly. In a way I felt more reassured leaving Karen in the house, as if its walls offered sanctuary from whatever lay without.

The ochre sky outside bled into the late afternoon as the clouds thickened and stole away the light. After we'd transferred the wounded man to the bedroom, David explained our intention to the party. Karen threw me a worried glance but I smiled in reassurance and nodded casually.

"We should be back before nightfall."

Within half an hour we were ready. Joel had decided to spend his time propped in a chair next to the unconscious man's bed, a solitary vigil. Before David and I left we all shook hands and he wished us well. I took my Sony Discman from my rucksack and pressed it to him. The look in his eyes meant he knew I was trusting him with much more than my Nirvana CD. David allowed me a brief moment with Karen, as he searched the rear outbuildings for anything of use. Her eyes scoured my face for any sign of nerves, although I managed to mask my true emotion. On the steps of the veranda we embraced. I kissed her, and then David and I turned and began heading towards the foot of the valley, beyond a grove of trees that extended as far as the farmland. Just as we reached a slope at the head of the canyon, I turned and looked back at the distant house. The veranda was empty.

5

Quite suddenly the rain came.

I heard the sound in the trees before I actually felt the drops. Huge, strong, splashes of rain that drenched us in seconds. In a way it was a relief; hopefully it would herald an end to the oppressive heat. Above us the heavy clouds glowered.

I drew my hood over and continued trudging, noticing that David's hood looked far more substantial than my own.

Soon we were descending into the crest of trees that lined the edge of the valley. The rain caused movement all around. A broad canopy of foliage sheltered us from the downpour, and I was grateful for the respite. In the deepening darkness of the afternoon, shadows seemed to press against us.

Our trek took us through the heart of the forest, where trees watched silently, obscuring the light. David insisted we break after about forty minutes. The air almost hummed with misty heat. From somewhere above, thunder rumbled a sinister growl.

We sheltered beneath a vast cam-wood tree. I tried to scrutinise the darkness of the forest floor, where I had the impression that things slithered and scuttled around my boots. Just before we set off I spied a huge black bird perched on a bowed branch. So intent was its gaze that I felt compelled to grab my camera and snap a photograph. It was an enormous crow, its feathers oil-black. But I must have been mistaken; when I had the pictures developed many months later, once the eventual horrors had faded, the photograph showed only a bare branch, exposed in its isolation. Perhaps the bird was just a product of my frenzied mind.

The weight of the Nikon around my neck was comforting so I tucked it beneath my rain protector, a light nylon poncho. As I strode it counted beats with my pace like a pendulum.

Eventually our progress through the forest—which so far seemed haphazard and meandering, although I had the utmost trust in David's navigation skills—took on a more resolved aspect as we came across a man-made trail that crossed the edge of the trees. Dewy shafts of light penetrated the periphery of the forest, illuminating the tangle of vines and broad leaves that inhibited our progress.

David turned to me, his voice low. "We're here."

I peered anxiously through the gap in the vegetation.

A large square building stood conspicuous in the basin of a shallow clearing. By its basic structure and the abandoned agricultural tools that stood in the yard, it was clear that the building had originally been a farmhouse. A makeshift fence surrounded the compound, though I could see several spots where the barrier had been breached. A sense of fear settled on me as I noticed several prone bodies scattered on the ground. Everything was ominously silent. We watched for several minutes but there was no movement from the site.

"Let's have a look." David stepped out of cover of the trees, moving with an assuredness that was startling. I hesitated for a split-second and then followed, catching up with him at the foot of the incline. He was carrying a vintage-looking pistol. I gripped my camera for support.

Puddles of rain speckled in the continuous downpour as we approached the fence. The wire had been flattened, one of the posts almost uprooted from the soil. We carefully made our way across the twisted fence. My heart was hammering.

A dead male Rwandan lay on his back, staring unblinking into the falling rain. Death had left his skin looking unnatural. There was a gaping wound in the man's chest, from which flies buzzed and swarmed. His hand was closed around a rusty machete.

As we drew close to the door I noticed the ground around the building was deeply scuffed and disturbed; strange undulating waves patterned the soil like ripples. David cocked his pistol and approached the open door.

I could see partway inside. There was a wooden rack standing just inside the threshold, cluttered with various implements. David flicked a switch on the wall and shrugged when nothing happened. The power was out. He began rooting through the tools on the rack. I noticed another machete half-buried in the disturbed soil and, on impulse I picked it up. David grunted in satisfaction and held up an electric torch. He clicked it on, and the strong beam sheared through the darkness.

We were standing in a small ante-chamber, not much more than a storage room really. Ropes and candles were stacked on the shelves, alongside a crowbar and some spare batteries. I poked around and was pleased to uncover another torch. My relief turned to dismay, however, when I realised the batteries had run out, so I quickly loaded another set from the storage supplies. My own beam pierced the darkness.

"What's happened here?" I peered along the corridor. "Maybe we should just move on?"

David shook his head. "No, this is what we've been looking for. This is the compound."

My instincts told me something was not right. I'd been in quite a few tricky situations over the years, some of them potentially life-threatening, but the sense of remoteness took away any control I pretended to feel. I wondered whether it was better to cut our losses and head back. Before I could vocalise my doubts, David made the decision for me.

"Come on." His whisper echoed along the corridor. He crept into the darkness.

I followed cautiously, sweeping my torch around. My beam

suddenly played across something on the ground and I knelt to examine it.

A pool of shiny mucus lay on the floor, like a huge snail-trail, extending for about four or five feet. David probed it with his finger and strands of the slime spanned the gap like glistening threads. He shrugged and we moved on, our progress sounding clumsy and conspicuous.

Pale light diffused through a window of opaque glass as the corridor opened into a small inner room, with a door ahead. I pressed my ear to the wood and I could hear a distant moaning coming from somewhere further inside the building. David opened the door and we stepped into what appeared to have originally been a kitchen. Oversized tins lined countless shelves that dominated the room from ceiling to floor. It was obviously now used as a food store. I took a couple of photos, hoping that the flash wouldn't overexpose the pictures; the light filtering through the grimy window was meagre. I was struck by how much food was stored here; before coming to Rwanda we'd heard stories of starving people and militia-controlled rationing. This stockpiling seemed absurd.

A door on the far wall opened into a wide hallway, with spindled stairs leading off to our left. It was clear that we were within the old farmhouse, and the prefabricated corridors and supplementary rooms that surrounded the original building had been recently added. Skeletal shadows swept across the walls as my beam touched on the spindles of the stairs. The moaning we'd previously heard was louder now, a low groan that seemed to come from both everywhere and nowhere.

I noticed David crossing the hallway to where a row of doors led away, feeling a sudden sense of alarm at his disjointed movement. It took me a few seconds to realise that his progress was hindered by fear, and I hurried close behind and let my beam support his own, which penetrated the darkness ahead. Then, instinctively, I gasped.

Beyond the climb of the stairs, over in the far reaches of the hallway, several figures watched us, motionless. The light bleached their features, casting a deathly pallor to their skin. I heard David's anxiety in the ragged exhalations of his breath.

Several seconds passed as I wrestled with the dread that was threatening to overwhelm me, before David let out a relieved laugh. I peered at him, incredulous.

He approached the figures and I saw him reach out and touch the face of the one nearest. "They aren't real." He looked at me. "They're statues."

I frowned and approached them. Up close I could see that it was true; there were four figures in total, all in different positions. I gazed in wonder at the lifelike detail, and my fingers felt the rough, cold shape of the stone. Something about the precise detail unsettled me, though. David poked around in the darkness while I examined the bizarre formations.

It wasn't just the detail that unnerved me, but the fact that it was inconceivable anyone would ever fashion a sculpture in such a way; one of them had a tongue lolling out of the corner of his mouth, stone spittle lining the contours of his lips. Another one had an open gash stretched across the extent of his back, from where his torn clothing stuck to the implied wetness of the wound. One was sitting with his head bowed, elbows resting on his knees. The final figure was frozen in the act of cowering back into the corner. A thin tear furrowed his neck. *Were these things simply pieces of art? Did they illustrate what was happening in Rwanda in the same way I hoped my photographs would?* I took several shots of the eerie stone formations.

David suddenly opened a door to our left, allowing the moaning suddenly to increase in volume. A short corridor ran away into the darkness, but an open trapdoor several feet over the threshold caught our attention. David stood and peered down, shining his torch into the hole.

A short metal ladder bolted to the edge of the pit descended to the corridor below, which appeared to run parallel with the floor passage. The groaning was coming from somewhere along there.

I swallowed and tried to catch David's eye but the light was too poor. I could just make out the square angle of his jaw and the determined nod of his head.

"Come on," he said.

He descended into the pit. The sounds of his boots on the metal rungs made me cringe, and I threw a quick scan around before hurrying after him.

The ladders were slippery. I felt my feet trembling on the rungs as I climbed to the bottom. Shining the torch onto them I noticed that much of the vertical wall was coated in the same slimy residue we'd seen upstairs.

The tunnel ran the length of the house for as far as we could see, eventually curving out of sight. It looked like it was originally built as a storage alley, though the heavy presence of dust and the emptiness of it now hinted that it hadn't been used as such in a long time. I noticed emergency lights fixed to the ceiling at intervals, and they flickered intermittently, throwing a sinister throb of shadows into the passage.

Just out of view, beyond the bend of the passage, someone moaned. The sound was unnatural and stark in the confines of the narrow tunnel. I felt the hairs on my neck stand on end.

David stepped forward, gaping at an angle so he could see round the bend. His approach obscured my own view of the curve, and I felt a surge of panic. I swallowed, and fought the terror that threatened to claim me.

The next few seconds were a blur of intense activity; movement and sound roaring at us all at once. Something rushed out of the shadows ahead of David, screams spiralling around us. Almost in slow motion, I winced. Instantaneously a shot rang out, halting the inhuman screeching. The gun's report sounded ugly in the narrow tunnel.

A man sat on his backside, staring at us in surprise. The light was enough for us to notice the crimson stain blooming across his chest. A thin ribbon of smoke drifted into view from the barrel of David's revolver, where it remained pointed at the man. The man's eyes followed the smoke for a moment before fading into milky, sightless beads. He dropped onto his back.

David turned to me. "I just pulled the trigger in surprise." He swallowed. "I didn't mean to shoot him."

I nudged the machete that was still gripped in the dead man's hand. "Lucky for us you did." Before we moved on, I took a couple of photographs. The squeal of the flash recharging added an element of alarm to our mood.

We edged further along the tunnel. I sensed there was now a degree of apprehension to David's movement. The moaning that had infused the house could now be heard more clearly, just ahead of us. As we approached a bend in the passage ahead I spotted the kid.

He was crouched in the corner, almost melting into the darkness that surrounded him. His chest was rising in shallow movements as the low moan escaped him. The eyes stared indifferently at the wall, unfocused and oblivious to our presence. He clutched something in the crook of his amputated arm, stroking it with trembling fingers. I peered closely and saw that it was a child's toy, a dog-eared stuffed harlequin. The material of its diamond clothing was grubby and soiled.

Over the previous few days my mind had been creating a powerful image of expectation based on the blurred polaroids we'd been shown. I was anticipating a mutilated monster wielding death and madness, but instead we saw a frightened kid cuddling a stuffed toy. There was something about how pathetic he looked, how utterly innocent he seemed, that made me feel bad about photographing him.

"Fabrice?" My whisper sounded deafening in the silence.

He flinched as I touched his arm. "Come on." I helped him up. His eyes continued to stare into the darkness. "He's catatonic."

Fabrice's mouth was moving soundlessly. David cocked his head closer to the kid's lips and listened for a second.

The older man's eyes glittered in the tunnel. "He said, '*It came from the ground.*' What does that mean?"

I shrugged. "He's delirious."

David began to lead him by the arm. "We'd better take him with us."

"Are you sure?" I was beginning to feel detached from reality. "I mean, he's dangerous, isn't he?"

They moved past me. "Does he *look* dangerous?"

Hysteria bubbled in my throat, and I fought hard to suppress a laugh. Where I'd been expecting a machete, the kid was carrying a soft toy. The situation seemed to be growing more absurd by the minute.

Between us we managed to guide him back to the end of the tunnel and up the metal ladder. He seemed withdrawn almost to the point of stupor.

The room with the statues had lost none of its weirdness. Fabrice's eyes held not a flicker of recognition; I wondered whether he actually noticed them. I hesitated, staring uneasily at the shadowy figures.

"This way." David motioned to a door at the rear of the room. I followed, relieved not to have to pass through that bizarre exhibition. We entered a deserted lounge, dusty and silent in neglect. I could hear the rain pattering the window, from where weak light diffused through the closed blinds. I dragged them down with a clatter, yellow light brightening the walls instantly. I unclipped the handle and pushed the window open.

David climbed out and I helped Fabrice through. His movement was vague and disorderly, the fingers of his right hand gripping the harlequin like a talisman. I clambered out of the window of the dusty farmhouse, breathing the damp air with a relief that edged towards hysteria.

Eerie statues—similar to the ones that were huddled inside— lay in frozen depictions of death. I examined one in the daylight.

The material was definitely stone; I scratched the surface of the thing with my torch, noticing the crumbling remnants that attached to the rubber. The actual detail was unreal; raised veins, skin blemishes, authentic touches of verisimilitude that increased the creepiness.

"Come on." David nodded to a jeep that was parked further up the incline. It seemed to shimmer in the rain like a beacon. I followed eagerly.

David let out a gasp of triumph when he spotted the keys in the ignition. I almost wept. We helped Fabrice into the back. I jumped into the seat next to him. David started the engine. "We can get back much quicker this way."

"What are we going to do? ..." I nodded my head towards the kid, "...*with him?*"

David stared into the trees as if searching for an answer. "I think they'll look after him at the convent."

I nodded uncertainly. "What's happened here?"

David pursed his lips. "I don't know. Something bad."

"What about the statues?"

He shrugged and shook his head.

The jeep spun in an arc on the grass and we were soon accelerating along the track that threaded around the perimeter of the farm. Lifeless bodies lay at intervals as we progressed.

"Brace yourself."

I peered ahead and saw that we were moving at high speed towards a locked chain-linked gate. I put my arm around the indifferent boy and braced myself.

We crashed through without fuss, bouncing over the struts of the gate. David righted the vehicle and we headed along the track that skirted the woods.

"It's longer this way," David indicated ahead with a nod. "But it would take ages trying to manage the boy between us."

I nodded, suddenly impatient to return to Karen and Joel. Darkness waited among the trees as we sped past, vague indistinct shapes huddled together under the canopy of leaves.

6

The kid rocked, continuing to stare into the distance. He looked to be beyond reach.

The mud track we were on circled back along the banks of a river that ran parallel with the perimeter of the farm. The fence had been breached at various intervals; tracks on the ground indicated a frantic mass of bodies had escaped the compound in a hurry, the posts left twisted and in disarray. Once again I was left to wonder what had caused such panic.

Rain continued to fall, disorientating me with its incessant patter. Constant drips from the overhang above reminded me that our shelter was transitory; that we'd soon have to brave the elements again.

David negotiated the track with a degree of reckless caution. Every so often I spotted bodies lying in the grass, but I found it impossible to take any photos with Fabrice next to me. Instead I simply averted my gaze.

Soon we were descending the track that ran into the valley. I knelt up as we emerged from the trees, studying the house.

It was just as we had left it.

We drew to a halt in front of the veranda. David and I managed to get the kid down from the back and up the steps. He was still catatonic.

As we entered the house I knew straight away that something was wrong. The house had taken on a different atmosphere.

"Karen? Joel?" My voice sounded invasive in the still air.

And then, almost creeping down the stairs towards me, I heard the barely audible sounds of Karen sobbing.

I was up the stairs in an instant, following the noise. There was a bedroom at the far end of the landing. I pushed the door open and stepped inside.

As soon as she saw me she leapt up and clutched wildly at me. She looked terrible. Her face was a pale mask of anxiety.

"Jason, he's gone—Joel's gone."

"Gone where?"

She took a series of deep raking sobs. "He came round for a while, that man downstairs. We managed to speak to him."

"Where is he?"

She ignored the question. "He told us what happened. He said he'd seen something in the forest—*something horrible*."

"Where's Joel?"

Her eyes widened as she spoke. "He went to find it."

I sat down on the bed. She resumed crying. Part of me wanted to escape, to get as far away as possible from this place. I was also irritated at Karen's behaviour. I thought about pointing out that he was probably just poking around the trees, looking for something in the woods. And then the reason for her trembling struck me.

"Karen." I held her face in my hands. "Where is the man we found? The one who was unconscious?"

She swallowed a low wail and motioned to the floor. *Downstairs.*

"Jason." David's voice was weighted with intent as it rose along the landing. "You'd better come and see this."

There was something in his tone that drew a shiver from me. I leapt up and hurried down the stairs. He was standing in the doorway of the sitting room, so my view was obscured. As I approached he stepped aside and I saw what he was looking at.

Curled in a foetal position on the low couch was the petrified figure of the farmer. The resemblance to the man we'd seen earlier was striking in its detail. Even the bulging madness in his eyes was captured. Veins stood out on his neck like tightened cords.

"Good God, what's happened?" I heard my voice raising the question at the same time as my brain raced ahead with insane theories.

David frowned. "It's the same …"

I touched the statue's cold cheek. It felt as solid and unnatural as the others at the compound.

"This has to be the man we found earlier." David sounded less than convincing. "Something's happened to make him like this— to calcify him."

He glanced at me. "Where are Karen and Joel?"

I fought a wave of nausea. "Karen's upstairs. She's pretty traumatised. She said Joel went into the forest looking for a creature that *he'd* spotted." It felt weird acknowledging that the statue in front of us had ever been alive, could ever have seen anything.

We left the effigy where it was and drifted into the main living quarters. I noticed the kid, Fabrice, perched on the edge of a chair. He maintained that same disconnected stare.

We hurried upstairs. Karen was crying on the bed.

"It's okay, it's okay." I stroked her hair. "Listen, we need to go and find Joel. What did he say?"

Tears were streaming down her face. "The farmer woke up. He was frightened. We calmed him down. He said that some kind of monster had attacked him in the forest. He said he needed to get some gasoline to burn it." The sobs overwhelmed her. After a moment she continued. "Joel got him to say where it was. He went to look."

"Where did he go?"

"He said…he said it was up near where the tracks crossed, quite a way into the forest."

David caught my eye.

"Karen, we're going to get Joel. You and me and Jason and Fabrice. We'll find him."

She nodded absently.

It took David and me nearly fifteen minutes to prepare for our final departure from the farmhouse. I guided Fabrice into the rear of the jeep, ensuring he was comfortably wrapped in the blankets and pillows that we procured from the house. He gripped the little harlequin doll in his only hand.

I ransacked the building from top to bottom. David managed to find a shotgun and a box of shells in one of the outhouses, and we stowed it in the front.

By the time we went to get Karen she'd composed herself somewhat. Her pallid face was streaked with tears, her eyes bloodshot. I put my arm around her and we walked to the jeep. She clutched at me with trembling hands. "Why did we come, Jason? Were we mad?"

"It's okay, Karen, it's okay," I soothed. "We'll get Joel, then go home."

She nodded.

Once we were all loaded into the vehicle, David started the ignition. I felt a sudden sense of trepidation. Karen's words had brought home to me the ridiculous nature of our trip; once again I was struck by how trivial our expedition actually was—to think we'd dared brave the insanity of this place just for a photo opportunity. Suddenly I wanted to be home more than anything else in the world.

The rain was still falling, although less heavily, but the minute we careered into the shelter of the trees I could no longer feel the drops on my head. Nevertheless, the foliage around us shivered and hissed with the drips. I felt the vehicle slide and judder as David crunched the gears, fighting to keep the tyres on firm ground. We skirted the slopes, accelerating up the grass incline that rose to a plateau, extending as far as I could see. I tried to glance back to see the farmhouse, but the pale trunks of the trees blocked my view.

The track led into the forest. We carefully traversed the muddy terrain, wheels bouncing to maintain purchase. Just as I felt we had gone too far, we reached the junction where the two paths intersected. The jeep slid to a halt and we paused, trying to listen, as the engine ticked and the leaves fluttered in the rain.

My thoughts had taken a macabre turn, and I was finding it hard to keep up with events; missing members of the team, petrified humans, the fact that we were in the midst of so much bloodshed and trauma. It felt like we were teetering on the brink of something far darker.

7

David stepped out of the jeep and started poking around in the undergrowth. I suddenly realised how tense I was, as I jumped down and felt the stiffness in my limbs.

For five minutes or so we searched the area. It was quite clear that the thing we were looking for—and I had no real idea what that might be, other than feeling a strange foreboding—would lie nowhere near the track, but somewhere rather more obscure. Eventually I discovered a series of rippled patterns in the soil, almost destroyed by the rain. The vegetation had been crushed, plant stalks broken, leaving a faint path cutting between the tall grass and bushes. I held back several wide fronds that extended from the trunk of a tree and noticed the mound of earth that rose sharply beyond the line of sight. Strands of mucus glistened on the loose soil, spanning the dapples that decorated its surface. I scaled the incline, my feet sinking into the barrow of earth. It was clear that this was soil that had been recently excavated. I squinted in all directions. The waist-high grasses did their best to obscure our target. And then I spotted a stretch of blackness hidden beneath the shadows of a conifer tree and my heart leapt.

"David." He looked over from where he was crouching by the trunk of a wisteria. I motioned him over.

As he drew near, I nodded towards the smudge of darkness. David gingerly swept his foot in an arc, parting the ground ivy and grass, revealing the yawning mouth of a tunnel.

I was starting to tire of this God-forsaken country, with its array of tunnels and darkness, strange vegetation and elusive places.

I suddenly realised that I had left my camera in the jeep. David shone his torch into the tunnel, illuminating the swathes of webbing that laced the edges. The size of the hole bothered me; the diameter was probably only two feet across, and the way David was kneeling indicated he was considering crawling into it.

"What are you doing?"

He dug at the rim of the tunnel with his hands, dislodging clumps of soil, pulling strands of vegetation from the edge. Very quickly he'd opened up the mouth of the tunnel, which I now realised was much wider beyond the first few feet. It appeared to drop down and then run horizontally. We both peered into the hole. I realised with dismay that it was wide enough for us comfortably to climb into.

"Joel?" David's voice seemed to be swallowed by the tunnel. He moved as if to climb down.

"What are you doing? He won't be down there."

David looked at me with eyes that glittered in the shelter of the trees. "This must be the place that the farmer described."

"But we've come to find Joel. He wouldn't have climbed down there."

David glanced into the hole. "He came to look for a creature in the woods. I think this is the thing's…nest, or lair."

I understood we needed to check down there, but I felt torn by the idea. It seemed cowardly to allow David to go down alone whilst I waited on the surface, yet the prospect of going down on my own felt repellent. Grudgingly I accepted that it was best if we both went.

I jumped down first, feeling my boots sink into the mud as I landed. David passed me the torch. I bent and shone the light into the tunnel, but the curvature of the walls meant that little of any interest was revealed.

"Joel?" My voice sounded feeble.

At least the torch beam indicated there might be enough room to bend and crouch, rather than having to crawl along the tunnel. I ducked my head and scuttled further into the burrow, while David joined me.

The light picked out glistening striations along the surface of the passageway. It reminded me of a photo I once saw of the chamber of a gun, where it had marked the exterior of a bullet as it passed through.

David's breathing behind me did little to calm my nerves; the sound seemed to spiral ahead. The arc of the light was sufficient to illuminate the entire width of the tunnel, banishing any possible surprises that might lurk in the shadows. That fact gave me a modicum of courage.

At one point the burrow dipped slightly and curved at an angle. Just as I shuffled far enough across for the torch to meet the perspective, I froze in my tracks.

The burrow ended abruptly about fifteen feet away, opening into a roughly circular chamber, wider than the rest of the tunnel. It might have been possible to stand fully in the hollow.

But there was no way in the world I was going any further.

The torch beam picked out several objects gathered together in bundles, propped against the wall of the burrow. A glistening cover of opaque mucus did little to conceal the odd human elbow or foot that protruded through the wrapping. I felt the first surges of panic rising in my throat.

And then a sound came to me very faintly from the surface. It was Karen, screaming.

8

We scrambled back along the tunnel. I was aware of the shapes behind us, wrapped in the mucus-shrouds, tried to force the meaning of their presence out of my head. David leapt out of the tunnel. I quickly followed.

I could see movement through the trees as we sprinted back to the jeep. Karen's screams injected me with a sense of terror. Through the tangle of shrubs and brush I could see a blur of motion. The air fizzed with a palpable sense of panic.

Just as we burst into the clearing, I collided against David's back with a gasp.

Karen stood screaming on the rear of the jeep, her hands covering her mouth, eyes wide with terror. I turned to get a better view. For several seconds I just blinked, trying to compute the information.

A monstrous insect writhed on the ground. It was a mass of legs and antennae, moisture glistening on the shell-like segments of its body. My first impression was of a pale, bloated centipede, the countless legs of its enormous length flexing in obscene ripples. It looked to be about eight or nine feet long, though it was difficult to tell because it was constantly coiling against the wheels of the jeep.

It must have sensed our approach, for its head angled towards us. It was at that moment that I feared my sanity teetering; even now I struggle to describe the sight.

The creature was something out of a nightmare, like a monster from the depths of Hell. The tip of its thorax bulged to accommodate the head. Between the grotesque mandibles I could see a pair of faceted eyes, insectoid, yet possessing a human-like semblance that was terrifying. A series of discs spanned the underside of its body. The glistening maw gaped, issuing a chitinous rattle. A shiver of muscular movement teased the legs into an undulating wave as it flexed against the back of the jeep. Karen screamed again and cowered against the glass of the cab. Fabrice remained motionless, still draped in the tarpaulin, silently moving his lips. The insect's mandibles twitched as if tasting the air. I could see a pointed barb protruding from its monstrous face.

Karen yelled again, breaking my reverie. I took a few steps back. David edged towards the border of trees that fringed the clearing, and scooted towards the front of the jeep. I moved towards the insect despite every fibre of my being urging otherwise.

The centipede scuttled forward with a hostile rattling noise, trying to grasp Fabrice's leg. He kicked desperately and recoiled. Karen attempted to drag him away. I could hear the driver's door of the jeep open, and it occurred to me that David might suddenly drive the vehicle away, abandoning me. I panicked. There was a machete in the back of the jeep, and I grabbed it and swung in a wild arc.

The blow connected heavily, cracking the shell-like carapace. Twisting and hissing, the creature reared up and flicked a set of antennae at me. I felt myself dropping back onto the ground, half delirious with terror. My hands grasped wet leaves, mossy undergrowth, desperately snatching at something to tether me to reality. Helpless, I bowed my head and awaited the strike.

Instantly a sharp crack split the air, closely followed by another. Almost in a blur I saw the creature jolt and jerk, coiling back on itself. I was only vaguely aware of David in the background as I scrambled out of reach. He continued his aim, the barrel of the shotgun remained constant even though both shells had been spent.

Then the creature was moving, scuttling low across the carpet of dead leaves with astonishing agility. I gasped at its speed. David cried out, urging me into movement. The creature seemed to be heading back towards its burrow, scurrying from side to side as its legs slid on the damp leaves. David was quickly reloading the shotgun. I ran through the trees, feeling the fronds and branches swipe at me. I arrived in the clearing just in time to see the tip of the monster's body disappear into the hole. The soil surrounding it was patterned by those ripples, only there was something different about the scene this time. I stopped suddenly as the realisation hit; the air was heavy with an overpowering smell of gasoline. An empty canister was lying half-covered by the grass; nearby a lighter glistened in the rain. The torch that I'd discarded as I'd clambered out almost leapt into my hands.

I peered into the burrow. "Joel!"

My voice was swallowed by a threatening hiss. I jumped down into the hole, staring intently into the darkness; a darkness that was punctured by a light from some frantically bobbing source.

Just then, from the far side of the tunnel, beyond the creature, a direct beam burst forth from Joel's torch, illuminating the nightmare creature in its path. I switched on my own torch and shone it along the burrow.

The monster rolled and arched its length as it sensed Joel's vulnerability. He was backing away, further into the burrow, almost reaching the point where the tunnel curved. It was clear he was trapped. He threw a canister at the centipede and it bounced off its body in a spray of gasoline. That's when I knew what to do.

Joel's eyes caught mine and an unspoken message passed between us. I clambered out of the tunnel and dived to one side. My fingers scrabbled around in the grass, before finally settling on the steel lighter. It took three strikes before the tiny flame caught. I dropped it into the hole and rolled away.

A roar erupted in my ears, threatening to burst my skull. I was aware of David grabbing and dragging me away from the hole. The air blistered with fire and, from the bowels of the earth, a shrill, desperate whistling.

I was almost unconscious by the time David loaded me into the jeep. The creature's dying *chittering* was still in my head many hours later.

The next few days passed in a fugue. Before we left I was vaguely aware of David telling Karen that we'd seen Joel's body in the tunnel, wrapped in the creature's mucus cocoon. He made no mention of what really happened. Joel's fate secured Karen's acceptance to leave. We paid David a small fortune, though no amount of money could possibly reward him for the expertise with which he guided us back to civilisation. It was only months later that I realised his resolve might have been strengthened by his experience of the country's religion. Maybe he'd seen so much madness that it had fortified his mind.

One minute we were perched on a brittle chair in Kigali airport—lost in a dream of uncertainty—the next we were home, being silently taxied to our apartment. I have little memory of the intervening events.

Karen and I endured the next year in fraught proximity. Our experience *could* have strengthened the bond that we'd shared, might have meant that we'd understood each other. Instead the madness and horror that we were exposed to simply accelerated the poison in our already-diseased relationship. Karen moved out. Her mind had remained in those farmlands and fields of Africa. The resentment that I'd harboured over her fling had swollen to gigantic proportions; Joel's loss did nothing to relieve that. If anything, it martyred him. There was no way I could compete.

The impact of what happened has lessened with time. I no longer have nightmares, although I can't watch documentaries about Rwanda or the civil war. I quit my job, and eventually found work at my local newspaper. It's a more sedate career. I met Joanne in 2004. Our relationship is fine, although I've only spoken briefly about what happened in Rwanda. We've been trying for kids, but we've had no luck so far; the miscarriages she's had have left us raw and emotionally fragile.

Even to this day, I find I'm claustrophobic. The thought of entering a tunnel leaves me with a tight chest and palpitations. There's something about the safety of the city that reassures me; concrete and glass, the constant sound of humanity, the ever-present reminders of society.

Sometimes I find my thoughts are wandering, covering the miles in a second, travelling back to the place where we almost lost everything.

My enduring image is not of the monstrous, bloated centipede that burned to death in its burrow, but the final look on Joel's face as he realised he was trapped, and the lighter offered the only answer. I feel no guilt at what happened; he'd have done the same thing if the situation had been reversed.

Occasionally I imagine someone nosing around in the tangle of vegetation—maybe a westerner, searching for riches to plunder—when he comes across those bizarre stone figures in the derelict farm. Perhaps instead he stumbles over the fire-stricken tunnels, and discovers the remains of that grotesque nest. What horror might that conjure?

And often I think of Fabrice.

He was the reason we went to Rwanda, after all. I no longer picture him as a fearsome warlord, mutilated by combat, wielding his machete in the scrabble for power. I think of him as I saw him last—just a young boy clutching a soft toy, terrified of the realities of life.

Just as we'd neared the road that began its wandering approach back into Kigali, Karen woke in the back of the jeep. She was violently ill. We'd pulled over and tried to soothe her. That was when she'd pointed to Fabrice.

He was lying in the back of the jeep, covered by the tarpaulin. I'd drawn it back and we'd stared at the stone image of the kid, frozen in the act of sleeping, his hand still grasping the harlequin to his chest. I'd examined the statue and discovered a rip in the calf of his trousers. A trickle of blood had leaked from the wound and pooled into his shoe. The gash looked consistent with the spike of the creature's barb.

David and I had lifted him from the back of the jeep and placed him on the ground, concealing his whereabouts with a screen of bushes. His face looked composed and relaxed. I like to think that he at last found peace in that short life of his.

As we'd driven away, I'd ignored Karen's hysteria. She'd wanted to take the stone thing with us, but I'd experienced enough madness to see me through the rest of my days; the last thing I needed was a macabre reminder.

Maybe one day I'll be watching some documentary on the Discovery Channel and see his serene face again, frozen in the act of eternal slumber, as some narrator speculates as to who created it. But I suspect that—like most of what happens in a country as steeped in mystical history as Rwanda—the only reminders of that horrific trip will remain forever in my memories.

For Paul Wright, who was keen to know what happened next.

Story Notes

The soundtrack suggestions to accompany each story should be thought of as a soundtrack to the anthology.

Cuckoo Spit - *Black Static*

I have often found cats and dogs creepy. Cats are silent and fleeting, like ghosts. My mistrust of dogs, I think, stems from two films I watched as a child—*Invasion of the Body Snatchers* and *The Mephisto Waltz*. One of them induced a nightmare several days later. Don't get me wrong, I love animals—especially dogs—but you can have a fondness for something whilst at the same time feeling apprehensive of it. Anyway, in this story I was aiming for a sense of dislocation. The central character's relationship with her mother is the key here, and I got the idea from a friend of my wife, who as a child had her face scarred by the family dog. No further action was taken and, unlike the characters in the story, there was no resentment created by this. However, my overactive imagination always wondered whether someone less understanding would accept what had happened without feeling that the dog was in some way responsible. The remoteness of the location lent itself to a suggestion of witchcraft. Old English folk tales of familars and animal transformations are extremely evocative, it was too good an opportunity not to touch on. I sold the story to Andy Cox at *Black Static*—my first sale to this illustrious publication—so it felt like a landmark point in my writing.

Soundtrack - An Acre of Land by PJ Harvey and Harry Escott.

None So Blind - *Shadows & Tall Trees*

I have always been fascinated by masks, and what they might conceal. There had been a spate of acid attacks in Britain, and the idea that someone might disfigure another human being by throwing powerful acid into their face seemed too horrific to comprehend, almost. I wrote the story to submit to Shadows & Tall Trees, a Canadian journal of disquieting weird tales, not even sure my entry was anything more than a very quiet crime story. But the editor, Michael Kelly, accepted it and it appeared in issue 3, going on to be selected by Ellen Datlow for *Best Horror of the Year 5*, my first appearance in an annual best-of.

Soundtrack - *Like a Hurricane* by Neil Young.

Apports - *Black Static*

This story was inspired by a news report I read about a father trying to enact out revenge on his estranged partner by attempting to commit suicide by jumping off a tall building with their child. It strikes me as a particularly selfish and bitter thing to do (not the suicide, but killing the child at the same time), and I couldn't get out of my head how anyone could feel justified in committing such a heinous act. The idea had lodged in my mind for several months before I managed to wrangle it into a story involving poltergeists and revenge from beyond the grave. Thanks to Gary McMahon for suggesting suitable place names in Leeds in which I could set the tower-block. The original ending had a little bit more to it but I think the finished version was much better. Andy Cox bought the story for *Black Static* and then it was picked up by Ellen Datlow for *Best Horror of the Year 6*.

Soundtrack - *The Numbers* by Radiohead,

Lord of the Sand - *The 11th Black Book of Horror*

The stories in the *Black Books of Horror* are usually great fun to read. I'd appeared in the series a couple of times before, and the editor Charles Black approached me to see if I'd be interested in writing one for his forthcoming edition. Many years ago, I worked with an old guy who was, in his younger years, a soldier in the army. He used to tell us stories of his exploits, no doubt filled with embellishments and exaggerations. Needless to say, one story that had stayed with me concerned a time when he was showering in one of the quarters while they were stationed out in the middle-east. A squaddie mate of his, for a lark, tossed a camel spider onto his back. His revulsion was suitably conveyed as he described the experience. I developed a macabre fascination with them. This story was the result of that, coupled with a separate idea I'd had for a twisted revenge tale. Charles accepted the story for the *11th Black Book of Horror*, and then it was chosen by Ellen Datlow for *Best Horror of the Year* 8.

Soundtrack - *Broken Boy Soldier* by The Raconteurs.

Somewhere On Sebastian Street - *Horror For Good*

The writer Gary McMahon wrote a story called "The Row", which I absolutely loved (which is nearly always the case with Gary's fiction) and I asked his permission if I could utilise one of the locations in the story for one of my own. I suppose I like to think of "Somewhere on Sebastian Street" as a sequel to Gary's original, but with my own slant on things. It appeared in a charity anthology, *Horror For Good*, alongside some of my favourite writers.

Soundtrack - *Your Ghost* by Kristin Hersh.

Bandersnatch - *Black Static*

This tale is a rather brief sojourn with a rather sick individual and his defective family. I decided to write in first person—a tense I usually enjoy—but in this instance it was quite a difficult experience due to the nature of the story. It deals with psychopathic tendencies, murder and incest, and yet the bit that most people mention to me is about the central character's cruelty to his sister's dog. As humans we are a very strange race. This was bought by Andy Cox for *Black Static*. By the way, if you aren't already aware of *Black Static*—or even subscribe to this brilliant magazine—you're doing yourself a huge disservice.

Soundtrack - *Strange and Beautiful (I'll Put a Spell On You)* by Aqualung.

Fear of the Music - *Something Remains*

At Fantasycon 2016 in Nottingham I heard from editor Peter Coleborn that Alchemy Press were interested in publishing an anthology of stories inspired by the great Joel Lane, who had sadly passed away in November 2013. Many of Joel's notebooks existed, containing fragments of stories, or opening paragraphs, or in some instances simply story idea, and Peter wondered whether other writers would contribute to finishing the stories, with the published book benefitting the charity Diabetes UK. Together with Pauline E Dungate they edited *Something Remains*. My story was taken from an opening paragraph originally written by Joel.
I couldn't profess to knowing Joel that well but I'd met him at Fantasycon around 2006 or 2007, back when I was a keen reader but had not yet taken any steps into writing. It was clear he was an intelligent speaker with a great deal to say. I'd been a fan of his writing for years, being brought up on a staple of Stephen Jones' *Best New Horror* annual anthologies, containing the best of the previous year's horror and weird fiction. Over the years Joel and I had met at various conventions and had corresponded quite a bit via email and even post. He'd been kind enough to read my first collection, *Peel Back the Sky*, and had offered support and constructive praise. So it was a huge shock to see him pass away so suddenly, robbing the world of a wonderful human being, as well as one of the best writers of weird fiction this country has ever produced.

Soundtrack - *A Forest* by The Cure.

The Summer of Bradbury - *Terror Tales of Yorkshire*

I was invited by editor Paul Finch to contribute a story to his long-running series of anthologies featuring tales linked to geographical locations. I am a huge fan of the books—which mix fiction with snippets of local myths and legends—so of course I jumped at the chance to be involved. As a native Yorkshireman I'd been fascinated by the notion that at times in the past whole valleys—including villages situated within—had been flooded to make way for the construction of reservoirs. Lady Bower Dam was one particular place near me where, during low water the spire of a subterranean church could be glimpsed. What an evocative concept. I decided to set my story around such a place, and tried to find parallels between Ray Bradbury's Greentown, Illinois and my fictional town. The theme of children being faced with an ancient supernatural presence is hardly a new one, but that was half of the fun of writing it.

Soundtrack - *Life in a Northern Town* by The Dream Academy.

The Devil's Only Friend - *Horror Uncut!*

I was invited by editors Joel Lane and Tom Johnstone to submit a story for an anthology that they were putting together called *Horror Uncut! Tales of Social Insecurity and Economic Unease.* Published by Gray Friar Press it was intended to reflect the rather sorry political state of the UK at that time, and offer a counter view to the economic issues relating to the coalition government—its enforcement of austerity, food banks, a gradual erosion of the NHS, the bedroom tax, cancer patients hounded by the DWP—a wide variety of modern-day problems were highlighted in the book, one that I was proud to be a part of. Sadly, Joel passed away before the anthology was published but Tom did a wonderful job of finishing such a worthwhile project. My story deals with a character who is recently released from prison, finding a Britain much-changed from the one he knew before his incarceration.

Soundtrack - *Glory Box* by Portishead.

Pennyroyal - original to this collection

Teenage pregnancy, under-age sex, backstreet abortions—all themes hopefully disquieting enough. But with the sinister aspect of the child's father I have tried to add an element of the supernatural to the proceedings. I have taken huge liberties with the timescales in relation to the development of the foetus but I hope you can forgive some artistic licence here.

Soundtrack - *Bronte* by Gotye.

Husks - *Murmurations*

Conrad Williams, one of my favourite British writers, ran an online writing class called Fiction Factory for a while, to which I was a member. The experience was extremely beneficial to my writing. Every so often he would have guests appear in our weekly 'cyber get-togethers' and we'd have the chance to question/answer and hear experiences from those writers with a greater insight into the publishing world. One week we were fortunate to have Nicholas Royle, who happened to mention that he was editing an anthology of weird bird stories to benefit the RSPB. Of course, I took the opportunity to submit something, and was lucky enough to have it accepted. Both Conrad and Nick were among those writers I mentioned earlier, like Joel Lane, whose work was brought to my attention by the annual *Best New Horror* series edited by Stephen Jones. To even have the chance to interact with these writers was an absolute honour so I was over the moon to appear in a Nicholas Royle anthology. The story itself is terribly sad. The kookaburra presence was inspired by a visit to a local wildlife park where I took my sons, when my youngest was still a toddler. We watched, horrified, as the keepers fed the kookaburras by distributing dead chicks around the cage. The kookaburras grasped the lifeless chicks in their pointed beaks and bashed them against branches or stones to tenderise them, before finally ingesting the carcases whole. Some of them had tiny chick feet protruding from their mouths for a moment or two as they swallowed them down. It was simultaneously macabre and fascinating.

Soundtrack - *The Man With the Child in His Eyes* by Kate Bush.

The Children of Medea - original to this collection

Many of my stories feature strangers in strange lands. A great deal of my characters are on journeys—sometimes emotional rather than physical ones—but the sense of being in an environment rather different to one's usual surroundings is a theme to which I'm drawn. One of the best examples of this is *The Wicker Man*, one of my favourite horror films of all time.
The schoolteacher in this tale is trying to forget his past by throwing himself into a new situation; one that's certainly troubling enough to allow him to forget what has happened to him back home. I pictured the schoolchildren looking like the classmates in Wolf Rilla's 1960 film *Village of the Damned*. The framework of the story is lifted from Greek mythology—or at least a version from the play by Euripides—the character of Medea, who murdered her own children to exact revenge on her estranged husband Jason.

Soundtrack - *Mykonos* by Fleet Foxes

What Grief Can Do - *Crimewave*

I have written in several speculative genres—horror, science fiction, fantasy—but the genre to which I'm drawn the most is crime, especially very dark crime where the boundaries between it and horror is blurred. This tale tries hard to be disturbing by touching on several themes—a child killer, guilt-induced suicide, the notion of a family member harbouring the darkest of secrets. I had a nice sense of satisfaction by how the antagonist met his match.
Andy Cox bought this tale for his occasional anthologies, *Crimewave*, published by TTA Press.

Soundtrack - *Precious Things* by Tori Amos.

The Ivory Teat - *The First Book of Classical Horror Stories*

This was another of those stories that started out with me just writing a paragraph of stream of consciousness that evolved into something more substantial and prose-like. I wanted it to speak about the way that music influences our moods. The story touches on loneliness and anxiety and how trapped we can all feel at times. The scene involving the tenant's grisly chain-saw suicide was based on a newspaper report of an actual real-life case. This story appeared in *The First Book of Classical Horror* Stories edited by Des Lewis, a fine man and a great writer.

Soundtrack - *Coffey on the Mile* by Thomas Newman.

Double Helix - *Ill at Ease 2*

I like the theme of regret and missed opportunities, something that I touch on in many of my stories. The characters in "Double Helix" reunite after a chance encounter, many years after they first had a relationship. By now they've both moved on with their lives but I was interested in the road never taken, the viewpoint looking back into the past. However, if they had a chance to change their futures, would they? Of course, anyone faced with death would, but I hope it's abundantly clear that Claire would probably take that choice, now matter what the future held. I think this story is probably my most romantic (I realise that's not saying much!). It appeared in the anthology *Ill at ease 2* edited by my very good friend, Mark West.

Soundtrack - *There is a Light That Never Goes Out* by The Smiths.

The Cambion - *Cemetery Dance*

Another 'fish out of water stories' where the protagonist finds themselves in unfamiliar surroundings, this time a tiny village in war-torn Chad. Some of the research I did for the story involved reading non-fiction accounts of daily life in countries like this, or National Geographic articles about the conflicts, or Wikipedia pages about Eastern mythology and superstitions. All fascinating but at the same time harrowing. I finished writing this story just as US publisher Cemetery Dance made the announcement that they would be opening up fiction submissions for their magazine for, as far as I'm aware, the first time in many years. I sent the story off and was thrilled to find it was accepted, eventually appearing in the same edition as a story from one of my heroes, Stephen King.

Soundtrack - *Angel Dust* by New Order.

Happy Sands - *Postscripts*

When I first set out with a vague idea to start submitting fiction, I had three specific publications that I wanted to appear in. These were the ultimate place-markers, outlets that I knew would be at the top of my list of ambitions. The first was *Black Static*, a magazine I had been reading for many years in its former incarnation as *The Third Alternative*. The second was the American publication, *Cemetery Dance*, originally formed by Richard Chizmar in 1988. The last was the bi-annual anthology put out by Peter Crowther's PS Publishing called *Postscripts*. I eventually managed to sell stories to the all three of my targets, with the achievement finally being attained in the very final issue of *Postscripts*. My story is a rather dark science-fiction tale, one that taps into how technology might be put to dark use by those members of society that look to exploit the vulnerable and the weak. This was a blast to write, the words almost poured out of me. Apologies to Bruce Springsteen for ushering in his early demise, but I wanted to show something to illustrate it was set in the near future. I think it was written, polished, submitted and accepted in less than four days. I believe I might have even nabbed the last spot in the anthology so I certainly was cutting it fine!

Soundtrack - *Nightcall* by Kavinsky.

Rapid Eye Movement - *Fear the Reaper*

Sleep has often fascinated me. It might be the way in which time seems to move at a speed quite unlike as it does during waking hours, it might be that sleep is the realm in which dreams occur. It's always felt a little magical to me. Sleep is something that we all need in order to continue living. So how would it be if an act so natural could cause a catastrophe on such a global scale? I filled the tale with horrible imagery to counterbalance the simplicity of the two central characters and their acceptance of what is going to happen. I wrote the story for editor Joe Mynhardt for his anthology of stories about death and the dying and the unstoppable inevitability of life reaching its end. The story's title is named after the state of sleep in which dreams are most prevalent.

Soundtrack - *(Don't Fear) The Reaper* by Blue Oyster Cult

It Came From the Ground - *Darkest Minds*

This story started with the opening line, a rarity in my experience. I knew I wanted to write a story that dealt with the Rwandan civil war and involved some kind of African spirit or djinn. Into my mind sprang the image of a one-armed child brandishing a machete, and I was off. Yet again this was a blast to write. Really plot heavy, almost pulp fiction in tone, it's nothing more than a creature feature embellished with a political backdrop. The monster itself is a gigantic version of something that strikes fear into my own heart—the centipede. There's something about the uncanny movement and its physical shape that evokes a deep sense of revulsion in me. I submitted the story to an anthology called *Darkest Minds* edited by Ross Warren and Anthony Watson, who fortunately accepted it, despite it being way over the word limit in the guidelines. The story seemed generally to go down well. Its title—like the titles of many of my stories—is borrowed from the name of a song, this time by Badly Drawn Boy.

Soundtrack - *It Came From the Ground* by Badly Drawn Boy

***

I'd just like to thank the editors that originally purchased or commissioned these stories, and the writers and editors that have inspired me to write – Ellen Datlow, Andy Cox, Michael Kelly, Richard Chizmar, Paul Finch, Paula Guran, Peter Crowther, Nick Gevers, Stephen Jones, Gary Fry, Joe Mynhardt, Mark West, Des Lewis, Ross Warren, Anthony Watson, Peter Coleborn, Pauline Dungate, Norman Prentiss, Brian Freeman, Joel Lane, Tom Johnstone, Nicholas Royle, Charles Black, Mark Scioneaux, RJ Cavender and Robert S Wilson.

Thanks for Priya Sharma for agreeing to write the introduction, Ben Baldwin for providing such a wonderful piece of art for the cover, and to Adam Nevill and Conrad Williams for the kind words of encouragement and support.

And I'll be eternally grateful to Francesca T Barbini and the people at Luna Press for taking a chance on publishing this collection. You guys do fantastic work in the speculative genres, and I'm proud to be a part of that.

www.ingramcontent.com/pod-product-compliance
Lightning Source LLC
Chambersburg PA
CBHW050835190726
48286CB00007B/2103